"Krentz's trademarks—fast plotting, snappy dialogue, hot sex—are all on display here, in a novel that ranks with her best."
—*The Seattle Times*

Raine Tallentyre always tried to heed her late aunt Vella's advice—and keep her paranormal abilities a secret. But when she journeys to Shelbyville, Washington, to clear out her aunt's house, Raine's highly developed sensitivity leads her to a horrifying discovery: a young woman held captive in the basement storage locker. And the kidnapper is on the loose.

Without warning, a new man enters Raine's life—investigator Zack Jones. While Raine hears voices, Zack sees visions, and suddenly Raine experiences an intense, thrilling intimacy with him that she never dared to expect. There's one complication, however: Zack is working for the secret Arcane Society. Dedicated to the study of paranormal phenomena, the organization lost Raine's trust long ago, when it shattered her family with an act of betrayal.

Now, as a killer makes her his target, and a cabal of psychic criminals known as Nightshade operates in the shadows surrounding them, Raine and Zack must rely not just on their powerful abilities but on each other as well.

"Entertaining."
—*Newsday*

"[An] addictively readable series . . . [a] brilliantly crafted novel that deftly fuses paranormal-flavored suspense with sizzlingly sexy romance."
—*Booklist* (starred review)

"It's quite simply a well-written, fun read that will entertain you from start to finish. . . . The passion between Zack
and Raine is enough to satisfy any romantic heart, and the
suspense only adds to it."   —*The State* (Columbia, SC)

"A 'sizzlingly' chilling story that takes readers on another
incredible journey into the riveting world of the Arcane
Society. Krentz continues her action-packed psychic paranormal series."   —*Library Journal*

**Praise for the novels of *New York Times*
bestselling author Jayne Ann Krentz . . .**

White Lies

"Intriguing suspense and captivating romance expertly
crafted."   —*The State* (Columbia, SC)

"Krentz adds an intriguing paranormal twist to her already
irresistible, deliciously dry humor."   —*Chicago Tribune*

"Spirited paranormal romance."   —*Publishers Weekly*

All Night Long

"In her signature sharp and witty fashion, Jayne Ann
Krentz mixes desire and danger to create a riveting novel
of romantic suspense."   —*Chicago Tribune*

"A master of romantic mystery and suspense novels."
                                         —*The Columbus Dispatch*

"Krentz is in top form here."   —*The Seattle Times*

"Superb romantic mystery."   —*The Oakland Press*

Falling Awake

"Will surely keep the sandman at bay. . . . Terrific."
—*The Roanoke Times* (VA)

"Romantic tension sizzles. . . . Tightly plotted . . . fully developed characters and crafty plot twists."
—*The Philadelphia Inquirer*

"Yet another winning tale of romantic suspense. . . . As always, Krentz creates an intelligent, likable couple, wonderful secondary characters, and a fast-paced story that will keep readers turning the pages." —*Library Journal*

Truth or Dare

"Compelling." —*The Age* (Melbourne, Australia)

"There's a reason Jayne Ann Krentz sells so many books. . . . [She] continues to exhibit a fine knack for entertaining her readers." —*Fort Worth Star-Telegram*

"Ranks with some of Krentz's most entertaining work."
—*The Seattle Times*

Light in Shadow

"If Krentz's newest thriller doesn't send your pulse racing, dial your cardiologist's number. . . . Packed with twists and shockers till the explosive ending." —*Publishers Weekly*

"One of Krentz's best." —*The Seattle Times*

Smoke in Mirrors

"Hearts will flutter. Spines will tingle." —*People*

"Passion smolders. . . . Krentz is a master. . . . The characters are the heart of the book and the reason why she has sold more than twenty-three million copies of her novels. This is vintage Krentz." —*The Seattle Times*

"Quick and witty and the romance sizzles. *Smoke in Mirrors* reads fast and will make you smile, wince, and sigh. What else could you want?" —*The State* (Columbia, SC)

Lost & Found

"Delightful." —*People*

"A compelling mystery laced with an equally compelling romance." —*The Newark Star-Ledger*

Soft Focus

"A healthy dose of suspense. . . . Krentz has so much fun sending up the noir genre that you won't mind going along for the ride." —*People*

"What could be more perfectly Krentz? . . . [Her] writing is clean and breezy, with many laugh-aloud chapter endings and a satisfyingly feel-good conclusion."
—*Publishers Weekly*

Sizzle

and

Burn

Jayne Ann Krentz

BERKLEY ROMANCE
New York

BERKLEY ROMANCE
Published by Berkley
An imprint of Penguin Random House LLC
penguinrandomhouse.com

Copyright © 2008 by Jayne Ann Krentz
Excerpt from *The Perfect Poison* by
Amanda Quick copyright © 2009 by Jayne Ann Krentz
Penguin Random House supports copyright. Copyright fuels creativity, encourages
diverse voices, promotes free speech, and creates a vibrant culture. Thank you for buying
an authorized edition of this book and for complying with copyright laws by not
reproducing, scanning, or distributing any part of it in any form without permission.
You are supporting writers and allowing Penguin Random House to continue to
publish books for every reader.

BERKLEY and the BERKLEY & B colophon are registered trademarks of
Penguin Random House LLC.

ISBN: 9780515145816

G. P. Putnam's Sons hardcover edition / January 2008
Jove premium edition / February 2009
Berkley Romance premium edition / November 2023

Printed in the United States of America
11   13   15   17   19   20   18   16   14   12

This is a work of fiction. Names, characters, places, and incidents either are the product
of the author's imagination or are used fictitiously, and any resemblance to actual persons,
living or dead, business establishments, events, or locales is entirely coincidental.

If you purchased this book without a cover, you should be aware that this book is stolen
property. It was reported as "unsold and destroyed" to the publisher, and neither the author
nor the publisher has received any payment for this "stripped book."

For Frank
As always, with all my love
Thanks for the sizzle and burn!

One

urn, witch, burn. . . .

The voice was a dark, ghostly whisper in her head. Raine Tallentyre stopped at the top of the basement stairs. Gingerly she touched the banister with her fingertips. That was all the contact she needed. The voice, thick with bloodlust and an unholy excitement, murmured again.

. . . Only one way to kill a witch. Punish her. Make her suffer. Burn, witch, burn. . . .

It was the same voice she had heard when she brushed against the counter in the kitchen a few minutes before. It whispered of darkness, fear and fire. The psychic traces were very fresh. A deeply disturbed individual had come through this house in the recent past. She could only pray that the freak was the type who limited himself to twisted fantasies played out in his head. But she'd had enough experience to know that probably wasn't the case. This bastard was the real thing, a human monster.

She shuddered, snatched her hand off the banister and wiped her palm against her raincoat. The gesture was pure instinct, a reflex. The coat, long and black, was wet because it was pouring outside but no amount of water could wash away the memory of the foul energy she had just sensed.

She looked back at Doug Spicer and heard another voice, her aunt's this time. The warning came straight out of her teenage memories. *Never tell them about the whispers in your head, Raine. They'll say you're crazy, like me.*

"I just want to take a quick look around the basement," she said, dreading what lay ahead.

Doug peered uneasily down into the darkness at the foot of the stairs. "Do you really think that's necessary, Miss Tallentyre? There will probably be mice or maybe even rats or snakes. Don't worry, I can take the listing without a thorough examination of the basement."

Doug was the proprietor of Spicer Properties, one of three real estate companies in the small town of Shelbyville, Washington. She had contacted him when she arrived that morning because he was the only agent who had bothered to get in touch with her after learning of Vella Tallentyre's death. He had inquired delicately about taking the listing. She was more than happy to give it to him. It was not as if she had been besieged by enthusiastic agents. For his part, Doug was relatively new in town and struggling to establish his business. They needed each other.

Dressed in a crisply tailored dark gray suit and a pale blue tie, a handsome brown leather briefcase in one hand, Doug looked every inch the professional real estate agent. Sleek, designer glasses framed his pale eyes. His car, parked in the drive, was a Jaguar.

She guessed him to be in his late thirties. His hairline was starting to recede and he had the solid, well-fed look of a man who, while not yet overweight, had definitely started to put on extra pounds. He had warned her that the gloom-filled house with its aging plumbing and wiring would not be an easy sale.

"I'll be right back," she assured him.

She couldn't tell him that she really had no choice now that she had picked up the psychic whispers of a man who fantasized about killing witches. She had to know the truth before she could leave the house.

"I did a little research and called Phil Brooks after I spoke with you," Doug said. "He told me that your aunt cut off his pest control service shortly before she, uh, left town."

Shortly before I took her away, Raine thought. She curled the hand that had just touched the railing very tightly around the strap of her purse. *Shortly before I had to put her into a very private, very expensive sanitarium*.

A month before, Vella Tallentyre had died in her

small room at St. Damian's Psychiatric Hospital back in Oriana on the shores of Lake Washington. The cause of death was a heart attack, according to the authorities. She was fifty-nine years old.

It dawned on her that Doug probably didn't want to get his pristine suit and polished shoes dirty. She didn't blame him.

"You don't have to come with me," she said. "I'll just go to the foot of the stairs."

Please be a gentleman and insist on coming with me.

"Well, if you're sure," Doug said, stepping back. "I don't see a light switch up here."

"It's at the foot of the stairs."

So much for the gentlemen's code. What had she expected? This wasn't the nineteenth century. The code, if it ever existed, no longer applied. After what she had just been through with Bradley, she should know that better than anyone.

The thought of Detective Bradley Mitchell proved bracing. The ensuing rush of feminine outrage unleashed a useful dose of adrenaline that was strong enough to propel her down the stairs.

Doug hovered at the top of the steps, filling the doorway. "If the light isn't working, I've got a flashlight in my car."

The ever helpful real estate agent.

She ignored him and descended cautiously into the darkness. Maybe she wouldn't give him the listing, after all. The problem was, neither of the other two agents in town was eager for it. It wasn't just that the house was in such a neglected state. The truth was that it was unlikely any of the locals would be interested in purchasing it.

For the past couple of decades this house had been the property of a woman who was certifiably crazy, a woman who heard voices in her head. That kind of history tended to dampen the enthusiasm of prospective clients. As Doug had explained, they would have to lure an out-of-town prospect, someone interested in a real fixer-upper.

The old wooden steps creaked and groaned. She tried to avoid touching the railing on the way down, and she was careful to stay close to the edge of each tread so that she would be less likely to step in *his* footsteps. She had learned the hard way that human psychic energy was most easily transmitted onto a surface by direct skin contact but bloodlust this strong sometimes penetrated through the soles of shoes.

As careful as she tried to be, she couldn't avoid all of it.

Make her suffer. Punish her the way Mother punished me.

The scent of damp and mildew intensified as she went down. The darkness at the foot of the steps yawned like a bottomless well.

She paused on the final step, groped for and found the switch. When she touched it she got a jolt that had nothing to do with electricity. *Burn, witch, burn.*

Mercifully, the naked bulb in the overhead fixture still worked, illuminating the windowless, low-ceilinged space in a weak, yellow glare.

The basement was crammed with the detritus of Vella Tallentyre's unhappy life. Several pieces of discarded furniture, including a massive mirrored armoire, a chrome dining table laminated with red plastic, and four matching red vinyl chairs, were crowded together. Most of the rest of the space was filled with several large cardboard boxes and crates. They contained many of the innumerable paintings Vella had produced over the years. The pictures had one unifying theme: they were all dark, disturbing images of masks.

Her heart sank. So much for taking a quick look around and retreating back up the staircase. She would have to leave her perch at the foot of the stairs and tour the maze of boxes and crates if she wanted to be certain there were no terrible secrets buried down there.

She really did not need this. She had problems enough at the moment. Settling Aunt Vella's small estate had proved remarkably time-consuming, not to mention depressing. In the middle of that sad process she had been forced to face the fact that the one man she thought could accept her, voices and all, found her a complete turn-off in the bedroom. On top of everything else, she had a business to run. Late October was a busy time of year for her costume design shop, Incognito. No, she did not need any more trouble, but she knew all too well that if she ignored the whispers, she would walk the floor until dawn for days or even weeks. For some reason she could never understand, finding the truth was the only antidote for the voices.

Stomach clenching, she stepped down onto the concrete floor and put out a hand to touch the nearest object, a dusty cardboard box. There was no help for it now. She had to follow the trail of psychic whispers left by the freak.

"What are you doing?" Doug called anxiously from the top of the staircase. "I thought you said you were just going to have a quick look around down there."

"There's a lot of stuff here. Sooner or later I'm going to have to clear it out. I need to get an idea of how big a job it will be."

"Please be careful, Miss Tallentyre."

She pretended not to hear him. If he couldn't be bothered to accompany her into the darkness, she was not interested in his platitudes.

There was nothing on the cardboard box but when her fingertips skated across the laminated surface of the old table she got another vicious jolt.

The demon is stronger than the witch.

Gasping, she jerked her fingers away from the table and took a quick step back. No matter how she tried to prepare herself, she would never get used to the unnerving sensation that accompanied a brush with the really bad whispers.

She looked down at the floor, searching for footprints. If there were any, they were undetectable. In the poor light the gray dust that covered everything appeared to be the same color as the concrete. In addition, the deep shadows between the valleys of stacked boxes left much of the floor in pitch darkness.

She inched forward, touching the objects in her path in the same tentative way she would have tested the surface of a hot stove. Psychic static clinging to the dusty armoire mirror made her flinch.

She looked around and realized that she was following a narrow path that snaked through the jungle of crates and boxes. The trail led to the closed door of the old wooden storage locker. A heavy padlock secured the sturdy door.

A very shiny new padlock.

She knew before she even touched it that it would reek of the freak's spore.

She came to a halt a step away from the locker, held her breath and put out her hand. The edge of her finger barely grazed the padlock but the shock was nerve-shattering, all the same.

Burn, witch, burn.

She sucked in a deep breath. "Oh, damn."

"Miss Tallentyre?" Doug sounded genuinely alarmed now. "What's wrong? Are you all right down there?"

She heard his footsteps on the stairs. Evidently her small yelp of pained surprise had activated some latent manly impulse to ride to the rescue. Better late than never.

"I'm all right but there is something very wrong

down here." She fished her cell phone out of her purse. "I'm going to call nine-one-one."

"I don't understand." Doug halted on the last step, clutching his briefcase. He peered around and finally spotted her near the storage locker. "Why in the world do you want the police?"

"Because I think this basement is about to become a crime scene."

The 911 operator came on the line before Doug could recover from the shock.

"Fire or police?" the woman said crisply.

"Police," she responded, putting all the assurance she could muster into her voice in an effort to make certain the operator took her seriously. "I'm at fourteen Crescent Lane, the Tallentyre house. Tell whoever responds to bring a tool that can cut through a padlock. Hurry."

The woman refused to be rushed. "What's wrong, ma'am?"

"I just found a dead body."

She hung up before the operator could ask any more questions. When she closed the phone she realized that Doug was still standing at the foot of the stairs. His features were partially obscured by the shadows but she was pretty sure his mouth was hanging open. The poor man was obviously starting to realize that there were reasons why the other local real estate agents hadn't jumped on the Tallentyre listing. He must have heard the rumors about Aunt Vella. Maybe he was starting to wonder if the crazy streak ran in the family. It was a legitimate question.

Doug cleared his throat. "Are you sure you're okay, Miss Tallentyre?"

She gave him the smile she saved for situations like this, the special smile her assistant, Pandora, labeled her *screw you* smile.

"No, but what else is new?" she said politely.

The officer's name was Bob Fulton. He was the hard-faced, no-nonsense, ex-military type. He came down the basement stairs with a large flashlight and a wicked-looking bolt cutter.

"Where's the body?" he asked, in a voice that said he had seen a number of them.

"I'm not certain there is one," Raine admitted. "But I think you'd better check that storage locker."

He looked at her with an expression she recognized immediately. It was the everyone-here-is-a-suspect-until-proven-otherwise expression that Bradley got when he was working a case.

"Who are you?" Fulton asked.

"Raine Tallentyre."

"Related to the crazy lady—uh, I mean to Vella Tallentyre?"

"Her niece."

"Mind if I ask what you're doing here today?"

"I inherited this house," she said coldly. He'd called

Aunt Vella a crazy lady out loud. That meant she no longer had to be polite.

Clearly sensing the mounting tension in the atmosphere, Doug stepped forward. "Doug Spicer, Officer. Spicer Properties. I don't believe we've met. I came here with Miss Tallentyre today to take a listing on the place."

Fulton nodded. "Heard Vella Tallentyre had passed on. Sorry, ma'am."

"Thank you," Raine said stiffly. "About that storage locker—"

He studied the padlocked door and then glanced suspiciously at Raine. "What makes you think there's a body in there?"

She crossed her arms and went into full defense mode. She had known this was going to be difficult. It was so much simpler when Bradley handled this part, shielding her from derision and disbelief.

"Just a feeling," she said evenly.

Fulton exhaled slowly. "Don't tell me, let me guess. You think you're psychic, just like your aunt, right?"

She flashed him her special smile.

"My aunt *was* psychic," she said.

Fulton's bushy brows shot up. "Heard she ended up in a psychiatric hospital in Oriana."

"She did, mostly because no one believed her. Please open the locker, Officer. If it's empty, I will apologize for wasting your time."

"You understand that if I do find a body in that

locker, you're going to have to answer a lot of questions down at the station."

"Trust me, I am well aware of that."

He searched her face. For a few seconds she thought he was going to argue further but whatever he saw in her expression silenced him. Without a word he turned to the storage locker and hoisted the bolt cutter.

There was a sharp, metallic crunch when the hasp of the padlock severed. Fulton put down the tool and gripped the flashlight in his left hand. He reached for the doorknob with gloved fingers.

The door opened on a groan of rusty hinges. Raine stopped breathing, afraid to look and equally afraid not to. She made herself look.

A naked woman lay on the cold concrete floor. The one item of clothing in the vicinity was a heavy leather belt coiled like a snake beside her.

The woman was bound hand and foot. Duct tape sealed her mouth. She appeared to be young, no more than eighteen or nineteen, and painfully thin. Tangled dark hair partially obscured her features.

The only real surprise was that she was still alive.

Two

Knives were always the worst. People did unpleasant things with them, and they did those things close up and in a very personal way.

"I don't like sharp objects," Zack Jones said.

He did not take his attention off the ceremonial dagger in the glass case. Elaine Brownley, director of the museum, leaned closer to study the artifact.

"Probably all that early childhood advice you got about the dangers of running with scissors," she suggested. "Leaves a lasting impression."

"Yeah, that must be it," Zack said.

This was not the first time he had found himself standing beside Elaine, looking at an unpleasant object housed in a glass case. His was a dual career path. Consulting for the Arcane Society's curators was one of his businesses.

Elaine removed her glasses and fixed him with a direct look. She was in her mid-fifties. With her short, graying brown hair, round glasses, intelligent eyes and slightly rumpled navy blue skirted suit, she looked like the academic that she was. Zack knew she had a number of degrees in archaeology, anthropology and fine arts. She was also fluent in several languages, living and dead.

At various points in Elaine's life her instructors, teachers and colleagues had labeled her "gifted." Most of them had probably never even had a clue how right they were, Zack thought. What she had was a psychic talent for finding and identifying genuine antiquities of any kind. No one could slip a fake past her, whether it was a Renaissance painting or a piece of Roman glass.

When she had left the university world to accept a position with a museum, most of her colleagues expected her to end up at the head of one of the many prestigious institutions that had made jaw-dropping offers.

Instead, she became the director of the Arcane Society's museum at the West Coast headquarters of the Arcane Society, USA. The museum was one of four the Society operated, three in the United States and one, the original Arcane House, in the United Kingdom.

The Society's museums were little known and mostly ignored by the mainstream world of archaeology and academic research. The Society liked things that way. Its highly specialized museums collected and studied artifacts and relics that were associated with the paranormal. They were not open to the public.

Elaine peered up at him. "Well?"

"It's old." Zack turned back to the dagger. "Lot of static on it. I can feel it from here."

"I know it's old." She made a soft, impatient sound. "I didn't buy it yesterday at Wal-Mart. It cost me a huge chunk of the museum's annual budget. Trust me, I wouldn't have authorized the acquisition if I wasn't certain that it was second century A.D. That's not what I'm asking."

"I'll have to handle it to know for sure. No gloves."

Her mouth pursed at that. Elaine did not like anyone to handle any of the objects in the collection with ungloved hands. But she knew his requirements. If she wanted him to verify her theory about the dagger, she would have to let him have direct physical contact.

Without a word, Elaine punched in a code that opened the case.

Zack readied himself for the shock he knew was coming and deliberately jacked up his psychic senses. He reached down and closed his hand around the jeweled hilt of the dagger.

The current of psychic energy that still clung to the blade even after so many centuries was faint but it had been laid down in blood and it was still strong enough to sear his senses. He locked his teeth together and closed his eyes. Not that shutting his eyes had any effect on the ghostly images that flashed through his mind.

The scenes, layers of them in this instance because the dagger had been used many times for similar purposes, came to him in the hues of nightmares. He was never able to explain the colors of the paranormal visions. They had no equivalent in the normal world.

. . . He thrilled to the act of driving the dagger downward, savoring the anticipation of how it would feel when it cut into human flesh, sensed the unholy lust and exultation that came with the killing blow, knew the terror of the victim . . .

He dimmed his psychic senses swiftly and dropped the dagger back into the case.

"Hey," Elaine yelped, outraged. "Careful with that thing."

"Sorry." He gave the hand he had used to grip the blade a little shake, as if the small action could rid him of the remnants of the grim visions. He knew better. Luckily the dagger was very, very old.

Elaine raised her brows. "Tell me."

"It was definitely used to kill people, not animals," he said. Calling on years of practice and sheer willpower, he managed to repress the visions. It was a temporary fix. They would be back, probably in his dreams that night. "A human-sacrifice scenario."

"You're sure it was a sacrifice, not just the killing of an enemy or a routine murder?"

He looked at her. "Routine murder?"

She rolled her eyes. "You know what I mean."

"The energy on the hilt was tinged with that special rush of sanctimonious power that goes with a blood sacrifice. The bastard liked his work and he got off on it. There's a reason they call it bloodlust, Elaine."

She remained skeptical but there was a sparkle in her eye that could only be described as a form of lust.

Archaeologists, he thought. *Gotta love 'em.*

"An execution, perhaps?" she suggested.

"No. Ritual sacrifice. There was an altar, and the killer felt he had a license to kill."

Elaine relaxed, smiling with intense satisfaction.

"I was right," she said, all but rubbing her hands together with glee. "This is the dagger used by the priests of the cult of Brackon."

He had never understood how collectors and curators could get so excited about objects and devices designed to kill and maim. But then, they didn't have to deal with the psychic visions left behind on those objects and devices.

"What's so special about that dagger?" he asked.

Elaine chuckled. "The director of the Sedona branch of the museum has been after it for years. He needs it to complete his collection of Brackon cult artifacts."

"A little friendly competition between curators?"

"Not so friendly." Elaine lowered the glass lid and relocked the case. "Milo has an Egyptian ring that I want very badly. I've begged him for years to consider a trade. He has always refused. But now I've got a bargaining chip. He'll have to deal on my terms."

"Got it." He surveyed the cases in the gallery. "You've built this into a fine museum, Elaine. I'm no archaeologist but I've spent enough time consulting in all four of the Society's museums to know that this is a world-class collection."

She laughed. "I am living proof that an obsessive personality and a keen sense of professional rivalry are the essential traits of a successful curator."

"Probably useful traits in any profession." He'd been on the obsessed path himself, most of his life. Until Jenna.

Elaine fixed him with a speculative look. He knew what was coming and readied his exit strategy. He liked Elaine and admired her professional skills. But she was a friend of the family and the family had been applying a lot of pressure lately.

On the surface, the invitation was smooth enough.

"Do you have time for a cup of coffee before you leave for the airport?" she asked.

"I was planning to spend a couple of hours in the museum library," he hedged.

"That was your excuse last time."

He considered his options and didn't like any of them. Elaine was a good client and a very smart woman. He liked the company of smart women. If she stuck to business, he wouldn't mind having coffee with her. It wasn't as if there was any great rush to return to his home in the northern California wine country. There was no one waiting for him.

For the most part he was okay with his new existence as a duo-job workaholic. The problem was that family and friends were becoming increasingly aggressive, pushing him to resume what they considered his destined career path. He knew damn well that they weren't applying pressure just because they were concerned about him, although that was part of it. The reality was that they had an agenda, and that agenda no longer coincided with his own.

He glanced at his watch. "My flight leaves at five-thirty. That gives me some time."

"Your enthusiasm is underwhelming."

He felt himself redden. "I've been a little distracted lately."

"By what?"

"Work."

"Ah, yes, the all-purpose excuse." She lightly patted his arm. "And there's no denying that it is excellent therapy after one has suffered a loss like yours. But it has been almost a year now, Zack. Time to move on."

He said nothing.

They walked toward the far end of the gallery. Moving down the aisle between the glass cases was like walking a gauntlet. The combined psychic energy buzz given off by the artifacts stirred his senses in an unpleasant way. He knew Elaine felt something, too, but she seemed to thrive on the sensation.

He had to exert a lot of raw willpower to keep the psychic side of his nature suppressed. He could never dampen it entirely; no level-ten sensitive was capable of shutting off his or her paranormal senses altogether. It would have been the equivalent of deliberately going deaf or losing his sense of taste. But it was possible to minimize one's parasenses.

"What are you working on?" Elaine asked.

"At the moment I'm finishing a paper for the *Journal*."

Among the curators and consultants associated with the Arcane Society's museums there was only one journal, *The Journal of Paranormal and Psychical Research*. Like the Society's museums, neither the print nor the online edition was available to the general public.

"I feel like a detective trying to interrogate a suspect who is waiting for his lawyer to arrive," Elaine said drily. "But I will persevere. What's the topic of this paper you're finishing?"

"The Tarasov camera."

She tilted her head slightly to look at him, her attention caught. "Never heard of it."

"According to the records, it was acquired in the 1950s during the Cold War. It was discovered in a Russian lab and brought back to the States by a member of the Society."

"Discovered?" she repeated, amused.

He smiled faintly. "A polite euphemism for stolen. That was back in the days when the former USSR was doing a lot of paranormal research and experimentation. Someone inside the CIA got nervous and wanted to find out what was going on. J&J was quietly asked to see if it could get an agent inside one of the Russian labs."

There was no need to explain what J&J stood for. Every member of the Arcane Society was aware that Jones & Jones was the Society's very private, very low-profile psychic investigation firm.

"J&J was successful, I take it?" Elaine said.

"The agent managed to get the camera out of the country. Brought it back and turned it over to the CIA. Their technicians examined it but concluded that it was bogus. They couldn't make it work."

"Why not?"

"Evidently it requires an operator who possesses a unique type of psychic talent. The Society wound up with the camera after the CIA decided it was a fraud. Our techs weren't able to make it function, either, so it went into a vault. That's where it's been sitting all these years."

"What made the camera unusual?" Elaine asked.

"The Tarasov camera was supposed to be able to photograph human auras."

"Nonsense." Elaine gave a disdainful sniff. "Human auras have never been successfully photographed, not even by the experts in the Society's labs. Something to do with the location of aura energy on the spectrum, I think. Auras can be measured and analyzed in oblique ways and some people can see them naturally, but you can't take pictures of them. The technology just isn't available yet."

"It gets better," Zack said. "According to the notes of the agent who brought the camera out from behind the Iron Curtain, the Russian researchers believed that a unique type of psychic photographer could not only take pictures of auras, he could use the camera to disrupt them in ways that would cause severe psychic trauma or death."

Elaine frowned. "In other words, it was meant to be some sort of psychic weapon?"

"Yes."

"But the experts say that no modern technology can interface successfully with human psychic energy. That's why no one has ever been able to build a machine or a weapon that can be activated by paranormal powers or one that can produce that kind of energy."

"True."

"In other words, the camera really is a fraud?" She sighed. "That's a relief. The world is already armed to the teeth. The last thing we want to do is introduce a new psychic technology designed to kill people."

"Uh-huh."

She beetled her brows at him. "What is that supposed to mean?"

"I was able to determine that the Tarasov camera had been used to kill at least once, possibly twice. The vibes from the first murder were murky, though."

Elaine's eyes widened a little. "In other words, the Russians had at least one sensitive who could operate the camera?"

"Looks like it."

She moved one hand in a small arc. "How is that possible?"

"The J&J agent speculated in his private notes that the Russian operator was probably a one-of-a-kind exotic. Some type of unusual level-ten talent that has never been classified by the Society."

Exotic was the Society's slang for those endowed with rare, extremely high-level psychic talents. It was not, generally speaking, a complimentary term. The truth was, people with exceptionally strong paranormal abilities often made other members of the Society uneasy. In fact, it was not uncommon for folks outside the Society—people who scoffed at the very idea of the paranormal—to find themselves unaccountably nervous or wary when they were in the presence of an individual endowed with powerful parasensitive abilities.

Power of any kind, including psychic power, was a form of energy. Most people, whether they were aware of it or not—whether they even wanted to acknowledge it or not—were capable of sensing it when there was a lot of it in the room.

"Wonder what happened to the exotic who could operate the camera," Elaine mused.

"She's dead."

Elaine gave him a quick, startled look. "Killed by the Jones & Jones agent who appropriated the camera?"

"Yes. It was close. She almost took him out first with the damned thing."

"Fascinating. Which one of the Society's museums got the device?"

"It's not in any of the museums. It's in the Jones family vault."

Elaine glowered. "I should have known. No offense, Zack, but your family's penchant for keeping secrets is extremely annoying to those of us who are in the business of encouraging research. That camera, if it has any historical significance at all, should be in the collection of one of the Society's museums."

"Hey, give me some credit here. I persuaded my grandfather to let me study the camera and write up the results for the *Journal*, didn't I? That was a major accomplishment. You know how he is when it comes to the family's and the Society's secrets."

"Bancroft Jones spent far too much time in the intelligence world before he accepted the Master's Chair, if you ask me," Elaine said, grimly disapproving. "If he had his way, he'd probably classify the guest list for the annual Spring Ball as *Top Secret, Council Eyes Only.*"

Zack smiled slightly.

Elaine stopped in mid-stride, rounding on him. "Good lord. Don't tell me he actually tried to do it?"

"Grandmother told me he mentioned the idea over breakfast one morning a few months ago. Don't worry, she talked him out of it."

Elaine made a *tut-tut*ting sound. "Talk about old school. Just another example of why we need new blood at the top. In fact, if you ask me, the entire internal organizational structure of the Society requires serious reform and modernization."

"It's not that bad. The changes that Gabriel Jones made in the late 1800s served the Society very well throughout the twentieth century."

"This happens to be the twenty-first century, although I sometimes think that certain members on the Council haven't noticed."

"Uh-huh." He resigned himself to the lecture. He'd heard it often enough.

"I predict that within the next twenty or thirty years, research and study of the paranormal will come out of the closet," Elaine continued forcefully. "It will move into the realm of mainstream science. When that happens, it's quite possible there will be some risks for those who possess any sort of psychic sensitivity. We need to start preparing now."

"Uh-huh."

"In the long term, it is the Society's fundamental duty to help move the study of the paranormal into the mainstream, to make the scientific establishment take it seriously. The last thing we want is another round of witch burning if and when that happens."

"Doubt if there's much chance of that," he said. Agreeing to have coffee had definitely been a mistake. He glanced covertly at his watch. Maybe he could get an earlier flight. "Today, people who claim to possess psychic powers don't go to the stake. They go on talk shows."

"Being treated as a carnival act or an exhibit in a sideshow is hardly an example of mainstreaming, and that's exactly what those silly talk shows are, if you ask me—modern carnival acts and sideshows."

"Right."

"To say nothing of all those poor people who end up in psychiatric institutions or on the streets because they've been driven mad by the psychic side of their nature or because someone decided they were crazy."

"Uh-huh."

"Take me, for example. Why, if I told any of my professional colleagues outside the Society that I could determine the age and authenticity of an object by the use of my psychic sensitivity, I'd become a laughing-stock among my peers."

"Right." It was definitely time to invent a belatedly remembered appointment.

But Elaine was in full flight now.

"It will take decades to prepare the scientific establishment and the outside world for the reality of the paranormal," she said. "It's the Council's job to guide the Society and its members during the transition period."

"The Council is pretty big on tradition, Elaine," he reminded her.

"Tradition is all well and good, but survival is the most important imperative. I'm telling you, Zack, the Society's antiquated ways could well come back to haunt us in the next few decades. People quite naturally fear secret societies. One can hardly blame them."

"I agree with you," he said.

And then, just as if he actually did possess a genuinely useful psychic talent for escaping from awkward social situations, his phone rang.

He unclipped it from his belt and glanced at the coded number. The hair stirred on the back of his neck. There was no such thing as precognition. No one could predict the future. The best you could do was a probability analysis. But it didn't take any keen paranormal talent to know that when Fallon Jones called, something interesting was about to happen.

"Sorry, Elaine," he said, "I'm going to have to take this. J&J business."

She gestured toward an empty conference room. "You can talk privately in there. I'll meet you in the coffee shop."

"Thanks." He walked into the room, shut the door and punched a button on the phone.

"Hello, Fallon."

"Where the hell are you?" Fallon demanded.

The head of Jones & Jones always sounded as if he were calling to inform you that the sky was falling, but today Fallon seemed even more grim and impatient than usual.

He was a strong psychic like almost everyone else in the Jones family tree but his talent was an unusual one. He could perceive patterns and connections where others saw only a bunch of dots or dangling strings, a natural born chaos theorist.

He was a descendant of Caleb Jones, who, together with his wife, established Jones & Jones in the late Victorian era. The firm still had an office in the United Kingdom. There were currently four in the United States, each responsible for a region. Fallon was in charge of the branch that handled the West Coast and the Southwest.

His base of operations consisted of a one-man storefront in tiny Scargill Cove on the northern California coast. During normal times he and his web of loosely connected agents were kept busy handling a wide range of security and investigative work for members of the Society. It was understood, however, that J&J's primary client was the Governing Council of the Arcane Society.

On rare occasions, someone who was not affiliated with the Society stumbled onto the existence of J&J and came looking for the services of a psychic detective agency. Once in a while—rarely—such clients were accepted. They included certain trusted investigators who worked for a handful of police departments and a highly classified, unnamed government security agency.

"I'm in LA," Zack said.

"The museum?"

"Right."

"You're supposed to be home." Fallon sounded deeply aggrieved.

"I know this is going to come as a shock to you," Zack said, "but strangely enough, I don't sit around the house twenty-four hours a day waiting for the phone to ring in the faint hope that you might call with a job for me. I have another business to operate, remember?"

As usual, the sarcasm went straight over Fallon's head, probably without even ruffling his hair.

"I need you in Washington ASAP," he announced.

"State or city?" It was sometimes necessary to be patient when one worked with Fallon Jones. He was always several moves ahead on an invisible chessboard that no one else could see. For some reason he expected those in his loosely knit network of contract agents to follow his unfathomable logic.

"State," Fallon snapped. "Town called Oriana. It's about twenty miles east and a little north of Seattle. Know it?"

"No, but I can probably find it."

"How soon?"

"Depends on whether or not I can get an earlier

flight out of LAX, how bad the traffic is on the drive home, how long it takes to pack a few things and then get a flight out of Oakland or San Francisco to Seattle," Zack said.

"Forget commercial. Head for the airport now. I'll have one of the company jets waiting when you get there. After you pick up your stuff from home, it will take you on to Seattle."

Company jet meant one of the Society's private, unmarked corporate planes. Fallon commandeered one only on those rare occasions when he had a very hot situation on his hands.

"I'm on my way," Zack said.

"That reminds me, when you pack?"

"Yes?"

"Be sure to add some hardware."

So Fallon thought he might need to be armed for the assignment. This was getting more interesting by the moment.

"Understood." Zack headed for the door.

"Why the hell do you sound so cheerful?" Fallon asked, immediately suspicious. "You haven't been in such a good mood in damn near a year. You smokin' something, Jones?"

"No. Let's just say your timing is better than usual." He lowered his voice. "You saved me from what was turning into a very long and extremely boring lecture on the future of the Society."

"Huh." With his usual preternatural ability to connect the dots, Fallon put it together instantly. "Elaine Brownley on your case?"

"Damn, Fallon, you must be psychic."

Fallon ignored that.

"I just e-mailed you a file with some background on the Oriana case," he said. "The data is sketchy. Sorry about that. You'll understand why when you read it. By the way, the file is encryption grade three."

Zack felt another little rush of adrenaline. An encryption grade three explained the company jet and the urgency in Fallon's voice. Lately he pulled out all the stops only when the matter involved the dangerous organization he had recently dubbed Nightshade.

Until the Stone Canyon case, Fallon had referred to the shadowy group of powerful psychic criminals as a cabal. But Stone Canyon changed all that. In the wake of the affair it became obvious that the group was not composed of a small number of closely linked conspirators. It was, instead, a highly disciplined mob-like organization run by a ruthless inner circle and a director. Nightshade had proven that it was willing to kill to achieve its objectives.

"I've got my computer with me," Zack said. "I'll read the file in flight."

"I wish you didn't sound so damn cheerful," Fallon muttered. "Makes me nervous."

Three

Zack finished the file shortly before the small jet touched down at the Sonoma County Airport. He spent the drive home to the quiet house in the wine country thinking about what he had read, searching for weaknesses, concocting a strategy.

He talked to Fallon while he threw some things into a duffel bag and retrieved his gun and holster from the small floor safe.

"You didn't tell me the subject of the file was Judson Tallentyre's daughter," he said.

"Didn't have time to go into detail. Figured you'd do better reading it in context."

"Some context." He zipped the duffel bag shut.

"Now you know why I'm in a hurry. This is big, Zack. I can feel it."

"I'm not arguing with you." He picked up the duffel bag and started toward the door. "Tell me about the trips to Vegas."

Fallon snorted. "Obviously Raine Tallentyre has a serious gambling habit."

"According to the file, she rarely went to Vegas until about a year ago. Then it became a monthly routine."

"She sure as hell wouldn't be the first sensitive to develop a taste for the casinos. Amazing how many folks forget that the laws of probability and plain old random chance are not automatically suspended just because someone with a little psychic talent decides to roll the dice."

"She plays cards, not roulette or craps. Blackjack. Never goes to the same casinos two months in a row. Never wins big enough at any one casino to draw the attention of security. But according to your info, she must have taken home close to a hundred thousand dollars during the past twelve months."

"Okay, so she's good." There was a shrug in Fallon's voice. "Maybe you'll be able to use that information."

"You're sure you don't have any more on the aunt?"

"You've got everything I've got. Vella Tallentyre was Judson Tallentyre's sister. She was a level-eight clairaudient. Heard voices. Started to suffer prolonged bouts of depression in her early thirties. She was eventually institutionalized last year. Died of a heart attack on the twentieth of last month."

"The same day that Lawrence Quinn disappeared from Oriana."

"You see now why I'm getting nervous here?" Fallon growled. "Doesn't take a psychic to connect those dots."

"I'm going to need the Judson Tallentyre file."

Fallon went uncharacteristically silent for a couple of beats.

"That's a grade-four classification," he said eventually. "Master and Council eyes only."

"Get it for me, Fallon."

There was another two-beat pause.

"Damn," Fallon said, thoroughly disgusted. "I knew this was going to happen."

"What?"

"Five minutes into the case and you're already giving orders. How many times do I have to remind you that I'm the boss here at J&J?"

"I'll try to remember that."

He ended the call and clipped the phone to his belt. Hoisting the duffel, he walked through the big, silent house and stopped briefly at the front door.

He turned and looked back at the gleaming stone tile in the foyer, the warm, Tuscan-style colors on the walls and the soothing views of green vineyards and mountains.

He'd been content in the house for most of the six years he'd lived in it. But then Jenna had arrived in his life. She moved in with him while they planned the wedding, living there just long enough to put her stamp on the place.

It would never be home again. When the Oriana case was finished, he would sell it.

Four

Over the course of his years in police work, first as a cop in San Diego and even once or twice during his short tenure as chief of police in Shelbyville, Wayne Langdon had encountered his share of strange folks. None of them, however, had given him the peculiar, downright eerie sensation he was getting from the woman seated on the other side of his desk.

None of them had ever had eyes like Raine Tallentyre, either.

"Is the girl all right?" she asked.

So cool and composed, he thought, as if she found the victims of serial killers every day of the week.

He finally realized what it was about her eyes that was so unsettling. The cat that hung around the back door of the station had eyes the same gold-green color.

Looked at you the same way, too. Raine wore a pair of severe, black-framed glasses but they didn't do a damn thing to soften the impression. You got the feeling that she saw things at midnight that other people couldn't see, didn't want to see.

"The ER doctor told me that, physically, she appears to be unharmed," he said, trying not to stare at her eyes. "But she's obviously been through an ordeal. Says her name is Stacy Anderson. A prostitute from Seattle. The kidnapper posed as a client. He brought her here sometime yesterday and put her in that storage locker. Told her she was being punished. Before he locked the door he took pictures. Used a digital camera."

A tiny, visible shudder went through Raine. She inclined her head once, as if he had just confirmed something she had already suspected.

"He's keeping a scrapbook," she said. "Souvenirs of his successes."

She was in her early thirties, he decided. Tall for a woman. She didn't try to disguise her height by wearing flat shoes, either, the way a lot of tall women did. The heels on her black boots had to be a couple of inches high. She wore her dark hair pulled back in a twist that emphasized those cat-like eyes and her cheekbones. Her black blazer looked like it had been created for a female mob boss by some high-end Italian designer. She wore it open over chocolate brown trousers and a matching brown turtleneck.

No wedding ring, he noticed. He was not surprised. An adventurous, maybe intoxicated man might
take a walk on the wild side with a woman like this but
he'd have to be a fool to marry her. The lady was dangerous territory. Everyone said that her aunt had been
certifiably crazy. Stuff like that sometimes went down
through the bloodlines.

At least Raine hadn't tried to tell him that she was
psychic. Not yet, at any rate. That was a relief. He hated
dealing with the quacks, frauds and phonies who frequently showed up in cases like this one, claiming paranormal powers.

"You say this is the first time you've been back to
Shelbyville since you moved your aunt to Oriana last
year?" he asked.

"Yes. Until then my aunt used the house here in
Shelbyville as a getaway."

He glanced down at his notes. "Evidently she liked to
get away several times a year for long periods of time."

"She enjoyed the peace and solitude of the mountains."

"According to my information, you drove up here
frequently to visit her when she was in residence, so
you're not exactly a stranger in town," he said.

He had never met Vella Tallentyre. She had been institutionalized a couple of months before he arrived in
Shelbyville to take over the tiny police department. He
had heard a lot about her, though. His secretary,
Marge, had told him that the local parents never let

their kids go trick-or-treating at the old house on Halloween. The youngsters thought Vella was a real witch. All the rumors about hearing voices had scared the heck out of them. Probably freaked out the parents, too, he thought.

"No," Raine said, "I'm not a stranger to the area but I don't really know anyone in town. Whenever I came up here I stayed with Aunt Vella, and as I'm sure you're aware, she did not have a lot of close friends in the community."

"I get the feeling you don't have any fond feelings for our fair town."

She shrugged. "The people of Shelbyville treated my aunt as if she were a freak. Why would I hold any of them in high esteem?"

He decided to ignore that. From what he'd heard, it was true. "When was the last time you were here?"

"A little over a year ago. That was when I helped Aunt Vella move."

Vella Tallentyre hadn't exactly moved. She had been institutionalized. He made a note.

"And you're back now because you've inherited the house and plan to list it with a local real estate agent?" he said.

"That's right. Mr. Spicer and I were going through the place to see what needed to be done to get it ready for sale."

"How did you know that something was wrong down there in the basement?"

He could have sworn her jaw tightened a little and her disturbing eyes narrowed ever so slightly.

"I noticed the padlock on the storage locker door. I knew that it hadn't been there the last time I was in the house."

"Why call nine-one-one? Why not call a lock-smith?"

"I was almost certain it had to be a police matter. There was no legal way that padlock could have been placed on the door. The house is private property and it has been locked up for a year. No one was author-ized to go inside except Ed Childers, the man who took care of the place for Aunt Vella. He worked for her for years. But he died some six or seven months ago."

"What made you so certain that Childers didn't put that padlock on the storage locker before he died?" he asked.

"I'll admit that I couldn't be absolutely certain but, frankly, it never occurred to me that he might have been the one who locked the door."

"You just leaped to the conclusion that a crime had been committed?"

"A crime *was* committed," she said drily. "Whoever entered my aunt's house and installed that padlock had, at the very least, broken into the place."

He sat back, thinking about it. His cop instincts were not entirely satisfied but at least he now had a rational explanation for her actions. That was a very good thing because the detectives from Seattle and Portland as well as the media were already on their way. He had a press conference to prepare for. It was going to be a zoo. Discovering the young woman alive in the basement of the old Tallentyre house was the biggest break yet in the unsolved murders attributed to the Bonfire Killer, and he was the man in charge.

"Thank you, Miss Tallentyre. That's all for now. How long will you be in town?"

"I'm going back to Oriana in the morning." She rose and paused with an inquiring expression. "Unless I can get into the house tomorrow? I'm really anxious to put it on the market."

"It's a crime scene now. Going to stay that way for a few days." He stood. "Sorry for the inconvenience."

"I understand." She hitched the strap of her dark green purse over one shoulder.

"Where are you staying tonight?"

"The Shelbyville B and B." She took her long black raincoat off a wall hook. "You have my contact information in Oriana."

"Right."

Belatedly he realized he should have helped her with the raincoat. But she already had it on. Strange how much it resembled a long black cape.

He did manage to open the door for her. She paused before going through it. He got the feeling she had decided there was something unpleasant she had to say before she left.

"Do you want to know what my intuition tells me about the killer?" she asked without inflection.

Here it comes. Damn. Just when he had begun to hope that she wasn't going to tell him she was psychic.

"Sure," he said, keeping his tone just as even as her own. "Tell me about the killer."

She seemed to draw even deeper into herself. Her eyes narrowed ever so slightly but he could see that she was determined to say whatever it was she had to say.

"He locked the woman in the basement because his mother used to punish him that way," she said quietly. "She left him in the dark for hours and then she beat him with a belt because he had befouled himself while he was confined. She told him that there was a demon inside him and that she had to drive it out."

"No offense, Miss Tallentyre, but that's the kind of useless crap every so-called profiler I've ever met says about the perp. Next you'll be telling me that he's an organized killer, right? That he's a white male somewhere between the ages of twenty-five and fifty-four. That he's an intelligent loner with no close ties to family, church or community."

"I don't know about those things," she said very steadily, "but I can tell you that you're looking for a man who is convinced that he has been possessed by a demon. He thinks of himself as a witch hunter."

He exhaled heavily. "I appreciate your insights."

"The first witch he ever killed was his mother. He covered up the crime by setting fire to her body. That should give you a starting point. He obviously got away with that murder, which implies that it is either a cold case or a death that was made to look like an accident."

He was not impressed. "They call this guy the Bonfire Killer because he kills his victims, dumps them in a field and sets fire to the bodies, destroying all the evidence. No big secret there." He paused, intrigued in spite of himself. "What makes you think he killed his mother?"

"Intuition," she said coolly.

She was really giving him the creeps now. Raine Tallentyre was either a consummate actress or a total nutcase like her aunt.

"Right, thanks, Miss Tallentyre. I'll be in touch."

Abruptly she turned on her heel, went back to the desk and picked up a pen. "I'm going to give you the name and number of someone you can call. Bradley Mitchell. He's a detective with the Oriana Police Department. He'll vouch for the fact that I'm not a likely suspect or a fraudulent psychic looking for publicity."

He frowned. "You've been involved in situations like this before?"

"Yes." She tore off the sheet of paper and handed it to him. "Call Detective Mitchell. He'll explain. Goodbye, Chief Langdon. Good luck with the press conference."

"How did you know about that?"

"There's always a press conference," she said, surprising him with a small, genuine smile. "Don't worry,

I won't try to steal your thunder. In fact, I would be extremely grateful if you would avoid releasing my name and identity to the media."

"No problem," he said, meaning it. The last thing he wanted to do was give the press the idea that he was working with a psychic. That kind of thing would make him look ridiculous.

"Thank you." She walked out the door, the long black raincoat swirling around her high-heeled boots.

He gave her a moment to leave and then he went into the outer office. Marge was at her desk. She was gazing over the rims of her reading glasses at the door through which Raine Tallentyre had just disappeared.

Marge was sixty-two years old. She had lived in Shelbyville all her life. She was his go-to source whenever he needed background on one of the local residents. He propped himself on the corner of her desk.

"What do you know about her?" he asked.

"Not much, really," Marge admitted. "Vella Tallentyre bought the house here over twenty years ago. When Raine was a little girl, a couple of men used to drive her up here to visit Vella. Later, she came by herself. She sometimes bought groceries at the local store and filled up her gas tank but other than that, we never saw much of her. She didn't seem to want to get to know any of us locals. I never even met her until today."

"What about the caretaker, Ed Childers? He have anything to say about her?"

"Ed wasn't much of a talker. But I ran into him at the post office one day not long before he died. He told me something about Raine that day that I never forgot."

"What?"

"He said he saw a photograph of Vella Tallentyre once. It was taken when Vella was younger, in her early thirties. Ed claimed that Raine Tallentyre was a dead ringer for her aunt at that age."

"No kidding."

"The only other thing I ever recall Ed saying about the Tallentyre women was that Vella had a downright obsessive fear of fire. Made him install half a dozen smoke detectors. Kept lots of fire extinguishers in the house. Had those little window emergency ladders in all the upstairs rooms. She wouldn't even allow a fire to be built in the fireplace."

"Phobic."

"For sure."

Five

"Her name is Stacy Anderson," Raine said into her cell phone. "They think she may be the latest victim of that freak the press calls the Bonfire Killer, the one that has been trolling among the prostitutes in Seattle and Portland."

"Damn." Andrew Kitredge sounded more resigned than surprised. "You can't even leave town for a day without stumbling onto a murder scene."

She almost smiled. Andrew was one of the few people in the world who was aware of her little *eccentricity*, as he called it, and took it in stride. His life partner, Gordon Salazar, was another who accepted her, voices and all.

Aunt Vella had understood her, of course, and her father, if he was still alive, would have considered her psychic side normal. But Judson Tallentyre died in a car accident when Raine was six and now Vella was gone as well.

She had no other close blood relatives. Her mother died when she was a year and a half old. Judson Tallentyre, forced to surface from his precious research in order to deal with the nuisance of caring for a baby daughter, had asked his sister to move into the household. Vella agreed, taking Raine into her heart immediately.

Child-care issues resolved, Judson immediately disappeared back into his lab.

The day of his funeral had been a turning point in Raine's young life. The small, sad ceremony was conducted in a gray, northwest mist. It was followed by what she had come to think of as the Night of Fire and Tears. She did not recall everything about that fateful evening but a series of frightening and disturbing snapshots had been forever etched in her mind.

A few months after the terrible night, Vella had sunk into the first of what would prove to be a number of long and extended depressive episodes. Aware that she could no longer care for a little girl on her own and terrified that the state would take Raine away and put her into the foster system, she turned to her best friend from childhood, Andrew Kitredge, and his partner, Gordon.

Andrew and Gordon never hesitated. They took Raine and Vella into their lives, assuming responsibility for Raine whenever Vella spiraled downward into one of her episodes. Somehow the four of them had formed a family, shielding Raine from the long arm of the state.

"You don't have to make it sound like I do it deliberately," she said to Andrew, trying to lighten the mood.

"I know you don't," Andrew said. "But you have to admit that your little eccentricities have a tendency to rattle nerves."

"Okay, I'll grant you that much."

She had been rattling Andrew's and Gordon's nerves ever since the summer of her nineteenth year, when she stumbled onto her first crime scene: that of a woman who had been murdered by her stalker-husband.

She settled deeper into the chair, propped her stocking-clad feet on a hassock and studied the view out the window. It wasn't quite six o'clock but night came early in the Cascades, especially at this time of year.

"Thank God that girl was still alive," Andrew said. "I can't even imagine what her family must have gone through after she disappeared."

"She told Langdon that she doesn't have any family, at least not one she wants to acknowledge. Evidently she's been living on the streets for the past couple of years. The chief says that fits the profile of the Bonfire Killer's victims. They've found three bodies so far, all young women with backgrounds like Anderson's. One was from Portland. The others were from Seattle."

"Classic serial killer victims," Andrew mused. "The kind of people no one misses when they disappear. I wonder why Stacy Anderson was still alive when you found her."

"She said the freak told her that she needed to be punished first by being locked up in the basement. She thinks he intended to finish the job tonight. It was just pure luck that I happened to go through the house today with the real estate agent."

"Do they think any of the previous victims were stashed in Vella's basement, too?"

"I don't know what the cops will conclude," Raine said, "but I didn't pick up traces of any other victims. I'm almost positive that Stacy Anderson was the first one the freak stashed in Aunt Vella's house."

"I don't suppose the local cops paid any attention to what you told them."

"No. I think I made Chief Langdon nervous."

Andrew's chuckle was dry. "You do have that effect on cops."

"What can I say? It's a gift."

"When are you coming home?"

Raine crossed one ankle over the other on the hassock. "I'll stay overnight, as planned, because Langdon said the detectives from Portland and Seattle might want to talk to me. But I can't do anything about putting the house on the market until the police

take down the crime-scene tape, so I'll be home tomorrow."

"I stopped by your condo this afternoon and fed
Batman and Robin. Played with them for a while.
They're doing fine."

"Thanks."

The cats tended to get anxious if they were left
alone for too long. Anxious cats could do a lot of damage in a small condo. That was especially true with Batman and Robin because Raine had refused to declaw
them. She hadn't been able to bring herself to deprive
them of their only natural defense just for the sake of
her very expensive woven wood window treatments.
She knew all too well how important it was to have
some defense mechanisms.

"I suppose Chief Langdon is going to take all the
credit for the big break in the case?" Andrew asked.
"The way Bradley always did?"

Andrew and Gordon had never entirely approved
of her arrangement with Bradley Mitchell.

"As it happens, Langdon is very photogenic," Raine
said, amused. "He's the rugged outdoor type. He'll
look good on the evening news."

"Bradley always looked good standing in front of a
camera, too. Going to be interesting to see how many
more interviews he gives now that you're no longer
solving his cold cases for him."

"Mmm." She kept her tone deliberately noncom-
mittal.

As hurt and pissed off as she was, she had not yet decided what to do about her working relationship with Bradley. Their personal relationship—what there was of it—was finished but she wasn't sure she could bring herself to stop assisting him on certain cases. In some way that she could not explain to Andrew and Gordon or even to herself, she *needed* to use the psychic side of her nature. Denying it was like trying to deny that she could see and hear and taste and touch and smell.

"Do you want Gordon or me to drive up to Shelbyville?" Andrew asked.

"No, don't worry, I'm not a suspect," she said quickly. "I spent an hour answering questions for Chief Langdon and I told him to call Bradley if he wants a character reference. He seemed satisfied. Glad to get rid of me, actually."

"You told Langdon to call the bastard?" Andrew demanded, outraged.

"Bradley's a professional when it comes to police work. He'll vouch for me."

"What about the real estate agent? What was his name? Spicer? How's he taking this?"

"He was pretty shaken. Got a hunch that after he gave his statement to Langdon, he went back to his office and had an attack of the vapors. One thing's for sure: if Aunt Vella's house was a tough sell before this, it's going to be almost impossible to move now."

"Maybe you can dump it on some unsuspecting buyer on eBay."

"You know, that's not a bad idea. But first I'm going to have to clean out the place. I'd forgotten how many crates of paintings are stashed in the basement. Aunt Vella always painted like mad when she was here in Shelbyville."

"It was her own personal form of therapy," Andrew said.

"I know."

The room phone rang.

"Sounds like you're getting another call," Andrew said.

"Probably Langdon with a few more questions."

"Better take it. We'll see you tomorrow. Love you."

"Love you. Bye."

She cut the connection and reached for the room phone.

"Yes?"

"Miss Tallentyre, this is Burton down at the front desk. There's a man here to see you. Says his name is Jones. Want me to send him up?"

The delicate cup she was holding, with its yellow-and-green floral motif, froze in midair.

"Jones?" she repeated, very carefully. There were a lot of Joneses in the world, but within her own private, tightly controlled and contained sphere the name stood out like the ominous light of an oncoming train.

"A cop?" she asked, hoping against hope that coincidences did, in fact, happen occasionally.

There was a low murmur of masculine voices. Burton came back on the line.

"Says he's a private investigator."

That gave her pause. Maybe the name really was a coincidence. Maybe one of the families of the Bonfire Killer's victims had hired a PI named Jones to look into a daughter's disappearance and somehow Mr. Jones had heard about the day's events and managed to track her down tonight.

And maybe she could hop on a broomstick and fly.

Adrenaline splintered through her. The primitive fight-or-flight rush left her edgy and profoundly wary. Briefly she considered asking Burton to tell the mysterious Mr. Jones to leave. But she had dealt with reality often enough to know that it was a remarkably stubborn force. It didn't go away just because one wished it away.

A thought chilled her to the bone. What if the Mr. Jones downstairs in the lobby was the same Mr. Jones who had frightened her and Aunt Vella so badly that night all those years ago? If so, he was in for a surprise. She was no longer a six-year-old kid scared out of her wits.

There was no help for it. She would have to find out why Mr. Jones had tracked her down here in Shelbyville.

"Send him up, please, Burton," she said.

She tossed the phone into the cradle, put the cup

down on the tray and rose from the chair. It dawned on her that she was wearing only her trouser socks. Quickly she sat down again and tugged on her boots. The added couple of inches of height fortified her confidence.

She went to stand at the window, stomach clenched, all her senses revved to the max, and listened for footsteps in the hall. It was full dark now. In spite of her determination to show no fear, she felt like a gazelle at the waterhole. The realization made her mad, which proved to be a good thing. Anger gave her strength.

She heard the footsteps only faintly and only just before the crisp, authoritative knock on her door. Mr. Jones did not make a lot of noise when he walked.

She took a deep breath, steeled herself and crossed the room to open the door.

She had no preconceived notions of what Mr. Jones would look like. Her memories of the Night of Fire and Tears were not clear on that point. The events had taken place against a backdrop of shadows, shouts and chaos. She had hidden her face against Vella's shoulder, afraid to look at the very dangerous Mr. Jones. Even at the age of six, long before the psychic side of her nature had developed, she had sensed the power in the man who stormed into her father's lab that night.

One glance told her that this Mr. Jones was not the same one who had frightened her and Vella all those years ago. The first Mr. Jones would be in his sixties by now. This man was only a couple years older than she was. She could not take any comfort from that fact, however, because the aura of power that surrounded him was as strong or stronger than the one that had emanated from the other Jones.

The Mr. Jones standing in front of her was tall. Even with her boots on she was a couple of inches shorter than him. He was lean and virile, a man who was centered and comfortable in his body and his masculinity, a man in full control of himself. His hair was short and dark and his eyes were a shade of blue that made her think of glaciers and gunmetal. He wore a black leather jacket, a black crewneck pullover, dark pants and low boots.

She knew immediately that this Jones was every bit as dangerous as the one who terrified her on that long-ago night but for some crazy reason, she wasn't frightened. The invisible energy he generated stirred the hair on the nape of her neck but she wasn't scared, she was curiously excited. A heightened sense of awareness fluttered through her. Mentally she groped for a one-word description of the unfamiliar feeling that was sweeping through her. Her brain supplied it immediately. She was *thrilled*.

"Raine Tallentyre."

He said her name as a statement of fact, not a question, as if he somehow recognized her, which was impossible because she was very, very certain they had never met. She would have remembered, she thought. There was simply no way she could have forgotten him or that low, controlled, compelling voice. It was a voice that could coax a woman into bed or challenge a man to a duel at dawn. It sent another shiver of raw sensation through her. She took a step back, trying to put some distance between the two of them while she pulled herself together.

"I'm Raine Tallentyre," she said.

"Zackary Jones. Call me Zack. I'm here to make a deal with you."

Okay, obviously she had just fallen down the rabbit hole.

"What kind of deal?" she managed.

"I need your help." He held up a manila envelope. "In exchange, I'll give you this."

She glanced at the envelope. "What's in there?"

He smiled the slow, confident smile of a man who is very sure he is holding all the high cards. "The missing pieces of your family history. Inside this envelope is your heritage, the one you were denied when your father was kicked out of the Arcane Society."

"I don't understand."

"It's simple. I'm the man with the answers to the questions you've been asking all these years."

Six

He'd chosen his strategy the way he always did, with cold, calculating psychic intuition based on what he knew and could sense about his opponent. The path across Raine Tallentyre's threshold had been clear to him as soon as he finished reading the files that Fallon Jones had provided. Very few people could resist the lure of learning the secrets of their past.

Figuring out a person's weak spots and anticipating their moves was part of his talent. He wasn't particularly proud of it but it was something he did very well. Most of the time.

What he hadn't factored into the equation was his personal reaction to Raine. Energy flooded through him, heating his blood and triggering an unfamiliar anticipation. He couldn't look away from her fascinating eyes, didn't want to look away. Her voice, soft and vibrant, was a siren's call to his senses. He could feel the power in her. It drew him as surely as her scent and the subtle challenge that she radiated.

He'd been waiting all his life to meet a woman who could do this to him. That, his level-ten mirror-talent intuition warned him, made her potentially the most dangerous woman he had ever met. And the most alluring.

"You're from the Arcane Society," she said. It was not a question.

"I'm a member of the Society," he agreed. "Just as your parents and your aunt were. So are you, for that matter."

"No."

He held up the envelope. "According to your file, your parents registered you at birth."

"My mother is dead and the Society expelled my father."

"True. But no one forced you or your aunt out of the community."

Her dark brows rose above the black frames of her glasses. "That's something of a technicality, isn't it?"

"Sure, but it's a big one. After your father's death it was your aunt's choice to keep you and herself away from the heritage that belonged to both of you." He moved the file in his hand ever so slightly, just enough to draw her attention back to it. "Well? Do you want answers, Raine Tallentyre?"

Her fantastic eyes focused briefly on the envelope he held. "That depends on the price I'll have to pay to get them."

He smiled and mentally rolled the dice, enjoying the rush that came with trying to outmaneuver her.

"What the hell." He held out the envelope. "The file is yours, whether you decide to help me or not."

She took it, even more wary now. "What happens if I refuse to help you?"

He shrugged. "Then I lose my bet."

She hesitated but he sensed her unwilling curiosity. He was counting on it. With her aunt gone, Raine had been deprived of the last link to the part of her family history that explained why she was different. How could she resist?

He knew, probably before she did, that he had won. His mirror talent picked up the faint tightening at the corners of her sensitive mouth and the small, almost imperceptible movement of one hand.

"You've got fifteen minutes," she said, opening the door wider. "If I don't like what I hear or if I don't believe you or what I read in this file, you'll leave."

"Deal."

He moved through the doorway before she could change her mind. She waved him to one of the chairs on either side of the table.

The room was larger than an ordinary hotel room. There was a comfortable sitting area and a gas fire that added warmth and atmosphere. He sat down but kept his jacket on. He didn't think she was ready to see the gun.

She took the other chair, crossed her legs and rested both arms on the upholstered sides. She did not offer him tea, but then, there was only one cup on the tray.

"How much do you know about the Arcane Society?" he asked.

She raised one shoulder in a small shrug, dismissing the question as though it were of little importance to her. But his talent told him that she was faking it.

"Very little," she said. "My aunt rarely talked about the organization. I tried to do some research online but I couldn't find anything useful."

"The Society is online but all of its sites are heavily encrypted."

Her mouth curved in disdain. "Just another secret society."

"Well, sure. Show me any group that can trace its origins back to the late sixteen hundreds that isn't secretive. On top of that, the founder was an alchemist."

"Sylvester Jones."

"Right." He smiled. "So you do know that much."

"My aunt mentioned him." She paused a beat. "One of your ancestors, I believe?" she added coolly.

"Right." He grimaced. "Those old alchemists were notorious for being reclusive, secretive and obsessed. I have to tell you that the Society prides itself on following those traditions."

"According to my aunt, Sylvester Jones's descendants have run the Society ever since it was established." She drummed her fingers on the arms of her chair. "The organization is not what anyone would call democratic."

"It's true that there has been a Jones in the Master's Chair ever since the Society was established," he admitted, "but as of the Victorian era there is an elected Governing Council that appoints the Master, who, in turn, answers to the Council, which can replace him. Or her."

"If you've gone all modern and semi-democratic, why the secretiveness?"

"There are reasons."

"Such as?"

"Think about it." He angled his head toward the envelope. "You're the real thing, a genuine psychic, but according to that file, you're not exactly sending out weekly press releases and signing up for talk shows."

She hesitated and then sank a little deeper into the depths of her chair. "Okay, I take your point."

"The Society was established and continues to exist for two primary reasons: to conduct research into the paranormal and to provide a community and a refuge for people who possess paranormal talents."

She stilled. "Refuge?"

"As a member of the Society you are automatically connected to other people like yourself, people with real psychic talents, not quacks and charlatans. You meet people who understand what it means to have additional senses." He smiled again, just a little. "Within the Society, being psychic is, for the most part, considered normal."

"What a concept," she said without inflection.

"Over the centuries the public's reaction to anything that smacks of the paranormal has varied from regarding it as witchcraft or magic to viewing the entire subject as sheer fantasy. In the middle you get all the gullible types who fall for fake gurus, mediums and fortune-tellers. Nowhere outside the Society is the paranormal considered a legitimate field of scientific study, and nowhere outside the Society are individuals with psychic talents considered normal."

"Yes, I did sort of figure that out on my own," she said drily.

"It's true some police departments and desperate families hire psychics when they run out of leads on tough cases. But that doesn't alter the fact that mainstream society thinks that folks who claim to have psychic talents are all gurus, frauds or sadly deluded."

Her smile was too bright and too brittle. "In other words, we're creepy."

He'd touched a nerve.

"I'm guessing that's how some people described your aunt?" he asked, probing gently.

"It's how someone described me."

"Someone you trusted?"

"Yes."

He nodded. "I'll level with you. Even within the Society, people who hear voices are considered to be pushing the envelope."

"I see."

"Try not to take it personally. Thing is, people with especially strong psychic abilities of any kind tend to make other people nervous."

"Including other people who have similar talents?"

"Yes. But I can guarantee you it's a hell of a lot better inside the Society than on the outside." He looked at the envelope. "According to that file, you've been assisting a detective named Bradley Mitchell in the Oriana Police Department for the past year and a half. You've provided information that allowed him to solve a string of cold cases and a recent kidnapping."

She tensed. "You know about my work with Bradley?"

"By all accounts, Detective Mitchell has become a rock star in the department, thanks to you. There is speculation that he will take over the department when the current chief steps down."

"Your file is very complete." She was clearly unhappy. "My name is never mentioned in any of Bradley's reports."

"I'm aware that you've taken great care to keep a low profile. Mitchell handles the media."

She rallied, brisk and certain of herself again. "That's the way I wanted it."

"Because you didn't care to be treated like some scam artist or a fraud or have people think that you were crazy like your aunt?"

For a couple of seconds she looked as if she might throw him out but then she gave him a brief, dazzling smile that did not touch her beautiful eyes.

"Those seemed like good reasons at the time," she said.

"They were excellent reasons," he agreed.

"You really do know a lot about me, don't you?" She stopped smiling abruptly and glanced at the envelope on the table. "Has the Arcane Society been spying on me and my aunt all these years?"

"No. To tell you the truth, you both fell off the Society's radar screen after your father was killed."

"Then how come you know so much about my current history?"

"What I know was put together over the past twenty-four hours. The agency I represent is very good at gathering information in a hurry. But I didn't have to read your file to guess how you would feel about being paraded around in front of the media as a police department psychic."

"No?" Her chin came up a little. "Why is that?"

"Because I would feel the same way."

She did not look impressed. "Is that so?"

"Given what you've been doing for the Oriana PD for the past eighteen months, I'm assuming you've got your aunt's talent or something close to it. You hear voices in your head, right?"

She went very still.

"Relax," he said. "I know where you're coming from. I see visions."

Seven

She was so stunned by his admission that it took her a few heartbeats to find her voice.

"Is that your idea of a joke?" she asked finally.

"No joke." He watched her with his striking, enigmatic eyes. "The ability kicked in full force when I was in my late teens. Everyone expected me to be another para-hunter like most of the other males in my family."

"What's a para-hunter?"

"It's a kind of psychic talent that jacks up an individual's natural ability to hunt. Hunters have preternaturally fast reflexes and the ability to detect the psychic spore left by violence. In addition, they can also see well in the dark."

She wrinkled her nose in disgust. "What do they like to hunt? Elephants? Moose? Snipe?"

He smiled. "Maybe, in ancient times, when the ability to hunt big game animals had a strong survival value. These days they tend to prefer to hunt their own kind. More of a challenge, I guess."

Shock reverberated through her. "They hunt *people*?"

"Calm down. Most of the hunters I know work in law enforcement." He paused a beat. "Although I have to admit that some go bad. None that I am aware of in the Jones family, however."

"I see." She glanced at the door, wondering if she should make a run for it.

"Take it easy," he said. "I just told you, I'm not a para-hunter."

She hesitated, annoyed. "Do you read minds, too?"

"No. The experts say that's impossible."

"What, exactly, are you?"

"Technically, I'm what's known within the Society as a level-ten mirror talent."

"What in the world is that?" she demanded.

"The best the experts can determine is that it's a rare type of psychometry."

"The ability to sense things by touch."

"Right. Your clairaudience is another form."

"Why do they call you a mirror talent?"

He rested his elbows on the arms of the chair and steepled his fingers. He had the air of an academic settling into a fireside lecture. "Ever heard of mirror intuition?"

She reflected briefly. "It's what provides people with social cues, isn't it? If we see someone frown or smile we understand intuitively what's going on. We don't have to stop and analyze the expression."

"Right. And if we see someone pick up a knife we can tell pretty fast whether the person intends to cut his steak with it or try to slit someone's throat."

"I read an article about the phenomenon," she said. "The theory is that it has something to do with special neurons in the brain. They allow us to mentally mirror the actions of others and make instant judgments. It's a bone-deep survival mechanism."

He tapped his fingers together once. "No one knows for sure how our mirror-intuition systems work but one thing is certain: almost everyone has the ability to some degree. In fact, we take it for granted until we meet up with someone who doesn't exhibit the talent, a person with autism or a mental illness like schizophrenia, for example."

"You're telling me that you have a paranormal version of that ability?"

He looked at her over the tips of his fingers. "With my form of the talent I can touch a knife or a gun or a rock that was used to kill or maim someone and intuitively mirror the reactions and responses of the person who used the weapon. I can sense what that person intended to do or what the victim anticipated. I'm also pretty good in a bar fight."

She stiffened. "I beg your pardon?"

SIZZLE AND BURN   69

He smiled. "My ability makes it possible to second-guess an opponent. But I try to avoid that kind of exercise."

"I should hope so." She frowned. "Am I a mirror talent, too?"

"No. Clairaudient psychometry works differently. It's not a visual talent. You are most likely a level ten like me, however."

"How do you know I'm a level ten, whatever that means?"

"Members of the Society are ranked on what's called the Jones Scale. It runs from one to ten, according to the level of psychic energy a person generates. The analysts came up with an estimate for you because your aunt never brought you in for testing when your psychic abilities developed in your teens."

She wasn't sure what to say. She could hardly believe that she was sitting there, discussing psychic talents with a man who acted as if such talents were the most normal thing in the world, like having brown hair or brown eyes. She had never had anything close to such a conversation with a stranger.

With the exception of Bradley, she had never even discussed the psychic side of her nature with anyone except Aunt Vella and her small, closely knit circle of friends. Vella had discouraged such conversations, reminding her always to keep her secret. Trying to explain herself to Bradley had been a serious mistake.

As if he knew what she was thinking, Zack gave her a

sympathetic smile. "Damn, you've missed a hell of a lot by growing up outside the Society. How many other people with genuine psychic abilities have you met over the years, aside from your aunt and your father?"

"I tracked down people who claimed to be psychic," she admitted. "Some worked as consultants to police departments. A couple made their living as fortune-tellers. One wrote a book on how to get in touch with your psychic side through your dreams."

His teeth flashed in a brief grin. "I read that one. It was pure crap."

"Yes, it was." She smiled suddenly. "Good to know someone else came to the same conclusion." She hesitated. "The book was on the bestseller lists for several weeks."

"There are a lot of gullible people out there and lots of frauds who are only too happy to take advantage of them." He regarded her with a thoughtful expression. "I'm getting the feeling that, with the exception of your aunt, every so-called psychic you've met as an adult has been either a fake or a flake."

"My aunt was a major exception."

"I know. And I'll bet every time you looked into her eyes you wondered if you were seeing your own future."

The intimate knowledge in his expression was a little unnerving. She wasn't accustomed to being around anyone who understood her this thoroughly. She couldn't think of a response.

"I'm going to tell you something that is not in that file," he said, glancing at the envelope. "One of our analysts constructed a psychological profile on you. The conclusion was that it was a miracle that you weren't confined to an institution or heavily medicated when you first came into your parasenses."

Ice formed inside her but she managed to keep her face politely expressionless. "Does that mean your analysts think I'm going to end up in an institution, like my aunt?"

"Hell, no." There was easy, absolute certainty in the words.

She held her breath, afraid to trust. "Why are they so sure of that?"

"Statistically speaking, psychological problems associated with parasenses kick in early, usually around the time the talents start to appear. Mid to late teens. If you were going to end up in a psychiatric ward or on heavy-duty meds because of your clairaudient abilities, you'd know it by now."

"But Aunt Vella didn't start having serious problems until she was thirty-two. The same age I am now."

"I won't kid you, no one knows why your aunt ended up in an institution. But it is extremely unlikely that it had anything to do with her talents. She managed those just fine into her early thirties."

"But you said your analysts were amazed that I haven't been confined to a psychiatric hospital?"

"Clairaudient psychometry, especially when it

reaches the level-ten category of power, is one of the most difficult of all talents to handle because the sensation is so intensely disturbing. Without someone to guide you through the learning curve, it's easy to believe you're going crazy. Other people around you usually come to that conclusion immediately and send you off to a series of doctors. You end up on a lot of drugs or in an institution. It becomes a self-fulfilling prophecy."

She gripped the arms of the chair so tightly her nails dug into the upholstery. "It's as if some stranger has invaded my mind. It's so horribly intimate and it's so evil. It makes me feel as if I've been . . . violated."

"Trust me, catching a glimpse or two of what that stranger experienced when he shoved a dagger into someone's chest is just as bad. It's as if I did the deed myself. For a while afterward, I feel—" He broke off abruptly.

She sensed that he hadn't expected to confide that much to her and wasn't sure he wanted to add to it.

Then, very deliberately, he tapped his fingertips together again. Once. Twice.

"I feel contaminated," he said quietly. "As if some of the darkness inside the killer has seeped into me."

She searched his face. "That's how it is for me, too."

His mouth curved in an odd, bemused smile. "I've never told anyone that before. The stuff about feeling the killer's darkness invading me, I mean."

"Neither have I." She took a deep breath. "I always

assumed it would be stupid to go around telling folks that I'm afraid I might be absorbing some of the dark energy produced by a bunch of murderers and freaks. I didn't want to alarm the people close to me, and it certainly doesn't make for scintillating cocktail party conversation."

"Those are the same reasons I've kept quiet about it, too."

Shared secrets, she thought. The exquisite intimacy of the situation was indescribable. How could she be having a conversation like this with a man she had only just met? Where would it lead? Perhaps more to the point, where did she want it to go?

"It's bad enough hearing the voices," she said. "I can't even imagine experiencing the visions."

"What are the voices like?" he asked, sounding genuinely curious.

"Whispers," she said slowly, searching for the words. "But not real whispers, not real voices. My mind understands the difference even though I can't explain it."

He nodded. Deep understanding shadowed his eyes.

"It's as if I'm standing in one dimension and there's a very thin veil between me and another dimension," she said. "Someone is on the other side of the veil, talking. If I pay attention I can make out occasional words. But I don't hear the voices, at least, not exactly. I feel them."

"When you pay attention, as you term it, what

you're really doing is opening yourself up to the stimuli your psychic senses are receiving, allowing your intuition to interpret the energy."

"It's like having a ghost walk through my mind."

"Sometimes you hear the victims' whispers, too, don't you?"

She shivered. "Those are the worst. I hate the freaks' whispers but when I hear the victims' voices, it's a million times more awful because I know it's probably going to be too late to rescue them."

"There are exceptions. That girl in your aunt's basement today, for example, and that kidnapping victim you helped Mitchell find a few months ago."

"True. But the happy endings are few and far apart. And with the cold cases there is never a good outcome."

"Except justice," he said quietly.

"Yes."

"This probably won't be much consolation but Arcane Society research indicates that it's not the actual voices of either the freaks or the victims that you hear. What you're sensing is the psychic residue of the emotions still clinging to the scene."

"I understand, but why do I only sense the dark, terrible stuff? I never feel the happiness or cheerfulness that people leave behind."

"The researchers believe there's an evolutionary explanation. The brain's primary job is to ensure your survival. Generally speaking, emotions like happiness or cheerfulness don't represent a threat so, with the notable exception of sex, the psychic side of your brain has evolved to ignore the good feelings and concentrate on the bad."

She felt heat rise in her face. "Sex?"

He looked amused. "Sex is directly connected to survival. Trust me, our psychic senses are very tuned into the vibes associated with reproduction."

"Oh." Probably best to let that subject drop.

"But powerful emotions such as fear and rage and twisted lust are all linked to danger, so our parasenses have adapted to be more keenly aware of them," he continued. "Our normal senses have, too, for that matter."

She absorbed that. "I see."

There was another silence. The sensation of intimacy in the small, firelit space grew stronger. She could sit here talking to this man for the rest of her life, she thought. The temptation was incredibly appealing and probably dangerous. Time to shatter the spell before it became unbreakable.

She straightened a little in her chair. "What do you want, Zack Jones? And please don't try to tell me that the Arcane Society suddenly gives a damn about me. If anyone cared they would have been in touch a long time ago."

His eyes narrowed faintly. She knew she had scored a point.

"I'm an agent for Jones & Jones," he said. "Ever heard of it?"

Shock lanced through her. So much for the aura of intense intimacy. She called on every ounce of self-control she possessed and gave him her very best *screw you* smile.

"Oh, yes," she said very softly. "I've heard of J&J."

He nodded as if he had suspected as much. "So you do remember. I thought so."

"I remember very well that it was a J&J agent named Wilder Jones who destroyed my father's life's work and burned his lab to the ground. I also think there is a very high probability that Aunt Vella was right in her theory that the man from J&J arranged for my father to die in that car accident. If you're with Jones & Jones, you've wasted your time tracking me down. I can't imagine any reason in the world why I would lift a finger to help you."

Eight

We have a deal," he reminded her.

Get a grip, woman, she thought. He was no longer the only other person she had ever met who truly comprehended what it felt like to live with her strange psychic talent. He was the man from J&J. She must not forget that.

"No, we do not have a deal," she said. Damn it, she could be just as cool and emotionless as him. "You entered my room a few minutes ago waving that envelope and I accepted it. But I made no promises in exchange."

"By taking the envelope, you gave me an implied promise."

"So sue me."

He smiled that easy, confident smile again. "Don't

worry, when you hear the story, you're going to want to cooperate with my investigation."

"Give me one good reason why I would want to help anyone from J&J."

"Only one reason?" He shrugged. "My investigation is going to involve your family history. Will that do?"

"*What?*"

"I think you're a lot like me when it comes to control. You like it and you're good at it. I can guarantee you that the only way for you to exert some control in this situation is by cooperating with me. You're smart and you'll figure that out real quick. Once you do, we become a team."

"You're investigating my family?" She was beyond dumbfounded, she decided. She was baffled.

"Indirectly." He glanced at the black steel watch on his wrist. "I'll tell you about it over dinner, assuming we can find a quiet place to talk in this burg."

"I'm not hungry."

"Using a level-ten talent takes an energy toll on the body. I'm always ready to eat after I've been jacked up."

He was right. She suddenly realized she was ravenous.

"I really don't think dinner is a good idea," she said.

"Shows how much you know. Eating dinner is one of the best ideas I've had all day."

There was no point fighting this. Now that he had

dropped the first shoe she would not be able to rest until she heard the second. Besides, she was hungry.

"Think of going out to dinner with me as a medical decision," Zack said.

"How does it get to be medicinal?"

"You really need a glass of red wine, don't you?"

She thought about that. "You know, you're right. This is very close to being a medical emergency."

"Let's go."

With a deceptively easy movement he uncoiled from the chair, scooped the envelope off the low table, and went toward the door. He didn't glance back at her. He knew she couldn't resist going with him, knew she had to get the answers that only he could give her.

For some bizarre reason she was almost overcome by the urge to laugh.

"Damn," she said instead. She pushed herself to her feet. "You're good."

He took her long black raincoat off the hook beside the door and held it for her.

"I know," he said. "It's a gift."

They went out into the hall and downstairs to the lobby. At the front desk Burton Rosser looked up from a magazine. Burton was about as nondescript as a man could get, Raine thought. Even his age was hard to pin down. She guessed him to be in his late thirties but he could have been much younger or older. He was a fidgety, slightly built man with dirty blond hair and eyes that never stayed still. She got the feeling that he spent a lot of time looking over his shoulder. She wondered who or what was pursuing him.

"Lucky you called ahead and reserved a room before you got here," he grumbled to Zack. "Place filled up all of a sudden."

Zack looked out at the small parking lot. Raine followed his gaze and saw a small herd of news vans.

"Didn't take long for the media to show up," Zack said.

"Yeah, they got the rest of the rooms," Burton muttered. "By the time the cops from Seattle and Portland rolled in, we were full." He appeared relieved by that turn of events. "Had to send 'em down the road to the motel."

Zack nodded, took Raine's arm and steered her toward the door.

Burton stared hard at Raine. "Heard you and Doug Spicer were the ones who found that girl in the basement of the witch's house today."

Raine stopped suddenly and swung around to face him. The long folds of the black raincoat flared out around her boots.

She said nothing, just looked straight at Burton.

Burton flushed a dark red. He blinked several times very rapidly.

"I—I meant in the basement of y—your aunt's house," he stammered.

She did not respond. When she turned back around on her heel she saw that Zack had the door open. Amusement and sincere admiration gleamed in his eyes.

"You're good, too," he said in a low voice as she swept past him. "Damn. I don't think I'm going to be able to resist a woman who can level a guy with one look."

Nine

She held the umbrella high enough to shelter both of them from the steady rain. The damp, cold night air stimulated all her senses. She felt gloriously alive, energized and *hungry* in ways she could not explain. She knew the cause of the exhilarating sensation was the man walking beside her. It was as though he had somehow drawn her into an invisible force field.

By unspoken agreement they turned toward the neon-lit windows of a nearby restaurant. A pickup truck and an SUV went past on the narrow, two-lane street that was the town's main thoroughfare.

Shelbyville was an old lumber town, typical of the many that were scattered around the heavily forested Cascades. The mill had closed years before, destroying the economic base of the community. In a desperate bid to survive, the residents had attempted a make-over, hoping to attract tourists, skiers and city folk looking for a quiet weekend getaway. The effort had been only partially successful. There was a sprinkling of shops and galleries along the three-block walk that separated the B and B and the restaurant. But underneath the thin veneer of updated storefronts you could still see the worn-out bones of the doomed logging town.

"How did you know that I like red wine?" she asked after a moment.

"The J&J analysts pulled up your credit card purchases for the past few months when they put the file together."

"I hesitate to point this out, but isn't that sort of illegal?"

"Probably. I leave that to Fallon Jones. I'm a strong believer in delegating when it comes to stuff like that."

"Who's Fallon Jones?"

"The head of the West Coast office of Jones & Jones."

"He's your boss, then?"

"He likes to think so."

"Is everyone in a position of authority within the Arcane Society named Jones?" she asked, not bothering to conceal her disapproval.

"Heck, no." He managed to sound amazed by the question. "Where'd you get that idea?"

"Gee, I don't know. Let me take a little stab in the

dark here. What's the name of the current Master of the Society?"

To her surprise, he hesitated a fraction of a second before answering.

"Bancroft Jones," he said neutrally.

"Has anyone with a last name other than Jones ever been Master?"

"You're really trying to put me on the defensive here, aren't you?"

"I think that answers my question." She glanced at the envelope he had tucked under one arm. "What else does the file say about me?"

"Let's see. You own a costume design and rental shop in Oriana and you have one full-time employee. You like to shop at Nordstrom and you go through a ton of peanut butter."

"At breakfast," she clarified. "I eat peanut butter on whole grain toast for breakfast almost every day."

"Okay, that explains the peanut butter."

"And if you live anywhere near Seattle, you shop at Nordstrom. It's sort of a rule."

"I'll be sure to annotate the file."

She shoved her free hand deeper into the pocket of her raincoat. "Is everything you know about me contained in that file?"

"Yes. There wasn't a lot of background data available on you and only twenty-four hours to collect it. Most of what was in the J&J files pertained to your father, not you and your aunt."

There was no apology in the words. Just a statement of fact.

"I realize," she said coldly, "that these days there is no such thing as a guarantee of privacy. Nevertheless, I have to tell you that knowing that J&J had the utter gall to create that file makes me furious."

"Figured it would. That's why I told you about it up front. I wanted to get it out of the way so we could talk about other things."

"Like this investigation you say you want my help with?"

"Right."

He pushed open the glass door to the restaurant and held it for her. She swept past him, long coat swirling.

Fifteen minutes later, with dinner ordered and a glass of red wine sitting on the table in front of her, she felt better equipped to deal with the man from J&J.

"Do you ever take off that jacket?" she asked.

"Sometimes."

She decided to let that go. There were, after all, more pressing issues.

"Tell me about this investigation you say involves my family history." She kept her tone as brisk and businesslike as possible.

He did a quick survey of the restaurant. She realized that he was double-checking to make sure there was no one seated nearby who could overhear their conversation. They had been lucky to get a booth at the back because the restaurant was crowded. Raine was pretty sure that most of the tables were filled with members of the media and maybe a couple of out-of-town cops, not local residents. Cell phones rang constantly. There was a lot of loud conversation involving the subjects of airtime and how to get interviews with Chief Langdon. The background din provided ample cover for a private conversation.

She heard Doug Spicer's name mentioned a couple of times but no one looked twice at her. Evidently Langdon had kept his word at the press conference. By now the entire town of Shelbyville undoubtedly knew that she had been with Doug Spicer when the girl was found but the out-of-town media was happily unaware of that bit of trivia.

Zack looked at her across the table. "Truth is, all I've got to work with is one hell of a coincidence."

"What's your coincidence?"

"Last month a researcher named Dr. Lawrence Quinn disappeared. Quinn was employed at an Arcane Society lab located in Los Angeles."

Her fingers clenched around the stem of the wineglass. "Like my father?"

"Yes. In fact, Quinn worked at the same lab where your father worked and he was in the same field. He's a biochemist who specializes in researching psychotropic pharmaceuticals." Zack drank some of his wine and lowered the glass with an expression of mild surprise. "This stuff isn't very good, is it?"

"You don't come to Shelbyville for fine wine and gourmet food."

"In that case, why did your aunt have a house here?"

"She liked the tranquillity of the mountains. Tell me more about Lawrence Quinn and his work."

"You probably already know that a lot of the standard antidepressants, tranquilizers and painkillers have unpredictable side effects on people who possess high-level parasenses."

She sighed. "We found that out when the doctors tried to treat Aunt Vella. Most of the drugs they used made things worse."

"Not an uncommon situation. Psychotropic meds, in general, have unpredictable effects on sensitives. The Society does a lot of work in that area, trying to determine which meds are effective and which are dangerous. And any sensitive who decides to experiment with illicit crap is really asking for nightmares."

"I see."

"Getting back to Quinn, it took a surprisingly long time before anyone noticed that he had vanished."

"Why?" she asked.

"There was some confusion initially because he had requested a large block of extended vacation time. It was only about a week ago that the lab director finally realized that Quinn wasn't coming back to work. No one else missed Quinn, either. He was a loner. No close friends or family. Eventually the director decided that something was wrong and notified J&J. By then a couple more days had passed. An investigation was launched immediately, but Dr. Quinn seems to have fallen off the face of the earth."

"I assume that made your boss extremely suspicious," she said.

He smiled slightly. "Fallon is a suspicious man by nature."

"Probably why he's running J&J."

"Probably. In any event, it didn't take him long to leap to the conclusion that Quinn may have been connected to an organization called Nightshade. The group has created a new version of the founder's formula."

She froze. "My father was expelled from the Society on the rumor that he was conducting research on that damn formula."

"What do you know about it?"

"The formula?" She set her glass down in the exact center of the cocktail napkin. "Very little. Just hints that I picked up from Aunt Vella over the years. I got the impression that the formula had the potential to greatly enhance a person's natural psychic talents."

"Theoretically it can boost a mid-range talent up to a level ten. It can kick a level ten like you or me right off the charts." He paused. "It would, in effect, make us very, very powerful sensitives."

She shivered. "I don't think I'd like that very much.

The voices are hard enough to deal with as it is. I don't want them to get any louder."

"Smart woman. I'm with you. But ours is an unusual and inherently difficult talent to handle. Trust me, there are a lot of intuitives, hunters and others who would kill for a drug that could jack up their talents. And Nightshade is happy to do just that."

"Kill?"

"It has already done so on several occasions that we know of during the past year."

She stared at him, nonplussed. "All because of that stupid formula?"

"It has caused trouble ever since it was recovered from Sylvester Jones's tomb."

"Why is the formula off-limits as far as the Society is concerned?"

His brows rose. "Aside from the fact that no rational person wants to see a whole bunch of superpowerful psychically enhanced criminals created, you mean?"

She winced. "Aside from that."

"The formula is inherently unstable and has always had one hell of a downside," he said.

"What's the downside?"

"Sooner or later, everyone who has ever taken any version of the drug has wound up dead or insane, invariably after turning into a ruthless killer first."

She cleared her throat. "I see. Okay, that definitely qualifies as an annoying side effect."

"We don't know a lot about the long-term effects of

the latest version of the formula that Nightshade has cooked up but one thing has recently become clear. It's seriously addictive."

"How?"

"Insanity followed by suicide ensues within two or three days if the individual is deprived of the formula. From what J&J has been able to figure out, Nightshade uses that nifty little feature to control its operatives."

She shuddered. "I can see where the tactic would be an effective way to keep discipline in the ranks."

"There haven't been any defectors or informants from the organization, that's for sure."

"What does Nightshade want?"

He shrugged. "What most bad actors want. Power and money."

She smiled. "Total world domination, huh?"

He didn't respond to her teasing. "Let's take one small example. Just think what you could do if you had the ability to slip a few very powerful parahypnotists, sensitives with the ability to install hypnotic suggestions in almost anyone, into various corporations and agencies of the federal government. We're talking the potential to control CEOs, governors, senators and the president."

She jumped a little, spilling a few drops of wine. Grabbing a napkin, she hastily blotted up the liquid. "Okay, I can see where that might be a very bad thing. You said the Society has had this problem before?"

"There haven't been many organized attempts to re-create the drug and use it for illicit purposes, but over the years there have been any number of individuals who were unable to resist the lure of experimenting with the formula."

"People like my father?" she said coolly.

Zack folded his arms on the table and fixed her with an unrelenting expression.

"Judson Tallentyre was the most notorious renegade scientist of his generation," he said evenly. "When he disappeared with the formula, the Master and the Council made finding him and destroying his lab and his research notes J&J's top priority. There was a collective sigh of relief in the higher echelons of the Society when Wilder Jones reported that he had completed his mission."

Well, he hadn't tried to sugarcoat that.

"I should probably give you points for honesty," she said, "but I don't feel like it."

"I understand."

She took a fortifying swallow of wine and slowly lowered the glass. "I didn't realize the Tallentyre name was so . . . so infamous within the Society."

"If it's any consolation, the name is well known only at the highest levels."

"Oh, gee, that's a relief."

"The reason that the Tallentyre name is not notorious throughout the Society is because the Master, the Council and J&J have deliberately tried to establish the notion that the founder's formula is a myth. It's part of the overall plan to discourage men like your father from deciding to become modern alchemists."

"My father wasn't an alchemist." Anger shot through her. "He was a scientist. And he was brilliant."

"He was brilliant, all right. No argument there. That's why when he went rogue, he became a serious threat. The Council had no choice but to deal with him."

"Murder him, you mean."

"There is nothing in the file that indicates Wilder Jones murdered your father," he said flatly. "By all accounts the car accident was just that. An accident."

"Just a dose of bad psychic luck?"

"It happens." His brows rose slightly. "And don't smile at me like that."

She blinked and stopped smiling. "Like what?"

"Like you're telling me to go screw myself. Pisses me off."

"Wow. I've managed to piss off the man from J&J. What's the penalty for that?"

"Keep it up and you'll find out. Now, do you want to continue playing games or would you like to hear why Lawrence Quinn's disappearance involves you and your family history?"

"Tell me about Quinn. If I get bored, I can always go back to pissing you off."

"I can promise you that you're not going to be bored. Yesterday Fallon Jones finally got a lead on the missing Dr. Quinn. Turns out Quinn popped up in Oriana last month."

She frowned. "He was in my town?"

"For about twenty-four hours, as far as we can determine. Then he vanished again. Now, here's the really interesting part. Lawrence Quinn paid his one-day visit to Oriana on the same day that your aunt died. You're a hotshot psychic. You tell me. What are the odds that confluence of events is a coincidence?"

Ten

Later he walked her back to the inn, exulting in the sensation of having her so close. In spite of the occasional bursts of fireworks at dinner, or, hell, maybe because of them, he was intensely aware of her femininity. It compelled and challenged him in all the ways that a man could be compelled and challenged. It felt very, very good to be with her, enveloped by the intimacy of the night and the rain and the subtle emanations of overlapping waves of psychic energy. It was like nothing else he had ever experienced.

"That's really all you have, then?" she said when they reached the top of the stairs and went down the hall. "Just the fact that Lawrence Quinn showed up in Oriana the day my aunt died?"

"That's all I've got at the moment, but you have to admit it's an interesting starting point."

She stopped in front of her room, a somber serious expression on her intriguing face. He didn't have to jack up his mirror-talent intuition to sense that she was about to confide one of her many secrets.

"Everyone thinks that Aunt Vella died of natural causes," she said quietly. "A heart attack. But I couldn't believe it at first. She was only fifty-nine and she was in good health. So I paid for a private autopsy before she was cremated."

"That wasn't in the file."

"I'm so glad to hear that J&J is not all-knowing and all-seeing."

"You're doing that smile again," he warned.

"Sorry. Can't help myself."

"What did the autopsy show?"

"Nothing sinister." She dug her key out of her purse. "No evidence turned up to indicate that her death was due to anything other than a heart attack. When you think about it, why would Quinn or anyone else want to murder her after all these years? She was no biochemist. She was an artist. She painted pictures and designed a lot of the masks I sell at Incognito."

"I'm not saying anyone killed her. I agree with you, there's no obvious motive. But the coincidence remains and it bothers me. Bothers Fallon Jones, too."

She opened the door, stepped inside and turned to face him. "I've made my decision. I'll cooperate with your investigation."

"I appreciate that."

She folded her arms and lounged against the door frame, studying him through the lenses of her black-framed glasses.

"You knew I would say yes, didn't you?" she said.

He shrugged. "Figured you'd have a personal interest in the case. I would if I were in your shoes."

"You figured right. But I want to make one thing very clear. It's true I've agreed to cooperate with you, but we don't share the same agenda."

The hair stirred on the nape of his neck. "Meaning?"

"Your objective and that of J&J is to find out what happened to Dr. Quinn. All I care about is my aunt. If she was murdered, I want the killer caught and punished. So long as you're willing to help me do that, we're a team."

He braced one hand on the outside of the door frame. "Deal."

"Good night, Mr. Jones."

She unfolded her arms, plucked the file out of his hand and closed the door quietly but firmly in his face.

Eleven

S on of a bitch," Fallon Jones said.

Zack cranked back in the chair, stacked his heels on the hassock and spoke into the phone. "Look on the bright side. Her goal and ours are aligned, at least for the moment. As long as that holds true, we've got her cooperation."

"And if it turns out there's no connection between Quinn's disappearance and Vella Tallentyre's death?"

"Then I think you can pretty much forget the whole cooperation thing. Raine has no fond feelings toward the Society and she doesn't trust J&J as far as she could throw you and your office. She thinks Wilder Jones murdered her father before he destroyed the lab."

"Son of a bitch," Fallon growled again. "Show her the damn file. It says that the accident was just that."

"She's in her room, reading the file as we speak.

Doubt that she'll believe every word in it, though. I wouldn't if I were her."

"It's the truth, damn it."

"How do you know? You weren't running J&J when the Tallentyre situation went down. We both know that good old Uncle Wilder wouldn't have blinked twice about a little thing like shading the facts for the record. They didn't call him Wild Wilder Jones for nothing."

"Huh."

They both contemplated that piece of family history in silence.

Wilder Jones had gone out the same way he lived, in a blaze of reckless glory. He had been working for J&J's unnamed government agency client at the time. He succeeded in taking down the bad guys and rescuing a number of people but it cost him his life.

In a family studded with individuals who often got involved in high-risk ventures, Wilder had been frowned upon for his penchant for taking outrageous chances. He had been addicted to fast motorcycles, fast women and cigarettes.

There were those in the Jones clan who held that he had always been unstable. Others maintained that, while it was true that he was born addicted to adrenaline, he did not go over the edge until the last few months of his life. That faction claimed that something dramatic happened to Wilder before he left on what amounted to a suicide mission. Zack's mother had always maintained that a woman was involved but that didn't ring true because everyone knew that Wilder changed lovers almost as often as he changed his shirts. Legend had it that he never looked back. Whatever the truth of the matter, Wilder took his secret with him to his grave.

"Do whatever you have to do to keep Raine working with you," Fallon said eventually. "I still think she's the key to this thing."

Zack didn't argue. There was no point. Everyone knew that Fallon's hunches had an accuracy rating well over 90 percent.

Didn't mean that he was always right, though.

Twelve

Burn, witch, burn.

Burn the whole damn lab to the ground.

Punish her. Then destroy her with fire. Got to be sure.

Get those two out of here. Then destroy everything. Can't take any chances. Got to be sure.

She came awake gasping for air, pulse pounding. Her nightgown was stuck to her back with perspiration. She was suffocating under the quilt. She had to breathe.

She sat up suddenly, shoved the covers aside, scrambled out of bed and leaped to her feet. For a couple of minutes she just stood there, trembling, trying to regain control.

She had known there would be nightmares. There always were when she came in contact with the sick psychic energy left by the freaks. She was used to living with the voices in her dreams for a few nights afterward.

But tonight there had been another voice interwoven with that of the freak, a dark voice from the Night of Fire and Tears. *Get those two out of here. Then destroy everything.*

She sank down on the side of the bed and looked at the clock. One-fifteen. She had stayed up until midnight, reading the file and learning just how notorious the Tallentyre name was within the highest circles of the Arcane Society. As far as the Master and the Council were concerned, she was the daughter of a man who had tried to create psychic vampires.

Screw them.

She did not hear the footsteps in the hall. The quiet knock on the door, when it came, made her jump. Edgy energy flickered through her. Briefly she considered pretending she had not heard the soft sound. But she knew him well enough after only a few hours to realize that he would not go away.

She went to the closet and took out the dark blue silk travel robe she had packed. She put it on and tied the sash around her waist. On the way to the door she ran her fingers through her hair, pushing it back behind her ears.

She checked the peephole first. Zack stood in the hall. He was wearing the black leather jacket again but this time he had on only a black T-shirt underneath.

The shadow of what would become his morning beard darkened his face. One hand was flattened against the doorjamb, just outside her narrow range of vision.

The sight of him had a very strange effect on her senses. All the unpleasant, nervy tension that had accompanied the nightmare seemed to convert into another kind of energy. Adrenaline made her shiver. Anticipation twisted inside her. She was aware of her pulse again but this time it was skittering with excitement.

She opened the door. The first thing she noticed was that Zack was barefoot. For some reason the sight of him standing there without any shoes on struck her as incredibly erotic. He had very nice, very strong feet. She had never noticed a man's feet before.

With an effort she raised her gaze to his face.

"Hi," she said, unable to think of anything more intelligent.

Zack regarded her with a knowing expression.

"How bad is it?" he asked, keeping his voice pitched to a low level that would not carry to the room across the hall.

No explanations were needed with him, she thought. A deep sense of longing swept through her. He understood as no one else ever could now that Vella was gone.

"Bad," she said. "But I've been through worse. The girl was alive, after all."

"Sure. But it's still bad because you know what he intended to do. What he did in the past."

"There is that," she allowed. He didn't know everything, she thought. He didn't know that tonight there had been another voice in her dreams. "Why are you here?"

"Figured that, between reading the file and the bad dreams, you probably weren't getting much sleep. I did some consulting work myself earlier today. A two-thousand-year-old dagger that had been used in human sacrifice."

"Yuck."

"Tell me about it." His mouth kicked up a little and his eyes darkened with intimate mystery. "Think maybe we could both use a little distraction?"

She was suddenly a bit breathless again. Her pulse leaped. Energy crackled silently in the atmosphere.

Out of nowhere, common sense reared its boring head.

He knew she was attracted to him, knew she was vulnerable tonight. He planned to use the sexual energy that flared between them to manipulate her. If he thought she was that easy, he could damn well think again.

"What kind of distraction did you have in mind?" she asked, putting as much ice as possible into the question.

He took his hand off the doorjamb and showed her the deck of cards he was holding. "How about a little blackjack?"

Braced for a blatant seduction line, she was thrown

off stride for a couple of seconds. She pulled herself together with an act of sheer willpower.

"You're suggesting we play cards?" she asked, bewildered.

"Thought it would take your mind off other things."

"I was going to turn on the television," she said weakly.

"In my experience, that doesn't work well. Too passive. You need something that makes you concentrate a little but not too much because you're too edgy to do that."

She pushed her initial suspicions aside. He wasn't here for sex. He knew what she was going through tonight. What's more, he was going through something very similar.

"You've been here and done this a few times yourself, haven't you?" she asked.

"The dreams go with the territory for sensitives like you and me. When I'm on my own I usually pour myself a couple of glasses of scotch and play some solitaire."

"I know an herbalist back in Oriana. He mixes up a special herbal tisane that I use. But I didn't bring any with me." She glanced hesitantly at the deck of cards in his hand. "I sometimes play solitaire, too."

He didn't say anything, just stood there, waiting.

"Okay," she said, feeling more reckless than she ever had in her entire life. "Let's play some blackjack."

He moved into the room. She closed the door. Abruptly they were enveloped in darkness. The sense of intimacy was almost overpowering.

She switched on the lamp that stood on the table near the window. In the warm glow, the bed—just another piece of furniture earlier in the day—now loomed very large. She was uncomfortably aware of the tangled sheets and rumpled pillows.

Inviting him into her room had probably been a very big mistake but she could not bring herself to ask him to leave.

Zack walked casually across the room. He didn't appear to notice the bed but she couldn't seem to get her mind off it.

She seized the bedspread and yanked it up over the pillows. The maneuver did nothing to reduce the aura of sexual intimacy that pervaded the small space.

Zack flipped on the gas fire. Instead of sitting down at the table, he lowered himself to the carpet in front of the hearth and sat cross-legged. He shuffled the cards.

"Let's make this interesting," he said.

She held her breath. "How?"

"We'll play for real money." He removed his wallet out of his back pocket and took out some bills. "My stake is twenty bucks."

So much for wondering if he was going to suggest a game of strip poker.

She went to the table, opened her purse and took

out her wallet. She counted out twenty dollars in ones and fives. With the money clutched in her hand she turned back to him.

It dawned on her that, attired in her nightgown with only the knee-length robe for modesty, she could not assume a similar cross-legged position. After a few seconds of close thought, she sank down onto the carpet and folded her legs, mermaid-style, to one side. In that position the robe covered her in what she hoped was a decorous fashion.

Zack dealt the first cards, one each, facedown.

She peeked at her hole card. It was the queen of hearts.

Zack dealt the next two cards, one each, faceup. The jack of diamonds for her. His up card was a three.

"Hold," she said. She shoved a one-dollar bill under the cards.

Zack shrugged and dealt himself a third card. They both looked at the red ten. He flipped over his hole card. Another ten.

"Busted," he said.

She smiled. "I've always been pretty good with cards."

He looked amused. "Yeah, I can see that."

He scooped up the cards and shuffled again.

She watched his hands, fascinated by the easy competence of the way he moved.

"Don't you ever take that jacket off?" she asked.

Good grief, where had that come from? If he removed the jacket he would be down to just his T-shirt and pants.

He paused in mid-shuffle and gave her a considering look. After a moment he seemed to make up his mind about something. He put down the cards and peeled off the black leather jacket.

She stared, transfixed, at the gun in his shoulder holster.

"Oh." She cleared her throat. "I see."

He picked up the cards and went back to dealing.

Twenty minutes later she had won his twenty-dollar stake and another forty to boot. She realized she hadn't been troubled by the freak's voice since Zack had arrived at her door.

"You're right," she said, delighted. "This is working. All I can think about is winning all of your money."

"You're doing a pretty good job of that."

She laughed. "You noticed, did you?"

"Good thing I put my room on my credit card." He gave her a slow, dangerously knowing smile. "But in my own defense, I can tell you that my mind is not on blackjack tonight."

The unmistakable heat in the words caught her completely off guard. He was watching her with a searing, undisguised sexual intensity that seemed to have come out of nowhere. A moment before he had been playing a friendly game of cards. Now he looked as if he wanted to strip her naked and take her right there on the carpet. No man had ever looked at her with that kind of heat.

Her initial suspicions had been correct. Zack had been very aware of the chemistry between them. He had been biding his time, letting her invite him into her space, putting her at ease. The blackjack game was a form of seduction. He'd used it to drive out the voice of the freak, leaving her open and vulnerable.

That knowledge ought to make her very wary, she told herself. And it did, it surely did. But it also increased the level of excitement shimmering through her.

"This is probably not a good idea," she whispered.

His smile got a little more dangerous. Invisible energy pulsed in the air around them.

"Thought you were a gambler," he said softly.

Not when it comes to this kind of thing, she tried to say. But for some reason she could not get the words out of her mouth. Her heart was beating very quickly now. Things inside her were threatening to melt.

Slowly, deliberately, he removed her glasses, reached up and put them on the table. Then he unfastened his holstered gun and set it aside.

He leaned toward her, giving her plenty of opportunity to avoid him. She did not even try to retreat. He caught hold of her and hauled her gently across the short space that separated them, scattering the cards.

Instead of informing him that she was not into one-night stands, she put her arms around his neck.

His mouth came down on hers, heavy, demanding a response. Her body gave it to him. The smoldering fire that had been burning inside her since she opened the door to him roared into a full-blown conflagration. She had never experienced anything like it, had never realized she was capable of such a raging response.

But what really made the blood run hot in her veins was the knowledge that Zack wanted her just as badly as she wanted him. *Not like Bradley*, she thought, elated. Zack wasn't afraid of the voices. A glorious sense of triumph arced through her.

She pressed herself closer, kissing Zack with all the pent-up energy of a woman who has never before been able to abandon herself completely to her own sensual nature. She was vaguely aware of his hands on the sash of her robe. The garment vanished.

With a husky groan, Zack rolled onto his side, taking her with him. He reached up with one hand and dragged the spare blanket off the chest at the foot of the bed. He spread it out on the carpet with a quick snapping motion, as though he were throwing out a fishing net.

The next thing she knew she was on her back on the blanket, looking up at Zack. He levered himself into a sitting position. She watched, utterly enthralled, as he pulled the black T-shirt over his head and tossed it aside.

Firelight gleamed on his sleek shoulders. Filled with a profound sense of wonder and discovery, she reached out and touched the sinewy curve of his upper arm. He caught her hand in his and dropped a warm, damp kiss into her palm, making her fingers curl in reaction.

Something curled deep inside her, too, something that ratcheted up the delicious tension several more degrees.

She circled his wrist with her fingers and tugged him down on top of her, needing to feel the weight and strength of him.

His low, soft laugh was intoxicating, empowering.

"I do like a woman who knows what she wants," he said against her throat.

He slid one leg between her thighs and kissed her deeply. All her senses were ignited now, normal and paranormal. Impulsively she clung to him, savoring the erotic feel of his muscled back beneath her hands. Deliberately she dug her nails into his warm skin.

"Sweet hell." He bit her ear very gently. "Got any idea what that's doing to me?"

In a heartbeat she discovered a new, sexy, sultry side to her nature, a side she had never even dreamed existed.

"Tell me," she whispered. "Tell me exactly what it does to you."

"Makes me hot." His voice had thickened noticeably in the past few minutes.

"Hot is good." She drew her thumb down his strong spine. "What else?"

"Hard." He nipped lightly at one nipple and let her feel his fierce erection pressing against the inside of her thigh. "Very, very hard."

"Hard works, too." She lifted her hips against his. "Go on."

He raised his head and framed her face between his bent arms.

"You know, I'm not feeling real verbal at the moment," he said. "I'm more into show than tell."

She smiled slowly and gripped his shoulders. "Then, by all means, show me."

"With pleasure."

He reached down. She heard the scrape of belt leather and then the rasp of his zipper. He sat up again, just long enough to get rid of his pants and briefs. He took another few seconds to remove a small packet from the pocket of his pants, extract the condom inside and sheath himself in it.

He settled down beside her, pulling her close. When he moved his hand between her legs she lost her own ability to communicate verbally. Within minutes she was clutching at him, trying to wrap herself around him, trying to get him inside her before the exciting tension dissipated.

"Hurry." She sounded desperate, even to her own ears. "Please. Hurry."

"Not so fast." He leaned over her, kissing her throat again, his hand still doing magical, tormenting things between her legs. "We've got all night."

This was a fine time for him to be regaining his verbal skills. She seized him by the shoulders and tried to shake him to get his full attention. It was like trying to shake a massive boulder.

"You don't understand," she got out through clenched teeth. "I think I'm going to come."

"Oh, yeah." His eyes gleamed in the firelight. "I know you are."

"You don't get it," she gasped. "I've never been able to do that with anyone before. Don't mess this up, Jones, or I'll never forgive you."

"You're in charge, babe." He moved on top of her. "This time."

The implied threat only heightened her anticipation.

"So close," she gasped. "So *close.*"

At last he was easing himself into her, stretching her, and somehow still using his hand.

"All you have to do is hang on tight," he whispered. "Real, real tight."

She squeezed her eyes shut and tightened herself around his rigid length.

"That's it," he said. "Squeeze me like you're never going to let me go."

He began to move slowly in and out of her. She was vibrantly aware of the psychic energy flaring between them. It was like being caught up in the eerie, shifting aura of the northern lights. They were creating their very own aurora borealis right here in room number six of the Shelbyville B and B.

And then she was *there*, catching one of the glorious, pulsating waves of night light, riding it across a starry sky. She couldn't breathe but it didn't matter. She wanted to laugh, wanted to cry, wanted to sing. But all she could do was allow herself to be flung away into the darkness.

She was vaguely aware that she was pulling Zack with her. The muscles of his back were marble hard beneath her hands.

She heard his long, drawn-out growl of triumphant release. For a timeless moment he pulsed deep inside her.

When it was over he collapsed along the length of her, crushing her into the blanket.

He dragged himself reluctantly out of the luxurious state of relaxation that had overtaken him following the climax to end all climaxes and opened his eyes. Raine was lying on her side, facing him, one arm tucked under her head. In the firelit shadows her eyes were deeper and more mysterious than ever. She was watching him as if he were some new, intriguing creature, one she had never before encountered. He figured he was probably watching her with a similar expression.

"Damn," he said, stretching his arms high overhead, "if I hadn't believed in the existence of the paranormal before tonight, I'd sure as hell be a believer after that experience."

She blinked, startled, and then she laughed, a light,

sparkling laugh that made him want to hug her close. He did just that.

She was still smiling a short time later when he picked her up and carried her to the bed.

Thirteen

She came awake to the insistent ringing of the room phone. Without opening her eyes she reached out and groped for the receiver.

Her hand collided with a solid masculine shoulder.

She did open her eyes then. Fast. She also sat bolt upright in bed, startled panic snapping through her.

"What?" she managed. The single word came out as a squeak.

"Take it easy." Zack levered himself up on one elbow and regarded her with sleepy-eyed amusement. "It's me. You do remember me, don't you? The guy who was rolling around on the floor with you last night?"

Reality and memories crashed through her. Mortified, she knew she was flushing a deep red.

"Sorry," she mumbled, snatching up her glasses. "I was a little disoriented."

Damned if she would tell him that she wasn't accustomed to waking up to a man in her bed. It was bad enough that she had let him know she'd never had an orgasm with one until last night.

"Don't worry," he said, yawning. "You'll get used to it. You want to answer that phone?"

She had her glasses on now. It dawned on her that the phone was still warbling.

"Right," she said briskly. "The phone."

The instrument was on the table on his side of the bed. To get to it she would have to reach across him. She went blank again at the prospect.

Amused, he picked up the receiver and handed it to her.

"Yes?" She held the phone as though she had never before had one in her hand.

"Miss Tallentyre? This is Burton at the front desk. Sorry if I woke you but I wanted to let you know there's a police detective on his way up to see you. I tried to make him wait until I called you but the sonofa—I mean the guy flashed a badge at me and headed for the stairs. Cops always act like they own the world, y'know?"

Burton sounded even more nervous than usual.

She forced herself to concentrate. "Is it Chief Langdon?"

"No. Guy said his name is Mitchell. Detective from Oriana. Says he knows you."

"Bradley?" She stared at the wall on the far side of

the room, trying to wrap her mind around the name.
"Here?"

"I just told you, his name is Mitchell, not Bradley."

"Right. Thank you."

She handed the phone back to Zack. He took it,
one brow raised, and gently replaced the receiver.

"Company?" he asked neutrally.

"Yes. Bradley Mitchell."

"The Oriana detective you've been working with?"

"Uh-huh." She pushed the bedding aside and swung
her feet to the floor. "For some reason, I seem to be very
popular all of a sudden."

"You'll be even more popular if you answer the
door dressed like that," Zack observed drily.

She glanced down and discovered that she was stark
naked. "Oh, damn."

She grabbed her robe and hastily pulled it on. Zack
uncoiled from the bed with an easy, masculine grace.
He was wearing his briefs. Crossing the room, he
picked up his black T-shirt and trousers.

She scurried into the bathroom and checked herself in the mirror. The disheveled creature gazing
back at her looked as if she had just climbed out of
bed after a night of extremely hot sex. She ran a brush
through her hair but that didn't do much to alter the
impression.

A knock sounded on the door.

"I'll get it," Zack said a little too casually. "Take
your time."

She rushed to the bathroom doorway but he was already on his way to the door, anticipation flowing off him in palpable waves. She noticed he had put on his leather jacket. When she glanced at the bedside table she saw that the gun and holster were gone. The testosterone level in the room was suddenly off the charts.

She went into full deer-in-the-headlights mode. Was letting Zack answer the door a good idea or a really bad one?

Then her head miraculously cleared and she suddenly felt extremely cheerful.

Letting Zack answer the door was an excellent notion.

She turned and went back into the bathroom.

"Thank you," she called over her shoulder. "I'll just be a minute."

She closed the door, whirled around and pressed her ear to the panel.

The door opened in the outer room.

"Sorry," Bradley said, startled. "Wrong room. Could have sworn the guy at the front desk said number six."

"Looking for someone?" Zack asked a little too helpfully.

"A woman. Must be the door across the hall."

"There's a woman in this room," Zack assured him. "Raine's in the bathroom at the moment, about to take a shower. We just got up."

"Raine Tallentyre?" Bradley was uncharacteristically flustered. "She's here?"

"Right," Zack said. "I'll tell you what, why don't you go back downstairs? I'll let Raine know you're here. If she wants to talk to you, she'll meet you in the lobby after she gets out of the shower."

"Listen, I don't know who the hell you are, but I can tell something's wrong here. I'm Bradley Mitchell with the—"

"Oriana PD. I know. Nice badge, by the way."

"I want to speak to Raine," Bradley said. "Now."

Raine winced. Bradley was using his hard cop voice. That was not good.

"Is this police business or personal?" Zack asked, politely curious.

"This is official business."

"In that case, maybe she should talk to her lawyer first."

"That's enough. I'm coming in."

"I don't think so." Zack's voice was suddenly ice cold.

"I don't know who the hell you are," Bradley growled, "but as far as I'm concerned, I've got probable cause to think you may have harmed Raine Tallentyre. Get out of my way."

So much for her little moment of feminine revenge. The adrenaline and testosterone in the other room had reached toxic levels. It was time to intervene.

With a tiny sigh of regret because she had just

begun to enjoy herself, she opened the bathroom door and put her head around it.

"Bradley," she said brightly. "I thought I heard your voice. What are you doing here in Shelbyville?"

Bradley looked past Zack, staring at her. Confusion and anger tightened his photogenic features. He looked like a homicide cop off a television series: hard-eyed and square-jawed. His dark hair was just long enough to touch the back of his collar. This morning he was dressed in jeans, an open-throated shirt and a slouchy sports jacket.

"What the hell is going on, Raine?" he asked. He seemed mesmerized by the sight of her in her robe. "Are you okay?"

"I'm fine," she assured him. She folded her arms and lounged in the doorway, going for total nonchalance. "What are you doing here?"

"I got a call from the local chief." Bradley frowned. "Guy named Langdon. He told me that you and some real estate agent found one of the Bonfire Killer's victims in your aunt's basement. That right?"

"Yes. I gave the chief your number as a reference. I thought that would be the easiest way of staying off the list of suspects. Do you mind if we talk about this later? I'm headed into the shower."

Bradley flicked a suspicious glance at Zack. "Who's he?"

"A friend," she said. She couldn't resist giving him her special smile.

"Good friend," Zack corrected helpfully. "The name's Jones. Zack Jones. By the way, does it piss you off when she smiles at you like that? It sure pisses me off when she does it to me."

Bradley rounded on him, looking ready to explode.

"Please go downstairs, Bradley," Raine said quickly. "I'll be down in twenty minutes."

Bradley's face tightened further but it was obvious he was out of practical options.

"Twenty minutes," he said.

"Or thereabouts," she said sweetly.

Without another word, he turned and stalked off toward the staircase. Zack closed the door very gently behind him and looked at her.

"I'm guessing the two of you did more than just find a few bodies and track down some killers together," he said without inflection.

"Not a great deal more," she said, choosing her words with exacting care. "My fault."

"What went wrong?"

"I'm what went wrong. Bradley and I had a nice little friendship thing going on. I made the mistake of thinking it had the potential to blossom into something else." She paused. "He knew about the voices, you see."

Zack nodded, comprehending immediately. "So you figured he was okay with your psychic side?"

"One night after a case I invited him to my place. I had a bottle of wine waiting. A little chocolate fondue.

A fire. Not to put too fine a point on it, I tried to seduce him."

"I sense a bad outcome here."

She flushed. "It was extremely awkward for both of us. In the end he finally had to tell me the truth."

"Which was?"

"That the thought of making love to a woman who hears voices really creeped him out."

"What do you know?" Zack shrugged. "Gets me hot."

Nonplussed, she just stared at him.

"Go figure," she finally managed.

He gave her a quick, wicked grin. "Yeah. Go figure. So where do things stand with you two now?"

"Nowhere. The debacle in my condo happened last month, shortly before Aunt Vella died. I'm surprised to see Bradley here today. I thought, given our mutual embarrassment, that he would want to avoid me just as much as I want to avoid him."

"What about your working relationship?"

"It would be extremely difficult to go back to being just friends or colleagues after what happened. At least it would be for me. I was humiliated beyond belief."

"Not to mention hurt?"

She winced. "Okay, I'll admit that being told I gave him the creeps was a little hard on the ego."

"Wonder why he drove up here today?"

"I have no idea. Last I knew he was fixing to become famous."

Zack raised his brows. "How's that?"

"Ever hear of Cassidy Cutler?"

He narrowed his eyes very faintly. "Why does that name sound vaguely familiar?"

"Probably because you've seen it on the bestseller lists. She's a true-crime writer."

"Right." He nodded. "She's the one who did the book about the freak who was stalking and killing members of a family in Florida. The cops couldn't figure out why he had targeted them. They finally arrested a cousin, I think."

"Did you read it?" she asked.

"Hell, no. I don't read stuff like that. Got enough nightmares of my own. I just know what I saw in the papers."

She smiled wryly. "Sounds like we have something in common when it comes to our bedside reading. Be that as it may, evidently Cassidy Cutler has decided that her next best seller will feature a certain small-town homicide detective who has recently closed a string of cold cases."

Zack laughed. "She's writing a book about Mitchell?"

"Bradley called me a few days ago. He was very excited. He told me that Cassidy Cutler had arrived in town with an assistant and had started background research."

"Interesting. I wonder if Mitchell plans to tell her that the reason he was able to close those cold cases was because he worked with a psychic?"

She shuddered. "I sincerely hope he never says a word about me. As far as I'm concerned, he can have all the credit."

"Because the last thing you want is to have your name appear in one of Cassidy Cutler's books?"

"The very last thing."

Fourteen

Bradley downed a long swallow of coffee, lowered the dainty china cup to the saucer and glowered across the table.

"What's wrong with you?" he asked. "Are you sick?"

"Good grief, no. Never felt better, in fact." Raine poured tea for herself from the pretty yellow-and-green pot. "Why do you ask?"

"I don't know." He searched her face, frowning. "You look like you're running a fever or something."

She stifled a smile. "Must have been the shower."

The inn's small dining room was packed with the same media-heavy crowd that had filled up the restaurant the night before. The din of cell phones and conversation assured privacy.

"It's not the damn shower," Bradley muttered. "There's something about you this morning."

"Well, I did get a good night's sleep last night," she said smoothly.

Bradley's jaw hardened. "How the hell did you meet Jones?"

She was seated facing the entrance to the dining room. Zack was at the front counter, collecting a cup of coffee in a plastic cup and a muffin from the harried-looking woman at the cash register. He saw her watching him and raised a hand in a casual greeting. She wriggled her fingers at him and then turned to Bradley.

"I'm sorry, what were you saying?" she asked.

He scowled. "Where did you meet Jones?"

"Good grief, you don't actually expect me to discuss my personal life with you, do you?"

"I didn't know you had a personal life," Bradley muttered.

"I do now," she said demurely.

"Does Jones know what you do?"

"Yes. Guess what? It doesn't creep him out."

Bradley had the grace to redden. "I said some stuff that night that I didn't mean, okay?"

"You meant it, all right."

She watched Zack take his coffee and muffin out into the adjoining lobby.

"Look," Bradley said, very earnest now, "even if our personal relationship wasn't meant to be, it doesn't follow that you and I can't still work together. We're a team, Raine."

The urgency that was vibrating from him was starting to make her curious. Bradley usually did the laid-back, wise-cracking, macho-detective thing very well. For the sake of her ego, it would have been pleasant to believe that he was wildly jealous of Zack but she was almost certain that was not the case. There was no doubt that he had been alarmed to find her with another man this morning but she was sure it wasn't because he had suddenly discovered that he wanted her after all.

"I don't know about that," she said quietly. "I've been under a lot of stress lately because of my aunt's death."

"I know," he said quickly. "But work can be excellent therapy."

"I need time to clear my thoughts and consider what I want to do next. Also, something else has come up. What with one thing and another, I'm just not ready to go back to working with you. Not for a while, at any rate."

He gripped the edge of the table with both hands. "Damn it, Raine, there isn't time for you to think it over. I've got a new cold case."

She was starting to get curious now. She had never seen him this tense, not even when he was about to make an arrest.

She picked up the teapot and refilled her cup. "What's the rush? By definition, there's no great urgency about a cold case."

"That's not how the families of the victims look at

it," he said, righteous indignation ringing in every word. "Some people have died waiting for justice."

In spite of her determination, guilt twisted inside her. "I realize that."

Satisfied that he had scored a point, his expression softened. "I'm sorry to put pressure on you like this. I realize your aunt's death hit you hard and that you've got your hands full dealing with her estate. But I'm in a bind here."

Now they were getting to the heart of the problem.

"Define *bind*," she said.

He exhaled heavily. "Here's the deal, honey—"

She raised her teaspoon as though it were a magic wand. "Don't ever call me honey."

"The thing is, this new cold case is very important. I need your help."

"What makes this particular case more important than any of the others?"

He glanced around the room a second time to make certain they were not being overheard and then leaned forward again and lowered his voice.

"Cassidy came up with this great idea for the book," he said.

She put the spoon down on the saucer. It made a nice little clatter.

"Cassidy Cutler," she said. "I should have seen that coming."

"Just hear me out, okay?" Bradley pleaded. "She wants to follow me through the process of closing a cold case from start to finish. We took a look at some of the files together and picked one that is tailor-made for you."

She choked on her tea. "For *me*?"

"Us," he amended swiftly. "It's a case that is ideally suited to your kind of, uh, observations and insights."

Observations and insights was his politically correct term for the clues she uncovered with her psychic abilities. After working together for more than a year he still couldn't bring himself to acknowledge that what she possessed was a true paranormal talent.

"Forget it," she said flatly. "I don't want to be in your book."

"Why not?" he demanded.

"For starters, I'd lose my anonymity. Oriana isn't New York or LA. I wouldn't be invisible there. The very last thing I want is for people in town to point me out on the street and whisper that I hear voices in my head."

"It would be great publicity for your business."

"Are you kidding? People will say that I'm crazy like my aunt. I don't need that kind of publicity, trust me. I want to be able to shop or attend the monthly meetings of the Oriana Business Association without worrying about what folks are whispering behind my back."

"Okay, okay," he said, raising a hand, palm out.

"Do you know what people here in Shelbyville called my aunt? They said she was a witch. And some of them really believed it."

"Look, I'll talk to Cassidy. Maybe she'll agree to give you another name for the book."

"I'm sorry," she said. "I've got a lot going on at the moment. I do not want to get involved in the book."

"It's him, isn't it? The guy in your room this morning."

"No," she said coolly.

"Bullshit. How long have you known him?"

She was getting seriously annoyed, she decided. She flashed her special smile. "Let's see, about sixteen hours."

"*Sixteen hours?*"

"Give or take an hour. I wasn't watching the clock too closely, to tell you the truth."

Bradley was dumbfounded. "You mean you just met him yesterday and already you're sleeping with him? Are you crazy?"

She paused, the teacup halfway to her mouth, and just looked at him, not speaking.

"I don't believe this," he continued, oblivious to her sudden stillness. "You must be out of your mind."

"But then, you've always wondered about that, haven't you?" she asked, keeping her voice perfectly even.

He frowned. "Wondered about what?"

"Whether or not I was crazy. That's why the thought of going to bed with me creeped you out, remember?"

He grimaced. "Damn it, Raine, don't put words in my mouth."

"The word *creep* came out of your mouth, not mine."

"Look, you don't hear voices." His mouth thinned. "You just think you do. What you have is a natural gift for observing things at a crime scene that other people miss, that's all."

"I hear voices, Bradley," she said flatly. "In some circles that's a working definition of crazy."

"That guy I found you with upstairs—"

"His name is Zack. Zack Jones."

"Jones. You really told him that you hear voices?"

"Yes."

Bradley looked at her with patent disbelief. "And he doesn't have a problem with that?"

"Says it turns him on."

"Something's wrong with this picture."

"Good-bye, Bradley. Good luck with the book."

She hitched her purse over her shoulder and started to rise.

"Please." The word sounded as if it had been ground out of him. "I need your help. This book is very important to me. If it works, I'll be able to use it to leverage myself straight into the chief's office. Hell, maybe I'll go private."

"Good luck," she said, meaning it.

"You owe me," he said.

"Excuse me?"

He leaned a little farther toward her.

"I did you a favor a year and a half ago when you

came to me with that wild story about a woman who was kidnapped and murdered by her husband, remember?" he said, his tone low and forceful. "Nobody else in the department was willing to give you the time of day. But I went into the old files and found one that matched the details you provided. I got the chief to authorize the DNA work. I tracked down the husband and got the confession."

"And you got all the credit for closing the first in the long string of cold cases that will soon make you famous. I'd say we're even, Bradley."

"Shit. We should have kept the relationship professional. Why did you try to make it personal?"

She flinched a little and then managed to rally. "My mistake. I thought we were more than colleagues. I thought you understood—" She broke off. "Never mind. I take full responsibility for the failure to communicate. Now, I've got to go. Chief Langdon said the detectives from Portland and Seattle may want to interview me this morning. As soon as that's over, I'm going back to Oriana. I've got a business to run."

He reached up and grabbed her wrist. "Damn it, Raine, we're a team."

Zack materialized in the doorway. He started toward the table. She could feel the dangerous vibes from halfway across the room.

She looked pointedly at her captured wrist. "I think you'd better let me go," she said quietly. "Now."

Bradley finally noticed Zack coming toward him. Hastily he released her. His expression hardened.

"Wise up, Raine," he said. "I don't care if Jones knocked your socks off in bed. He didn't just appear out of thin air. Whoever he is, he wants something from you, too, doesn't he? And it isn't just hot, sweaty sex."

"That's none of your business."

Bradley was in full interrogation mode now.

"I can't believe you met him yesterday," he said. "What's his connection to you?"

"I guess you could say he's an old friend of the family."

Fifteen

An hour later Zack leaned a shoulder against the inn room wall, folded his arms and watched Raine place a toiletries kit into her small overnight suitcase. She had looked different after that conversation in the dining room, he thought. She was back inside her safe zone.

"The interview with the detectives didn't last long," he said.

"Mostly because they weren't interested in talking to me." She zipped the small suitcase closed. "They're too busy working the crime scene. Also, I got the feeling that Chief Langdon had warned them that I wasn't quite right in the head."

"Did he tell you when you could get back inside the house?"

"No, but it will probably be several days, at least."

She made a face. "For all the good it will do me to put it on the market now."

"You never know. You might get some wack job of a buyer who will get a little thrill out of owning a genuine house of horror."

"In Shelbyville?" She made a small, derisive sound. "Fat chance."

"Well, at least you did a good job staying out of the limelight. This place is filled with reporters and camera crews. I counted two more news vans in the parking lot this morning. But no one is paying any attention to you."

"Thank goodness."

"According to the local morning paper, Spicer is getting the credit for rescuing the girl."

"He's welcome to it. Langdon probably finessed things to throw the spotlight his way."

"What are you going to do about Mitchell?"

"Nothing, at least not right away." She put on her raincoat.

"He's not going to give up."

"Probably not." She took a last look around the room, checking to see if she had missed anything. "He thinks that the book Cutler wants to write will make his career."

"He's going to have a hard time maintaining his glittering track record without your help."

"Bradley solved a lot of cases before he met me," she said quietly. "He's a good cop."

"What did he say to you this morning that made you go back behind your barricades?"

She looked at him, eyes widening. "I don't know what you're talking about."

He said nothing, waiting.

She gripped the handle of the suitcase very tightly. "Okay, he pointed out that my relationship with you had gone from zero to sixty in a very short length of time. He seemed to think that I had allowed myself to be seduced and that you probably wanted something from me other than hot, sweaty sex."

He whistled softly. "Had a feeling that might be it. A comment like that would definitely account for the dimming of the postcoital glow."

She flushed and stalked toward the door, suitcase in tow. "I'm leaving now. See you in Oriana."

"You'll see me in your rearview mirror." He dropped his arms and straightened away from the wall. "I'll be right behind you. Couple things before you leave."

She paused at the door and regarded him with steady suspicion. "What?"

He moved closer and caught her chin on the edge of his hand.

"Mitchell was right," he said. "I do want something from you."

"I know." She lifted her chin free of his hand. "But it's okay because I've got an agenda, too."

"You want to find out if your aunt was murdered."

"Yes."

"In other words, when it comes to using each other, we're even," he said.

"Right," she agreed.

"The other thing you should remember," he said deliberately, "is that the hot, sweaty sex came after we made our deal."

She blinked twice, watching him cautiously through her dark lashes.

"So?" she said, her voice laced with subtle challenge.

"I didn't go to bed with you in order to get you to cooperate. You had already agreed to help me because there was something in it for you. I went to bed with you because I wanted to have hot, sweaty sex with you. I was under the impression that you wanted to have hot, sweaty sex with me. Was I wrong?"

"No," she said, cornered and defiant. "You're not wrong. The hot, sweaty sex had nothing to do with our business arrangement."

He kissed her quickly, before she could pull away.

"Glad we got that settled," he said.

She stepped back, opened the door and moved out into the hall.

"But the more I think about it," she said, speaking over her shoulder as she walked toward the stairs, "the more I agree with the old advice on the subject of mixing business with pleasure. It's never a good idea."

"Shows how much you know," he said softly.

She pretended she hadn't heard him and went down the stairs. But he knew she'd heard every word.

Sixteen

The witch hunter let himself into the room with the electronic lock pick. There was no real security at the Shelbyville B and B. No need for any. Until today the town had enjoyed a reputation for an almost imperceptible crime rate. It was one of the reasons he had chosen Shelbyville as home base for his most recent round of witch hunts.

The first time he saw the remote, tree-shrouded Tallentyre house at the end of the long, lonely lane he knew it was perfect for his purposes. It had belonged to a genuine witch. It was only fitting that it be used to destroy others of her kind. He had spent months making certain that it was safe for him to use. It had taken several more weeks to select the first witch to be punished in it. Now all his work had been wasted.

Like aunt, like niece. Clearly Raine Tallentyre had inherited her aunt's dark powers. She, too, was a witch, the most powerful one he had yet encountered.

Rage poured through him, swamping every other sensation. In the blink of an eye the Tallentyre witch had ruined everything he had worked so hard to establish in Shelbyville. Now he would be forced to find a new location for his work.

But first he had to learn more about what he was up against. Raine Tallentyre was a threat he had never anticipated. She had to be destroyed but he must move cautiously. She was clearly very dangerous.

Fortunately, the girl he had put in the storage locker never saw his face. He always wore a ski mask when he went about his work. But the very fact that she had been found before her punishment was complete had jolted him badly. He assured himself again that she would not be able to tell the cops anything that would lead them to him. Nevertheless, for the first time in his career as a witch hunter, he was very worried. In the past he had always been able to count on the purifying effects of fire to destroy all the evidence.

After a long, sleepless night, however, he had finally understood. This was a test set by the demon.

He comprehended that his work would no longer be as easy as it had been in the past. He was moving to a new level of power and he would be hunting more powerful witches. He must be ready.

It was clear that Raine Tallentyre's arrival in Shelbyville and her discovery of the captured witch was no accident. If he wanted to survive and grow stronger, he would have to prove to the demon that he was more powerful than Raine. He would have to hunt her and destroy her, just as he had hunted and destroyed all the lesser witches he had punished.

He stood quietly, looking around the small space. It had been a risk coming here today before the room had been cleaned but he needed something personal, an object that she would recognize when he began to hunt her. It was important that a witch knew fear before he came for her. He had discovered that satisfaction early on in his work. He sometimes spent weeks and months stalking them in order to make them afraid.

He prowled the room, searching for what he needed. He considered one of the pillowcases for a moment and then rejected it. He wanted something more interesting.

There was a damp washcloth on the towel rack in the bathroom, but it was a very ordinary white washcloth. There was nothing distinctive about it. She might not even recognize it. That wouldn't do.

He hurried out of the bathroom. His eyes fell on the tea tray.

He reached down and picked up the delicately painted cup.

Perfect.

Later that afternoon he discovered to his horror just how much progress Langdon and the detectives from Portland and Seattle were making on the case. At the post office there were rumors of DNA and hair samples and even his precious photos. The stupid girl was remembering all sorts of things, things that could come back to haunt him.

Panic and rage roared through him. This was all the fault of the Tallentyre witch. He picked up the teacup and hurled it at the wall. The fragile china shattered.

Shaking, he went down on one knee to pick up the pieces.

Burn, witch . . .

Seventeen

I can't believe you're working on a case with someone from Jones & Jones," Andrew said. He opened
the oven door to check the paella.

"It's not like I had much choice," Raine said. "Not
after he told me how that Arcane Society researcher
showed up here in Oriana the same day that Aunt
Vella died."

The kitchen had been remodeled recently. It
gleamed with the latest in high-tech appliances. The old
countertops had been replaced with green granite, and
the cabinet doors were fitted with sparkling glass fronts.

No amount of superficial change could alter the
feeling Raine got whenever she walked into the room.
This was home. Although, growing up, she and Vella
had lived across the street, the truth was that she had
spent most of her time here, wrapping herself in the

security and warmth that Andrew and Gordon provided. She had done her homework and learned to
bake cookies in this kitchen.

She and Zack had arrived in Oriana a few hours before. The invitation to dinner had come as soon as she
called Gordon to tell him what was going on.

"Bring him over for dinner tonight," Gordon said.

*"But you two are busy packing for that travel conven-
tion,"* she reminded him. *"You have to leave for the airport
at five in the morning. You don't want to entertain us tonight."*

*"If you think we're leaving town without checking out
your Mr. Jones, think again."*

Zack had taken the summons to dinner with surprising equanimity. *"They want to get a look at me.
That's what families do."*

Raine had experienced a little rush of pride and satisfaction when he said that. She had a family, just like
he did. True, hers consisted of only two people, neither
of whom shared any of her DNA, but that didn't matter. The three of them were linked together with other
kinds of bonds. Tonight her clan was circling the wag-
ons, gathering protectively around her, sending a not-
so-subtle message to Zack. Andrew and Gordon were
making sure he knew that she was not alone, not vulnerable.

The saffron-scented aroma of the paella wafted out
of the open oven. Raine sniffed appreciatively.

"Smells great," she said.

"It's coming along nicely." Andrew closed the oven door. "The rice is almost done. Another ten minutes and I'll toss in the shrimp and clams."

In his late fifties, with a receding hairline, he was a neatly made man, trim and distinguished.

"I can't believe that after all these years, J&J is suddenly interested in you," he said.

"It's not me they're interested in," she said. "All they care about is their missing researcher. They're trying to track him down."

"The way they tracked down your father?" Andrew said, his face grim.

"Yes." She opened a drawer and took out a whisk. "They gave me a file to read. I have to admit that it does look like Dad was involved in some potentially dangerous research."

"Doesn't matter, Raine. J&J isn't the FBI. It's nothing more than a private investigation firm. It doesn't have the legal authority to invade a man's private property and destroy it."

"I know."

"I just can't see any way Vella's death could be connected to that missing researcher. Not after all these years."

"You have to admit it's a little weird that he was here in town on that day."

Andrew's eyes tightened with disapproval and concern. "I don't like any of this, Raine. Jones makes me very uneasy."

"You don't like him?" she asked, paying close attention, because although Andrew claimed no psychic gifts, he was an excellent judge of people.

"To be honest, I'm not sure what to make of him." Andrew picked up the wineglass on the counter and took a sip of the expensive cabernet. He lowered the glass. "He's not anything like Bradley, though, is he?"

"No."

"I could tell that much just meeting him tonight. With Bradley, everything is on the surface. But Zack is a thousand miles deep. You only see what he wants you to see." Andrew looked at her. "He's a lot like you in that regard."

Raine focused on whisking the rich balsamic vinegar into the pricey olive oil that Andrew insisted on using for everything from cooking to salad dressings.

"If I was a bad guy," she said, thinking about it, "I wouldn't want either one of them on my trail."

"But of the two of them, which one would you worry about the most?"

Raine stopped whisking. "Okay, now that's a strange question."

"Got an answer?"

She shrugged. "I'd worry more about Zack."

"Why?"

She tapped the whisk lightly against the bowl. "Probably because I know he wouldn't quit, even if the trail went cold on him. Bradley would be more pragmatic. He'd cut his losses and go look for some other bad guy."

"I got the same impression." Andrew exhaled slowly. "I'll tell you something, though."

"What's that?"

"Even though I'm suspicious of Zack's reasons for contacting you, I must admit I think we all owe him."

Raine widened her eyes, amazed. "Good heavens, why?"

"Gordon and I have been concerned about you lately."

"You knew I was feeling a little low."

"You weren't just a little down," Andrew said meaningfully. "We were starting to wonder if you were flirting with full-on depression."

"Hey, I wasn't that bad off." She stopped, thinking about it. "Was I?"

Andrew smiled. "It wasn't as if you didn't have some legitimate reasons. In recent weeks you've lost your only known blood relative, the woman who was the closest thing you had to a parent. Then Mitchell dumped you. On top of that, you had to deal with Vella's estate. Last but not least, you stumbled into another crime scene yesterday."

"At least that last situation had a more or less happy ending. Could have been a lot worse."

"True. But yesterday evening when we talked on the phone, I could tell that even though you found that young woman alive, you were bracing for the usual nightmares. I could hear it in your voice."

She shrugged. "The nightmares are part of it."

"You always say that. Tonight, though, when you walked through the front door with Zack Jones, you looked different."

"I did?"

"It was as though you had bounced back and were ready to take on the world again."

Raine tossed the whisk into the sink. "Zack told me that Aunt Vella's depressive episodes were not related to her psychic talents."

Andrew took a moment to absorb that information. Then understanding lit his face.

"I'll be damned," he said softly. "So that's why you're feeling so much better. Jones reassured you that your little eccentricities aren't going to land you in an institution."

"He seemed very certain. He said that psychological problems related to psychic talents manifest themselves much earlier in life. Late teens or early twenties. Evidently the Arcane Society studies that sort of thing." She hesitated. "He also said that if Aunt Vella had contacted the Society, their experts might have been able to help her."

"You know, I once suggested to Vella that she do just that," Andrew said.

"Really? What did she say?"

He swirled the wine in his glass, looking troubled.

"She just cried and said that wasn't possible. Something about it being too late. She feared the Society and J&J. Didn't trust anyone connected to either organization. She'd have been horrified if she knew about Zack Jones."

"I know."

He exhaled deeply. "I think there's something you should know. When you told me that a man from J&J had contacted you, Gordon and I both went cold to the bone. We were afraid that history was about to repeat itself."

She wrinkled her nose. "Hardly. It's not like I'm engaged in any illicit drug research."

"That's not what I meant. Wilder Jones didn't just show up out of the blue one night and burn down your father's lab. He and Vella had an affair."

Shock rendered her speechless for a couple of beats.

"They were lovers?" she finally got out.

"For almost two months. Wilder Jones seduced Vella, lied to her and used her to find your father and the lab."

She sagged back against the counter, utterly floored. "Why don't I remember him? The first and only time I recall seeing Wilder Jones was the night he and his men stormed into the lab."

"Vella was afraid that if you knew she was dating you would become anxious about the possibility that she might leave you. She would never have done that, of course. She would have found a way to keep you with her, even if she had married. She would not have left you with your father. But until she was certain that the relationship with Wilder was going somewhere, she thought it best to shield you from it."

She shook her head. "I'm stunned. I had no idea."

"Vella fell for him hard. She told us she was in love for the first time in her life. Gordon and I used to take care of you on the nights when she and Wilder wanted to be alone."

"No wonder she went hysterical the night Jones and his men destroyed the lab. She was betrayed by the man she loved. She blamed herself for everything: my father's death and the destruction of his work."

"Yes."

"That certainly explains a lot," Raine said quietly. "She was never really herself again after that night."

"No," Andrew said, "she wasn't."

"What happened to Wilder Jones? Did he ever come around again?"

"No. He disappeared."

"Poor Aunt Vella," Raine whispered. "At least I now know just why you're so worried about my relationship with a man from Jones & Jones."

"Yes."

"But this time around things are different," she said quickly.

"Because you think that Zack has been honest with you?"

"Yes."

"Maybe he's just using a different approach to manipulate you."

"I may resemble Aunt Vella, but I'm not her. My eyes are wide open, Andrew."

"I know, but—"

Raine walked to him, put her arms around him and hugged him.

"Now there's something I want to tell you," she said.

Andrew smiled wryly. "Is this going to be another shock to my system? Because if so, I think I'd better have a second glass of wine first."

"Remember what you said a few minutes ago? About how when I lost Aunt Vella I lost the person who was the closest thing I had to a parent?"

"I understand." Andrew patted her shoulder gently.

"You were wrong," Raine said.

Andrew's hand stilled on her shoulder.

"I loved Aunt Vella with all my heart and I know she loved me," Raine said. "She did her best to take care of me. But you and Gordon are my real parents. Everything I need to know about life I learned from you."

"Oh, Raine."

Tears glittered in Andrew's eyes. He put his arms around her.

They stood together in the kitchen for a long time, holding each other very tightly.

Eighteen

Mitchell is a complete bastard as far as I'm concerned," Gordon said. "He took advantage of Raine, used her to make himself look like a brilliant detective. Allowed her to think he cared about her. She started to fall in love with him. When she made her feelings clear, he humiliated her."

"I know," Zack said. "I got the whole story in Shelbyville."

He and Gordon were in the living room sitting in deep leather chairs in front of the fire, drinks in hand. The sounds and smells of dinner emanated from the kitchen along with the low murmur of voices. If it weren't for the interrogation he was undergoing he would have been able to settle back and enjoy a cozy, comfortable evening and a home-cooked meal. Instead, he was running the gauntlet.

He knew it was no accident that he and Raine had been separated almost immediately after they walked through the door. Smart, streetwise cops always split up the suspects for interrogation purposes.

Gordon was silver-haired and solid-looking. Something about his eyes, his haircut and the way he carried himself shouted ex-military.

"So you're from J&J?" Gordon said.

"Yes," Zack said.

"You know there's some evil history between Raine and J&J."

"Heard that."

"She was in her father's lab the night those SOBs stormed in and smashed everything in sight. She was just a little kid. I remember she had nightmares for months afterward. Between that and losing her father, she was badly traumatized."

"I'm aware that J&J didn't handle the situation well," Zack said.

"Vella always maintained that Wilder Jones was responsible for Judson Tallentyre's death."

"I'm almost certain that's not true."

Gordon cocked a brow. "Almost?"

"There's nothing in the files that indicates that Tallentyre's death was anything other than a car crash." He tasted the excellent wine and lowered the glass. "Besides, J&J doesn't operate that way. It's not some secret mafia-style organization or a firm that supplies hit men. It's an investigation agency. It investigates."

Gordon snorted indignantly. "It did more than investigate Raine's father. Vella told us the men from J&J destroyed his life's work."

"That was an extreme case," Zack said.

Gordon settled into his chair. "You know, there's something we never did understand. Why the hell did J&J go after him so aggressively in the first place? Vella was never clear about that. We got the impression that he had stolen a formula for some kind of proprietary drug from the Arcane Society. Is that true?"

"I'm not at liberty to give you the details," Zack said. "But yeah, that's the bottom line. The Society has very strict rules governing research. Tallentyre violated those rules. He knew damn well what he was doing and he knew that if J&J found him, it would do whatever it had to do to shut down his lab."

Gordon frowned. "If Judson Tallentyre was operating an illicit drug lab, the Society should have informed the police and let the authorities handle the problem. It had no right to send a bunch of vigilantes after a man."

Zack examined the wine in his glass while he decided what to say next. As a matter of policy, J&J, like the Arcane Society community, kept a low profile where the general public was concerned. But Gordon was not a member of the general public. He and his partner had accomplished an amazing feat. Between the two of them they had somehow managed to accept Raine and her wild, disturbing talent. They had given her a family and a reasonably normal life instead of institutionalizing her. Gordon had a right to some answers.

"In most cases involving criminal actions, J&J operates as a regular investigative agency, calling in the cops when necessary," he said quietly. "But there are some internal affairs that it handles on its own."

"I don't care if the Arcane crowd is some kind of secret society," Gordon said. "No group is above the law. And I'll tell you something else."

"What's that?"

"You break Raine's heart, Andrew and I will break both your legs."

Zack nodded. "Fair enough." He contemplated the fire. "What happens if she breaks my heart?"

"Not our problem. You're on your own."

Nineteen

Cassidy Cutler stared at Bradley Mitchell, unable to believe her bad luck.

"What do you mean, Raine turned you down?" she said. "You told me there wouldn't be any problem convincing her to help you with the Dellingham case."

It was after nine o'clock. They were sitting in Bradley's big black SUV. She had been waiting anxiously to talk to him all day but after he returned from Shelbyville he was immediately called out to deal with a shooting. By the time he finally showed up at the hotel where she and her assistant, Niki Plumer, were staying, she was seething with impatience.

The news that he had failed to get Raine Tallentyre on board with the writing project was the final straw. It had never dawned on her that he wouldn't be able to persuade Raine to work with him again for the sake of the book. Who didn't want fifteen minutes of fame?

Bradley turned in the seat to face her. He gripped the wheel tightly with his left hand. "It's not my fault, damn it. When I found Raine in Shelbyville, some guy opened the door of her room."

"She was with another man?" Cassidy pondered that complication briefly. "But I thought she went to Shelbyville to deal with a house her aunt left her."

"That's right."

"How in hell did she find time to shack up with some stranger?" Cassidy frowned. "Or was it a man she already knew?"

"She said he was an old friend of the family but that's hard to believe."

"Why?"

He shrugged. "With her aunt gone, Raine hasn't got any family left. I have a hunch she picked him up just to get some revenge against me. I think she got a kick out of throwing him in my face."

"But she didn't even know you were on your way up there to see her."

Bradley rubbed his jaw with his right hand. "Coincidence, then."

"I'm an author. I don't believe in coincidences. Editors won't buy them."

"I'm a cop. I'm not big on them, either."

Cassidy drummed her fingers on the seat. "This is a disaster. The psychic angle is absolutely perfect. My editor loves the idea. Niki has already started the background research."

"The thing is, Raine doesn't want any publicity," Bradley said. "She's afraid people will think she's crazy if it gets out that she hears voices."

She studied him in silence for a moment. He really was nice to look at. The light from the streetlamp revealed the exceedingly well-chiseled planes and angles of his face. His picture, alone, on the front of the book would sell out the entire first printing, she thought. The talk shows would love him. Damn, damn, damn. There had to be a way to salvage the deal.

"I'll give her a fake name," she said.

"I suggested that to Raine. She still wasn't interested. She hasn't ever wanted any of the credit for closing those cases. I told you, she doesn't want people to wonder if she's a wack job."

"Great. Just great. A seven-hundred-and-fifty-thousand-dollar advance and a potential TV series in the toilet all because Raine Tallentyre is pissed at you."

Bradley went very still. "You never said anything about a TV series."

"My agent mentioned it today. I didn't want to tell you about it until it's a sure thing."

"Damn," he muttered. "A TV series."

Cassidy thought about the problem some more. "All right, Raine doesn't want the publicity. How does she feel about money?"

"Huh?"

"She's a businesswoman. An entrepreneur. She must be interested in money. Did you ever pay her for the work she did with you?"

"How the hell was I supposed to pay her? Not like I got any bonuses for closing those cold cases. Besides, she never asked for money."

"There's a lot riding on this book," Cassidy said. "Maybe I should point out the financial advantages to her."

Twenty

The drive back to Raine's condominium complex took about five short minutes. Zack didn't try to break the silence in the car until he pulled into a parking space and shut down the engine. He folded his arms on the wheel and contemplated the lobby entrance.

"All in all, I thought that went well," he said. Might as well go for a positive spin.

"Gordon threatened to break both your legs," she said without inflection.

He grinned. "You heard that?"

"Yes."

"He's just looking out for your best interests. That's what family does. Sometimes they screw up the job royally, but it isn't for lack of trying to do the right thing."

She shot him a speculative look. "Has your family ever screwed up that way?"

"Let's just say they're applying a lot of pressure at the moment. They want me to pursue a different career path."

"You mean, they don't approve of you working for J&J? I can understand that. Sounds like it's risky work at times."

"It's not that so much, although Mom has never been happy with that aspect of my work. The thing is, they all want me to go into the family business."

"Ah, got it. The old tradition of following in your father's footsteps."

"My grandfather's, in this case. Dad escaped. He's a high-grade sensitive with a talent for strategy. He owns a law firm."

"What's the family business?" she asked.

"It's a mid-sized corporation. A holding company with a lot of diversified interests."

"No offense, but it sounds boring."

"No," he said, not taking his eyes off the entrance. "It isn't. Until a year ago I thought I wanted to run the business when the time came. I'd planned on taking Granddad's place ever since I was a kid. You could say I was trained for it from the cradle."

"What changed your mind?"

He shrugged and unbuckled his seat belt. "I finally realized a year ago that I wasn't cut out for the job."

He opened the door and climbed out before she could ask any more questions.

By the time he got around to her side of the car she seemed to have understood that he no longer wanted to discuss his future career prospects. That was a very good thing. He'd come damn close to telling her about Jenna. He never talked about Jenna. Not with anyone.

They walked toward the building entrance.

"What did you tell Andrew about your reasons for working with me?" he asked when she paused to dig out her key.

"I explained that there's a chance I might find out what really happened to Vella. He and Gordon know I was never satisfied with the natural-causes verdict."

"So you didn't mention the hot, sweaty sex angle?"

She gave him a severe glare as she unlocked the security door.

"It isn't a sexual thing," she said crisply. "Not anymore. I told you, it's not smart to mix business with pleasure."

"Who said anything about me being smart? I could be a lot dumber than I look."

She laughed. "Not a chance."

He pushed the door open for her. "But it was a hot, sweaty sex thing for a while," he said as she went past him. "Right?"

"One night, that's all," she said gruffly. She started toward the stairs to the second floor. "Tell me, where does Wilder Jones fit on the Jones family tree?"

An ominous sense of impending disaster swept over him.

"Wilder was one of my uncles," he said, cautious now. "I've got several."

"Were you aware that your uncle and my aunt had a red-hot affair? Andrew told me that Wilder Jones seduced Vella in order to find out the location of my father's lab."

I'm doomed. Mom was right about you, Uncle Wilder. You were a real pain in the ass.

"That wasn't in the file," he said aloud. He seemed to be saying that a lot lately.

"I suppose it would have been kind of embarrassing for a hotshot J&J agent to admit that the only way he was able to get to his target was to seduce and manipulate the target's sister. Doesn't sound like a real heroic, manly thing to do, does it? More like sneaky, underhanded and conniving."

He took a deep breath. "Maybe that's not how it was."

"According to Andrew, that's exactly how it was."

He said nothing.

Raine stopped outside a door. "Now, at least, I know why Aunt Vella cried so hard that night. She trusted the man she loved and he betrayed her."

"I'm sorry, Raine."

She gave a visible start. Her hand stilled on the doorknob. "That's what he said."

"Who?"

"Wilder Jones. Aunt Vella held me in her arms while the men from J&J tore the place apart. All I remember was the noise and the flashlights and the way Vella was raging and crying. I didn't know what was going on. I was terrified."

"Hell of an experience for a kid to go through."

"One of the men—it must have been Wilder—stopped in front of Vella and me. He said, *I'm sorry, Vella*. She screamed at him. Called him a lying bastard. He ordered someone to take us out of the building and put us in the backseat of a car. The next thing I recall was hearing an explosion. The night sky was suddenly filled with flames, and Aunt Vella wouldn't stop sobbing."

"What happened after that?"

"One of the men drove Vella and me back to our house. That was the end of it. I never saw anyone from J&J again until you showed up at my door in Shelbyville."

He exhaled slowly. "I can see how you came by your opinion of the agency."

"After that night Aunt Vella developed a serious phobia about fire. She never burned a single log in the fireplace in the Shelbyville house. Even burning candles made her nervous."

She opened the door and moved into a small foyer. When she flipped on the light, two cats appeared out of the darkness, one silver and gray, the other a mix of brown and gold shades. She put her purse down and scooped up a cat in each arm. The combined purring sounded like a couple of miniature Harley-Davidson engines.

"This is Robin," she said, indicating the brown-gold cat. "The other one is Batman."

He rubbed each cat behind the ears. "I can see why you named them after a couple of superheroes. With those markings around their eyes they look like they're wearing masks."

"I got them from a shelter when they were a few months old. Their pasts are a mystery, just like Batman's and Robin's."

"Like your own?"

"I seem to be learning a lot about my own past now that I've started hanging with you."

"That's the reason you're calling a halt to the hot sex, isn't it?" he asked softly. "You're afraid that history might repeat itself."

"I just think it would be best if we kept things on a businesslike footing from now on. Good night, Zack."

She closed the door.

He stood there for a few seconds, listening to her throw a couple of bolts. Then he went back downstairs to his car.

Twenty-one

The homeless man was curled up in the limited shelter of the motel's dimly lit breezeway. He had covered himself with a ragged purple blanket and an insulating layer of newspapers. Zack stopped a short distance away. The man's face was hidden by the blanket pulled up over his head. The sole of one running shoe poked out from beneath the lower edge of a newspaper.

Some street people were so disturbed by their own unstable thoughts that they radiated a kind of chronic psychic chaos in the form of an aura that even nonsensitives could often detect. Zack opened his senses cautiously.

He waited a couple of seconds but didn't get any crazy vibes from the homeless man. He removed his wallet from his back pocket and took out a five-dollar bill. He dropped the money into the curve of the man's body where it would not be visible to an opportunistic street thief. The night guard in the small pickup that patrolled hourly would be around soon. The sleeper would be shaken awake and sent on his way. With luck he would notice the five.

You weren't supposed to give money to street people. It was a safe bet that the cash would be wasted on booze or some other form of self-medication. But it was always possible that the sleeper was one of those unfortunates who had been saddled with a strong psychic talent that eventually drove him to alcohol and the streets. If enough people labeled you crazy, the prediction usually came true.

He walked past the sleeper, heading for the locked wrought-iron gate that secured the side entrance closest to his room. Who was he to deny the sleeper whatever it took to dull the sharp edges? After the really bad cases, he often went home and used a little scotch and solitaire to hold the visions at bay.

He switched his thoughts back to Raine. Objectively speaking, it was probably a good thing that she had not invited him to spend the night. He needed to do some serious thinking. That didn't make the prospect of going upstairs to an empty bed any more appealing but it did force him to concentrate on the job.

First on the list of priorities that night was a call to Fallon Jones. It was unlikely that the news of Wilder's affair with Vella Tallentyre all those years ago would affect the current situation but it constituted a missing fact in the file. Fallon should be made aware of it. He was forever harping on how even a tiny, seemingly insignificant detail could ripple through a case and cause an explosion. Chaos theorists called it the butterfly effect.

Tiny, seemingly insignificant details.

Small details like the sole of a new, clean, expensive running shoe poking out from beneath a blanket of newspapers.

He heard the faint indication of movement behind him even as he started to turn around.

The sleeper was wide awake, coming up off the bench like a striking cobra. The blanket and newspapers fell away, revealing an elderly woman with a helmet of gray curls. She wore a baggy, flower-print dress. In her right hand she gripped a small, folded umbrella.

The frail senior citizen launched herself in a low, preternaturally fast rush, the point of the umbrella extended and aimed like a rapier at his midsection.

Twenty-two

I t was for the best." Raine switched on the automatic kettle, leaned back against the counter and looked down at Batman and Robin. "Last night in Shelbyville was just one of those things. It shouldn't be allowed to happen again. Can't let physical attraction interfere with this investigation."

Robin twitched one ear but on the whole did not seem interested in her analysis of the decision not to invite Zack into the condo. Batman was focused on the large ceramic biscotti jar. Andrew had given it to her. It was decorated with a cheerful blue-and-yellow Raffaellesco design and was one of the few touches of exuberance among her otherwise minimalist furnishings.

She filled a tea strainer with some of the herbal tisane that she purchased from a local tea shop. The voices would be back tonight. It usually took a few days before they finally dissolved into the dark swamp where such memories were stored.

She was in her nightgown and robe. The lights throughout the condo were turned down low. A Mozart concerto played softly in the background. Mozart usually worked. What worked even better was the loud, head-banging rock music played at Pandora's favorite nightspot, Café Noir. But she didn't feel like calling up her assistant and asking if she wanted to go to Noir. She wanted to be by herself for a while and contemplate all that had happened in the past twenty-four hours.

"Life, as we know it, is changing," she said to the cats. "Got to stay in control here."

Batman meowed softly and continued to stare at the biscotti jar. Robin wandered over and joined him.

She raised the lid of the jar. Robin's tail flicked. Batman concentrated harder, probably using some kind of weird cat psychic power on her to encourage her to take out a treat. It was working.

"Have you any idea what it was like to finally meet a man who actually understands how it feels to hear the voices in my head?" She selected two of the cat munchies inside the jar and replaced the lid. "Last night was the combined result of the aftereffects of adrenaline and the thrill of knowing there is a sexy man out there who knows I'm psychic and who doesn't think I'm creepy."

Batman meowed again.

"Okay, okay."

She gave the cats their snacks. They set to work on them with polite greed.

The water in the kettle began to boil. She switched off the pot and poured the hot water into a mug. The gentle, soothing aroma of the herbs in the strainer wafted upward.

"One thing about blackjack and sex with Mr. Jones," she announced to the cats, "they definitely took my mind off the voices last night."

Batman finished his treat and looked hopeful.

"You know you only get one at night," she told him.

The cats gave up trying to use their psychic powers on her.

She removed the strainer from the mug and set it on the small dish beside the kettle. Carrying the mug in her right hand, she went into the living room. Her black ballet-style slippers made no sound on the bare hardwood floor.

The translucent origami shapes of the wall sconces cast a subdued glow across the low black leather sofa and chairs. The gas fireplace was outlined in gleaming black tiles. A deck of cards stood waiting on the black granite coffee table. Two elaborately designed climbing trees for the cats, complete with secluded sleeping quarters and a cat gym, stood near the window that overlooked the condo gardens. Batman and Robin liked to look out at the view.

The only colorful objects in the room were the three art glass sculptures. Each was positioned on a white pedestal and lit with a tiny, low-voltage halogen lamp suspended from the ceiling.

Gordon and Andrew complained that the place, with its white walls, uncarpeted floors and black furnishings, looked like a modern art gallery or a meditation center. But she liked the calm, tranquil, uncluttered effect. On bad nights it was an antidote to the voices.

She went to stand at the window, mug in hand, and looked out at the condominium gardens. She wondered if Zack had gone to bed yet or if he was on the phone to Fallon Jones, trying to find out more about what had happened between Wilder and Vella. She could tell the revelation that the two had been involved in an affair had caught him by surprise, just as it had her. He hadn't been faking it.

A chill sparked down her spine. It was as if someone had touched the nape of her neck with a live wire. The mug in her hand trembled. Several drops of hot liquid dampened her fingers, making her draw a quick, startled breath. Some of the tisane splattered on the hardwood floor.

"Oh, damn."

She stared down at the spilled liquid, baffled by the sudden attack of nerves. Zack had been on her mind virtually all day but this was the first time the thought of him had rattled her like this.

She turned around and hurried back into the

kitchen. Setting the mug down on the counter, she yanked a couple of white paper towels off the stainless steel holder and returned to the living room.

Crouching, she mopped up the spilled tisane. When she was satisfied that she had got it all, she went into the kitchen again, opened the cupboard door beneath the sink and dropped the crumpled towels into the trash.

Now her pulse was racing. She looked at her fingers. They were shaking.

What was happening to her? She had been feeling fine only a few minutes before. Now something was very wrong, something involving Zack.

It was ridiculous, but she couldn't overcome the overwhelming urge to call him, just to make sure he was okay. He'd written the number of his cell phone on a card and given it to her before they left Shelbyville. *Just in case we get separated and you need to reach me*, he'd said.

What had she done with the card? It was imperative that she find it. She tried to think. It wasn't easy because the adrenaline was pounding through her now, filling her with a sense of frantic urgency.

Batman meowed loudly at her feet. Robin wrapped himself around her legs. The cats were channeling her anxiety.

This is crazy. Oops, wrong word. Not crazy. Just weird. Really, really weird. For Pete's sake, slow down and focus.

She had dropped Zack's card into her purse before

getting behind the wheel. Her purse. Where else would one put a card with a phone number?

Okay, that made the next step simple.

She hurried into the foyer and opened the closet door. Her purse was right where it was supposed to be, on the shelf next to her keys, a pair of gloves and a stack of neatly folded scarves.

When she reached for the purse, the back of her hand brushed the side of her black raincoat hanging nearby. Dark psychic energy splashed through her, acid hot.

. . . *Let the witch know she's being hunted. Make her afraid* . . .

"No."

Instinctively she jerked back, promptly tripping over Batman, who had come up behind her. She staggered and fell against the wall. She grabbed for the door handle to keep her balance, missed and landed on the floor in a distinctly undignified position.

For a moment she just sat there, trying to get her nerves and her senses under control. Batman and Robin prowled around her, restless and agitated.

"Don't look at me," she whispered. "I don't know what's going on, either."

Maybe the incident in Shelbyville followed by the revelations about the mystery of Vella's death had been too much for her psychic nerves.

Don't think that way. Zack told you you weren't going to go crazy because of your psychic side. Pull yourself to-

gether. Find out what the hell just happened to you. You had that raincoat on earlier this evening and there were no psychic zingers from the freak.

"Some kind of fluky psychic echo effect," she told the cats. "Maybe Zack can explain it. He has all the answers."

Zack. She had to call him immediately. That was what had started this whole thing.

She gave Batman a pat and scrambled to her feet.

Gingerly she reached back into the closet and touched the raincoat.

. . . Punish her like the others. Burn, witch . . .

She snatched her hand away again. It *was* the freak. But what she was hearing in her head was not an echo of what she had heard earlier. This was something else, something new.

Clenching her teeth against the invasion of the voice, she took the coat out of the closet and examined it closely. There was something in the pocket that was giving off the bad vibes.

She opened the pocket cautiously and looked inside, afraid of what she might find.

A piece of broken china gleamed. She recognized the dainty green-and-yellow floral pattern. She was looking at a broken cup from the Shelbyville B and B.

Twenty-three

There was something wrong with the little old lady. She was blurry. And then, in mid-stride, she morphed into a man clad entirely in black. A black ski mask covered his face. Instead of an umbrella, he gripped a military-issue knife.

Zack's eyes were confused by the abrupt transformation but his psychic senses were fully jacked and had no difficulty whatsoever interpreting the situation. Intuitively, as he always did when the chips were down, he went with his parasensitive instincts. His mirror-talent abilities recognized a would-be killer regardless and telegraphed the assailant's next move in a nanosecond.

He slid to the right, *knowing* that the attacker expected him to shift to the left. The ski-masked man blurred again. In the next instant the elderly woman reappeared. She adjusted with dazzling speed, whipping around to run down her prey.

The old lady was a para-hunter.

That was not good news. He had spent a lot of time in the gym and the dojo, sparring with his hunter relatives. He was good but he lacked the preternatural speed and lightning-fast reflexes of a level-ten hunter. Ski Mask was definitely level ten.

He yanked the gun out of his holster. The elderly woman lashed out with a slashing kick. He managed, just barely, to evade the killing force of the blow but the toe of the woman's shoe caught him in the ribs and sent him reeling back. A second strike numbed his shoulder. The gun flew out of his fingers. He heard it clatter on the concrete. There was no time to search for it. He could not take his eyes off the old woman.

In the next instant she morphed back into Ski Mask. This time Zack's mirror talent caught the cues just before the transition and telegraphed the information to his brain in a neurochemical way that was literally faster than the speed of thought. He suddenly understood something very important. The constant morphing came with a price. Switching from ski-masked killer to little old lady and back again slowed the guy down a little. So why was he wasting the psychic juice it obviously required to shift back and forth?

Even with the faint hesitations that occurred when he jumped from one identity to the other, the attacker was still hunter-fast. It was all Zack could do to avoid the slashing knife. There was no way to escape the assault. The wrought-iron gate was at his back. The assailant blocked the only exit out of the breezeway.

The old woman came at him again in another lethal charge. His mirror talent noted the way she was balanced and he knew without being able to explain how he knew that she expected him to dodge right. He waited until the last possible second and went left.

The old woman slammed into the iron bars. For a fraction of a second or so she seemed disoriented.

Zack seized the opening and ran toward the far end of the breezeway. If he could reach the parking lot, he could use the parked cars as shields.

Ski Mask was suddenly behind him, running him down the way a predator runs down prey.

Zack whipped around in a small, tight circle. When he came out of it, he had one foot extended.

Caught in mid-morph, Ski Mask stumbled over the foot and went down. But he rolled to his feet as the old lady with paranormal speed.

Zack grabbed the purple blanket that was lying on the concrete. He flung it at the woman's face.

The blanket found its target, wrapping around the attacker's eyes for a few critical seconds. The old woman leaped back, swiping wildly at the fabric with her free hand.

Lesson Number One from the gym and the dojo: luck and surprise beat even the best reflexes every time.

The woman switched back to the ski mask persona.

Zack made no attempt to close with him. There was no way he could win in hand-to-hand combat with a hunter. He had to stay out of reach. The gun was his only hope. He could see it out of the corner of his eye. It lay on the concrete about ten feet away.

He was edging toward it when headlights suddenly flared, illuminating Ski Mask and himself in a blinding glare. A car was pulling into a nearby parking slot.

The black-clad figure hesitated again. Then he whirled and raced out of the breezeway into the shadows of the parking lot. Zack scooped up the gun and went after him, but he knew that the fleeing man's superior reflexes and speed were going to trump his mirror talent.

Ski Mask arrived at a dark SUV that had been sitting at the far side of the lot. The passenger door was already open and the vehicle was in motion when he leaped up into the passenger seat. The big engine roared as the driver stomped down on the accelerator.

The vehicle, running with the lights off, slammed forward, aiming straight at Zack. It didn't take any high-grade mirror talent to figure out that if he stayed where he was he was going to get flattened.

He leaped into the safety of the narrow valley between two parked vehicles.

The SUV sped past him, out of the lot and onto the street. It vanished around the next corner. He was not greatly surprised to note that there was no license plate.

He heard a familiar ring tone. He reached into his pocket, pulled out the phone and flipped it open.

"Jones," he said automatically, his attention on the streetlights at the intersection where the SUV had disappeared.

"Zack?" Raine's voice was tight and urgent. "Are you all right?"

The anxious edge in her voice distracted him immediately.

"What's wrong?" he asked sharply.

"I'm not sure. I got a little panicky a few minutes ago. For some reason I thought you were in trouble."

"Huh."

"You're breathing hard. Oh, good grief." She sounded utterly chagrined. She cleared her throat. "Am I, uh, interrupting something?"

It took him a second to figure out what she meant. "No. What's going on, Raine?"

"Don't snap at me like that. Pisses me off."

"Damn it, what the hell is wrong?"

"I went to the closet to get your number out of my purse and I found something weird. If I'm not hallucinating, then I may have a serious problem."

"What kind of problem?"

She drew a deep, shaky-sounding breath.

"I think the Bonfire Killer may have followed me home," she said quietly. "He was in my condo tonight. Left a little souvenir."

Twenty-four

He was at her door in less than ten minutes, which meant he'd broken every speed limit in Oriana.

When Raine let him into the condo her eyes went straight to the duffel bag in his hand. It was a straightforward clue that he intended to spend the night. She did not raise any objections. That spoke volumes about her common sense, he thought.

The two cats circled him a few times with interest and then allowed him to rub their ears. Satisfied, they trotted off into the living room.

That was when he realized that Raine was staring at him, her mouth open in shock.

"What happened to you?" she whispered, eyes widening.

He looked down and saw that his shirt was hanging

loose beneath his jacket. His hair was probably mussed but, all in all, not too bad. He wondered why she looked so stricken. Then it dawned on him that she was picking up the energy created by adrenaline and violence.

"There was a fight," he said. "The other guy got away."

"You got into a *fight*?"

"It's a long story. I'll explain later."

She glowered. "You told me you tried to avoid bar fights."

"This fight wasn't in a bar. Tell me about the cup fragment you found in your coat. Are you sure it's a piece of the one you used in Shelbyville?"

For a moment he thought she was going to insist on pursuing the bar fight lecture but she reluctantly focused on the cup instead.

"I can't be certain it's the same cup that was on the tea tray," she admitted. "But there was one just like it in my room. It was still there when I checked out."

"I remember it."

"He must have entered the room, found the cup, smashed it and left a piece here tonight."

He looked at the locks. "How did he get into your condo?"

"I don't know." She hugged herself tightly. "There was no sign of forced entry. I didn't pick up any bad vibes off the doorknob."

"You wouldn't," he said absently, "not unless he was in a killing frenzy when he broke in. Also, I wouldn't be surprised if he wore gloves when he let himself in here. Psychic energy transmits most readily with direct skin-to-object contact. Gloves are fairly effective barriers."

She shuddered and looked at the black-lacquered shelf positioned beneath a wall sconce. "He must have been in a rage when he smashed the teacup. That piece of china reeks of panic and fury."

He followed her gaze and saw a fragment of broken china on the shelf. Steeling himself, he reached out and picked it up.

Dark energy crackled across his senses. A scene appeared and then disappeared in his mind like a film clip from a nightmare. It lasted only a couple of heartbeats. In that brief span of time he felt the cup in his hand, experienced the rush of rage and panic, abandoned himself to the sheer release of hurling the delicate china against a hard surface.

He set the china fragment back down on the shelf, trying to dampen the fresh surge of biochemicals shooting through his bloodstream. He'd already OD'd on that particular drug mix tonight.

"The freak was here, all right," he said. "Or maybe I should say *a* freak was here. I never went into the basement of your aunt's house in Shelbyville, so I don't have a basis for comparison."

"Trust me, it's the same person." She stared unhappily at the broken bit of china. "This is the first time one of them has followed me home."

"Unnerving," he agreed.

"Try scared out of my wits."

He caught her by the shoulders and pulled her gently against him, wrapping her close. "Scared out of your wits is good. Scared people tend to be more careful."

"No offense," she said, pressing her face into the front of his shirt, "but that wasn't quite the positive, upbeat approach to this situation that I was looking for."

"Sorry. Probably a J&J thing. Fallon Jones holds with the everything-that-can-go-wrong-probably-will-go-wrong theory of psychic detecting. He becomes annoyed whenever his agents get too positive and upbeat."

"Sounds like a real fun guy."

"Look up the definition of *fun* in the dictionary and you'll see Fallon's picture right next to it."

She made a strange, half-muffled little sound that could have been a choked laugh. Some of the tension went out of her. She raised her head.

"Tell me what you saw," she said.

"I got a visual of what you heard. The bastard smashed the cup in a fit of red-hot rage and panic. He's running scared. Blames you for ruining his plans."

"He must have been watching me in Shelbyville,

waiting for me to leave. But he took a risk going into my room. I wonder if anyone noticed him."

"Good question. But there's another possibility."

"What's that?"

"Maybe he wasn't afraid of being seen. Maybe he had a right to be in the B and B." He thought about it a little more. "Could have been one of the employees or a guest. The inn was crammed with news crews. It wouldn't have been hard for someone to blend in with a crowd of strangers in town."

"True."

"The big question here is what made him focus on you? As far as everyone back in Shelbyville is concerned, you and that real estate agent stumbled onto the victim by accident."

She pulled back a little and looked at him with a shadowed expression.

"I don't know about you," she said, "but in my experience, the real freaks don't make allowances for coincidence. Everything is a sign to them."

He exhaled slowly. "You're right."

"The girl was found in my house, a *witch's* house. He knows that I'm the witch's niece. That makes me a witch, as well. Last but not least, he knows that I was there when his victim was discovered. The upshot is that he holds me personally responsible for ruining his latest witch hunt."

"Any other traces here in your condo?"

"No. I did a quick tour while I was waiting for

you." She wrinkled her nose in disgust. "Doesn't mean he didn't have a good look around."

"I doubt if he stayed for more than a few minutes. Too risky." He took out his phone.

"Who are you going to call?" she asked.

"First guy on my list is Chief Langdon in Shelby-ville. Got a number for him?"

"Yes, but why bother?" She swept out an arm. "We haven't got a scrap of proof. Langdon made it very clear that he doesn't believe in psychics. What's more, I got the distinct impression that he thinks I'm a leather-and-whip-style bitch. I don't think he cares for that type."

"Obviously a man of limited imagination. Get me the number."

She rewarded that with the severe glare he no doubt deserved but she obediently reached into the closet and took out her purse. He watched her dig out a card.

"Personal issues aside," she said, handing him the card, "all we've got in the way of hard evidence is that fragment of a teacup, which proves nothing. I wouldn't be surprised if Langdon concludes that I broke the stupid cup and brought the pieces back with me so I could stage an attention-getting scene for the media. I could tell when I talked to him that he was just waiting for me to claim to be psychic."

"But you didn't give him the satisfaction?"

"Are you kidding? If I pushed that angle, he

wouldn't have listened to anything at all that I had to say about the killer. As it was, I'm pretty sure he thought I invented everything I did tell him."

"I'll call him, anyway. He may not pay attention but he can't say that he wasn't kept informed." He punched in the number on the card.

A gruff, sleep-heavy voice answered on the fourth ring.

"Langdon here."

"Wake up, Chief. Looks like your killer was in Oriana tonight."

"Who the hell are you?" Langdon was fully awake now.

"Zack Jones. I'm a private investigator." It was his standard ID when he was on a case and it was true. He had the license to prove it. All J&J agents did. The agency was a legitimate firm, duly registered as such in every state in which it maintained an office.

He gave Langdon a terse version of events.

Langdon was not impressed.

"You're telling me that Miss Tallentyre believes the killer followed her back to Oriana just because she found part of a broken cup in her coat pocket?" he asked.

"She didn't break it herself," Zack said patiently.

"How do you know that?"

"I'm very sure of it."

"Is she your client?" Langdon asked, suspicious.

"Yes."

"Then you've got a reason to believe her. I don't. I've got a lot of solid leads to follow up. I can't waste time."

"The freak was in her condo tonight."

"Why would he focus on her?" Langdon demanded.

"Excellent question."

"Look, as far as the media is concerned, Doug Spicer, the real estate agent, was the one who was responsible for finding the girl. I didn't give Miss Tallentyre's name to the press."

"Shelbyville is a very small town, Chief. Everyone there knows that she was with Spicer when the girl was found. More to the point, the girl was found in her aunt's house. It makes sense that the killer would aim his rage at her. Although, come to think of it, you might want to check on Spicer and make sure he's okay. It's possible he's in danger, too."

"I'm not buying any of this," Langdon said wearily, "but I'll tell you what I'll do. I'll call that detective with the Oriana PD and ask him to stop by Miss Tallentyre's place tomorrow and check out the broken cup."

That was as good as it was going to get. At least Bradley Mitchell would be predisposed to believe Raine.

"Thanks," he made himself say, employing an unbelievable amount of willpower to remain civil.

"No offense, Jones, but your client is a strange woman. Got a feeling the polite term is *unbalanced*."

"Good night, Chief."

He ended the call without waiting for a response and looked at Raine. "He's going to have Mitchell come by and take a look at your cup."

"Well, at least Bradley will probably believe me."

"Yeah, that's what I'm thinking, too." He punched in another number.

"Who are you calling now?" she asked.

"Fallon Jones."

"Why?"

"Because about twenty minutes ago some SOB of a para-hunter tried to gut me like a fish with a really big knife. Never did like knives."

She stared at him, horrified. "The man who attacked you was one of those hunters you told me about? The kind that can see in the dark?"

"Yeah. Looks like Fallon got it right."

She went from appalled to incensed in about half a second.

"How does any of this make Fallon Jones right?" she demanded.

He looked at her while he waited for Fallon to pick up. "He hoped that sending me here would draw some of the bottom feeders to the surface. Looks like his plan may be working."

Fallon answered the phone on the first ring, sounding gruff and ill-tempered as usual.

"Give me some good news, Zack."

"This will put the cherry on your ice cream sundae.

A hunter with a twist tried to take me out tonight in a motel parking lot."

There was a short silence on the other end.

"You're all right, I assume, or you wouldn't be making this call," Fallon said eventually.

"You're a real people person, Fallon. Yeah, I'm okay."

"What about the other guy?"

"He got away."

"Damn."

"I agree. But I did learn a few things that you'll want to factor into that computer you like to call a brain."

"Such as?"

He knew he had Fallon's full attention.

"The guy was a hunter, but he has this really cool trick where he morphs into a sweet little old lady right before your very eyes while he's coming at you with a knife. Ever try to beat up on someone who looks like your great-grandmother?"

"Describe *morph*," Fallon ordered in a voice that was as sharp as the knife in the attacker's fist.

"The guy started out as a homeless man sleeping in a breezeway. I think that was just a standard-issue disguise. The tip-off was his fancy running shoes. The next thing I know there's this little old lady coming at me with an umbrella, a really fast old lady. But it was hard to focus on her. Then, in mid-stride, the old lady transforms herself into a guy in black tights and a ski mask. Ever hear of a para-talent who could pull off that kind of illusion?"

Fallon was silent for a time. You could almost hear the synapses firing.

"Maybe," Fallon said eventually. "I think there are a few old legends in the historical records. I'll have to do some research and get back to you. Anything else?"

"Hell, no. Haven't even gotten to the exciting part yet. Been a busy evening here in Oriana. Looks like the Bonfire Killer followed Raine back here from Shelbyville."

"Listen up, Zack, I don't want you getting distracted by a secondary investigation. Is that understood?"

"Sorry about that, but finding out that Raine is now the focus of a sadistic killer is going to be a little hard to ignore. We don't all have your ability to compartmentalize, Fallon."

"So? You stick close to her. That's what you're being paid to do, anyway. Given your talents, she's safer with you than she would be with an armed cop standing at her side. You can guard her while the two of you concentrate on finding out what happened to Lawrence Quinn."

"You're a very focused man, Fallon."

Fallon pretended he hadn't heard that. "If you're finished, I have something for you. It's not much but I've got a feeling about it."

"I'm listening," Zack said. Actually, he was listening

very carefully. Whenever Fallon said he had a feeling, his agents took notice.

"My analyst just came up with one small but interesting insight into Lawrence Quinn. Turns out he's a serious fan of the blues. I did some checking. There's a nightclub there in Oriana that features a lot of jazz and blues. Place called the Alley Door."

Twenty-five

Houdini. He hated the code name they'd given him. His name was Sean Tanner and not so long ago that name had been in lights. It was true that when the Nightshade operative had approached him he was a small-time Vegas magician, but he was moving up fast. He was destined to become a headliner at a major casino on the Strip. No one else could do what he did. His magic was the real deal.

Nightshade, however, had promised him more, a lot more. And they'd delivered. The organization had another, more formal name, but it had adopted the nom de guerre that the Society used. He liked it. *Nightshade* suited his theatrical nature.

He was way beyond being a low-rent stage act now. The drug had not only given him the additional talents of a para-hunter, it had also enhanced his already existing powers of illusion. They told him that he was something new and different in the world of paranormal talents: a level-ten hunter-illusionist. He deserved some respect but he wasn't getting it from January.

"Failure is not tolerated within Nightshade," January said.

Rage, infused with the frustration that resulted from the missed kill, twisted through him. It was all he could do not to break January's neck. It would be so easy.

Unfortunately, January was the source of the drug. Until he figured out how to obtain the formula from someone else within Nightshade—the mysterious person January reported to, for example—he was stuck having to take orders.

"I didn't fail," he said. He stared hard through the SUV's windshield at the night-darkened street. "You saw what happened. A car pulled into the lot. I was caught square in the headlights. I had no choice but to leave the scene. You said yourself we can't afford to attract the attention of the cops."

"I was watching you. Jones had you on the defensive. Obviously the old-woman illusion wasn't working."

"It worked."

It had slowed him down, though, and it had been out of control. That really worried him. He was afraid to tell January that in the heat of hand-to-hand combat, he had been unable to hold the illusion. It had winked on and off erratically like a broken flashlight.

"You tripped and fell," January said.

There was a reason January had been given that particular code name, he thought. Cold as a glacier.

"Things like that happen in a fight," he said. "It wouldn't have changed the outcome. Jones isn't anywhere near as fast as me."

"He's a mirror talent. He was anticipating your every move."

"That's not true. I was closing in. The problem was that damned car."

"I hope you understand that your failure to perform to expectations reflects poorly on me. Jones survived tonight. That means I will have to have an unpleasant conversation with a certain individual. Need I remind you that both of us are dependent on that individual for our supply of the drug?"

He forced himself to remain silent. He had one critical advantage. January could be replaced but that was not the case with him. He was a one-of-a-kind lab experiment. They had explained to him that illusion talents of any level were extremely rare. An illusion talent who possessed a psychic profile that could, with the right chemical stimulation, be expanded to include a high-level hunter talent was the stuff of myth and legend.

He was on the way to becoming a walking legend within the organization. Nightshade needed him.

"I'll take care of Jones next time," he said.

"I'll decide whether or not you get a second shot at Jones."

He did not argue. Instead, he started to make his own plans.

Twenty-six

By the time Zack ended the call she was sim-
mering.

"Mr. Jones, I take it, is not a sympathetic
employer," she said. It had been all she could do not to
yank the phone out of his hand and give Fallon Jones
the benefit of her opinion.

Zack shrugged. "I think of him as a client, not an
employer. I work for him on a contract basis. As far as I
know, all of his agents and analysts handle it that way.
He doesn't have a regular staff. Doubt if he could get
anyone to work for him full-time. He calls in whatever
talent he thinks he needs."

"That's not the point." She spread her arms wide,
exasperated. "You almost got killed tonight. Judging
by your end of the conversation, it didn't sound as if
Fallon Jones cared a jot about your welfare."

"Fallon is all about the bottom line. As long as I'm alive and kicking, he's only interested in the next move."

"He doesn't sound like a very nice person at all."

"Fallon is . . . Fallon. To know him is to appreciate him."

"Bet he doesn't have a lot of friends," she muttered.

"Well, no, but that doesn't seem to bother him much."

She sighed. "What happens next?"

He looked down at his duffel bag and then raised his eyes to meet hers. "Given recent events, it looks like I'll be staying with you for a while. Where do you want me to put my stuff?"

She had known this was coming, she reminded herself. And he was only here because of the danger. This was business, nothing more. Nevertheless, the reality of having him here, under her roof, sent little shivers of anticipation through her.

"Okay," she said, opting for cool and composed.

"Not going to argue, huh?"

She raised her brows. "A serial killer invaded my home tonight and more or less announced that he is targeting me. I am not an idiot. I am delighted to have a houseguest who knows how to cope with people who attack other people with knives."

"Gotta love it when common sense prevails. Are you going to call Gordon and Andrew and tell them what's going on?"

She shook her head. "There's no point. They'll cancel their trip and sit around worrying about me. There's nothing they can do. In fact, if they stay here in town they might be in jeopardy. If the freak finds out how important they are to me he might—" She broke off suddenly.

"Your choice. Where do I sleep?"

"I made the second bedroom into a library. There's a pullout sofa bed in there."

"I was afraid you were going to say something like that. Lead the way."

She turned and went down the hall. He followed her, duffel and jacket in hand. Batman and Robin padded after them, interested in the unusual situation.

"Maybe you should think about getting a dog," he said. "Cats are great but they have their limitations when it comes to guarding a household."

Raine looked at him over her shoulder. "I'll let you bring up the subject with Batman and Robin. Something tells me they're going to be a tough sell."

She led the way into the library. Bookcases lined the walls. There was a sleek glass-and-wood desk near the window. The sofa bed, black leather like the rest of the furniture, was in the center of the room.

She got some sheets and pillows out of a closet. By the time she returned to the library, Zack had pulled out the bed. They made it up together. It was an oddly intimate experience, she thought. But then, everything she did with Zack felt that way.

"There are two baths," she said, indicating the door across the hall. "That one is all yours."

"Thanks."

Unable to think of any reason to linger, she went to the door.

"Good night," she said.

He made no move to stop her but she knew from the heat in his eyes that was what he wanted to do.

Was that what she wanted? To have him lunge toward her, scoop her up and toss her down onto the sofa bed? Take the decision out of her hands?

Well, sure. What woman with blood in her veins wouldn't have wanted to play out that scenario? Life was getting complicated.

She made it out into the hall without succumbing to the urge to fling herself into his arms. So far, so good.

Two steps beyond the door he spoke.

"Almost forgot to tell you. Fallon gave me a lead on Lawrence Quinn. He's a big blues aficionado. Evidently there's a club here in town."

She turned and went back to the entrance to the little library. "The Alley Door. I've never been there but I've heard it's quite popular."

"Fallon thinks it's worth checking out, and since hunches are his specialty, I'd better take a look. Tomorrow night—" He checked his watch. "Make that tonight, you and I are going to spend the evening at the Alley Door."

Her curiosity stirred. "Sounds interesting."

He watched her with a knowing expression.

"You like the hunt, don't you?" he said. "Even though there's a heavy downside."

"*Like* isn't the right word," she said slowly. "But yes, I do get something out of it. Using my talents is satisfying. I can't explain it but in a way I need to do it occasionally."

"So do I. I've come to the conclusion that finding justice for the victims is the way we exorcise the visions and the voices."

A sense of intuitive wonder swept through her.

"Yes," she said. "That's it. I've never thought about it in those terms but that's the way it works for me, too."

He walked to her and cupped her face in one hand and kissed her slowly, taking his time. When he finally raised his head, excitement was sparking through her.

"Good night," he said.

She managed to make it all the way to her bedroom without looking back over her shoulder. She didn't need to do that. She knew he was watching her from the doorway. She could feel his eyes on her. Everything inside her got very, very warm.

A few minutes later she climbed into bed, took the deck of cards out of the bedside table drawer and propped herself against the pillows.

Robin and Batman curled up beside her.

She dealt herself a game of solitaire and tried to tune out the dark voice that whispered to her.

. . . *Burn, witch, burn.* . . .

Twenty-seven

The figure at the end of the bed was silhouetted against the window. She knew it was a man but she could not see his face. She tried to move, to cry out, but neither her limbs nor her voice responded. She was frozen with terror.

"Mother tried to drive out the demon but every time she punished me she only made him stronger. Now I serve the demon. He has made me more powerful than any witch. You will be punished, and then you will burn . . ."

She came awake to the feel of something warm and soft against her cheek. She opened her eyes and saw Robin standing over her. Batman was on the other side. He touched his small nose to her shoulder and meowed softly.

Her nightgown was damp. She shivered with the ice-and-flames sensation she always got when the voices invaded her mind at night.

She sat up, gathered both cats in her lap and buried her face in their fur.

"Thanks, guys," she whispered.

"Had a feeling it would probably be bad tonight," Zack said from the doorway. "Didn't think the solitaire would do the trick. It's bad enough when the voices are talking about someone else, a stranger who is usually already dead. You can get a little distance. Puts an entirely different spin on things when you're the target and the voices are talking about you."

She raised her head and looked at him. In the low glow of the night-light she could see that he was wearing pants but nothing else.

"Has it ever happened to you?" she asked.

"In a way."

"Very cryptic."

"Sorry," he said. "Long story."

"And one you don't like to tell."

"It doesn't improve with repetition, trust me."

He had a right to his secrets, she thought. She'd only known him a little over twenty-four hours. How was it possible that a man she had met just yesterday was standing there, only inches outside her bedroom?

How was it possible that a serial killer had gotten inside her condo tonight and left a warning?

Her life was tumbling into chaos.

"Didn't mean to wake you," she said.

"I wasn't asleep." He did not move out of the door-way.

"I actually got to sleep but then I started dreaming. I think I had a mini panic attack."

"No surprise there."

"No." She stroked Robin. "In hindsight, I was definitely overdue."

"Remember, your psychic side is hardwired directly into your intuition. When your senses perceive a threat, it stirs up all those good old and extremely primitive fight-or-flight reflexes."

"You certainly do know a lot about this kind of thing."

"That's because I had the advantage of being raised—"

"Within the Arcane Society community," she finished crisply. "Yes, you have mentioned that on one or two occasions."

"Just trying to explain."

"I know. I seem to be a little prickly when it comes to that subject."

"Then let's change the subject." He waited a beat. "Want to play some blackjack?"

Why not? She certainly wasn't going to get any more sleep tonight.

"Okay," she said. She started to push the quilt aside, intending to stand and put on her robe.

"No need to get up." He glided into the room, pausing long enough to switch on the bedside lamp. He left it on its lowest setting. Then he sat down on the edge of the bed. "We can play right here."

Based on previous experience, playing cards in a room that contained a bed was probably not a good idea, she thought. But Zack was already dealing.

"Are we going to play with real money again?" she asked.

"I can think of only two things that make a game of cards interesting." He gave her a slow, wickedly sexy smile. "Money's one of them."

She awoke to the gray light of a rainy morning and the sensation of a warm, heavy weight pressed against her back. Not Batman or Robin. She could feel the cats at her feet. Also, neither of them possessed a long arm like the one wrapped around her waist. She looked down. That was not a cat's paw positioned just south of her right breast, either. It was a very large, very powerful, very masculine hand.

She spent a few seconds exploring memories. There had been several games of blackjack. She had been on a winning streak for quite a while. They had kept score on a pad of paper.

At some point Zack had gone into the kitchen and brought back the bottle of scotch that she kept in a cupboard for Andrew and Gordon. She recalled drinking one or two glasses, possibly three. Shortly afterward things had gone pleasantly vague.

She levered herself up on her elbows and looked at Zack. He had pulled the bedspread up to his waist for warmth but he was still on top of the quilt and still wearing his pants. She could see the broad expanse of his bare chest.

Shock jolted through her. "*Zack.*"

He opened his eyes and regarded her with lazy, masculine appreciation.

"We didn't play strip poker last night, if that's what's worrying you," he said.

She surged to her knees to survey his chest more closely. "My God, you look like you've been hit by a bus."

He looked down and grimaced when he saw the bruises. "Purple isn't my color but it's not as bad as it looks."

"That's hard to imagine. I had no idea it was this bad. We should have taken you to the emergency room last night." She started to scramble off the bed. "I'll get dressed and drive you there right now."

He caught hold of her wrist, chaining her easily. "Relax. Nothing's broken."

"Are you sure?"

He seemed amused by her concern.

"I'm a little sore, that's all."

"A *little*." She looked at him in disbelief.

"Okay, kind of sore." He touched his ribs in a gingerly manner. "A few anti-inflammatory tablets will take care of the worst of it. How's my face look?"

She scrutinized him carefully. "No black eye, amazingly enough."

"Good. That will save answering a lot of questions today. Black eyes always draw a lot of attention." He used the grip on her wrist to tug her slowly toward him. "You know, if you're sincerely interested in speeding my recovery, I have a suggestion."

A kiss was not a good idea but she could not seem to stop herself from leaning toward him.

She brushed her mouth lightly against his.

"Oh, yeah," he said, eyes darkening. "That's the magic cure, all right."

His arm started to tighten around her.

She resisted. "I wouldn't dream of taking advantage of an injured man."

"It's okay. I know you'll be gentle with me."

"You don't need sex," she said sternly, enjoying the banter more than she wanted to admit. "What you need is a good breakfast and those anti-inflammatories."

"See, that's where you're wrong." He raised a finger and assumed a lecturing tone. "Sex releases all sorts of endorphins into the bloodstream. It makes you feel good. Like a tonic."

Laughing, she got to her feet, found her glasses and pulled on her robe. "Breakfast sounds safer."

"You gamble for big money in Vegas and you hunt bad guys for a hobby, lady. Since when do you play it safe?"

She stopped short at that. She had always thought of herself as risk-averse, having spent her entire adult life concealing her talents from all but a tiny, close-knit circle of acquaintances. She had played it safe, just as Aunt Vella had taught her, so that others would not label her crazy. Until Zack, she had never even experienced anything close to genuine intimacy with a lover because she had been afraid to reveal the truth about herself.

The concept of herself as a woman who was not afraid to take a few risks was nothing short of dazzling.

She was about to give Zack the sort of snappy comeback a bold, assertive, risk-taking woman might make to the man she had allowed into her bed when she noticed the notepad on the nightstand.

She stared at the numbers written on the top sheet of paper, outraged.

"What's this?" She snatched up the pad and held it right in front of his eyes.

He pushed himself up on his elbows and studied the numbers on the pad, brows furrowed in concentration. Then he smiled.

"That's the result of our friendly little game of blackjack last night," he said.

"According to this I owe you ten thousand, four hundred and fifty dollars."

"My luck turned after you drank those three glasses of scotch."

"The heck it did. I never lose at blackjack. You got me drunk and took advantage of me."

"Three itty-bitty glasses of scotch are enough to put you under the table? I'll have to remember that."

"It was the scotch on top of the stress that did it," she shot back indignantly. "I've been under a lot of stress lately."

"I dunno." He shook his head, unconvinced. "Sounds like an excuse to me."

"Hah." She tossed the notepad onto the nightstand and fitted her hands to her hips. "There is only one other possible explanation."

"What?"

"You cheated."

"Does this mean you're going to try to wriggle out of your gambling debt?"

"If you think you're going to collect ten thousand, four hundred and fifty bucks from me, think again."

"Maybe we could come up with alternative payment arrangements," he suggested smoothly.

She beetled her brows at him. "Such as?"

"I believe I mentioned last night that there were only two kinds of bets that make a game of cards interesting."

She picked up a pillow and tossed it at him. He fell back, laughing. She turned on her heel and flounced off into the bathroom.

It occurred to her that it was the first time in her entire life that she had actually flounced. It was quite invigorating.

Twenty-eight

Bradley examined the fragment of broken china he was holding in his hand. "You're sure this is from the Shelbyville B and B?"

He had arrived shortly after eight, wearing his slouchy jacket, his mirrored sunglasses and his cop face. He had removed the sunglasses and he and Zack were both behaving themselves but Raine was uneasily aware of the tension in the room.

In an effort to avoid a scene, she had made a large pot of coffee. She then instructed the men to *sit*, using the same tone of voice she used with Robin and Batman when they got a yen to exercise their claws on her delicate woven wood window shades instead of their cat trees.

Zack lounged in one of two chairs that bracketed

the coffee table. Bradley had taken the opposite chair. That had left the sofa for her.

"I'm positive that cup fragment is from the B and B," she said, answering Bradley's question. "He was here, right inside my condo."

Bradley looked dubious. "Why would he leave a broken cup in the pocket of your coat? It's not exactly a dramatic message. I guess it could be symbolic of something but it's a little vague. There was a good chance you wouldn't even recognize the shattered cup, let alone realize he had left it there for you."

She concentrated on pouring coffee. "He has started stalking me but he doesn't want to leave any hard evidence behind that I can take to the police."

"He feels safe," Zack said, watching Bradley very steadily. "He's sure that even if Raine went to the cops with that piece of broken china, no one would take her seriously."

Bradley ignored him to focus on Raine.

"How did he get your name? As far as the media was concerned, you were just an unnamed client of a local real estate agent. Doug Spicer and Chief Langdon got the credit for the rescue."

"I didn't land on the six o'clock news, thank heavens," she said. "But everyone back in Shelbyville knows that I was the person with Spicer when we found the girl. They also know that my aunt's house now belongs to me."

Bradley looked seriously thoughtful. "Are you telling me that you think the killer is a Shelbyville resident?"

"A resident or maybe someone who spends weekends and vacations in the area. I think he almost has to be a person who knows the community well, not just because he picked up my name so fast after the girl was found, but because he felt comfortable coming and going from my aunt's house."

"I get why he may have focused on you," Bradley said. "There's a twisted logic to it."

"He hunts witches. I'm the niece of the Shelbyville witch. That makes me a witch, too. I think he fears me."

She realized she was no longer regarding Bradley from the standpoint of a hurt and humiliated would-be lover, and, for his part, he wasn't fixated on manipulating her with guilt in an attempt to obtain her assistance with the Cassidy Cutler book. They were working together again.

Bradley rubbed his jaw. "If he's afraid of you, why not just pick up a gun and shoot you?"

Out of the corner of her eye, Raine saw Zack go dangerously still. Energy pulsed in the small space. Bradley must have picked up on it unconsciously because he stirred as though suddenly uncomfortable.

"You know better than to attribute normal reasoning processes to freaks like this," she said quickly. She gave Zack a warning frown.

Zack did not take his eyes off Bradley but she felt the powerful energy dim a little.

"Can't argue with that," Bradley said. He turned the bit of china with his fingers. "He took a risk leaving a chunk of evidence behind, though."

"How many people would interpret that broken cup as a threat or a clue?" Zack asked. "Chief Langdon sure as hell wasn't interested."

"That's for damn sure," Bradley agreed. "He told me he was busy chasing down the hard leads they got from the latest victim and at the scene. When he called me he apologized for asking me to waste my time. Said he was only doing it because he didn't want Raine going to the media and making a lot of wild claims about being a psychic."

"He thinks I'm either borderline delusional or full-on crazy," Raine said neutrally.

Bradley chuckled. "Oh, yeah."

She gave him her special smile. "Not a unique opinion among members of the law enforcement community."

Bradley had the grace to redden.

"You sure that smile doesn't piss you off?" Zack asked with polite interest.

Bradley looked confused and annoyed. He closed his fingers around the shard and kept his attention firmly fixed on Raine. "I've worked with you often enough to know better than to blow off your, uh, observations and insights."

She allowed herself to relax a little. "Thanks, Bradley."

"What happens now?" Zack asked.

"I can arrange to have more patrols in this neighborhood at night to keep an eye on things," Bradley said, "but I can't give Raine a twenty-four-hour guard. No money for bodyguards in the city budget."

"Not a problem," Zack said. "She's got one."

Bradley gave Raine a quick, searching look and then turned back to Zack. There was wary respect and silent acknowledgment in his expression.

"Yeah, sort of figured that," he said.

"What are you going to do?" Zack asked.

"The usual routine. I'll talk to the neighbors. See if anyone saw a stranger in the vicinity last night. Maybe someone noticed an unfamiliar car in the lot." He took a notebook and a pen out of the inside pocket of his jacket. "I've got tomorrow off. I'll drive up to Shelbyville, see what breaks in that direction. Maybe someone saw the guy entering or leaving Raine's room."

"Langdon isn't going to be real happy to have you asking questions on his turf," Zack said.

"We'll work it out," Bradley said. He flipped open the notebook and looked at Raine. "Take me through it from the start. I want to hear everything you saw and felt in your aunt's basement the other day. You know the drill."

"Sure," Raine said.

She knew the drill but Zack was right. It was different

when you were the one at the top of a killer's To Do list.

By the time Bradley finally left, notebook crammed with every detail Raine could recall, she felt mentally and emotionally drained. She flopped against the back of the sofa. Batman and Robin jumped up beside her and settled down, purring loudly.

"Whew." She stroked the cats. "I think I need another cup of tea."

Zack was at the window. "I'll make some for you."

"Thanks."

"You're right." He turned around, his expression thoughtful. "Mitchell did take you seriously."

"Told you so. He may think I'm creepy but he knows better than to ignore me."

"He's also got a damn good reason to work this case hard. Bagging the Bonfire Killer would do a hell of a lot more for his reputation than solving a hundred cold cases."

She smiled wryly. "Hadn't thought of that."

"Judging by the gleam in Mitchell's eye when he left, I've got a hunch it's pretty much all he's thinking about at the moment."

Twenty-nine

John Stilwell Nash stood at the bank of windows that lined one wall of the corner office and watched a steady rain fall on Portland. As far as he was concerned it could pour until the whole damn city washed into the Willamette River. He did not like anything about the place. Every aspect of it, from the too relaxed, too nice, too polite, too environmentally conscious locals to the annual rose festival made him want to hurl the heavy Victorian inkwell on his desk through the plate glass.

But nothing outside the window was as infuriating as the conversation he was having on the phone.

"What went wrong?" he asked.

He was enraged by this latest failure. But he managed, with some effort, to maintain the cold, utterly flat tone that he always used with members of his staff. It was vital to conceal all emotion from one's underlings. The barest hint of the fury that threatened to consume him could be taken as evidence of loss of control. Within the organization, loss of control was viewed as a weakness.

"Houdini claims that he was interrupted before he could complete his assignment," January said.

The voice on the other end was as icy as his own. Nash had considered that an asset at the start of the operation in Oriana. It was the reason he gave the operative the code name January. After exhaustive analysis, he had concluded that the disaster in Stone Canyon was due to the use of agents who succumbed to the emotional sides of their natures. Lust, envy and greed contributed to the unsatisfactory outcome of that project. He could not afford a repeat.

"In other words, Houdini failed," he said. "That means that you failed."

"There will be other opportunities," January said, sounding not the least bit ruffled by the implied threat. "In the meantime, I have come up with a new approach to the problem, one that is more . . . subtle."

Nash ground his teeth. The implication was clear: January was reminding him that it had been his idea to use Houdini to take the J&J agent out of the picture. He had envisioned a quick, surgical strike. The kill was to have looked like a routine parking lot mugging gone bad. No clues. No witnesses. One dead Jones.

His intense hatred of the Jones family was in his blood, bequeathed to him by John Stilwell, his Victorian-era ancestor. Stilwell had been destroyed by Gabriel Jones and the woman who later became Jones's wife.

The Jones family had probably forgotten all about the first John Stilwell. What the bastards had not counted on was the fact that in the year preceding his death, Stilwell pursued his own personal breeding program. His secret journal detailed how he deliberately seduced and impregnated at least two female psychics in London, women he believed had genuine paranormal talents. John Stilwell had been fascinated with the discoveries of Darwin. He had been curious to see if his own psychic abilities could be passed down and strengthened by mating with women who also possessed such powers.

Darwin's theories had proved valid, although John Stilwell had not lived to see the results.

Phone pressed tightly to his ear, Nash started to pace the office. It was true that using Houdini to deal with Zackary Jones had been his idea. The Stone Canyon project had been wrecked by a Jones. He did not intend to allow another member of that damned family to interfere again. But now that things had gone wrong, he had to make certain that he did not take the blame. If anyone went down, it would be January. Fortunately, he had been careful to insulate himself from any fallout if there was a disaster, just as he had after the Stone Canyon affair. He was certain that members of the Inner Circle had not learned about his connection to that operation. Nevertheless, a second cover-up would be extremely risky.

The members of the Inner Circle had little patience with failure. He did not blame them. When he assumed his rightful position as head of the organization, he intended to enforce a zero-tolerance policy as well. The Darwinian approach to management ensured that only the strongest and the most powerful survived. But meanwhile, he had to protect himself.

"You are in charge of this operation," he said. "It is imperative that you recover what Quinn failed to deliver to us."

"It's unfortunate that Houdini was ordered to dispose of Lawrence Quinn before the data on Quinn's computer was analyzed and discovered to be false," January said. "If Quinn had been kept alive he could have been interrogated."

He fought back another wave of rage. When this was over, January would most certainly have to go. An unpleasant accident, perhaps.

"I anticipate that the next time you call, it will be with news of success," he said evenly. "Otherwise I shall be forced to replace you."

"One more thing," January said, ignoring the threat. "Houdini is asking for a higher dose. He claims that the reason he missed the target was because he was given too little of the drug."

Nash stopped in mid-stride, fear streaking through him.

"What's your opinion?" he made himself ask.

"Judging by what I saw last night, I'd say he's losing control. He couldn't hold the illusion. Kept switching it on and off. That's what slowed him down. The experiment is a failure and should be terminated."

Cold fear knifed through him. Houdini wasn't the only experiment the organization had produced. Hell, they were all, to one degree or another, experiments.

"You're in charge of the Oriana project," he said. "It's your decision to make. But I would remind you that Houdini is a tool, a very expensive one. The particular version of the formula that was prepared for him required a significant financial investment. It would be unfortunate, to say the least, to see that investment wasted. However, if the project is a success, the loss of Houdini could be written off."

He ended the call before January could respond, aware that his pulse was racing and he was breathing too rapidly. Fear and adrenaline shivered through him. It took longer than it should have to regain control.

After a while he crossed the room, opened the door and went into the outer office. His attractive administrative assistant looked up from her desk.

"Yes, Mr. Nash?"

"I'm going down to the lab," he said.

"Yes, sir. Shall I cancel the meeting with the people from the online supplements company?"

"No." Shit. It was one thing after another today. He paused at the door, concealing his impatience. "What time are they due to arrive?"

She checked the clock. "Forty-five minutes from now."

"I'll be back by then."

He went out into the hall and headed for the stairwell. His office was on the third floor of the aging three-story brick building but he rarely used the elevator. He liked to set an example of fitness for the staff.

He passed a cheerful wall banner announcing that Cascadia Dawn Natural Food Supplements had achieved record profits for the sixth quarter in a row.

The director of marketing emerged from an office and nodded respectfully. Two women from publicity saw him and greeted him with formality. He acknowledged them, then pushed open the stairwell door.

The top floor of the building was reserved for offices. Online and catalog sales were handled on the middle floor. The first floor served as a warehouse for the wide variety of nutritional products sold under the Cascadia Dawn Natural Food Supplements label.

The company was successful but it was not large. That was intentional. He planned to see to it that it remained a regional niche player in the nutritional supplement business. It was the perfect cover for an illicit drug lab.

Cascadia Dawn did not manufacture and package its own products in bulk. It hired an outside firm to do that. But it did possess a state-of-the-art research and development lab where new nutritional formulas were developed and older ones were updated. The lab occupied a large portion of the basement of the building. It was divided into two sections.

He went down the last flight of stairs, opened a heavy steel fire door and walked into a small office.

An attendant in a white jumpsuit was seated at the desk. He got up quickly.

"Good morning, Mr. Nash. Do you want to enter the lab?"

"Yes, please, Miller."

"I'll get a suit for you, sir."

Miller opened a cabinet and took out a sealed plastic packet containing a disposable lab coat, elastic-brimmed hat, gloves, mask and booties.

Nash stepped into a small chamber and donned the clean apparel quickly. When he was ready, Miller pressed a button that opened another door.

Nash walked into the pristine space beyond the door. The stainless steel workbenches and equipment gleamed beneath the bright industrial lights suspended from the ceiling. Technicians and assistants gowned in white from head to toe nodded and murmured greetings as he went past.

Everyone in the room was working on a variety of supplement products of the type found in health and fitness stores across the country. Nash knew that some companies in the field had gone under over the years but for the life of him he didn't see how anyone could lose money in the nutritional supplement business. Sheer incompetence was the only way he could imagine going bankrupt. It was astonishing how much money consumers were prepared to throw at any product that promised to help them lose weight, get an erection, reduce stress or improve their immune systems. And all the stuff could be legally sold without any evidence of effectiveness backed up by clinical trials.

Amazing. And profitable.

He nodded to several technicians and then went to the far end of the room. There he stopped in front of another stainless steel vault door and paused at the computerized lock. He was one of only two people in the entire building who knew the code. As far as the vast majority of the staff was concerned, the door to the second, smaller lab was secured in order to protect against industrial espionage and theft. The Cascadia Dawn supplement formulas were highly prized proprietary secrets.

Only a handful of people knew the true value of the unique formulas concocted inside the inner lab.

This secret facility was not the only lab funded by the organization. There were a few others, equally well disguised, scattered around the country. But he intended for this one to become the most important and successful of all the labs. It was going to be his ticket to the ultimate seat of power, the one held by the director of the organization. As John Stilwell's descendant, that position should have been his by now. He had a far more legitimate claim to it than the current director. But he knew how to bide his time. He had been born a level-seven hunter. Thanks to the drug, he was now a ten. In addition, the latest version of the formula that had been specially engineered for him was expanding his range of powers. His natural business acumen had been enhanced to the level of a mid-range para-strategy talent. He was also developing some hypnotic abilities.

Now, however, after learning what had happened to Houdini, it was clear that it would be wise to back off from the attempt to expand his range of psychic talents.

The steel door opened. He stepped into the room and waited for the door to relock behind him.

Three people were at work at the lab benches. They all looked up when he entered. One of them, Dr. Humphrey Hulsey, regarded him with pale, emotionless eyes. Hulsey was a tall, thin skeleton of a man, with spindly arms and legs. Nash thought the safety glasses he wore made him look like an oversized insect.

"Well?" Hulsey demanded. "Did your operative get that information for me yet? I can't proceed with the new experiments until I see the Tallentyre data. According to Quinn's notes, it's critical to stabilizing the formula."

Nash resisted the impulse to pick up a nearby microscope and smash it against Hulsey's shiny skull.

Hulsey was the only person in the building who dared to speak to him as if he were an employee rather than the CEO. Hulsey got away with it because he was a brilliant research chemist. He was also a level-eight intuitive with a psychic talent for analyzing patterns—the kind that were hidden at the molecular level.

Hulsey was also the only other person on the staff who was a high-ranking member of the organization. The combination of his intellectual and paranormal abilities made him invaluable. Unfortunately he was all too well aware of his critical importance to the members of the Inner Circle.

"No," Nash said. "I'm here to talk about the latest version of the X9 that you prepared for me."

Thus far Hulsey's greatest contribution to the ongoing research on the founder's formula was a breakthrough that had made it possible to genetically tailor the drug to an individual's specific psychic profile.

"I just altered the drug for you again a few weeks ago." Hulsey sounded disgusted. "What's wrong now?"

Nash moved closer to him and lowered his voice. His assistants had been cleared to the highest security levels but Nash made it a policy not to trust anyone any further than absolutely necessary.

"The surges haven't stopped," he said quietly. "They're coming more frequently."

Hulsey snorted. "Don't blame the drug for your anger management issues. If you've got a problem with self-control, I suggest you take a close look at your own psych profile. You know the old saying 'It's in the blood.' "

He turned back to his microscope.

Nash managed, just barely, to clamp down on the tide of white-hot rage that threatened to consume him.

"You will prepare a new batch," he said, "without the additional enhancement capabilities. I want to return to the original version, the one that jacks up only my hunter talents. Do you understand, Dr. Hulsey?"

Hulsey did not look up from his microscope. "Of course I understand. You can't handle the other talents."

Nash forced himself to leave the lab without giving in to the urge to slit Hulsey's throat.

For the time being he needed Hulsey but eventually that would change. No one was irreplaceable, not even Dr. Humphrey Hulsey.

Thirty

Zack stopped on the sidewalk outside Incognito and studied the window displays. On the other side of the glass were two mannequins dressed in Victorian-era attire, an astronaut, a pirate and a familiar superhero. An array of elegant and fanciful masks dangled on long ribbons secured to the ceiling.

"No offense," he said to Raine, "but I would never have guessed there's a large market for costumes except at Halloween."

"Halloween has become a major adult party night," she said. "People spend small fortunes on their costumes."

He pushed open the door for her. "That's just one day a year."

"Add to that the annual Oriana charity fund-raiser,

which is traditionally an old-fashioned costume ball, a variety of kids' parties during the year, several high-end private bashes and events, contracts with some regional theater groups and an online site and you've got a viable business."

He smiled. "Okay, I'll take your word for it." He followed her into the shop. "Got to tell you, though, I find it hard to believe that anyone over the age of ten would want to put on a costume."

"Aunt Vella used to say that everyone wears a mask."

The sales floor of the shop was not large. It was dramatically decorated in vivid colors and lit with theatrical lighting. There were several more costumes on display, including a mannequin dressed in a tutu and one wearing an elaborate gown that reminded him vaguely of the big, ornate dresses worn by women in the eighteenth century.

A series of paintings in sleek, modern frames hung on the walls. Each one featured a haunting image of a mask.

"Aunt Vella did them," Raine said. "Painting was one of the few things that calmed her. She could lose herself in a picture for hours and days at a time. I could only hang so many of them here in the shop. Most are stored in the Shelbyville house."

"You don't have any hanging in your condo."

She gave him an enigmatic look. "Would you want any of those masks on your walls at home?"

He studied the nearest painting. He was a good three feet away from it but he could sense the faint, disturbing energy.

"No," he said.

"Luckily most of my customers don't notice the bad vibes," she said quietly. "People think the pictures are fascinating. I've had several offers for them."

"Ever sold any?"

"No," Raine said. "They're all I have left of Aunt Vella."

There was a sales counter to the right and an opening draped in red velvet set in the far wall.

"Is that you, Raine?" a voice called from the other side of the crimson curtain. "I was just about to call you."

"Sorry I'm late," Raine said. "Things got complicated this morning."

The velvet curtains parted. A short, round woman in her early twenties appeared. She looked as if she had just walked out of a vampire film.

"This is Pandora, my assistant," Raine said. "Pandora, Zack Jones."

"How do you do," Zack said. "I didn't catch your last name."

"I don't use one," Pandora said, eyes slitting in a not-so-subtle warning.

"Right," he said. "That explains it."

He managed, just barely, not to smile.

Pandora was dressed in a long, flowing black gown

with wide sleeves. Massive platform shoes with five-inch heels graced her feet. A heavy necklace decorated with an odd design wrought in some silvery metal hung around her neck.

Her artificially black hair was parted in the middle and fell halfway down her back. Pale makeup gave a ghostly pallor to her skin. Dark lipstick and elaborately painted eyes provided a startling contrast. Small rings and studs gleamed in her nose, ears, brows and lips.

Pandora looked at Raine, expressionless. "New boyfriend?"

To Zack's amazement, Raine blushed.

"No," Raine said quickly. "New, uh, acquaintance."

Zack looked at her. She turned even pinker and hastily cleared her throat.

"Like I said, my life has become somewhat complicated lately," she added smoothly. "Zack wanted to see the shop and meet you. He's going to hang out here with us today."

"Why?" Pandora asked, still suspicious.

Raine made a face. "Because the Bonfire Killer has decided I'm his nemesis. Zack is playing bodyguard for a while."

Pandora was horrified. "That freak has targeted you?"

"Looks that way," Raine said.

"Damn it, I was afraid this would happen someday. Didn't I tell you that getting involved in all those cold cases would come back to haunt you?"

"Yes, you did."

"Where did you find him?" Pandora angled her head at Zack. "You don't know any professional bodyguards."

"Zack is sort of an investigator," Raine said.

Zack smiled. "Actually I'm a real investigator."

Pandora crossed her arms and looked disgusted. "Not another guy in law enforcement. Thought you learned your lesson with Mitchell."

Raine frowned. "I told you, Zack is not a boyfriend."

Zack looked at Pandora. "I don't worry about enforcing laws. I just ask questions and try to get answers."

"Yeah?" Pandora did not appear convinced but she shrugged a plump shoulder.

"Mind if I take a look around the back room?" Zack said to Raine.

"No." She went toward the velvet curtain. "Follow me."

Pandora gave Zack one last, suspicious glare and then went behind the counter and sat down in front of the computer.

"By the way, Marie Antoinette called," she said over her shoulder to Raine. "She rescheduled her fitting for Thursday."

"No problem," Raine said, moving through the curtain.

Zack followed her. "Marie Antoinette?"

"Joanne Escott, the mayor of our fair town. She's

getting a costume from us for the annual charity ball I mentioned. She doesn't know quite how to deal with Pandora so I make it a point to be here when she comes in for her fittings."

"Why the Marie Antoinette name?"

"This year Joanne wanted to wear an elaborate eighteenth-century gown, complete with the big, powdered wig like the costume out front. I told her she'd look like Marie Antoinette and that was probably not the image she wanted to project as mayor. She was very determined. I finally pointed out that if she wore the costume, her critics at the *Oriana Journal* wouldn't be able to resist printing a picture of her at the ball with a *let 'em eat cake* caption."

"I assume that observation made her change her mind?"

"Yes, but unfortunately, I don't think her second choice was particularly wise, either. Couldn't talk her out of it, though. She's going as Cleopatra."

"With or without an asp?"

"Oh, she'll have one. We here at Incognito pride ourselves on attention to detail. Wouldn't dream of letting our mayor attend the ball in a half-asped costume."

He laughed.

"Here it is." She waved an arm. "Our back room."

He walked slowly around the space, opening his senses. There was a dressing room and a three-way mirror to his left. The rest of the room was filled with a number of long, rolling carts outfitted with hanging rods. He estimated that there were a couple dozen costumes on each cart. A wide variety of elaborate masks were displayed on several rows of plastic heads arranged on shelves.

"You keep quite an inventory," he said.

"This is a busy time of year for us."

"Do you design all of these yourself?"

"Just some of the creative sketches and ideas. Pandora is the genius when it comes to costume design. When Aunt Vella was alive she did a lot of the masks."

He went down an aisle between two of the long costume display carts, picking up nothing but the usual dull static.

"No hot spots," he said.

"Well, that's good news."

He glanced at the door at the back of the room. "I assume that leads out into the alley?"

"Yes. We keep it locked at all times. There's a good, solid bolt on the door and an alarm. I'm very aware of the fact that Pandora and I are here alone a lot. We don't take chances."

He nodded, then went to the door and checked it, making sure.

When he was satisfied, they went back out into the front room of the shop. Pandora was hunched over the computer, typing swiftly.

"Another twenty orders for the new corsets," she said to Raine, her attention on the screen. "Told you they were going to be hot."

Zack glanced at the screen and saw a tight, black vinyl corset. It was displayed with a pair of stiletto-heeled boots and an Egyptian style ankh necklace.

He looked at Raine. "The online business you mentioned?"

Her eyes sparkled with laughter. "You know, until I met Pandora I had no idea that the neo-goth market was so huge."

Thirty-one

The interior of the Alley Door was a midnight-dark cave studded with the fragile lights of tiny candles placed on the tables. The lone guitarist on stage was singing about the delights of illicit sex. As far as Raine could tell the entire song was based on a series of metaphors, all of which appeared to be related to shopping in a candy store.

She toyed with the swizzle stick in her sparkling-water-and-lime drink, impatient for the musician to take a break so she could talk to Zack. Out of respect for the performer, no one in the audience was conversing except occasionally and in very low tones with the wait staff.

Zack seemed absorbed by the music. He lounged in the booth beside her, one hand wrapped around his glass of sparkling water. He was so close that he was touching her at shoulder and thigh, so close that she was stirred by his scent. On the psychic level she was intensely aware of little frissons of excitement.

She reminded herself that they were both here to work, hence the sparkling waters. That fact, however, had not prevented her from taking a lot of time with her wardrobe selection for the evening. She had never been to a jazz club but she was fairly certain she would be safe with black. The dress she had decided to wear did not qualify as working attire by any stretch of the imagination. It was very sleek-fitting and featured a top that was cut lower than anything else she owned. Somehow it managed to look both elegant and outrageously sexy. She would never have bought it if Gordon hadn't been with her at the time. He insisted that the dress had her name on it. She had intended to wear it on her first real date with Bradley.

Zack's reaction to the dress had been very rewarding.

"That definitely works," he'd said when she walked into the living room wearing very high heels and clutching a little purse in one hand.

It wasn't the words that had made her blood zing. It was the heat in his eyes. She'd never seen that look in any other man's eyes. It fired up her own temperature.

The guitarist finally finished his song about a trip to the candy store and announced that he was taking a break. The sound system was switched on. Recorded music and the buzz of conversation filled the room.

"What happens now?" she said.

Zack straightened in the seat. "Now I do a little detecting."

"How?"

"I'm going to wander over to the bar and have a little chat with the bartender."

"Why?"

"I did some checking earlier. The night that Quinn was here, there was a sell-out crowd. I'm guessing that the tables and booths would have been reserved for two or more people. If Quinn came here alone, there's a good possibility he sat at the bar."

"Got it," she said. "You're hoping the bartender remembers him."

"Worth a shot. Be back in a few minutes."

He slid out of the booth and paused.

"That really is a great dress," he said.

She realized that he was looking down the front of it.

"Better go talk to the bartender," she said.

"Right. The bartender. Now if I could just remember what it was I wanted to talk to him about—"

She smiled. "Focus, Jones."

"Yes, ma'am."

She watched him make his way through the maze of tables, aware of a fizzy sensation. Most women her age had acquired some experience with the flirting game but it was all new and exciting to her. She had never practiced the fine art with any degree of success because she had dreaded the inevitable result. She had always felt deeply uneasy sending out the subtle signals women used to attract a man when she knew that, in the end, she would never be able to allow herself to get emotionally close. To do that she would have had to explain about the voices. Telling a guy you heard voices had a chilling effect on a relationship.

But that wasn't true with Zack.

She lost sight of him and settled back into the booth to sip her drink. The noise level was fairly high now. People talked and chattered, pitching their voices above the background music. Others came and went from the hallway that led to the restrooms.

A short time later Zack returned. When he slid back into the booth she sensed at once that he was no longer in a flirting mood.

"The bartender remembers him, all right," he said. "Quinn had a laptop that he held on to as if it were pure gold. He ordered a beer and paid for it in cash. Then he ordered a second. Figuring he was good for it, the bartender let him start a tab. After the third beer Quinn went to the restroom and never returned."

"You mean Quinn ran out on his bar bill?"

"That's the way the bartender interpreted events. Quinn didn't pay for the beers. Didn't leave a tip. Just went to the restroom and never came back."

She realized that Zack was studying the opening that led to the restrooms.

"What are you thinking?" she asked.

"I'm thinking that, according to Fallon, the trail Quinn left stops very abruptly in Oriana. Maybe it came to an end right here in the Alley Door."

"You think Quinn might have been kidnapped out of this club?"

"All we know for sure at this point is that he was here on the evening of the twentieth. After that, he vanishes."

She could feel the energy shimmering around Zack. It was the same kind of dangerous aura she had sensed emanating from him the night before, when he showed up at her door fresh from combat.

The weird part was that his heightened psychic energy was stirring all her senses, too. Anticipation and an excitement raced through her.

She leaned closer. "What are you going to do now?"

"What Quinn did after he had three beers. I'm going to the restroom."

She put her hand on his arm, needing to touch him. "Please be careful. I've seen a lot of movies that feature scenes in the men's room. Things always go badly."

"Don't worry." He patted her hand reassuringly. "I've seen some of those movies, too."

Thirty-two

He chose a path to the restroom that looked like it would have been the logical route for a man who had been seated at the bar. He was running hot now, all his senses, normal and paranormal, aroused and humming with anticipation. The cold thrill of the hunt was upon him.

He knew Raine had sensed the energy burning through him, knew that it had triggered a response from her own parasenses. The bond between them was growing stronger, whether she realized it or not.

He went down the dimly lit hall and pushed open the door marked MEN. There were three people inside—two at the urinals, one in a stall. He walked across the small, tiled room, trying not to look like some kind of pervert while he searched for traces of old violence.

The problem wasn't the lack of residual psychic

energy. It was a typical restroom and it had seen its share of dramatic human moments. Jacked up like this, the visions were disorienting but, for the most part, faint and unfocused. He detected the dull miasma left by years of hastily staged sexual encounters, illicit drug use, violent, stomach-churning illness and rage.

The last caught his attention. The violent anger was startlingly new, maybe from tonight. It emanated from one of the sinks. He washed his hands while he concentrated on it for a few seconds. The visions were those of a man who had just learned that his wife was sleeping with another man. He hoped the poor bastard had gotten himself back under control before he returned to the table.

As he had expected, the door handle gave off so many layers of static that it was impossible to sort them out. Door handles collected psychic energy like sponges.

By the time he had concluded his brief survey the two men at the urinals were giving him uneasy looks. He let himself back out into the hall.

Well, it had been a long shot, he reminded himself.

He continued along the hall to the emergency exit door. It was an obvious way out of the building for someone bent on evading a bar tab.

The door was not alarmed. He tested it cautiously with one hand and picked up only the usual door handle mush.

He went out into the alley. The door closed heavily

behind him. He stood for a moment, absorbing impressions across the spectrum. The crisp night air carried the scent of garbage from a large, commercial-sized steel container. There was a second bin marked GLASS ONLY. It reeked of stale wine and beer. A couple of rats studied him from beneath the shelter of the garbage container and then scurried away into the night.

He hadn't picked up any traces inside the restroom or hallway so searching the alley was probably a waste of time. Nevertheless, he started walking slowly toward the far end.

Thirty-three

Raine checked her watch for the fourth or fifth time. The weak glow of the table candle revealed that only another minute had passed. Not that much time, in the grand scheme of things. How long could it take to search a restroom?

Almost immediately after Zack had disappeared in the direction of the men's room her own edgy excitement had given way to an ominous sensation. What she was feeling now was disconcertingly similar to what she had experienced the night before at about the time Zack encountered the killer in the motel breezeway. She didn't like it but she was not sure what she could do about it except go down the hall and knock on the door to the men's room.

Not a bad idea, come to think of it.

If they both disappeared from the table, the waiter

would probably assume they had left for good. Zack had paid for the drinks when they arrived, so the bill was taken care of but he hadn't tipped because they had intended to buy another round.

She opened her small purse to search for some tip money. The hair on the nape of her neck lifted a little as though stirred by an invisible, ice-cold draft. Goose bumps crawled up her arms.

She was aware of two things simultaneously. The first was that someone very dangerous had just walked past the booth where she sat alone. She could feel not only the presence of the man directly behind her but his malevolent intent as well.

The second thing she knew with unshakable certainty was that the man's malevolence was directed at Zack.

Zack was in trouble. She knew it as surely as she knew she heard voices.

She forced herself to remove some money from her wallet in what she hoped was a calm, unhurried manner. Her instincts were screaming now. It was all she could do to appear calm.

She put the cash on the table. Only then did she allow herself to turn slightly in the seat, as though searching for the waiter.

She was just in time to see a figure go into the shadowy hall that led to the restrooms. Something about the purposeful way he moved told her he was the one who had set her inner alarm bells clanging.

The man vanished into the restroom hallway.

She snapped her purse closed, slid out of the booth and hurried toward the restroom. She reached the hall just in time to see the dark figure pause briefly beneath the emergency exit sign that marked a rear door.

In the eerie glow of the sign she saw him jerk a ski mask out of his pocket and pull it down over his face. Then he reached for the door handle with one hand. With his other hand, he drew a knife out of a concealed sheath.

Thirty-four

The terrible visions slammed through him without warning when he touched the corner of the steel garbage container. The images were searing and fairly fresh, no more than a month old.

Suddenly he knew what had happened in this alley. He saw it all from Lawrence Quinn's perspective.

. . . A dark figure approaching swiftly out of the shadows. Confusion and then skyrocketing terror. The sickening knowledge that he had been a fool to believe them. A death's head loomed. Eyes like bottomless black holes . . .

. . . Then there was an unearthly cold seeping into him. He was on the ground. The death's head reached down, leaning over him, snatching something from his numb fingers . . .

The door to the nightclub opened. He jerked his

hand away from the metal, turning quickly. The visions evaporated the instant he was no longer in contact with the metal but he could still feel the emotional punch of a man who knew he was facing his own imminent, violent death.

Raine plunged out of the doorway, moving incredibly fast in her fragile high heels and tight black dress. She came straight at him, her small clutch purse extended in her right hand. She did not speak as she closed the distance between them in long, lethal strides.

Not Raine, his para-instincts screamed. Everything was wrong.

But the disconnect between the physical appearance of the attacker and what his senses were telling him created an instant of jangled chaos in his mind, slowing his reaction speed.

A second figure flew out of the doorway.

"Look out," Raine shouted. "He's got a knife."

The real Raine.

She threw her purse at the attacker. It bounced off the fake Raine's back and landed on the pavement. The blow couldn't have done any real damage but it caused the phony Raine to glance back over a shoulder for a split second.

The distraction must have interfered with his control because for a couple of heartbeats the fake Raine wavered and disappeared. A familiar-looking figure in a black ski mask appeared.

Ski Mask dismissed the real Raine as a source of

danger in the blink of an eye but that gave Zack time to get his gun out of his shoulder holster.

It was impossible to line up a clear shot, however. The hunter-illusionist was moving too fast. In addition, Raine was behind him. If the bullet missed its target, which it probably would under the circumstances, there was a chance it might strike her.

Ski Mask morphed back into Raine. He was only a couple of feet away now. Zack intuitively *knew* what he was going to do next and managed, just barely, to evade the lunge.

He reeled back behind the end of the steel container marked GLASS ONLY, reached inside and grabbed the first empty bottle he touched. Then he crouched low.

The fake Raine rounded the corner, black clutch purse extended. Too late the apparition realized that his target was no longer on his feet. He tried to adjust, slashing downward with the purse. The clutch purse changed into a knife in mid-thrust. Ski Mask was back but the transformation disturbed his balance for a second or two.

Zack seized the opening, going in low. He slashed the bottle against a black-clad leg. The blow shattered the glass. He was already rolling out of range. He didn't have a chance to see if he had drawn blood because Ski Mask abruptly danced back out of reach. He was switching back and forth between the fake Raine and his ski mask persona so quickly now that Zack couldn't focus long enough to get a clean shot.

It was obvious that the attacker had completely lost control.

"*No*," Ski Mask/Raine wailed in a high, keening shriek of panic and rage.

He whirled. Still clutching his knife/purse, he fled toward the mouth of the alley.

Zack pounded after him, going straight past a stricken Raine. But it was hopeless. There was no way he could catch the fleeing man. Ski Mask might have lost control of the psychically induced illusion, but he still had a hunter's speed.

The running figure raced out of the alley and onto the sidewalk. He turned left and vanished from sight, footsteps echoing in the night.

A heavy engine roared. Tires shrieked.

The getaway car was waiting for him.

But this time there was a sickening thud and then the sound of a highly revved engine.

Zack hesitated a few seconds at the mouth of the alley. There was no point running straight into an ambush. But when he risked a quick look around the building, there was no sign of the getaway car.

All he could see was the body sprawled on the pavement in the intersection.

Thirty-five

The cops are calling it hit-and-run," Zack said into the phone. "He was dead when I got to him. No ID. No one saw the car."

"What about you?" Fallon asked.

"I didn't see it, either." He paced Raine's serene living room, trying to work off some of the excess energy that was still pumping through him. Batman and Robin trotted at his heels, trying to figure out if this was a new game. "But it sounded like the same SUV that was waiting for him in the motel parking lot last night."

"Are the police paying any attention to you and Raine?"

"Not at this stage. They read it as an attempted robbery gone bad. I told them I went to the restroom and then stepped outside to get some fresh air. The guy surprised me. Had a knife. He took off running when Raine came outside to see what was going on."

"All true," Fallon said.

He sounded satisfied. Everyone knew the Number One Rule. *Stick to the truth as much as possible but don't try to explain the Arcane Society and its problems with Nightshade to the authorities.*

On the whole, it was a good rule, Zack thought. There was just no way a conversation about the Society and Nightshade would go well with a cop. *See, Officer, I work for a psychic detective agency that's on retainer to an organization devoted to paranormal research, and there's this other crowd that stole a secret alchemical formula that can enhance a person's psychic powers . . .*

Yeah, right.

Once in a while the Arcane Society found itself in the pages of the tabloids, right next to breaking news about new appearances by Elvis and innocent women getting impregnated by strange creatures from other planets. That was bad enough, as far as Fallon was concerned. He had no intention of compounding the problem by allowing J&J to become a joke among law enforcement agencies.

"The cops are, of course, very interested in the car that hit the robber," Zack said.

"Even if they find it, I doubt it will lead them anywhere. Whoever took out Ski Mask will make sure of that. The way I see this, his handler inside Nightshade gave him one more chance to remove you from the equation. When he failed, they had a Plan B ready, just for him."

"Any theories on what was going on with all that morphing?"

"Looks like he may have possessed two high-grade talents," Fallon said. "But he couldn't control them both."

Raine walked in from the kitchen, carrying a bamboo tray that held a delicate pot and two fragile-looking cups. She had changed out of the sexy black dress into a white spa robe. Slippers had replaced the stiletto heels. Her hair was still up in a sultry twist but several silky tendrils had come loose during the excitement in the alley. They dangled around her ears and down the nape of her neck in an incredibly sexy way. Zack's body, still abuzz with leftover adrenaline, reacted immediately.

"I thought the appearance of multiple high-level talents in any one individual was supposed to be impossible," Zack said, unable to take his eyes off Raine. "The experts claim that one talent always becomes dominant."

"Like everything else, there's an exception to the rule," Fallon growled. "The historical record indicates that there have been a few cases in which certain individuals displayed strong levels of more than one type of talent. But yes, the phenomenon is extremely rare. According to the experts, there is a logical explanation for why one talent is almost always dominant."

"Something to do with overstimulation of the brain, right?"

"The brain is designed to process a vast amount of incoming data supplied by all the senses. It is also engineered to tune out unimportant or unnecessary information coming in from those senses. We call it the ability to focus. But if that ability is overridden, the brain can short-circuit, for want of a better term."

"Information overload."

"You yourself know that it's hard enough to handle the stimuli provided by a level-ten psychic sensitivity," Fallon said. "Takes a lot of willpower and self-control. Just imagine what it would be like to deal with two equally powerful talents."

"The guy in the ski mask was definitely losing control. It was worse tonight than last night. He was blinking on and off like a bad neon sign."

"I checked out every reference I could find," Fallon said. "In each confirmed instance, and admittedly there were only a handful, the double-talents died at an early age. Probably nature's way of ensuring that those folks don't become super predators who, in turn, breed more super predators."

"If you're right, what are the odds that Nightshade came up with one of those extremely rare multitaskers who didn't die young?"

"Slim to nothing," Fallon said. "My gut tells me that Nightshade didn't find a double-talent; they created one using some new variation of the formula."

"Makes sense. But if they went to all that trouble to produce one, why destroy such an expensive tool?"

"Obviously because he proved unreliable," Fallon said. "He went up against you twice and failed both times. Nightshade seems to be a very Darwinian organization. Only the strong and the successful survive and advance to the higher ranks."

"Sure hope they don't have a whole bunch of high-level double-talents lined up to fill that guy's shoes."

"Not likely." Fallon sounded very certain. "Cost issues aside, the analysts assure me that, statistically speaking, there are very, very few people who possess the sort of parapsych profile that could be chemically stimulated to create a functioning double-talent."

"Statistics wasn't my favorite subject. Too many ways they can be manipulated."

"Look on the bright side," Fallon said, dourly cheerful. "You're obviously making progress with the assignment. At least we now know that Lawrence Quinn is dead and that the double-talent you encountered tonight is probably the one who killed him."

"We also know that Nightshade stole something from Quinn before taking him out. His computer, I think. The bartender at the club said he had one with him."

"Probably contained his research notes or whatever information he intended to sell to Nightshade," Fallon mused. "But something must have gone wrong. The folks who arranged to kill Quinn and steal the computer didn't get whatever it was they expected to find so they're back in Oriana. And Raine Tallentyre is the only lead we've got. Whatever you do, don't let her out of your sight."

Zack heard a click and realized he was holding a handful of dead air. He clipped the phone back on his belt, stopped pacing and looked at Raine. She was seated on the sofa, pouring tea with a sensual grace that made the breath catch heavily in his chest. Everything deep inside went tight and hard.

Get a grip, Jones. It's just the aftermath. You've been here before and survived.

Raine set the pot down on the tray and looked at him with a shadowed expression. "What did Fallon have to say?"

He forced himself to concentrate and managed to give her a quick summary of Fallon's comments.

The cats, having concluded that the pacing game was over, wandered over to the sofa and hopped up onto the cushions on either side of Raine.

Zack shoved his fingers through his hair, trying to concentrate. "One good thing. Fallon doesn't think we need to be worried about another double-talent hanging around the vicinity of Oriana."

Raine used both hands to raise the tiny cup to her lips. "What about the person who just murdered the one we did have?"

"Him, we probably should worry about." He realized he was staring at her mouth. *Focus, Jones.* He started moving again, prowling the room. "But maybe not for a while."

She paused before taking a sip of the herbal concoction. "Why do you say that?"

"Fallon may be right. Maybe Nightshade did remove their double-talent because he failed to get rid of me. But there's another possibility. Maybe the real reason for the termination was that Ski Mask slipped out of control and became a problem."

She pondered that briefly.

"You mean you don't think he was ordered to make another attempt to kill you tonight? You believe he was acting on his own?"

"He was running very, very hot. It's hard to explain but I sensed that he wanted to kill me for his own, personal reasons. He just didn't have the kind of detachment that a pro is supposed to have. Fallon thinks they were giving him some variation of the formula. It may have affected his sanity."

She shuddered. "From what you've said, the founder's formula has a long history of driving users crazy."

"Yes."

"It's hard to believe that my father was secretly working on something so dangerous."

"Raine—"

She put the little cup down very carefully. "No wonder the Council expelled my family from the Society and sent J&J to burn down the lab."

He crossed the room and halted in front of her on the opposite side of the coffee table.

"I thought I made it clear, the Council kicked your father out of the Society," he said quietly. "It didn't expel you or your aunt. Remember that."

She shrugged. "Not like either of us had much choice after that night when J&J destroyed everything."

"You didn't have a choice because you were too young. But your aunt did. She's the one who made the decision to raise you outside the Society and to deny you your heritage."

"In her place, I would have done the same thing. She didn't have a lot of reason to trust the Society or J&J."

He moved around the end of the coffee table, reached down and wrapped his hands around her wrists. He pulled her up off the sofa.

"What about you?" he said.

"I have no reason to trust the Society or J&J, either. They've got their own agendas."

"And you have yours."

"Yes."

"You don't trust the Society and you don't trust J&J," he said. "What about me?"

She searched his face. "Does it matter?"

"Yes," he said. He could hear the rough, gritty edges in his own voice but there was nothing he could do to soften them. "It matters."

SIZZLE AND BURN   259

"I trust you," she said. She looked as if the statement surprised her but she didn't back away from it. "You have been honest with me since the start of this thing."

He felt something deep inside him ease.

"Okay," he said. He made himself release her wrists. "Okay, thanks."

"Do you trust me?"

"Yes." He answered without even thinking about it.

"Even though you know I've got my own reasons for helping you find out what Nightshade is after?"

"I know where you're coming from. Not like you've kept it a secret. You've been honest from the beginning."

"So have you." She sank back down onto the sofa. "I'll pour you some of my special tea. We'll play some cards."

He did not want to sit down. He wanted to keep moving. Tea and solitaire weren't going to cut it tonight. The images of Lawrence Quinn's last seconds on earth were still too vivid, too intense. The attack by Ski Mask had compounded the usual problems of the aftermath.

It was going to be a bad night and he couldn't risk dampening his senses with a couple of shots of scotch. Probably better not to even try to sleep.

Raine poured the brew into the small cup and handed it to him. "Here. Drink some of this."

To please her, he downed half the contents of the

cup in a single swallow. The slightly astringent, herbal flavors were not unpleasant but he didn't think they were going to have any effect on the visions. There was only one thing that could distract him from the death scene and that was the one thing that was not available to him tonight.

Raine picked up the deck of cards and started to deal. He made a valiant effort to concentrate but he knew it was a waste of time. His brain insisted on jumping wildly from images of oncoming death to a raging need to affirm life in the most primitive way possible.

"I appreciate the effort but it's not going to work."

"It's going to be one of those nights, isn't it?" she asked. "One of the bad ones."

"I'm used to it. Don't worry about me."

"I'm not feeling very sleepy myself. Watching that man try to kill you left my nerves on edge, to put it mildly. And then, seeing his body in the street—"

His hand stopped with the cup halfway to his mouth. "How did you know that the guy was coming after me?"

"I'm not sure. He passed very close behind the booth where I was sitting. I was just suddenly aware of him. And not in a good way. It was like looking over your shoulder and seeing a tiger waiting to pounce."

He nodded. "That happens with hunters when they're running hot. The energy they put out is preda-tory. Most people can sense it, even if they aren't consciously aware of it. Another sensitive like yourself wouldn't have any trouble at all picking up the vibes."

"You're sure that the visions you picked up tonight were connected to Lawrence Quinn's death?" Raine asked quietly.

"Yes."

"And you're also sure that the killer was Ski Mask?"

"Can't be absolutely certain, but it seems logical. The last thing Quinn saw was a face that his panic-stricken brain interpreted as a death's head. Two black holes for eyes. I'm betting it was really a ski mask."

"Fallon Jones still thinks I'm the key to this thing," she said.

He drank a little more of the tea. "Unfortunately, I agree with him."

"But it's been a month since Aunt Vella died. No one has made any move to contact me."

"Fallon thinks they've been sitting back, watching you."

"Watching me do what?" she asked, bewildered.

"Let's think about this," he said. "What's the main thing you've been doing in the past month?"

"You mean, aside from running my business?"

"Yes."

"Settling my aunt's estate. It's amazing how much paperwork there is associated with death."

"Right."

"So?"

"So, it all comes back to Vella Tallentyre," he said.

Thirty-six

The dream was a bad one.

. . . A death's head coming at him out of the darkness, black holes where the eyes should have been. He was paralyzed, fingers clutching the corner of the steel garbage container. He desperately wanted to turn and run but he was unable to move. There was no point trying to flee. The terrifying figure would run him down . . .

. . . The death's head morphed into Jenna's beautiful face. She smiled at him and held out her hands.

"I was perfect for you. What more could you want in a woman?"

He came awake, heart pounding. Sweat dampened his

T-shirt. He sat up abruptly, swinging his feet to the floor, and breathed hard.

Just a dream, you idiot. Get over it. You can handle this. You've done it before. What are you complaining about? You didn't expect to get any sleep at all tonight, anyway.

He glanced at the clock. Two forty-five. He had gotten a whole hour and a half of rest. The trouble was, he felt worse now, more wired than if he had just stayed awake.

The herbal tisane had worked but not for long. He really hated the damn dreams.

A pale, ghostly figure materialized in the doorway.

"Zack?"

He could deal with the sight of her standing there in the opening, looking ethereal and untouchable as hell, just pretend it was another vision, an antidote to the images of death. But the sound of her voice was too much for his already wired senses.

"I'm all right," he said, aware of the harshness in his own words. "Go back to bed."

"I heard you through the wall. You called out."

"Just the usual junk dreams."

"Zack—"

"I don't want to play cards, damn it. Go back to bed. Now."

Great. He was snapping at her like a dog with a sore paw.

She walked into the room, came to a halt directly in front of him and put her arms around his neck.

"I don't want to play any more games, either," she said. "I realized that tonight when I watched you almost get killed."

"Raine." Violent desire slammed through him. "Please don't do this. Not unless you really mean it. I don't need your sympathy."

She kissed him, not a gentle, soothing, reassuring kiss. This was a full-on, pull-out-all-the-stops, open-mouthed kiss, letting him know that she wanted him, just as she had wanted him the other night in Shelbyville.

Sensual energy—normal and paranormal—flared, wild and hot. He was swept up in a whirlwind. The force of it obliterated the ghastly visions of the nightmare, at least temporarily.

Temporarily was good enough for now.

He dragged her down onto the bed, getting her under him where he needed her to be. Her foot glided along the side of his leg. He got a grip on the front of the prim, white cotton nightgown, intending to peel it off her but somewhere along the line he heard buttons pop and fabric rip.

The front of the gown was suddenly open down to her waist and that was a very good thing. He found her breasts and feasted on them, enveloping himself in the heat of her body and her scent.

He reached down, discovered that the inside of her

leg was even warmer and softer than her breasts. He moved his hand upward along her thigh. The nightgown crumpled and gave way beneath the relentless onslaught.

When he found her hot core with his fingers she made an urgent little sound. He felt her nails on his back beneath the damp T-shirt, scoring his skin. Come morning he would be wearing her marks. The knowledge sent another wave of raw lust through him.

His briefs could no longer contain his erection. She took one palm off his back and wrapped it around him. It felt good to have her touch him so intimately but he needed to be closer, needed to be inside her.

She opened herself to him, welcoming him. When he entered her she was still a little dry and very tight. He groaned and started to retreat but she wrapped her legs around his waist, urging him deeper. He started to thrust, hard and fast, unable to hold back.

"*Raine.*"

"Yes," she whispered, clutching at him. "Yes, it's okay. I want you inside me like this."

His release crashed through him almost immediately. The heavy waves washed away the nightmarish images and the edgy energy that had fed on them.

The cleansing climax seemed to last forever. When it was over he collapsed onto the pillows beside Raine, utterly exhausted. He knew she hadn't come, wanted to make it right. But he was so damn tired.

She kissed him gently. "Go to sleep."

He was vaguely aware of her reaching down to pull the covers up over both of them. The last thing he remembered was the feel of her arm sliding around his waist.

He slept.

Thirty-seven

He opened his eyes to a damp, gray dawn, feeling relaxed and refreshed. Beside him, Raine stirred.

"Who was Jenna?" she asked gently.

The relaxed, refreshed sensation evaporated in a heartbeat. For a couple of seconds he debated lying to her. But he hadn't lied to her yet. He did not want to start now. She had a right to know.

"My fiancée." He put his forearm over his eyes. "She died a year ago."

Raine touched his arm. "I didn't realize. I thought . . . never mind. I'm so sorry."

He uncovered his eyes and turned his head on the pillow to look at her.

"How do you know about Jenna?" he asked.

"You called out her name while you were dreaming.

That's what brought me to your room to see if you were all right."

He winced. "I was afraid of that. Jenna got mixed up with a dream about Lawrence Quinn."

"That explains it."

"Explains what?"

"When you shouted her name my first thought was that Jenna, whoever she was, might be one of the bad guys you tracked in the past. I didn't realize she was someone close to you."

He looked straight up at the ceiling, knowing he was going to tell her everything.

"A year and a half ago Jenna and I were introduced by the matchmakers at www-dot-arcanematch-dot -com. It's a matchmaking agency run by the Society to help members find mates. Relationships can be tricky for people with strong psychic natures."

"I've noticed that," Raine said drily.

"According to arcanematch, Jenna was the perfect woman for me. And, damn if it wasn't true."

Raine said nothing. He sensed her withdrawing a little, pulling back into her safe zone.

"Jenna was very beautiful," he said, determined to plow on to the end now that he had started. "But she was so much more than merely beautiful. She was smart. Well educated. She seemed to know what I wanted even before I knew it myself, in bed and out."

Raine tugged the sheet up to her chin. "I see."

"She charmed my family and my friends. She could

be sexy or sultry or glamorous or playful, depending on my mood. She enjoyed the same things I enjoyed from music to food to vacations. We never argued. We laughed at the same things. She never complained when I was obsessed with a case for days or weeks on end. She was always—"

"Perfect," Raine supplied neutrally.

"Yes. She and my mother planned the perfect wedding together. And the perfect honeymoon. I told myself that I should be the happiest man on the face of the earth. But I wasn't."

"Perfection wasn't enough for you?" There was a noticeable edge in Raine's voice now.

He met her eyes. "Things were just too damn perfect. I finally decided Jenna was a little too good to be true."

"You tried to find flaws in the perfect woman?"

"Yes."

Raine sat up, still clutching the sheet. "For heaven's sake, why?"

"Because at some point I finally acknowledged that I wasn't in love with the woman everyone said was perfect for me and I had to know what was wrong."

"With her?"

"No," he said. "With me."

"Well?"

"I started looking into her perfect past. When I got beyond the data in the computers, which was pristine, I finally began to spot some holes in the pattern of perfection. My first thought was that she had simply covered up a few secrets."

"You took that as a good sign?"

"Believe it or not, it came as a relief to know that maybe she was human."

"What happened?" Raine was looking reluctantly fascinated.

"I was careful but Jenna was a high-level intuitive talent. She began to suspect that I was having doubts about her. She got very worried."

"Did she confront you?"

"You could say that. She tried to poison me."

Raine stared at him, dumbfounded. "Are you serious?"

"The only thing that saved me was my talent. She put the poison in a bottle of my favorite scotch, the kind I drink when the visions are really bad."

"How did you discover the poison before you drank it?"

"She took the bottle down from the cupboard for me that night. There was just something about the way she handled it. I watched her pour the scotch and I knew she intended to kill me."

"Good grief. I don't know what to say." Raine paused, frowning. "What happened when you refused to drink the scotch?"

"She went a little mad. I don't know how else to describe it. She threw herself at me, going for my eyes with her nails. She screamed she was perfect for me over and over again. I finally managed to restrain her. I called one of the Society's doctors. He concluded that she'd had some sort of psychotic break. We took her to a private clinic run by the Society."

"What happened?"

"Two days later she was certifiably insane. She was put on a suicide watch but she managed to kill herself anyway."

Raine's eyes widened in horror. "You said that kind of sudden spin into insanity is typical of what happens when someone who is addicted to the formula is deprived of it."

"Yes."

"Zack, are you telling me that you were almost poisoned by a member of Nightshade?"

"Nightshade didn't want to poison me," he said quietly. "The intent was for Jenna to marry me."

Understanding dawned on her intelligent face. "Of course. If they could have married off an agent to a member of the Jones family, they would have had the perfect spy."

"They had prepared a near-perfect cover for her and managed to hack into the arcanematch files to plant it. In addition, they got into the Society's genealogical database to set up a solid history for her, too."

"How did Nightshade figure out how to construct the perfect woman for you?" Raine asked.

"They hacked into arcanematch and got my profile out of the database. Then they built a profile for Jenna that appeared to be nearly one hundred percent compatible. Jenna was chosen because she was not only very beautiful, she was also an excellent actress. She was also a high-level intuitive talent like my mother. They jacked up her natural abilities with the formula."

"And turned her into the perfect woman," Raine whispered.

He folded one arm behind his head. "Until she tried to poison me. Amazing how a little thing like that can ruin an otherwise ideal relationship."

"Guess there's just no pleasing some men."

Her lips twitched at the corners and the tension inside him eased.

"Call me picky," he agreed.

"You said she tried to kill you because she was afraid you were getting suspicious of her?"

"Yes."

"What was the point? If the plan had failed, why take the risk of murdering a Jones? She must have known J&J and the Council wouldn't stop until they caught her."

"She was desperate. I told you, failure is not an option in Nightshade. The poison she used would have imitated a heart attack. She hoped that if I died of natural causes, her handlers would not hold her responsible."

"Tough crowd."

"Very tough."

Raine pulled her knees up under her chin and

wrapped her arms around them. "Does everyone in the Society know what happened between you and Jenna?"

"No. The entire affair was hushed up by the Master, the Council and J&J. The official story is that my fiancée committed suicide."

"Which is the truth," Raine said.

"Sort of. As far as I'm concerned, though, Nightshade murdered its own agent."

Raine studied him with troubled eyes. "You had one heck of a close call."

He smiled grimly. "Perfection isn't all it's cracked up to be."

"You really didn't love her?"

"I was dazzled for a while," he admitted. "But eventually I had to face the fact that there was something missing."

"It shook your self-confidence, though, didn't it? Made you question your own intuition."

"Yes."

She nodded. "In a much less extreme way, that's what happened to me after the debacle with Bradley. I keep wondering how I could have convinced myself that he was Mr. Perfect."

He reached up and caught her wrist. "You're sure he's not?"

She smiled. "Not a doubt in my mind."

He tugged her gently down onto the bed and levered himself up on his elbow.

"No doubt in my mind, either," he said.

He lowered himself along the soft, warm length of her.

He made love to her slowly in the dawn light, savoring the sheer pleasure of watching her eyes grow hot and unfocused with passion. When she turned to molten fire in his arms he sank deeply into her. Her legs closed around him and the bedroom was suddenly filled with the effervescent energy of life.

Thirty-eight

They ate vibrant red raspberries with their whole wheat toast and peanut butter. Zack made coffee for himself. Raine prepared tea and privately concluded that it was one of the finest meals of her entire life, maybe the best. She knew she would treasure forever the warmth and intimacy that pervaded the kitchen.

"You know," Zack said, munching a bite of toast, "I think I could get used to peanut butter for breakfast."

She could certainly get used to seeing him sitting across from her at the breakfast table, she thought. A pang of wistfulness whispered through her. *Don't go there.*

The doorbell rang an hour later, just after she put the last of the breakfast dishes into the dishwasher.

"I'll get it," Zack said, setting down his coffee cup. "It's probably Mitchell. He must have heard about the incident at the club last night."

She straightened. "I thought he said something about driving up to Shelbyville today."

"Maybe he changed his mind."

Robin and Batman trotted after Zack, evidently anticipating another new game.

She listened to the sound of the front door being opened. Zack greeted someone. The next thing she heard was a woman's voice, charming and vivacious.

"Oh, how cute," the woman said warmly. "I adore cats."

"I'm allergic to them," a second woman stated.

She walked into the living room. A petite woman in snug black jeans, high-heeled boots and a black turtleneck stood chatting with Zack. She had delicate, elegantly fashioned features and vivid eyes. Her face was framed by a wild mane of amber brown curls. A large chunk of turquoise hanging from a silver chain reflected the color of her eyes.

"Cassidy Cutler," she said to Raine before Zack could explain who she was. She waved a hand at the woman standing a little behind her. "And this is my assistant, Niki Plumer."

"How do you do, Miss Tallentyre," Niki Plumer said. She eyed Robin and Batman uneasily.

Niki was taller than Cassidy and a few years older, probably thirty-six or thirty-seven. She was dressed in a rumpled-looking pantsuit. Tortoiseshell glasses framed her dark eyes. She clutched a heavy-looking leather briefcase in one hand and wore a perpetually harried air.

Raine scooped up Batman and Robin. "I'll put them in the library," she said.

"Oh, please don't worry about the cats," Cassidy said quickly.

"I'll be right back," Raine assured her.

Niki gave her a pathetically grateful look.

She hurried down the hall and deposited Batman and Robin in the library. They were not pleased.

When she returned to the living room, Cassidy and Niki were seated on the sofa.

"I'll get some coffee," Zack said.

Cassidy turned to Raine.

"Bradley has told me so much about you," she said. "I'm thrilled to meet you. I've never talked to a genuine psychic before. Bradley says you do amazing things at crime scenes."

Out of the corner of her eye Raine saw Zack emerge from the kitchen. She knew he was working hard to conceal his amusement. She ignored him and Cassidy's comment.

"What can I do for you?" she asked, keeping her voice smooth and cool.

"I apologize for showing up unannounced like this," Cassidy said. "As I just told Mr. Jones, I hope I'm not interrupting breakfast. I took a chance coming here early today because I wanted to catch you before you went to work. Bradley mentioned that you own a costume rental shop here in town."

"You want my help with the book you're writing about Bradley," Raine said.

Cassidy did not seem the least bit disconcerted by the directness of the statement.

"Yes, I do," she said, assuming a more businesslike tone. "What's more, I'm prepared to make it worth your while." Her brows rose in gentle disapproval. "I understand that Bradley never compensated you for assisting him with those cold cases."

"I didn't do it for the money," Raine said quickly.

"Obviously. But I believe in paying for services rendered. And, believe me, given the advance my agent got for this book, I can afford to make it worth your while to take part in the project."

"I'm a little busy at the moment, Miss Cutler."

"I understand. Bradley told me that there was a recent death in the family. Please accept my condolences."

"Thank you."

Cassidy folded her hands in her lap and looked at Raine with a very serious expression. "I also realize that you use your psychic talents not for money but because you feel a responsibility to help the families of the victims find closure. All I'm asking is that you help Bradley give that peace of mind to the Dellingham family. You are the only one with the power to do it."

The damn guilt card, Raine thought.

"I'm afraid I don't have the time right now," she said. She knew she sounded weak.

Righteous indignation seemed to crackle through Cassidy. Her chin came up, her shoulders stiffened and steel glinted in her eyes. "I'm afraid that's exactly what the Dellingham family has heard from law enforcement for the past five years, Raine. Are you going to shatter their hopes again?"

Raine snapped out of her guilt trance. She smiled coolly. "We just went over the part where you stand to make a lot of money on this book project, remember? That's the real reason you're here today, isn't it?"

Cassidy's mouth tightened. "I won't deny that I make money on my books, but that isn't the main reason I write them. I would have written crime fiction, not true crime, if money was the only thing that interested me. I write my books for the same reason that you assist Bradley. I, too, feel compelled to speak for the forgotten victims."

Another wave of guilt rolled through Raine. "I'm sorry," she said. "I didn't mean to imply that you don't have a personal interest in the cases."

Cassidy's expression softened. "There's another reason I do what I do. We, as a society, need to examine criminal behavior and figure out ways to identify and deal with vicious psychopaths before they slaughter their victims. Do you know what Lynda Dellingham's murder did to that family? It absolutely shattered those poor people."

"I'm not saying that you don't have a calling to write true crime," Raine said hastily. Damn it, she was feeling the pressure, the way she had when Bradley tried to talk her into helping him.

"I'll be honest," Cassidy said. "I won't pretend I wasn't skeptical when Bradley told me that you claim to be psychic. You can't blame me. In my line I meet a lot of frauds. In fact, I even wrote a book about a fake psychic."

"*Cruel Visions*," Raine said.

Cassidy blinked, pleased. "You read it?"

"Yes." She had read it in the hope of finding someone like herself, someone who understood. But the psychic in the book was, indeed, a phony.

"Well, then, you know where I was coming from when Bradley told me that you claim to hear voices," Cassidy said. "He tries to tell himself that you simply have special powers of observation and that you can pick up tiny details at a crime scene that others miss. But I believe you're the real deal, Raine, and I want to write about you and your gift. I want to follow you and Bradley and tell the story of bringing justice to the Dellingham family."

"You don't understand," Raine said. "The last thing I want is to have my name show up in one of your books."

Cassidy softened visibly. "I respect that. I promise I'll use a pseudonym for you."

"I don't think that would work. It would be too

easy for bloggers or the tabloids to figure out my identity."

Cassidy leaned forward earnestly. "I guarantee I'll preserve your anonymity. Trust me. I have always protected the identities of my sources."

"No," Raine said. "I'm sorry, but I just don't want to get involved in the project."

For the first time, Cassidy displayed a hint of impatience. Raine could tell that the slight shift in mood worried Niki. She watched her boss with an uneasy expression.

Cassidy drummed her fingers on the black leather sofa cushion and fixed Raine with a determined look. "The problem is Bradley, isn't it?"

"No," Raine said.

"I understand." She flicked a quick glance at Zack and then turned back to Raine. "Bradley explained that you misinterpreted his friendship. Read more into it than was there. Don't worry about it. These things happen."

Raine glanced at her watch and jumped to her feet. "You'll have to excuse me. I've got to go to my shop now. Good luck with your writing project."

Cassidy made no move to rise from the sofa.

Niki was starting to look downright nervous. She blinked several times and cleared her throat. "Uh, perhaps we should leave, Miss Cutler. Don't forget you're supposed to call your agent at nine."

Cassidy hesitated a few seconds longer, clearly annoyed. Raine contemplated throwing her out bodily.

It wouldn't be difficult. She had the advantage of height and weight.

But Cassidy finally seemed to comprehend that the situation had become awkward. She rose reluctantly and held out a hand to Niki.

"Card," she said brusquely.

Niki hastily opened the leather briefcase and took out a gold card holder. She extracted a business card and placed it in Cassidy's outstretched palm.

Cassidy handed the card to Raine. "I want you to think about this, Raine. Regardless of the status of your personal relationship, you and Bradley share a very special working partnership, one that enables both of you to make a unique contribution to justice. Please keep my card. When you're ready to consider my offer, give me a call at that number. It's my cell phone."

Raine took the card. It seemed the quickest way to get Cassidy out of the condo.

Zack was already in the foyer, opening the door. Cassidy walked outside very quickly. Niki threw Raine an apologetic grin and followed.

Zack closed the door and looked at Raine. "That is one very determined woman."

"She thinks the reason I won't help with the project is because of what happened between me and Bradley," she said.

"I know."

"That's got nothing to do with it. I just don't want to take the risk that I'll end up named in her book."

"You don't trust her to keep you anonymous?"

"Nope. My cover would start falling apart the first time a blogger got curious."

"Got a hunch you're right."

Raine looked at him. "What's the next step in your investigation?"

"Well, to begin with, you're not going in to work today. I assume Pandora can handle the shop?"

"Yes. What are we going to do?"

"I think it's time we talk to the last people to see Vella Tallentyre alive."

Thirty-nine

Dr. Baxter Ogilvey looked at Raine across the expanse of a desk piled high with files, papers and scholarly journals. He was the director of St. Damian's Psychiatric Hospital. Over the course of the year that Vella had been a patient at the hospital Raine had come to like and respect him.

He was a compassionate man steeped in traditional medical and psychiatric practices. She knew that he'd never had a clue as to the true nature of Vella's mental illness. To fully comprehend her pathology, he would have been forced to believe that Vella possessed psychic senses. Raine knew that he had never been able to make that leap. To the end Ogilvey had considered Vella's claim of hearing voices a symptom of her illness.

Nevertheless his approach to what had to have been

one of his more unusual and challenging cases had been surprisingly open-minded and wide-ranging. It had included nutritional aspects such as vitamin supplements as well as cutting-edge psychotropic medications, traditional talk therapy and, above all, a tranquil environment. Raine knew that she would always be grateful to him. Ogilvey had done what she and Gordon and Andrew had been unable to do on their own in the past year. He had given Vella a degree of mental and emotional peace for the first time in years.

He had clearly been surprised to see Raine and Zack walk into his office a short time before but he had offered condolences again.

"I understand that you are still grieving," Ogilvey said to Raine. He folded his hands on the desk and studied her through a pair of gold-rimmed glasses. "Sometimes the process makes us demand answers where there are none, at least none that the medical world can provide. You might want to consider consulting a religious or spiritual adviser."

"We're not here to ask those kinds of questions," Raine said quickly. "We want to know more about what happened the night my aunt died."

Ogilvey began to look troubled. "As I recall, you requested and were given a copy of the file relating to your aunt's case."

Zack looked at him. "We know that Vella Tallentyre suffered cardiac arrest shortly before midnight. We also know that extreme resuscitation attempts were made but failed. We're not questioning the cause of death or your staff's efforts to revive her."

Ogilvey frowned, bewildered. "Then what do you want from me?"

"We'd like to talk to the members of your staff who had contact with Vella during the twenty-four hours before her death," Zack said.

There was an edge to his voice. Raine knew that it wasn't just because he was now in full investigator mode. Like her, he was dealing with the swirling chaos of psychic energy that permeated the lobby and the office. Like any hospital, St. Damian's had absorbed the psychical essence of desperation, fear, anxiety, rage, pain and just plain craziness given off by patients and their families over the years. The energy had literally soaked into the very walls.

Ogilvey stiffened in reaction to Zack's tone. "Surely you don't expect me to subject the members of my staff to questioning by a private investigator? If you suspect criminal negligence, there are procedures that must be followed."

"No," Raine said, interrupting before Zack could alarm Ogilvey any further. "That's not what this is about. We understand that you have an obligation to protect your staff. But, as you probably realize, I have been dealing with my aunt's estate for the past month and certain questions have arisen."

Ogilvey was watching her with grave caution now.

She knew he was giving serious consideration to calling his lawyer. At this rate she and Zack would soon be asked to leave.

"You should be able to answer the single most important question we have," Zack said. "Did Vella Tallentyre have any visitors on the day of her death?"

Ogilvey hesitated, dubious but uncertain.

Raine leaned forward earnestly. "Please, Dr. Ogilvey. It's very important. I know you keep careful records. As far as I am aware, in the year that my aunt was here at St. Damian's the only people who came to see her aside from me were Gordon Salazar and Andrew Kitredge. We always had to sign in and show identification."

"The family has a right to know if the patient received any other visitors," Zack said with an air of quiet authority.

Ogilvey's jaw flexed but he nodded once, brusquely. "Yes, I can give you that information." He punched the intercom on his desk. "Mrs. Thomas, would you please bring in the log of all visitors who came to see Vella Tallentyre on the twentieth of last month?"

"*Right away, Dr. Ogilvey.*"

A short time later the assistant walked into the office, a computer printout in one hand.

"Is this what you want, sir?" She handed him the sheet of paper.

He glanced at it quickly, gray brows bunching a little. "Yes, thank you."

The assistant left, closing the door behind her. Raine realized that Ogilvey was staring intently at the printout.

"I was out of town on the twentieth," Raine said. "But I know that Gordon stopped by for a few minutes around lunchtime. Is there anyone else on that list?"

"Yes," Ogilvey said, not bothering to conceal his surprise, "there is."

Zack did not move but Raine felt the sudden, heavy pulse of his psychic aura. He probably felt something from her, too, she thought, because she was clenching the arms of the chair with enough force to leave small gouges in the wood.

"Who was the visitor?" she made herself ask in as calm a tone as she could manage.

"Nicholas J. Parker. He put down his relationship to the patient as *friend*."

Raine's stomach did an unpleasant little flip. "As far as I know, my aunt was not acquainted with anyone named Parker."

Ogilvey's brows rose. "Are you certain that you knew all of your aunt's acquaintances?"

Her first impulse was to say yes. Then she remembered that, until recently, she hadn't even known that Vella had been engaged in a torrid affair with Wilder Jones all those years ago.

"No," she admitted. "But I can ask Gordon and Andrew. They might recall if there was someone from her past named Parker."

"When did this Nicholas J. Parker arrive and leave?" Zack asked.

Ogilvey checked the printout. "He signed in at three-thirty in the afternoon and left forty minutes later."

"Did he visit my aunt in her room or in one of the lounges?" Raine asked tensely.

"I can't tell you that by looking at the log." Ogilvey put down the sheet of paper with a decisive air. "But one of the staff will probably remember, since any visitors other than you and Mr. Salazar and Mr. Kitredge would have constituted an unusual occurrence."

"I'd appreciate it if you would ask whoever you talk to for a description of Parker," Zack said.

Ogilvey nodded, punched in a number on the phone and spoke to someone in a businesslike manner.

Raine waited, intensely aware of the kick of her pulse.

After a short, one-sided conversation, Ogilvey replaced the phone. He did not look pleased.

"Nicholas J. Parker met with Vella Tallentyre in her room," he said.

"Number three-fifteen." Raine flexed her hands on the chair arms. "It was a private room. She never left it willingly. She had to be coaxed out. She said she felt safe there."

"Yes," Ogilvey said. "In any event, the two of them were alone together for the most part during those forty minutes. However, because Parker was unfamiliar to the staff, one of the orderlies made an excuse to go into the room a couple of times just to make certain that Vella was not agitated or disturbed."

"She must have known Parker," Raine said, bewildered by the widening mystery. "Otherwise, I doubt she would have allowed him to stay so long. She didn't do well with strangers."

"No," Ogilvey said. "She did not know him. When the orderly escorted Parker into the room and told Vella that she had a visitor, she started to object. However, Parker then informed her that he had been a colleague of her brother's at some research lab. That's why Vella allowed him to stay."

Raine felt something squeeze tightly in her chest. "Parker knew my father?"

Zack looked at her, his expression stone cold. "That's what he told your aunt. He might have lied in order to gain access to her."

She shook her head, dazed by the revelations. "Either way, the question remains. Why did he show up out of the blue after all these years?"

"I regret I can't answer that," Ogilvey said, deeply concerned now. He turned to Zack. "I got only a very limited description, I'm afraid. The orderly described Parker as being of medium height, mid-forties, bald and twitchy."

"Twitchy?" Zack repeated with cold interest.

"That was the word the orderly used. I gather Parker was the nervous type."

"Did the orderly remember how Parker was dressed?" Zack asked.

"There was nothing memorable about his attire, apparently. The orderly recalled that he wore glasses, but that was all." Ogilvey exhaled heavily. He looked at Raine. "In hindsight, the visit appears to have been somewhat out of the ordinary. I can assure you that Parker was monitored, however, and that it was your aunt's decision to allow him to remain as long as he did."

"Thank you," Raine said quietly.

"I can tell you something else, as well," Ogilvey said, quietly serious. "Something that may ease your mind. The orderly assured me that after Parker left, Vella seemed tired but very calm. She dozed for most of the rest of the afternoon and evening. Took her normal medication at ten and went to sleep almost immediately."

"An hour and forty-five minutes later she was dead of a heart attack," Raine said.

Zack folded his arms on top of the steering wheel and studied the building and the grounds through the gray, misty rain. He could feel the case coming together rapidly now, like pieces of a puzzle snapping into place. There were still some missing bits but they would show up soon. He knew it.

"The description of Parker wasn't very exact but

what there was definitely fits Lawrence Quinn, especially the twitchy part," he said.

Raine turned her head very sharply to look at him. "Are you certain?"

"There was a note about the twitchiness in his file."

She wrapped her arms beneath her breasts and contemplated the hospital. "Why would Lawrence Quinn go to see her?"

"There was only one connection between them, and we both know what it was."

She gave a sad little sigh. "My father's version of the founder's formula."

"Yes." No point trying to soften the hard truth. She could handle it. "Did you ever go back into room three-fifteen after your aunt's death?"

"No. Her body was moved immediately to a morgue. Gordon and Andrew packed up her things that night. By the time I returned from Vegas and dealt with the funeral arrangements, there was no reason to go back into the room. To be honest, I didn't want to go there."

"I understand."

She glanced at him. "What are you thinking?"

"That you were right to be suspicious about Vella Tallentyre's death."

"You heard Ogilvey. He said she was fine after Parker or whoever he was left. She was very calm. Drowsy, even."

"Maybe unnaturally so."

Raine went very still. "You think he drugged her?"

"Quinn was a brilliant research chemist. If there was one thing he knew, it was drugs. He knew something else, too."

"What?"

"He was an expert on how psychotropic drugs of all kinds affect people with strong parapsych senses. It was his area of expertise."

"But why would he drug Aunt Vella, let alone kill her, after all these years?" Raine asked. "She was in no position to be a threat to anyone."

"I can't answer that yet. All I know is that Fallon was right. There's a connection."

They both looked at the hospital for a few more minutes.

"How did she stand it?" he asked after a while.

"Being confined in a psychiatric hospital?"

"Must have been hell," he said. "We were in there for only about thirty minutes and I was ready to climb the walls."

"She could tolerate it because toward the end, her psychic senses became very faint. She said it was like going deaf or losing her eyesight. For all practical purposes, during the last year of her life she was no longer clairaudient. But instead of giving her peace, the loss of her talent flung her into a deep and enduring depression. Ogilvey managed to deal with the depression but she never recovered her parasenses."

He started the engine. "One more thing."

"What?"

"St. Damian's is an exclusive private facility. Must have cost a fortune to keep your aunt there for a year."

"Mmm."

"Vegas?"

"Turns out I'm good with cards."

Forty

Her phone rang just as she unlocked the front door to the condo. She took it out of her purse and glanced at the familiar incoming number. Bradley.

Zack followed her into the hall and closed the door. He watched her take the call.

"Hello?" she said warily. She was not in the mood for another argument about the Cassidy Cutler book.

"It's Bradley. I'm still in Shelbyville. Got some good news for you. Thought you should be the first to know."

"What's going on?"

"Langdon just arrested the Bonfire Killer. Press conference will be on the six o'clock news."

Relief poured through her. She held the phone

away from her mouth to speak to Zack. "It's Bradley. He says they've got the witch hunter."

Zack whistled softly. "That was fast."

"This time he didn't have a chance to destroy the evidence with fire." She pulled the phone closer to her mouth to talk to Bradley. "Is the killer a Shelbyville resident?"

"Yes. New in town. Burton Rosser. Maybe you remember him. Worked the front desk of the B and B where you stayed."

"Oh my God. When I think of all the times I walked past him in the lobby—" She broke off. "How did Langdon nail him?"

"Found the souvenir photos of the victims on Rosser's laptop. In addition, there was a belt in Rosser's bedroom that was identical to the one that was with the girl in the storage locker in your aunt's basement. They're running a DNA analysis on some hair they found in your aunt's house now. Should have the results soon."

"What made Chief Langdon look at Burton Rosser as a suspect in the first place?"

"Rosser came up on the radar screen right away. Langdon had been keeping an eye on him because he knew that Rosser had done time for rape and burglary. When Langdon started to question him, Rosser tried to run."

Forty-one

Pandora's lips moved but Raine couldn't hear what she was saying. She leaned across the small table and eased the earplug out of her right ear.

"What did you say?" she yelled above the thundering music coming from the band on the stage.

"I said, why did Zack leave you here with me this evening?" Pandora shouted.

"I told you, he's an investigator. He's off investigating. Couldn't take me with him this time. Didn't want to leave me alone at the condo."

They were sitting in a black vinyl booth in Café Noir. Pandora was drinking espresso. Raine had ordered an herbal tea. The club's name was no accident. Just about everything inside was draped in black, including the walls and the ceiling. Glowing neon sculptures in strange shades of green, purple and red provided an otherworldly lighting effect. It was one-thirty in the morning and the place was crowded. Raine was very aware of the fact that she was the oldest person in the room. Even the bouncer out front and the bartender were younger.

She was pretty sure she was also the only one in the place wearing earplugs. The young people would regret not taking care of their hearing when they got older, she thought, feeling elderly and righteous. On the other hand, the crowd was having a lot of fun, at least as much fun as a group of goths could allow themselves.

Like the clientele at the Alley Door, everyone in Noir wore a lot of black. The difference was that instead of the traditional coffeehouse/jazz-club style of attire favored at the Alley Door, the denizens of Noir went in for black leather accented with steel jewelry. There were a lot of elaborate tattoos. Hair color tended to be either jet black or platinum white, although electric blue showed up here and there.

Heavy metal music boomed out of the speakers. The members of the band were dressed a lot like the audience. The lead singer wore an unfastened leather vest that displayed the coiling demons and snakes on his arms and chest to interesting effect.

Raine felt decidedly underdressed, as usual, in a pair of black pants and a black pullover but Pandora was a work of goth art in a long, flowing gown that would have graced any vampire queen. The dress was slit to mid-thigh to display her black fishnet stockings and sky-high black platform heels. The high, flaring collar framed her artificially pale face and dramatic makeup.

Pandora raised her pencil-thin black brows and put her mouth close to Raine's ear. "Sure glad they caught that freakazoid in Shelbyville."

"Not nearly as glad as I am."

"Lots of times those serial killers get away with murder for years. They would never have caught this one if it hadn't been for the information you gave them. I still say you should get more credit."

"No thanks."

"Gordon and Andrew are going to have a fit when they get back and find out what's been going on."

"Tell me about it. I'm already working on my story for them."

"You know," Pandora said, "I used to think it was cool working for a psychic who helped the cops find murderers. Never really believed that there was such a downside to your little hobby."

"Neither did I," Raine said.

Forty-two

St. Damian's was a reasonably secure facility but the emphasis was on making certain the patients did not get out. Zack quickly discovered that far less consideration had been given to preventing unauthorized intrusions. With the assistance of a small J&J alarm-negating tool, he had no trouble slipping into the building through a basement window.

In spite of the reassuring news from Shelbyville, he had not been comfortable with leaving Raine on her own tonight so he had deposited her with Pandora at a goth hangout she seemed to know well. Perhaps he was feeling a little overprotective. So what?

He hoped that the hospital laundry would turn out to be in the basement and luck was with him. At that hour of the night the facility was not staffed. He borrowed a set of freshly washed gray scrubs, pulling the top over his black T-shirt. The loose-fitting pants felt bulky and awkward over his trousers but with the hospital lights dimmed for the night, he didn't think anyone would notice. His soft-soled running shoes and a plastic ID badge finished the look. The badge was on backward, concealing the fake ID. Just an accident. Could have happened to anyone dressing in a hurry.

St. Damian's maintained a large staff. In addition, a little research earlier in the evening had turned up the fact that, like most hospitals, it occasionally relied on temporary agency help to fill in when there was a staffing crunch. It seemed reasonable that an unfamiliar orderly in the hall would not cause undue concern. The plan, however, was to avoid any such encounters, if possible.

The most serious problem was that he was running hot, all his senses jacked up to the max. That meant there was no way to tune out the background static that infused the entire building. He was primarily sensitive to the darker passions—violence and fear and the adrenaline rush that came with the anticipation of the kill—but other stuff sometimes seeped in as well, stuff like despair and psychic pain. There was plenty of that in a psychiatric hospital.

He knew that once he got upstairs into the wards, just walking across the floor would be uncomfortable. The thick soles of his running shoes would not be able to block out all the bleak energy that would cling to every surface.

Tensed against the psychical shock waves that awaited him, he loped up the stairs to the third floor. At the door he paused, listening intently. He heard no sound in the corridor. When he stepped out into it, he found it empty.

Bright lights marked the small nurses' station at the far end of the corridor. All but a few of the overhead fluorescents in the corridors were off, however, as he had anticipated. The doors to the patients' rooms were mostly closed, although one or two were open partway.

Raine had told him exactly where 315 was located. Luckily it was at the end of the hall farthest from the nurses' station. He started toward the room and found out immediately that he had been right about the floor.

Some sensitives claimed that walking through a hospital or a police station or any other highly charged environment was like walking through a graveyard and discovering that the occupants were still partially alive. He disagreed. He always found graveyards to be relatively peaceful places. Hospitals, on the other hand, were anything but.

The door to 315 was closed. He opened it as quietly as possible and walked into the room, moving with the confidence of an orderly who has just entered to do a routine check. He closed the door gently behind him.

Moonlight spilling through an uncovered window

revealed a figure in the bed. Zack could see that the patient, a teenager, was watching him with wide, frightened eyes. It didn't take a psychic to pick up the raw energy of terror. For some reason the kid was looking at him like he was the monster from under the bed.

"I'm sorry," Zack said softly. "Didn't mean to scare you. Just a routine check to make sure you're okay."

The frozen kid did not move or speak.

This was not going well. He would have to come up with a Plan B.

"I'm leaving now," Zack said, holding up both hands in what he hoped was a reassuring manner. He took a step back.

"Are you going to kill me?" The boy's voice quivered so badly it was barely audible.

Zack stopped edging toward the door. "No. I'm not here to hurt you. I just wanted to take a quick look around the room. Make sure everything is okay."

"I don't believe you," the boy whispered. "You're glowing too hot. None of the other orderlies do that."

Understanding slammed through him. "Well, damn. You're picking up my aura, aren't you?"

The boy did not respond. He just continued staring with those big, frightened eyes.

Zack shut down his parasenses. "Is that better? I'm no longer jacked up."

"What does that mean?"

"It means I've closed down my paranormal senses. I can't shut them off entirely, but I can dial them back.

I'm not putting out nearly as much energy now. Most folks wouldn't be able to detect an aura when I'm running cold like this. My name is Zack, by the way."

"Are you a vampire or something?"

"No such thing as vampires. I've got some psychic abilities, that's all. And I think you do, too. You know what they say, takes one to know one. What's your name?"

"Josh."

"Nice to meet you, Josh. How come you're in this place?"

"I'm crazy."

"Yeah? What did you do? Set fires? Torture small animals?"

"*No.* Nothing like that. I like animals." Josh levered himself up on one elbow, shock and outrage overcoming his fear. "I sort of see light waves around people."

"Yeah, figured that was it." Zack went closer to the bed. "Who put you in here?"

"My stepmom. She got my dad to go along with it. Told him that if I stay with them, I'll traumatize her kids and the new baby."

"Because you see auras?"

"Is that what they are? The light waves?"

"Uh-huh."

Josh hesitated. "Yours are really strong. I thought you said you shut them down."

"I did. But level tens give off a lot of energy, even when we're in neutral. Not everyone can sense that

energy, though. Only other people with highly specialized parasenses."

"You sound as crazy as me."

"People who don't have a strong paranormal nature
often think that those of us who do are wack jobs. You
got access to a computer in this place?"

"Sure. Dr. Ogilvey let me bring one with me when
I checked in. My stepmom said I spend too much time
on it. But Dr. Ogilvey told my folks that it was important to me and that I should be allowed to do normal
things that other kids my age do, like go online."

"Dr. Ogilvey seems like a pretty decent guy. He just
doesn't believe that it's possible for folks to have paranormal senses."

"I know. I told him that he has a good aura, sort of
warm and bright. He thought I was either hallucinating or making it up."

"He wouldn't be the first person to suppress his
own psychic nature. Lot of folks do that rather than
deal with the fact that they've got extra senses."

"You sure you're not another crazy?"

"If I am, at least I'm not living here at St. Damian's.
I've got a life. Even got a lady friend who's also psychic."

"Huh. Isn't that sort of weird?"

Zack pulled out his wallet and removed a card.
"Seems normal to me. But then, I know some stuff you
don't know."

"Like what?"

"I know about an organization for people like us.

I'll give you a link and the password you need to access the site online."

"Cool."

"I need a pen."

"There's one over there on the desk," Josh said, sounding awed.

Zack looked around. There was just enough light to make out the pen and a pad of paper on the small desk near the window.

"I see it."

He walked to the desk.

"Man, you give off a lot of energy," Josh whispered. "All kinds of colors but they don't have names."

"That's because paranormal energy comes from a different part of the spectrum than visible light. It emanates at wavelengths that the human eye can't see."

"So, I'm like one of those birds that can see ultraviolet light that people can't see?"

"Exactly. The average psychic can't detect that kind of energy, either, at least not as visible light. Only certain individuals—you, for instance—who happen to have a special type of sensitivity can detect other people's aura patterns. It's a gift."

"Some gift. It landed me in a loony bin."

"Don't worry. I'm going to talk to some people. We'll find a way to get you out."

Josh made a soft, derisive sound. "Think so?"

"I know so," Zack said.

"You don't know my stepmom."

"Trust me. There are people who specialize in this kind of work."

"What kind of work?"

"Helping people with psychic abilities adjust to their senses and figure out how to act normal so they can live in the real world."

"Yeah?"

There was so much aching hope in the single word that it was all Zack could do not to take him down the stairs and drive him straight to the nearest Arcane Society office. But there were rules against that kind of thing, not to mention a few laws. Fallon didn't like it when a J&J agent was accused of kidnapping. Fortunately, there were other options. The Arcane Society had a whole team of experts trained to handle situations like Josh's.

"No problem," Zack said. "Just takes a little time because we have to work through the system, for everyone's sake. Meanwhile, though, I want you to check out this Web address I'm going to give you. You'll find out that you're not alone and that you're not crazy."

He picked up the pen on the table.

Searing, frantic, desperate psychic energy screamed through him. Faint, ghostly images flashed across his mind.

He jacked up his senses and the visions became sharper and more vivid.

. . . He saw his hand closing around the pen—no, a woman's hand. He sensed a feminine essence . . .

. . . Felt her struggle to write a message, the fierce determination to write the note before . . .

. . . before she died . . .

"Mister?" Josh was scared again. "Are you okay? Your aura's going all weird."

"I'm all right." He dialed back quickly. The images faded from his head. He was able to grip the pen, although he could still sense an electric trickle of energy.

He wrote the Internet address and the password for the Arcane Society site that had been established for trusted outsiders who showed a serious interest in the paranormal. There were other sites for members only but Josh wasn't ready for that. He would find the basic facts and, most of all, the reassurance he so badly needed at the first stop.

He handed the card to Josh. "Next time you go online, take a look at this site. Meanwhile, I'll talk to some people who should be able to convince Dr. Ogilvey and your folks that you'd do better with some different therapy."

Josh took the card, gripping it very tightly. "What happens if they can't convince Ogilvey and my parents?"

"Then we take more drastic measures. But these guys are experts, and Dr. Ogilvey really does want what's best for you. They'll know how to talk to him in his professional language."

"Okay," Josh said, still afraid to believe.

Zack gripped his shoulder. "Are you going to be okay here while this process works itself out? Could be a while. A few weeks, maybe."

"Yeah, sure. It's not so bad. First thing Dr. Ogilvey did when I arrived was start cutting back on my meds. I went off them altogether on Monday. I'm feeling a lot better now. I can handle this place."

"Good. Meanwhile, for what it's worth, my advice is to stop seeing auras."

Josh gave him a quizzical look. "You mean pretend to stop seeing them?"

"Right. With luck, Ogilvey and his staff will conclude that the reason you were seeing them in the first place was because you were overmedicated. Overmedication gets blamed for all kinds of stuff."

"Should have thought of that myself."

"Look, I hate to leave you. I know you've got questions. But I've got to get out of here before someone comes around to check on you."

"Don't worry. They only cruise through a couple of times at night. Last bed check was about an hour before you got here."

"You sure?"

"Trust me, I've had plenty of time to figure out the routine here," Josh said.

"In that case, mind if I take a quick look around before I leave?"

"Sure." Josh hesitated. "Uh, why?"

"Because I'm a private investigator and I'm looking into a case that involves the woman who was in this room before you."

"Oh, man, that's what you do? You're a for-real private investigator?"

"Pretty real. Most of the time."

Josh folded his legs, tailor fashion, under the sheet. "So what's your psychic power? Is it like mine?"

"No." There was a glass on the table. He picked it up. Nothing. "I can sometimes sense someone else's aura in a very vague, unfocused way if the person generates a lot of power and is standing fairly close. But I can't see it clearly the way you do. I can't read it."

"What about if you were standing close to a crazy person?"

"Crazy people sometimes give off wild, chaotic energy that I can sense."

"Do I, uh, give off that kind of energy?" Josh asked uneasily.

"No." He put his hand on the base of the lamp. It was silent.

"What are you looking for?" Josh asked.

He moved on to the closet, braced himself for a jolt and eased the door open. "My talent allows me to pick up the psychic residue left by someone who was in the grip of a violent or powerful emotion."

There was nothing on the handle of the closet door except the usual layered static.

"You felt something when you touched that pen a moment ago, didn't you?"

"Yes. A woman used it to write a note."

"What was violent about that?"

He didn't want to scare the kid to death, he reminded himself. "She was very worried about something at the time and desperate to leave a message for someone."

"That is so weird."

"Not any more weird than seeing auras."

Josh smiled for the first time. "Guess not. So, what do you think you'll find in here?"

He could not tell him that he was looking for traces of a killer who murdered a woman in this very room. Josh wouldn't be able to sleep in that bed again.

"Just seeing if there was anything else left behind," he said.

He wrapped his hand around the bed railing.

. . . and jumped straight into a nightmare.

He released the railing with a reflexive action.

"Find something?" Josh asked, fascinated.

"Yes," he said. "I did. I have to go now, Josh."

"Okay." Josh waited until he was almost at the door. "Zack?"

He turned at the door, waiting. "Yeah?"

"I can see how a guy with your talent could do some cool things like be a private detective or a cop. But what happens to people who see auras?"

"Believe it or not, some of 'em become shrinks."

Forty-three

The relentless pounding of the heavy metal rock music penetrated the restroom walls. Raine could feel the floor vibrating beneath her feet.

She exited the graffiti-decorated stall and went to the sink to wash her hands. It was almost 2 A.M. and there was still no sign of Zack. On the positive side, she hadn't experienced any more of the disturbing episodes like the semi panic attack that had alarmed her so badly when he encountered the knife-wielding illusion talent. On the negative side, she had no idea how much she could rely on such a sensation to warn her that he might be in trouble again.

She readjusted her earplugs and then, taking a deep breath to fortify herself against the roar of the music, she opened the door.

The restroom was dimly lit but the hallway was even darker. The route back to Noir's main room was a narrow corridor draped in black. The only illumination was a string of eerie blue lights embedded in the floor beneath heavy glass. She looked down, watching where she placed her feet.

A figure brushed past her and vanished into the men's room. In the gloom he was little more than a dark shadow. With her attention focused on her footing, all she saw was a leather-clad pant leg and a heavy black boot.

The scent of smoke laced with a strong, acrid-sweet herb drifted around her. Someone in the men's room was either burning incense or smoking something strange. She had a hunch it was the latter. She wrinkled her nose, trying to avoid taking a deep breath.

But the smoke grew stronger, not fainter. Out of the corner of her eye she thought she caught a hint of movement in the heavy black drapery to her left. It undulated as though a powerful current of air had moved over the fabric.

No, not over the curtain, under it. The motion was caused by something or someone standing between the drapery and the wall. One of the club's patrons had ducked behind the curtain to take a quick hit of something that was no doubt highly illegal.

Out of nowhere a tide of voices rose in her head. She recognized the screams of rage and pain and sick, euphoric elation.

. . . Need to swim in the blood. Need to bathe in it . . .

. . . Die-die-die. Want to feel it when she finally stops breathing. Need it. Need to know I have the power to take her life . . .

Old voices from a cold case she had worked with Bradley, she realized. They were intermingled with a lot of blurred static that clung to the hallway.

. . . Need another hit. Gotta have it now, now, now. Don't care what I have to do. Gotta have the stuff. Nothing else matters. Nothing . . .

. . . Stupid bitch. Has it coming. She deserves to suffer. Make her pay . . .

. . . Going to kill him this time . . .

Panic welled up, as disorienting as the sea of ghostly voices. Zack was wrong when he'd promised that she wasn't going to go crazy like Aunt Vella. It was happening. She was losing control. Her internal psychic defenses were crumbling. Everything was coming up out of the secret swamp.

Suddenly there was another voice riding the swelling wave of screams. Zack, casually telling her something every member of the Arcane Society already knew.

. . . Any sensitive who decides to experiment with illicit crap is really asking for nightmares . . .

Okay, maybe she wasn't going crazy. Maybe it was the herb-scented smoke. The stuff was doing something to her parasenses. She had to get away from it.

She tried to hurry out of the hall but couldn't seem to find her balance. When she looked down she saw that her feet, complete with high heels, had disappeared into the glowing blue light beneath the thick glass. She could no longer tell where she was stepping. The smoky drug was throwing both her normal and her paranormal senses into chaos.

The heel of her invisible shoe skidded on the glass, twisting beneath her.

She stumbled and started to fall. Instinctively she grabbed a handful of the black curtain to steady herself. But the thick drapery could not support her weight. It tore free of the hooks that secured it to the wall.

She went down hard on the illuminated floor, still clutching the curtain. Yards of heavy fabric cascaded on top of her, threatening to suffocate her.

A rush of adrenaline shot through her. This was ridiculous. She was not going to die here on the floor outside the restroom of a goth club. Clamping down savagely on the riot of horrible voices, she planted both hands on the illuminated floor and managed to push herself up onto all fours.

The change in position allowed a draft of air in under the shroud of cloth. She could still smell the tainted smoke but it was not nearly as strong as it had been a moment before. *Smoke rises*, she thought. The air was less tainted here near the floor. The dust embedded in the curtains was another problem, however. She sneezed.

There were more voices. Thankfully, they were not

coming from inside her head. Two young men who had just emerged from the restroom were talking.

"Hey, man, floor look a little weird to you?"

"I told you that new shit was some righteous stuff."

"No, man, it's, like, the curtain that used to be on the wall. What's it doin' on the floor? Can't see the lights."

She drew another cautious breath. "Help."

"I think there's somebody under there, man."

"You sure it ain't the shit?"

"Don't think so."

The drapery was abruptly snatched away. She straightened to her knees and discovered two figures peering down at her. She couldn't see their faces clearly in the deep shadows but the floor light illuminated two pairs of heavy leather boots.

"Thank you," she managed between sneezes.

One of the young men bent over her, concerned. The blue floor light gleamed on the rings in his nose, eyelid and lower lip.

"You okay?" he asked.

"Yes, thanks," she said. The scent of the drug was almost gone. The air tasted relatively clean. "Could you give me a hand? I think I broke the heel of my shoe."

"Sure." Ring Guy took a firm grip on her elbow and hauled her upright. "Hey, you're Pandora's boss, aren't you? I've seen you in here before."

"That's right." Standing, she could see that both men were wearing leather vests that left their arms and chests bare. The better to exhibit their extensive tattoos, no doubt. Ring Guy's hair was cut and gelled into a shark's fin on top of an otherwise shaved head. His companion wore his hair in a long black ponytail.

"I can't tell you how much I appreciate the two of you coming to my rescue," she said, giving them both a grateful smile. "That curtain weighed a ton. Thought I was going to suffocate under it."

"No problem," Ring Guy said, pleased to play hero.

"Yeah, sure," Ponytail said enthusiastically. "Anytime. You gonna be okay now?"

"I think so, yes." She looked around, wondering why the noise level had gone up so dramatically. "You two weren't behind the curtain, were you?"

"Huh?" Ring Guy seemed confused. "No. We just came out of the restroom."

"I thought so," she said. "There was someone else here a moment ago, hiding behind the curtains. Did you see anyone leave?"

"No," Ring Guy said. "But it's sorta hard to see much in here."

"I know. Well, thanks again."

She tried to take a step and realized that walking was going to be an issue. Her ankle was throbbing. She put one hand on the wall to steady herself and limped slowly back to the main room. She heard the voices of her rescuers floating out of the hallway behind her.

"Is she walkin' sort of funny?" Ring Guy said to his companion.

"Probably the shit. Told you it was good."

She made it back to the booth where Pandora was waiting.

"There you are," Pandora shouted over the roar of the pounding music. "What's wrong? Did you hurt your foot?"

"Fell coming out of the restroom." She slid into the booth, relieved to get off her feet. "Broke a heel. Twisted my ankle."

"Bad?"

She wiggled her foot cautiously. "No. I'll put some ice on it when I get home."

She realized that the reason the decibel level had climbed to the point of pain was because she had lost her earplugs. She was reaching into her purse to find another set when she sensed the wave of paranormal energy. It stirred everything within her. Zack. She realized that she would know his invisible psychic aura anywhere. She could also tell that he was running very hot. Something was wrong.

She turned to search for him. He wasn't hard to spot. For an instant he was silhouetted against a flash of strobe light. She caught a glimpse of his hard face and the black leather jacket he wore over his black T-shirt. He looked a thousand times more dangerous than anyone else in the vicinity.

He cut purposefully through the crowd with the

ease of a wolf carving a path through a flock of sheep, clearly intent on reaching the booth where she sat with Pandora. The club's patrons got out of his way without seeming to be aware of why they were moving. She realized they were acting on instinct, responding on a primitive level to the strong vibes that formed an invisible aura of power around Zack. The Arcane Society experts were right, she decided. Most people did have some degree of psychic talent. They just preferred to call it intuition or, maybe, plain old common sense.

Zack reached the table and stopped, looking down at her. In the next flash of a strobe she saw that his face was a grim, intimidating mask.

"Are you all right?" he demanded.

"Yes," she said automatically, startled by the savage intensity of the question.

"She twisted her ankle," Pandora explained.

"Bad?" he asked.

"No, really, I don't think so," Raine said hastily. His edgy mood was making her very uneasy. Her feminine instinct was to calm him down, the way one would soothe a guard dog poised to attack.

He relaxed a little and nodded at Pandora. "Thanks for keeping an eye on her."

"Sure," Pandora said. "Anytime. How'd the investigating go?"

"It was interesting," Zack said. "Raine and I are leaving now. Can we give you a ride home?"

"No thanks." Pandora waved him off. "Music's

great tonight. I've got plenty of friends here. I'll go home with one of them. Don't worry about me."

Raine grabbed her purse and worked her way out of the booth. Without a word, Zack took her arm and started to steer her through the crowd.

Pain shot through her ankle. She gasped and staggered a little, clutching at Zack for support.

"You *are* hurt," he said. "Damn it, I knew something had happened."

"Broke a heel, that's all."

"Damn high heels."

"You know you love 'em."

"I'd love you in flat, sensible shoes just as well."

She wondered if he realized what he'd just said.

"I don't believe that for a moment," she managed airily. "Men are fools for high heels."

"There is that," he agreed.

Okay, neither one of them was going to refer back to the *I'd love you* remark. Just a slip of the tongue, no doubt.

Before she realized what he intended, he scooped her up in his arms. The sea of tattooed-and-pierced club patrons parted as if by magic, creating a path to the lobby entrance.

"So, you come here often?" Zack asked, amused.

"Just on the really bad nights after a case. The nights when my herbal tisane and solitaire aren't enough."

"I can see how this place would work for you. A little hard on the hearing, though."

"You're showing your age."

They paused long enough to collect her raincoat, then Zack carried her out into the cold night.

"Remind me to take you with me the next time I hit the January sales at the mall," she said. "You're really nice to have in a crowd."

"You know what they say, everyone's got a talent."

He carried her to the car, setting her carefully on her feet before opening the door. She scooted into the passenger seat and waited until he went around to the driver's side and got behind the wheel.

She realized that, although she was still very much aware of him with all her senses, she was no longer picking up the hot, flaring energy that had raised the hair on the nape of her neck a few minutes before.

"What did you mean back there in the club when you said you knew something had happened to me?" she asked, deeply curious.

"Just a feeling." He put the car in gear, rested one arm on the back of the seat and turned his head to check the rearview.

"Like the feeling I had the other night when you were attacked?"

"Maybe." He reversed out of the parking slot with smooth competence and aimed the car toward the exit. "I should probably tell you that the experts claim there's no such thing as telepathy, though."

"These experts of yours. Do they know everything?"

"Hell, no." He drove out onto the street. "In fact,

they're the first to tell you that scientific investigation of the paranormal is still in its infancy. The Society has made a lot of progress in the past few decades but there are some major barriers."

"Such as?"

"Technology, for one." He slowed for a light. "It's hard enough coming up with reasonable theories to explain psychic phenomena. Figuring out how to detect and measure it is even more difficult because modern technology isn't designed to explore the paranormal."

"Hmm. Hadn't thought about that problem."

"How's the ankle?"

"Hurts a little," she admitted.

He did not say anything, just concentrated on driving.

"You discovered something at St. Damian's, didn't you?" she asked.

"Vella Tallentyre was murdered."

She swallowed hard. As often as she had let her imagination play with that disturbing possibility, it was, nevertheless, very hard to take in the reality of it.

"How?" she whispered.

"I think Quinn gave her a lethal injection."

A sick horror, followed by a tide of guilt, rose inside her, threatening to make her ill.

"Nothing came up in the autopsy," she reminded him, trying to quell another tsunami of guilt.

"There are a lot of drugs that can trigger a heart

attack and leave no trace. Remember, Lawrence Quinn was an expert on meds. He also knew how they affect people with strong parapsych profiles."

"You're sure he gave her something?"

"I saw his hand," Zack said quietly. "Sensed the syringe in it. I could feel his anticipation of the kill. He was . . . excited."

Tears leaked out of her eyes. "Dear heaven. He *enjoyed* killing her?"

"No. When I said *excited*, I meant jacked up. He was very, very nervous. Scared that someone would catch him, probably. But I could tell that he was also thrilled because he believed he had gotten whatever it was he wanted from Vella. The combination of emotions was so strong they left a lot of residue on the bed railing."

"But what could he possibly have wanted from her?"

"I don't know but I got the impression that he killed her to protect the secret, whatever it was. He didn't want to risk that she might tell someone else what she told him."

She blinked back more tears.

"Are you okay?" Zack asked.

"Not really." She took a deep breath and tried to concentrate. "But whatever he gave her obviously didn't work right away. The orderly said Aunt Vella was calm after Quinn left."

"I think that's true. I got no sensation of resistance.

Vella didn't fight back. In fact, she seemed to welcome the injection. Quinn must have tricked her, convinced her that whatever he was giving her would help her."

"She wouldn't have been able to pick up any warning signals on the psychic plane because her clairaudient talents had all disappeared," Raine said. Sadness mingled with the guilt, roiling her insides. "On top of that, even her normal senses were probably dulled because of her regular medications. She had no natural defenses left at all."

The night seemed to grow heavier and darker, closing around the moving car.

"There's something else," Zack said. "Something that may be very, very important."

"What?"

"I picked up a hospital pen. It was like touching a live electrical wire. Female energy."

"Aunt Vella's?"

"I think so. Whoever it was sensed that she was dying. She was desperately trying to leave a message for someone she loved."

Stunned, she twisted around in the seat. "Are you sure?"

"As sure as I can be." He flexed one hand on the wheel in a small gesture of irritation. "You know how it works."

"Not as well as you do," she reminded him. "I haven't had the advantage of all that fancy Arcane Society research, remember?"

"I told you, our brand of psychic talent is hard-wired to our sense of intuition. On some unconscious level we interpret the energy we pick up and translate it into the images that I see and the voices you hear. But as is the case with any interpretation or translation, there's room for nuance and outright error."

"Nuance," she repeated evenly.

His fingers tightened on the wheel but when he accelerated through the intersection, the car moved smoothly, under full control. "Always plenty of room for nuance and misinterpretation."

She knew then that he was thinking about how he had allowed himself to be deceived by his fiancée.

"Do you think it's likely that you didn't translate the nuances correctly in this case?" she asked.

"No. I think your aunt aroused briefly from the effects of the drug that Quinn gave her. Dr. Ogilvey told us that she received her evening meds around ten o'clock and that she died less than two hours later. Her regular drugs may have temporarily counteracted the effects of the injection. Or maybe the sense of impending death produced a burst of adrenaline. It happens that way sometimes. Whatever the cause, she managed to get up and find a pen."

"Did she actually write a note to me?"

"That's the part I can't be sure of because what I picked up was her absolute determination to write some kind of message." He hesitated, thinking. "But there was also a trace of overwhelming relief in the mix. She believed that she had succeeded. I can tell you that much."

"But there was no message. Gordon and Andrew would have noticed it when they collected her things that night."

"Would have been easy to overlook a small piece of notepaper lying on the table," he said.

She clasped her hands together in her lap. "Or the message might have been meaningless gibberish that made sense to her disordered mind but not to anyone else."

"In which case it would have wound up in the trash."

"Yes."

They both fell silent for a while.

"What happened to the things that Gordon and Andrew took away from her room?" Zack asked eventually.

"They kept the items that they knew would have sentimental significance to me. Everything else was thrown away."

"Where did they put the stuff they saved?"

She tensed a little, thinking about the task she had put off for the past few weeks. "They're in a box at Gordon and Andrew's house. To tell you the truth, I haven't been able to gear myself up to go through her things. It's been hard enough just dealing with the paperwork and the legal side of death."

"I understand." He shifted gears. "I assume you have a key to Gordon and Andrew's place?"

"Yes, of course."

"Know where the box is stored?"

She braced herself for what she knew was coming. "You want to pick it up tonight, don't you?"

"We're fighting time here, Raine."

"I know." She rested her head against the back of the seat and closed her eyes. "I've got the key with me on my ring."

Zack cradled her in his arms while she used her key to open the front door to the house. Then he moved into the hall with her so she could punch in the code that deactivated the alarm system.

"You don't have to carry me around, you know," she said, reaching out to switch on a light.

"I like carrying you around." He settled her into a chair. "Stay here while I get something to ice that ankle."

He disappeared into the kitchen and returned a short time later with a large packet of frozen spinach that he draped around her sore ankle. When he was satisfied with the makeshift ice pack he straightened and took his phone out of his pocket.

"You're going to call Fallon Jones right now?" she asked.

"Couple of things I have to tell him." He punched in a number.

"It's two-fifteen in the morning."

"So what?" He put the phone to his ear. "Figure if we're awake, he might as well be awake, too. Besides, Fallon doesn't sleep much when he's working a case, especially one that involves Nightshade."

"He's not the only one who isn't getting much sleep lately."

Zack ignored her to speak into the phone. "And a cheery good morning to you, too, Fallon. Got a little news here but first I need to tell you about a seventeen-year-old high-level aura talent. At the moment he's doing time in a psychiatric hospital."

He spoke quickly and succinctly, as usual showing little strong emotion but she sensed the urgency beneath the surface. She was aware of something else, too. There was quiet authority, a cool but unmistakable edge of command, in his voice.

"It's going to be complicated by the fact that the new stepmother is afraid that the kid's crazy and that he'll be a bad influence on the other children," he concluded. "But the director of the hospital is a good man. Probably a fairly high-grade intuitive. Just doesn't know it or won't acknowledge it. An extraction team should be able to work with him."

There was another pause as Fallon responded.

"I know I sound like I'm giving orders again," Zack said patiently. "That's because I am. Now I'm going to update you on the Oriana situation. There have been some new developments."

When he was finished he ended the call and looked at Raine, politely inquiring.

"What?" he asked.

"Why is it," she said, "that every time I listen to you talk to Fallon Jones it sounds like you're giving him orders?"

Zack smiled a cheerfully serene smile. "It works better that way."

"Why?"

"Probably because I'm good at giving orders. Never did take them very well myself."

Forty-four

The box that contained the things that had surrounded Vella Tallentyre during the last year of her life at St. Damian's was pitifully small. He found it in an upstairs closet, next to an easel. He picked it up and carried it downstairs and outside to the backseat of the car. He went back inside to retrieve Raine and a fresh packet of frozen vegetables. Peas this time.

When she was belted into the passenger seat she turned her head to look at the small box.

"There wasn't a lot of storage space in her room at the hospital," she said wistfully. "I only took the things I knew meant a lot to her. The rest of her stuff is still at the Shelbyville house." She settled back into the seat with a tiny sigh.

He took one hand off the wheel and briefly touched her knee. "How's the ankle?"

"Better, thanks. The cold packs are helping."

"You didn't tell me how you twisted it."

"Just one of those things. The hall outside the restroom was very dark. Someone was smoking something behind a curtain. The stuff affected my parasenses. I lost my balance and went down. Took the wall drapes with me. It was very embarrassing."

A small chill went through him, a faint but disturbing echo of the cold thrill that had iced him to the bone just as he parked the car in the lot outside Café Noir. He would never forget that sensation, he thought. He had never felt anything quite like it. Screw the experts. On some deep level he had *known* that Raine was in trouble.

But she had just slipped and slightly sprained an ankle. It was not as though she had been in grave danger. Why had he reacted so intensely?

"Tell me about the smoke," he said.

She shot him a startled look that said more clearly than words that his tone of voice must have been a little on the rough side.

"Why?" she asked. "What's wrong?"

"I don't know," he said. "Nothing, probably. I'm just curious about the smoke."

"I don't know what it was."

"Marijuana?"

"No, something else. More like incense. There was an herbal scent to it that I didn't recognize. Not that I'm an expert."

"Recognize the person who was smoking the dope?"

"Never saw him." She stopped for a second. "Or her."

"You never saw the smoker?"

"It was very dark in the hallway outside the restrooms. The person was hiding behind the wall drapery. Disappeared when I did my swan dive and pulled the curtains down on top of myself."

He felt ghostly fingers caress the nape of his neck.

"The guy was hiding behind the drapery?" he said, fighting to keep his tone level.

"Probably afraid of being caught with an illegal substance. Café Noir has what you might call a bit of a reputation in town. Pandora says the cops occasionally conduct sting operations there."

"Let me get this straight. You never saw the smoker because he was hiding behind the curtains and you only caught a few whiffs of the smoke but that was enough to affect your parasenses?"

"Well, yes, I guess that pretty much sums it up."

"Shit."

"Which reminds me," she said, very earnest now, "I want to thank you for telling me about how psychotropic drugs can have unpredictable effects on a person with a strong psychic profile. That little gem of wisdom kept me from freaking out entirely when I realized that the smoke was destroying my ability to control my clairaudient talents."

"Shit."

"You said that once already."

He drove faster.

"Zack?"

"Yeah?"

"You think we have a new problem, don't you?"

"That's pretty much what I'm thinking, yes."

He prowled the living room, phone nailed to his ear, and talked to an eternally irritated Fallon.

"I need someone here in Oriana as soon as possible," he said. "Preferably a hunter."

He was intensely aware of Raine watching him. She was ensconced on the sofa, her injured, freshly re-iced foot propped on the cushions. Batman and Robin were curled on her lap. The box that he had carried out of Gordon and Andrew's house sat unopened on the coffee table.

"Why the hell do you need a bodyguard for Raine?" Fallon demanded. "They arrested that Bonfire Killer freak. I even had one of the analysts check it out. Ninety-six point three percent probability they got the right guy. That's as good as it gets. You know that. No such thing as a hundred percent with that kind of thing."

"If I'm right, this has nothing to do with the freak.

Doubt if a guy like that would have known how to use a drug to screw up Raine's parasenses, anyway. This was someone connected to Nightshade."

"Huh."

He knew he now had Fallon's full attention.

"There's no way to be absolutely certain," he added. "I'm going with gut-level intuition here."

"There's no logical reason for Nightshade to risk kidnapping Raine Tallentyre." Fallon sounded very thoughtful now. "You told me she doesn't know anything about her father's work."

"Until tonight we didn't have any logical reason to think that someone murdered her aunt."

"I'll be damned. You're sleeping with Raine, aren't you?"

That was Fallon for you. Always connecting dots.

Zack looked at Raine. "Beside the point."

"Not if your personal relationship with her is warping your judgment."

"Get someone here tomorrow, Fallon. There are things I need to do and I can't leave Raine alone while I do them."

"You really think she's in danger?"

"Yes."

"Huh."

"Stop right there, Fallon. I'm warning you right now, we're not going down that road."

"What road?" Fallon asked, doing a very poor imitation of an innocent man.

"You're thinking that if someone from Nightshade is after Raine you can use her as bait. Not going to happen."

"If I throw another J&J agent into the situation, there's a risk the Nightshade operative will decide the game isn't worth the candle and pull the plug on the whole operation. I may never get the answers I need."

"I want a hunter standing here on Raine's doorstep by eight o'clock tomorrow morning, Fallon."

He ended the call before Fallon could come up with another argument.

Raine's hand stilled on Robin's furry head. "Do you really think someone tried to kidnap me tonight?"

"Yes."

"For heaven's sake, why?"

"I don't know," he admitted. "There's a lot of stuff I don't know. But we've played the waiting game long enough. As soon as your bodyguard gets here, I'm going to start looking for answers."

"Where?" she asked, bewildered.

He walked across the room and stopped in front of the coffee table. "In my experience, they are usually found very close to home."

"I don't understand."

"I know." He circled the table and sat down beside her, his leg not quite touching hers. "And you won't like it if I explain."

"No secrets, Zack."

"Right. No secrets." He leaned back into the sofa

cushions and thrust his legs out under the coffee table. He laced his hands behind his head. "I need to take a closer look at the people who are close to you."

She stiffened, as he had known she would. "Not Gordon and Andrew. Surely you can't believe that either of them would want to hurt me."

He looked at her, saying nothing.

"Damn it, Zack, you can't possibly suspect either of them. There's just no way."

"I doubt if Gordon or Andrew is involved in this," he agreed neutrally.

"But you aren't writing them off as possible Nightshade agents, are you?"

"The fact that both of them are supposedly at a conference in San Diego is definitely a vote in favor of their innocence."

"Supposedly?"

"It will be easy enough to check to be certain they're both in their hotel tonight."

"This is ridiculous." She started to pet Batman, somewhat forcefully. The cat twitched his tail. "I can't believe you actually think they might be Nightshade operatives."

He said nothing, waiting. He had known this was going to be bad.

"Who else are you going to check out?" she asked grimly.

"Bradley Mitchell and Pandora."

She sighed. "You're going to be busy."

"Which is why I ordered up the bodyguard for you," he said.

"Do you think Fallon will send one?"

"He knows that if I say I need a bodyguard, I have a good reason."

He looked at the box on the coffee table.

She followed his gaze. "Guess it's time to open it."

He stomped hard on the guilt that was unfurling inside him. He did not want to put her through this but it had to be done.

"I think so," he said.

Forty-five

She unsealed the box and looked at the meager contents. There were three volumes of poetry, paints, brushes, a framed photograph, toiletries and a few other small, personal items.

"So much for a secret message," Raine said. "There's no envelope. No piece of paper. Not even the hospital room notepad."

She lifted the photograph out of the box and looked at it for a moment, tears burning her eyes. The picture showed the four of them—Gordon, Andrew, Vella and herself. They were gathered in Vella's room at St. Damian's. There was a brightly illuminated birthday cake in the background.

"We tried to get her to leave St. Damian's for the day." She set the photograph on the table. "But she refused. She felt safe there."

Zack unlaced his hands from behind his head and sat forward to study the photograph. "She looks peaceful in that picture."

"Thanks to Dr. Ogilvey and the fact that the voices had finally stopped."

He removed the photograph from the frame, working carefully. When he had it out, he turned the picture over to examine the back. She looked at it, too. It was blank.

"If Aunt Vella wanted me to find a message," she said, "I doubt she would have hidden it someplace I might never look."

"It was just a thought." He tucked the picture back into the frame.

She picked up one of the volumes of poetry and flipped through the pages. No notes fell out.

"This isn't going to get us anywhere," she said. "If there was a message, it must have been tossed out as trash."

She put the book down on the table and reached back into the box for one of the other volumes.

The instant her fingers touched the second book psychic electricity crackled across her senses. Instinctively she sucked in her breath and released the small volume, letting it drop back into the box. But she wasn't fast enough. The voice in her head was a spectral echo of Vella's, low and throaty and desperate.

. . . Keep you safe. You're the innocent one . . .

She clamped down on the eerie echoes from

beyond the grave and twisted her hands together in her lap. She stared at the book as though it were a cobra. Tiny claws sank through the fabric of her pants, into her thighs. Robin and Batman were restless, reacting to the tension that gripped her.

"You okay?" Zack asked.

"Yes." She could not take her eyes off the volume of poetry. "The book. She was frantic when she touched it. Terrified."

"For herself?"

"No. For me."

Batman butted his head against her arm, demanding her attention. She hesitated, then, relaxing slightly, she started to pet him again. Satisfied, he settled back down in her lap.

Zack picked up the book, glancing at the title. *Winter Journey.*

"It was her favorite book of poetry. Personally, I find the poems extremely depressing but they seemed to comfort her."

The corners of his mouth and eyes tightened. She knew he was registering the same energy she had picked up.

"She was frightened, all right," he said. "For you."

He opened the book. Vella had made no attempt to conceal her message. It was written on the flyleaf. A yellowed business card was also tucked into the book.

"She was panicked but she knew what she was doing," he said. "She wrote a message to you in this book because she knew it would end up in your hands. A message on a hospital notepad might have been tossed away but not the personal effects of the patient."

He put the book, open to the flyleaf, on the coffee table. Picking up the business card, he turned it over. The simple black print had faded but the name of the firm was still legible. There was a phone number scrawled across the bottom edge of the card.

"It's a Jones & Jones business card," Raine said. "Wilder Jones must have given it to her. I can't believe she kept it all these years."

She leaned forward, not touching the book, and read the message aloud.

My Dear Raine,

   I am dying and I believe you may be in terrible danger. A man calling himself Parker came to see me today. He told me that he had found Judson's notes and studied his work. He said that he could cure me. But now I know that he lied. Soon he will realize that I lied to him, as well. As if I would ever trust my secrets to a stranger.

   Oddly enough, the drug he gave me has provided me with the first clearheaded moments I have known in years. But I can feel my heart pounding. There is something wrong. I must get this down quickly.

   My fear is that when he learns I deceived him, Parker will go after you. You cannot give him the answers he seeks because I never told you the whole truth. But he may not believe that.

There is no help for it now. You must contact Jones & Jones. The Agency will protect you. There will be a price. There is always a price when one deals with J&J. They will demand the same thing Parker wanted. Give it to them, Raine. It is not worth your life. What they want is hidden behind Wilder Jones's mask. Just remember your birthday.

The blame for everything that happened all those years ago falls entirely on your father and me. You are innocent, Raine. J&J will understand that.

I love you. Please tell Gordon and Andrew I love them, too. I owe you all more than I can ever repay.

Vella's signature was barely legible.

Raine could not hold back the tears any longer. She eased Batman and Robin off her lap, jumped up from the sofa and hobbled to her room. Once inside, she closed the door, sank down on the side of the bed and gave herself up to the storm of grief and guilt.

She did not hear the door open, but a moment later Zack was beside her, pulling her into his arms. It was too much. Unable to resist the comfort he offered, she pressed her face against his shirt and sobbed. He did not try to console her. He just held her close until the tempest had passed.

When it was over she felt utterly drained. She rested her head on his shoulder.

"I was in Vegas," she whispered. "Lawrence Quinn was murdering her here in Oriana and I was playing blackjack in Vegas."

"Is that what this is all about?" Zack said into her hair. "You're feeling guilty because you were in a casino when she was killed?"

"Maybe if I was here—"

"No." The single word rang with finality. He held her gently away from him. "You weren't partying in Vegas. You were doing what you had to do in order to keep her in St. Damian's."

"Yes, but—"

"Even if you were here, it would have made no difference. There was nothing you could have done. She let Quinn give her the drug. She was aware that she was taking a chance. Hell, she knew she couldn't trust him. That's why she lied to him."

"I wake up at night sometimes, wondering if I could have done something."

He slid his hands up her arms to her throat and cradled her head between his palms. "You were so accustomed to your role as her primary caregiver that you can't allow yourself to deal with the facts. And the facts in this case are very clear. You could not have saved her."

"Just as you couldn't save Jenna?"

His jaw tightened. For a few seconds she thought he was going to contradict her. Then he pulled her back into his arms.

"Yes," he said. "Just as I couldn't save Jenna."

They wrapped each other close. Neither spoke for a time.

"You think this is nature's way of teaching us that neither one of us can save everyone?" she said eventually.

"Looks like it."

"Hard lesson," she said.

"Yes," he said. "It is."

Forty-six

Raine pushed aside the remains of her peanut-butter-on-toast breakfast and studied the message on the flyleaf of *Winter Journey*. "I hate to tell you this, but it turns out I may not be an ace psychic detective after all. I still haven't got a clue what Aunt Vella meant by the references to Wilder Jones's mask and my birthday."

Zack was at the counter, pouring coffee into a mug. "Did Wilder leave any of his things with Vella?"

"Not that I know of." She tapped the end of the pen against the tabletop, thinking. "But then, I hadn't even realized she had an affair with him until Andrew told me. If Vella kept any souvenirs of her time with Wilder Jones, they would be at the Shelbyville house."

"You said the basement was filled with boxes and cartons."

"Yes. Most of them contain her paintings. I suppose we'll have to go through them. It's going to be a job. There must be two or three hundred pictures in that basement. As far as I know they're all masks."

The doorbell chimed, startling Raine into dropping the pen. "It's six-thirty in the morning. Who in the world?"

"Got a hunch that's your babysitter."

Zack put down his coffee mug and went into the living room. Robin and Batman trotted along at his heels, ears perked and tails high. They had adopted him, Raine realized. As far as they were concerned, Zack was now part of the gang. She tried to recall the name for a group of cats. Clowder. That was it. Unfortunately it didn't sound very exciting, let alone cool. No wonder people didn't use it to describe those of the feline persuasion.

She heard the front door open and the rumble of a deep bass voice that sounded like it came from the heart of a mountain. She got to her feet, exercising some caution because her ankle was still tender, and went to stand in the doorway.

A big, dark-skinned man a few years younger than Zack occupied a considerable amount of space in her small living room. His head was completely shaved and gleamed as though it had been waxed. Dark glasses veiled his eyes. A gold ring flashed from one ear. He was dressed in khakis, a dark blue pullover shirt and a battered suede bomber jacket. She caught a glimpse of a shoulder holster beneath the jacket.

He gave her a smile that could have lit up the stage of a large theater.

"You must be the client," he said.

She didn't even try to resist the smile. "You must be the bodyguard."

"This is Raine Tallentyre," Zack said. "Raine, meet Calvin Harp."

Raine extended her hand. "A pleasure, Mr. Harp."

"Call me Calvin." He shook her hand and then looked down at the cats, who were sitting directly in front of him, gazing upward with unblinking stares. "Who are these guys?"

"Batman and Robin," Zack said.

Calvin beamed. "What do you know? Couple of my favorite masked avengers."

He went down on his haunches and held out his hand. The cats sniffed his fingers in an assessing manner and appeared to be satisfied. Calvin rubbed their ears gently with one huge hand and straightened.

"Looks like you're in the club," Zack said. "How about some coffee?"

Calvin's smile got even bigger. "Excellent idea. Any chance of some food? I've been a little busy since I got Fallon's call a few hours ago. Wasn't anything to eat on board the company plane except a couple of boxes of doughnuts. Had to share 'em with the pilots."

"How do you feel about peanut butter?" Zack asked.

"Works for me." Calvin looked toward the kitchen with great interest. "Hell, I'm hungry enough to eat the cats' food."

Zack looked at Raine. "The only downside of working with Calvin is that you have to feed him. A lot."

Forty-seven

Zack used a gadget from his J&J tool kit to let himself into the small studio apartment. He did not expect to find anything that pointed to Pandora as a member of Nightshade but he had learned the hard way not to let the personal get in the way of the logical.

The tiny space was decorated in what could only be described as High Goth. The ceiling was an elaborately detailed night sky, complete with crescent moon and stars. The walls were painted midnight blue, the window and door trims picked out in a paler shade. The furnishings were eclectic and mostly black, punctuated with the occasional bloodred pillow.

He checked the refrigerator first. One of the things they had learned in the Stone Canyon affair was that

Nightshade's version of the formula had to be refrigerated. With luck, that was still true.

He opened the door with gloved hands. There was an assortment of leftover takeout, several bottles of water and a couple cases of soda. He took the small metal stick Fallon had given him out of its leather case and inserted it into the milk carton, just to be sure. It did not change color. He rinsed it off at the sink and tried the bottle of vinegar. No change.

He went through the rest of the apartment carefully but there was nothing to indicate that Pandora was anything other than what she appeared—a creative young woman with a flair for the offbeat and the dramatic.

He went out of the apartment, made his way down the three flights of stairs and walked the two blocks to where he had left the rental car.

Pandora emerged from the back room shortly before noon. "How does pizza sound?"

Calvin, sprawled in a chair with a cup of coffee, gave her a mockingly earnest look. "Don't toy with me, woman. You never want to ask me a question like that unless you're serious."

Pandora's answering laugh was light, almost a giggle, and so unexpected that Raine, standing behind the counter, could only stare at her in disbelief. She had never heard Pandora laugh like that.

"The restaurant at the end of the block makes great pizza," Pandora assured Calvin. "I'll go pick one up."

"Oh, man," Calvin said, big hand covering his heart. "The perfect woman. You with anyone?"

To Raine's astonishment, Pandora actually blushed.

"Not at the moment," she said lightly.

"This is definitely my lucky day," Calvin declared.

Pandora looked oddly flustered. She turned hastily to Raine. "The usual? Olive and veggie?"

"Sounds good to me," Raine said, still trying to get used to the sight of a sparkling-eyed Pandora. "If that's okay with you, Calvin."

"Sure." Calvin took out a wallet. "Get two. Make sure one of 'em's extra large."

"That's okay," Raine said. "Lunch is on the house."

"Nah, let's let J&J pay for it." Calvin crammed a fistful of cash into Pandora's hand. "I'll bill the pizzas as expenses."

With a last lilting giggle, Pandora hurried out the door with the money.

Calvin watched her go with a besotted expression. "I think I've just met the girl of my dreams."

Raine folded her arms on the counter. "I thought you Arcane Society folks relied on your own in-house matchmakers to find partners."

"I like to do my own hunting." He went back to watching the street in front of the shop. "Besides, arcanematch-dot-com isn't what you'd call one hundred percent reliable. Just ask Zack about his fiancée."

"He told me about Jenna," she said.

"No telling what Nightshade might have been able to do if they had succeeded in marrying an operative off to Zack," Calvin stated.

"I can see where it would have been a big coup for Nightshade to have an agent married to a member of the Jones family."

Calvin snorted softly. "Not just any member of the family, the Number One Jones."

She stilled. "I beg your pardon?"

Calvin glanced at her. Surprise and then amusement dawned on his broad features. "Sorry about that. I forgot."

"Forgot what?"

"When Fallon called me he said something about you having been raised outside the Society. Guess you don't know much about the politics of the organization."

"I'm aware that the Society was founded by a Jones and that the Jones family has always been extremely influential."

"That's putting it mildly. In the last century the Society went through some major changes. Members of the Governing Council are elected now, for example. But one thing hasn't changed. The head of the organization has always been a Jones, usually a Jones from Zack's branch of the family tree. Society's pretty strong on tradition."

She nearly collapsed on the counter. "Are you

telling me that Zack is slated to be the next Master of the Arcane Society?"

"The U.S. branch," Calvin clarified. "The UK has its own Master."

"Another Jones?"

"Afraid so."

"Good grief. I had no idea."

"Zack's appointment is supposed to be confirmed by the Council anytime now. It gets officially announced at the Society's annual Spring Ball. Problem is, ever since his fiancée died, Zack's been telling everyone that he's decided to opt out of the job. No one's taking him seriously, though."

She frowned. "Zack doesn't strike me as the kind of person who changes his mind once it's made up."

"True, but in this case, folks figure he just needs some time to get past what happened last year."

"Don't know about you, but speaking personally, I can see how finding out that you nearly married a Nightshade operative and then having said operative try to poison you might make you reconsider your goals and objectives in life."

"Nah. Zack was born for the job. Sooner or later he'll realize it."

"Would it be the end of the world if he did opt out?"

Calvin shrugged. "Like they say, no one's irreplaceable. And lord knows, there are plenty of other Joneses around. Thing is, Zack's grandfather, the current

Master, and the majority of the Council, which includes a lot of intuitives, by the way, feel that Zack is the best guy for the job. There's a lot of pressure on him."

"What makes him so unique? You said yourself there are a lot of Joneses."

"He's the first Jones in a long time who is a level-ten mirror talent."

"So what? Why does that make him the best person to take on the Master's responsibilities?"

"Mirror talents are so rare they're the stuff of legend within the Society," Calvin explained. "The Council and the old man at the top are thrilled with Zack. See, the ability to intuitively second-guess the opposition is just exactly the kind of talent you need in the Master's Chair when you're up against some real bad guys. And Nightshade is definitely a world-class collection of bad guys."

Forty-eight

He left the car in the herd of vehicles clustered in a lot that served a small city park and walked a block to a sprawling six-story condominium complex.

Bradley Mitchell's home security was stunningly low-end. Then again, maybe hotshot detectives assumed that the bad guys wouldn't dream of burglarizing a cop's home. Talk about a state of denial.

He deactivated the simple alarm system with the same J&J gadget that he had used to open the front door.

Once inside, he found himself in a one-bedroom apartment decorated in surprisingly good taste. He had been expecting a cluttered, dust-laden bachelor pad filled with cheap rental furniture, a lot of high-tech media equipment and the kind of artwork that was ripped out of girlie magazines.

The state-of-the-art television and sound system were present but the sofa, chairs and coffee table were comfortable and modern in design—clearly several steps above rental quality. The pictures on the walls were Ansel Adams prints. Maybe the biggest shocker of all was the well-stocked bookcase.

Okay, so he had been hoping that Mitchell would prove to be a knuckle-dragging Neanderthal with no redeeming traits. He should have known that Raine would never have been attracted to a man who didn't exhibit some civilized behavior patterns and a degree of intelligence.

He brushed against the first ghostly images when he took off a glove and touched the bed. The scenes were very faint, little more than gossamer flickers slicing through his mind. His powerful intuition conjured up a vision of two people engaged in heated sex. One of them—the one who left the strongest impression— wasn't enjoying the act, at least not in a normal, healthy way. For one of the two lovers, sex was a weapon—no, a tool—that had been used to achieve some objective far more vital than a momentary release. Power was the goal.

He steeled himself against the visions long enough to absorb the few clues they offered and then sup-pressed them, temporarily at least.

Moving more quickly now, he pulled the glove back on and went into the kitchen. Disappointment shafted through him when he found no unmarked vials inside the refrigerator but he used the little metal stick to sample a carton of orange juice and the milk, just to make sure.

He closed the door and stood quietly in the middle of Mitchell's neat, tidy kitchen, thinking about things. All his parasenses were yelling at him, telling him that the drug had to be somewhere in the apartment.

He went back into the living room and stood listening intently. Nothing. Then he went down the hall and opened a closet door. There was a stacked set of apartment-sized appliances inside, a washer and dryer. He finally heard it: the high-pitched whine of a miniature refrigerator, the kind designed for a den.

The little unit was sitting in the corner, plugged into a wall socket. When he touched the handle, another whispery vision slashed through him, strong enough to penetrate the glove. He opened the door and saw a small, unlabeled vial. There was a trace amount of clear fluid inside.

Bradley shoved the key into the lock of his front door. He moved into the foyer and looked at the small white control panel on the wall. The security system was off. That wasn't right. He was sure he'd set it before he left the apartment. The damn thing was broken again. One of these days he would have to get around to replacing it.

He thumped the panel box a couple of times. The lights didn't come on. He was about to hit the box again when he sensed a presence behind him.

He spun around, hand going inside his jacket. But Zack Jones already had his gun out.

"Guy in your line of work should probably get a better security system," Zack said.

"What the hell are you doing here?"

Zack held up a small glass vial. "You and I need to talk."

Forty-nine

Mayor Joanne Escott parked her Mercedes sports car in a no-parking zone in front of Incognito shortly before noon and rushed inside. Calvin did not appear to be paying much attention but Raine was sure she caught a whisper of power. He had jacked up his senses when Joanne flew into the shop, assessing her with his hunter talent.

Joanne stopped short, removed her dark glasses and gave him a blatantly appraising look.

"New employee?" she asked, brows rising with unconcealed interest.

"This is Mr. Harp, a freelance costume designer," Raine said before Calvin could respond. "He brought in some sketches for me to look at."

Joanne's interest faded immediately. "Oh. Probably gay, then, hmm?"

Calvin gave her his sunny smile.

Raine cleared her throat. "Calvin, this is Joanne Escott, our mayor."

Calvin inclined his head, gravely polite. "Your Honor."

"Do you live here in Oriana?" Joanne asked brightly.

"No, ma'am. I'm from out of town."

"I see." Assured that Calvin was not a potential voter, Joanne rounded on Raine. "I've only got fifteen minutes for my fitting," she announced, checking her diamond-studded watch. "I have an appointment with my stylist at twelve forty-five. I don't dare be late. Roger is so temperamental and I absolutely have to get my hair done for the fund-raiser tonight."

"Your costume is finished," Raine said. She held the red velvet curtain aside. "It won't take long to try it on."

Joanne gave Calvin one last regretful glance, and then, with a tiny sigh, she dropped her dark glasses into an oversized purse and followed Raine.

Calvin rose from his chair in a seemingly leisurely fashion and ambled after them. He lounged just inside the doorway, arms folded.

Raine brought the Cleopatra gown out from behind a long row of costumes and started to remove the plastic covering.

"We took the hem up another two inches and tightened the bustier," she said.

Joanne watched, pleased, as the finished gown was revealed. "It looks fabulous."

She reached into her purse. Raine assumed she was going to take out another pair of glasses. Instead she removed what looked like a milky white jar.

Power jumped. Calvin moved so quickly, Raine didn't even realize he had left the doorway until he seized Joanne's right wrist.

But Joanne, serene and unruffled, had already dropped the jar. It shattered on the floor. White smoke erupted in a foggy cloud of vapor.

Hand grenade, Raine thought. *We're all dead*.

Instinctively she dove for the floor behind a rack of costumes, bracing for the inevitable shock wave and the flying bits of metal, knowing there was nothing she could do to shield herself.

But there was no shock wave. No metal bits pierced her body. There was only the cool, white smoke. It roiled through the room, filling the small space with a familiar herbal scent.

Joanne stared at the swirling vapors, frowning in baffled confusion.

"What in the world?" she said.

She crumpled, unconscious.

A torrent of voices rose out of the swamp of nightmares inside Raine's head. Familiar screams of rage, agony and hellish panic smashed across her senses.

"Get down," she shouted to Calvin.

He seemed to comprehend but he did not follow

her instructions. Instead, he lashed out with one foot, kicking the smoking canister beneath another rack of costumes. Then he backed toward the door, fumbling for his phone.

But it was too late. He had been standing virtually on top of the canister when it struck the floor. Raine knew he had taken the worst brunt of the initial explosive blast of smoke. It was amazing he had remained upright as long as he had. There was no telling what effect the drug might have on a powerful hunter whose parasenses had been running wide open when the herb-laced fumes hit them.

Calvin coughed but managed to punch in a number on his phone.

"Get out of here," he roared to Raine. "Back door. Now."

Then he went down. The floor shuddered when he landed. He did not move again.

The phone landed on the floor beside him. She had no way of knowing whether he had managed to punch in 911. Her own phone was in her purse in the other room.

Breathing shallowly, she yanked her shirt out of the waistband of her pants. The smoke was thickest in the center of the room. She did not dare try to crawl through it to get to the safety of the front part of the shop. The alley door was closer.

Holding the edge of her shirt over her nose and mouth, she wriggled awkwardly on her belly toward the rear door. The smoke was doing what it was supposed to do according to the laws of physics: rising. The air near the floor smelled strongly of herbs but the vapors were not as thick as they were a few inches higher. She knew she was still taking in a lot of the drug, however. The demonic cacophony in her head was getting steadily worse.

The costumes around her began to come alive. She was suddenly in the midst of a nightmarish masquerade ball that was taking place in a room filled with funhouse mirrors. Capes and gowns swirled, making her dizzy. Malevolent eyes peered down at her through the empty sockets of the masks. Panic drenched her senses. The urge to leap to her feet and make a run for the door was overpowering.

It's the drug. Ignore it. Stay low.

The voices were changing. Some of them seemed to be coming from the mouths of the masks.

". . . Kill her. Torture her. Burn, witch, burn. . . ."

She told herself that she was making progress through the ranks of dancing costumes. She could see the rear door but to her smoke-warped vision it kept shifting position. The masks were closing in around her.

". . . Hurt her—hurt her—make her suffer . . ."

A bell chimed somewhere in the distance. She dimly recognized it. Pandora returning with the pizza. Thank God.

Then she heard more voices, not the ghostly cries inside her head.

"They should all be unconscious by now," Cassidy Cutler said.

"We've got to be careful." Niki Plumer sounded worried, as usual. "That smoke is very strong. If it gets to us, we'll be in trouble."

"We'll give it a couple of minutes to clear. Lock the front door and turn over the closed sign. We'll take her out the back."

Fifty

"She set you up," Zack said.

"This doesn't make any sense." Bradley reached the end of the living room, turned and paced back in the reverse direction. "She's Cassidy Cutler. She's written four books." He stopped in front of a bookcase, yanked out a copy of *Cruel Visions* and showed Zack the back cover. "Her picture is on every damn one of them."

"I'm not saying she stole Cutler's identity, although it's a possibility. I think it's more likely that she really is Cassidy Cutler."

Bradley shoved the book back into the case. "Why in hell would she want to hurt Raine?"

Zack chose his words carefully, sticking to the truth as much as possible.

"My agency believes that she's involved with a

crowd that manufactures and distributes exotic designer drugs," he said.

Bradley dropped down onto one of the chairs, eyes narrowing. He knew drug dealing and the crimes associated with the business. "Okay, let's say for the sake of argument you're right. What does she want with Raine?"

"Raine's father was a brilliant chemist."

"Yeah, I know. She told me."

"When Raine was a little girl, Judson Tallentyre worked for my firm's client, a company that invented and patented a unique psychotropic drug." Zack slipped easily into the familiar cover story, blending truth and fiction into a seamless whole. "The company abandoned research and shelved the drug after initial trials revealed that it was extremely dangerous. But Tallentyre suspected that the formula would be worth a fortune on the black market. It needed some tweaking, however. There were some extremely serious side effects. He left the company and took the formula with him. He continued to experiment on his own."

"Raine said he died when she was little. Traffic accident."

"That's right. The company he worked for investigated and concluded that the secret of the formula died with him. That was the end of the matter until a few weeks ago, when another researcher named Lawrence Quinn suddenly disappeared. The client called in my agency again. We discovered that Quinn had been doing unauthorized research on the same proprietary formula that Judson Tallentyre had stolen. We traced Quinn here to Oriana."

"Yeah? Where the hell is he, then?"

"Disappeared. Based on what I've been able to piece together, I strongly suspect that he's dead. I think he came here to interview Raine's aunt, Vella Tallentyre. After he got the information he wanted from her, he vanished."

Bradley was starting to look interested. "You think he was murdered by someone who wanted whatever it was he got from Vella Tallentyre?"

"Yes."

Bradley held up a hand, palm out. "Let's go back to Vella Tallentyre. Got any proof that she was murdered?"

"She left a note for Raine. We found it last night among her things. It was written on the night of her death. In it she said she'd had a visitor that day who gave her an injection. She knew she was dying and wanted to warn Raine. The description of the visitor that we got from the hospital fits Lawrence Quinn."

"What did Quinn want from her?"

"We don't know but we suspect it had something to do with the formula for the drug that Judson Tallentyre stole all those years ago."

Bradley looked thoughtful. "You think Quinn intended to re-create the formula and set himself up in the illegal drug business?"

"Yes. But it looks like he didn't get what he wanted

from Vella Tallentyre. In her note to Raine, Vella said she didn't trust him and lied to him. Presumably she gave him some kind of false data about the drug."

"But Quinn figured he had the answer he wanted so he got rid of her. Then he tried to make a deal with some bad guys. It did not go well. That's it?"

"That's it. Except that I'm sure Cassidy Cutler is one of the bad guys. Niki Plumer, too."

"Any others?"

"I think she had some muscle with her when she first came to town," Zack said. "The guy tried to take me out in the alley behind a local jazz club, but he managed to get hit in an intersection. Never made it to the hospital."

"Heard about the hit-and-run when I got back from Shelbyville. Meant to talk to you about it. They're still trying to ID the victim. You're telling me you think Cassidy killed him, too?"

"Yes."

"Why?"

"Probably because he failed to get rid of me."

Bradley eyed the little bottle of clear fluid sitting in the ice bucket on the table. "You really believe she left that stuff here to implicate me, don't you?"

"She knows I'm in town. She needs to point me in another direction. You were convenient. She was already using you to get close to Raine. Guess she figured you for a dual-purpose tool."

Bradley's mouth curved in a sour grimace. "Why use me? Why not approach Raine directly?"

"Think about it," Zack said. "Raine's a very private person. Her inner circle of friends is small and tightly knit. It's not easy breaking into it."

Bradley hesitated, then nodded once. "I see what you mean. But Raine's no research chemist. Neither was her aunt. Besides, according to you, Cassidy and her crowd already have this drug you're talking about. What the hell did they expect to get from Vella Tallentyre? What do they want from Raine?"

"I'm still working on that angle. What I know is that there are some serious problems with the current version of the drug. Someone may have been convinced that Vella Tallentyre knew something important about her brother's version that would be useful. Now that she's dead, those same people may think that Raine has the information."

Bradley shot back to his feet and resumed pacing. "You're making me look stupid here, Jones."

"No," Zack said. "Stupid would be refusing to believe the facts when they're put in front of you."

Bradley looked at him. "If you want me to arrest Cassidy Cutler and Niki Plumer, you're going to have to give me some hard proof."

"I don't have a lot of that," Zack admitted. "But you could start with her SUV."

"What about it? She's driving a rental."

Zack raised a brow. "The same one she had a couple days ago?"

"No. She said the heater wasn't working on that one. She had to exchange it."

"Got a hunch it never made it back to the rental agency. It's probably been abandoned in one of the big mall parking garages. She didn't have a lot of time to get creative."

"You think she used it to run down that guy who attacked you?"

"Yes. Probably wiped it clean but she may have missed something. You never know."

Bradley reached for his phone. "I'll have someone contact the car rental agency."

Zack smiled slightly.

"What?" Bradley asked, brows bunching.

"Raine told me you were a good cop," Zack said.

An electrifying sensation shivered across his parasenses. Adrenaline splashed through him.

He was on his feet before he had made a conscious decision to move, heading for the door.

"What the hell?" Bradley yelled after him. "Where are you going?"

"Raine. She's in trouble. Get someone to her shop. Now."

His phone rang. He yanked it out of his pocket as he opened the door and ran toward his car.

One ring. Calvin's code appeared on the small screen. Then silence.

Fifty-one

The poisoned smoke was dissipating but the masks still taunted her and the costumes still swayed to music only the ghostly dancers could hear. The room whirled around Raine. Her stomach roiled. She could not be sick. Not now. She had to get out of there before Cassidy and Niki decided it was safe to enter the room. The alley exit was her only chance.

She inched forward, trying not to make any sound on the carpeted surface. The gleaming knob that spelled escape was almost within reach. A draft of fresh air was coming in under the bottom of the door. All she had to do was jump to her feet, yank the door open and run for her life.

Another peculiar sound intruded on the silently

screaming voices. Someone was pounding on the front door of the shop, demanding admittance.

"It's the clerk," Cassidy snapped from the far side of the red curtain.

"She sees us," Niki said, her voice rising. "Probably thinks the door got locked by accident. If we don't open it, she'll know something's wrong."

"Let her in. We'll have to get rid of her. The other two didn't see us but she'll be able to give a description to Jones and the cops."

"You said no guns."

"I said no guns. I didn't say no weapons. I've got a company product with me. A double dose will be more than enough to stop her heart."

They were going to murder Pandora simply because she was an innocent bystander who had seen them. Rage crashed through Raine.

She heard the outer door open.

"Hey, thanks," Pandora said. "Who locked the door? Where's my boss? And the big man who was sitting in that chair?"

"Back room," Cassidy said coolly. "They'll be right out."

Raine took one last gulp of the relatively untainted air seeping in under the door, surged to her feet and, holding her breath, half-stumbled, half-ran through the wispy vapor toward the crimson curtain.

Adrenaline drowned most of the pain that shot through her injured ankle. Not all.

She thrust the velvet curtain aside. Pandora was in the act of crossing the threshold into the shop. She held the pizza boxes in both hands. Cassidy and Niki were on either side of the front door waiting to jump on her as soon as they could get the door closed.

"Run, Pandora!" Raine burst out of the opening, heading toward the front door as fast as she could on her bad ankle. "They're going to kill you. Get the cops. *Run*, damn it!"

Pandora hesitated, mouth open in surprise and confusion. Cassidy reached for her.

"*Run*," Raine shouted again, putting every ounce of authority she could muster into the single word.

Pandora dropped the pizza boxes, whirled and fled straight out into the middle of the street. Horns honked. Tires shrieked. Drivers shouted. Somewhere in the distance a siren wailed.

"Forget her," Cassidy said to Niki. "We've got to get out of here. The back door. Help me with the bitch."

"Guess that would be me," Raine said. She gave Cassidy a really super version of her special, patented *screw you* smile.

She did not stop. Fueled by desperation and fury, she continued her unsteady headlong rush. Cassidy and Niki were directly in her path. The plan, such as it was, consisted of ramming through them with enough force and momentum to carry her outside onto the sidewalk.

But her injured ankle gave out just as she reached

the pair. She lost her balance and staggered wildly to one side, colliding with Niki.

The impact sent them both down in a tangle of arms and legs. Raine lashed out, frantically trying to free herself.

"Hold her still, damn it," Cassidy ordered.

Raine caught a glimpse of a silver, pen-like object aimed at her neck.

But nervous Niki was in a full-blown panic now.

"This is crazy," she screamed. "The cops are on the way. Do whatever you want, I'm getting out of here."

She freed herself from Raine, lurched to her feet and streaked out through the front door.

Raine rolled away from Cassidy and grabbed the feet of the nearest mannequin, the one used to display the ballerina costume. She yanked hard and managed to topple the figure. It fell between her and Cassidy, who was forced to jump back out of the way.

"Damn you." Cassidy's face was a snarling mask of rage and frustration.

Raine rolled again. This time she grabbed Marie Antoinette's elegantly shod feet and pushed with all her might.

"Eat cake and die," she yelled at Cassidy.

Cassidy barely avoided tripping over the elaborate skirts. She suddenly seemed to become aware of the commotion going on outside the shop. She hesitated a fraction of a second, then evidently arrived at the sensible conclusion that the situation was not going well.

Whirling, she ran toward the red velvet curtain, whipped it aside and vanished into the back room.

Raine lay on the floor, trying to catch her breath. She heard the back door of the shop open, followed by frantic, scuffling sounds.

"No," Cassidy shrieked. "Let me go, you fucking *bastard*."

"If you hurt her, you're a dead woman," Zack said. His tone was lethally cold.

"Watch out for her pen," Raine shouted.

There was a dull thud.

Zack appeared in the opening, an elegant black and gold fountain pen in one hand.

"Got one of my own," he said, slipping it back into the pocket of his leather jacket.

Bradley slammed through the front door of the shop, gun in hand. Two uniformed officers followed him. One of them had Niki in handcuffs.

Bradley looked at Raine. "You okay?"

"Yes," she said, sitting up cautiously. "I'm okay." She decided to ignore the pain in her ankle for the moment.

"Cutler's in the back room." Zack jerked a thumb in that direction.

Bradley ran toward the other doorway, one of the officers on his heels.

Zack's hands closed around Raine's shoulders, his face hard. "Did she inject you with anything?"

"No." Raine shook her head. "She used the smoke

again, a lot of it, but she didn't get a chance to shoot me up with anything."

He pulled her close and hugged her so tightly she had to struggle to breathe again.

"There's something very dangerous in that silver pen of hers," she mumbled into his shirt. "She said two doses would kill Pandora."

"I've got her pen. Bradley will search her for other weapons."

"What about the smoke in the other room?"

"You can still smell it but there wasn't enough left to affect me when I came through."

"Calvin and the mayor?"

"Unconscious but alive," Bradley announced from the doorway. "So is Cassidy. What the hell did you do to her, Jones?"

"Nothing permanent," Zack said. He eased Raine slightly away from his chest, no more than an inch. "It'll wear off in a few hours."

"Guess I won't ask any more questions on that subject." Bradley moved farther out into the front portion of the shop. "Which one of them tossed that damned smoke bomb?"

"Probably Cassidy," Zack said.

Raine blinked, startled, and opened her mouth to correct him. His arm tightened a little around her. She closed her mouth.

"How did you know we were in trouble here at the shop?" she said instead.

"Don't ask me." Bradley smiled wryly. "It was Jones who realized something was going down. Must be psychic." He paused and then added quietly, "Like you."

Fifty-two

Much later Raine sat on the sofa, one leg curled under her, and sipped the tisane that Zack had brewed for her. She had showered and washed her hair as soon as they returned and now she was wrapped in her white spa robe. Robin was a warm, comfortable weight in her lap, Batman snuggled against her thigh. A medic had taped her ankle. Another package of frozen vegetables was wrapped around the badly abused joint.

Zack and Calvin sat in the twin chairs, drinking coffee.

Raine looked at Zack. "I'm very glad Bradley took your suggestion and agreed to let me give a full statement tomorrow. I really didn't feel up to it this afternoon."

Calvin snorted, amused.

She raised her brows. "What's so funny about that?"

"Hate to disillusion you," Calvin said, "but I doubt that Zack was thinking of your comfort when he persuaded Mitchell to wait for the statement. Zack here is what you might call a real focused kind of guy when it comes to details."

Raine suddenly understood. She looked at Zack. "You wanted to make sure I got my story straight first."

"Hey, give me some credit for thoughtfulness," Zack said, managing to appear offended. "You were exhausted."

"Hah. I'm not buying it. You felt I needed a little assistance with my facts. Admit it."

Calvin grinned and drank some more coffee.

"Okay," Zack said. "In my experience, I've found it's usually best not to confuse the police with too much information."

"In other words, we aren't going to tell them that they got caught in the middle of an ongoing turf war between two secret organizations devoted to psychic research, is that it?" she asked politely.

"As a general policy, J&J prefers to let the bad guys give that version of events to the cops," Calvin said.

She raised her brows. "Because it makes the bad guys look like nutcases while J&J preserves its image as a legitimate private investigation agency?"

Calvin's grin widened. "You got it."

"It's not as if there aren't plenty of legitimate charges to go around," Zack said. "What's more, Mitchell has a strong personal incentive to make them stick. He doesn't like the fact that Cutler played him."

"Assault, attempted kidnapping and possibly attempted robbery will make a good start." Calvin wrapped one big hand around his coffee mug. "Got a feeling Mitchell will dredge up some others."

"Not that he'll need them," Zack said, watching the fire. "At least, not for long."

Raine looked at him, startled. "What do you mean? Are you saying Cassidy and Niki will walk?"

"Yes. Straight into an institution for the criminally insane, and that's assuming they make it that far," Zack said.

She frowned. "I don't understand."

"From what we've seen, Nightshade doesn't tolerate failure." Zack swallowed some coffee and lowered the mug. "I told you, one of the ways it keeps its operatives in line is by making them dependent on a version of the formula that is specifically tailored to them. If they're deprived of it, they go insane and usually commit suicide within forty-eight hours."

Horror shivered through Raine. "Like Jenna?"

"Yes," he said, watching the fire. "Like Jenna. One way or another, insanity has always been the big downside to every version of the formula ever created."

"What about the stuff you found in Bradley's apartment?"

"The vial was nearly empty. There was only a trace of the drug left in it. Not even enough for one dose. Cassidy left just enough to make sure I could identify the formula and leap to the conclusion that Bradley was the guy I was after."

Raine swallowed hard. "So Cassidy and Niki are probably going to go crazy soon. Do you think they know that?"

Zack shrugged. "I doubt it. We don't know how much the Nightshade leaders tell their operatives but the best guess is that they lie to them. No profit in telling them the truth. Might put off new recruits."

She closed her eyes for a couple of seconds and shivered. Then she remembered something.

"What about the mayor? This afternoon when Bradley asked who threw the smoke bomb, I got the impression you didn't want me to tell him about her role in this thing."

He gave her an approving smile. "You were right."

"But if she was involved—"

"She wasn't," Zack assured her.

"Explain," Raine ordered.

"When I came through the back room I got a quick look around. The mayor's purse was unfastened. The contents were scattered across the carpet. I realized that she was probably the one who brought the smoke bomb into the shop but there were no hot spots around her or her purse. She didn't know what she was doing."

"Then why in the world did she set off the smoke bomb?" Raine demanded.

"The most likely explanation is that either Cassidy or Niki is a parahypnotist," Zack said. "Probably formula-enhanced."

"In other words, you think that one of them hypnotized the mayor into carrying the smoke bomb into my shop and exploding it," Raine said.

"Right." Zack shrugged. "Which is why, when Her Honor came around, she had no memory of what she had done."

Raine looked at him. "What are we going to tell her? What are we going to tell Bradley, for that matter?"

Zack stretched his legs out toward the fire and rested his elbows on the arms of the chair. He put his fingertips together.

"The simplest story is usually the best," he said. "Mitchell will soon realize he can't do anything with a drug charge because there is no evidence of illegal drugs. But what do you think about promoting the notion that Cassidy and Niki planned to kidnap the mayor and hold her for ransom?"

Raine blinked. "I think Mayor Escott would love it. Talk about great publicity for the upcoming election."

Calvin grinned. "Very creative, Jones."

"Cassidy and Niki will deny it," Raine pointed out.

Calvin uttered a half-amused little sound. "They'll

deny everything. So what? They'll both be in padded cells within a couple of days."

"Wonder why they decided to grab me," Raine said.

"Sheer desperation," Zack said. "The idea was to watch you as closely as possible to see if you inherited whatever it is that Lawrence Quinn hoped to get from Vella. You were the only link left. When I showed up, it merely confirmed their theory that you knew something vitally important. They decided they couldn't afford to wait and allow J&J to get the secret from you."

"Those poor women," Raine whispered.

The men exchanged looks. Neither spoke.

Raine sipped her tea and lowered the cup. She frowned a little at Zack. "You said the Arcane labs have a sample of the formula that they've been studying. They must know a lot about it by now. Isn't there anything your experts could do to save Cassidy and Niki?"

Zack looked at her over the tips of his fingers. He seemed baffled by the question. "You want to save that pair? Cassidy Cutler is probably indirectly responsible for the murder of Lawrence Quinn, and it's a good bet she's the one who ran down the illusion talent the other night. She tried to kill Pandora and kidnap you. Niki was her accomplice in everything that took place."

Raine pulled her robe more tightly around herself. "It's just that the prospect of going insane is so terrifying. My aunt believed that she was hovering at the edge of it for years, and it was my own worst nightmare for a long time. The thought of letting someone else, anyone else, face that abyss makes me ill."

Zack glanced at Calvin.

Calvin raised his massive shoulders. "Don't look at me. How the heck should I know if they've come up with an antidote?"

Zack hesitated a moment longer, then, reluctantly, he unclipped his phone. "I'll see if Fallon knows anything about the status of the research."

Fifty-three

She was in bed, Batman and Robin curled up at her feet, when she heard his phone ring. The sound was muffled by the closed door of the hall bathroom and the rush of water in the shower. The water was turned off abruptly. She heard the low rumble of Zack's voice.

A few minutes later he walked into the bedroom. He was naked except for a towel around his waist. His hair was damp. He stopped beside the bed, grim-faced.

"That was Fallon," he said. "He checked with the head of the lab that is studying the sample of the drug that turned up in the Stone Canyon case. The most they've been able to determine is that the stuff is inert on its own. They think it has to be combined with some other ingredient in order to work. No one knows what the missing ingredient is or how it's taken."

"In other words, the researchers haven't even begun to think about an antidote," Raine said.

"No."

She closed her eyes and leaned back against the pillows. "Niki and Cassidy are doomed to go insane and probably kill themselves."

"Yes."

There was a long silence. She opened her eyes and saw that he was watching her with the expression of a man who knows he has failed.

"I'm sorry, Raine," he said wearily. "I know this was important to you."

She sat up abruptly, appalled. "Oh, for heaven's sake, don't look at me like that. It's not your fault. I knew it was a long shot. Thank you for making the call."

He said nothing. She reached up, grabbed his hand and tugged at him until he sank down on the side of the bed.

"I thought we agreed last night that we couldn't save everyone," she said gently.

"You want the truth? I didn't give a damn about saving Cutler and Plumer. They tried to kidnap you. They would have killed you once they got what they wanted from you. Or even if they didn't get it, for that matter. Far as I'm concerned, they can jump out a window or rot in an institution for the rest of their lives."

Sometimes she forgot about the ruthless streak of icy pragmatism that ran through him. It was probably one of the reasons everyone thought he would make an excellent Master. Compassion and vision were all well and good in a leader but they tended to be useless qualities unless they were coupled with a will of steel.

"I understand," she said quietly. "You made the call to Fallon for my sake. It didn't work so that's the end of it. In addition to not being able to save everyone, you're going to have to learn another lesson."

"What's that?"

"Unlike inside Nightshade, failure actually is an option in life. Failure happens. It's how we learn and change and grow. If you don't give yourself room to fail, Zack, you'll live your life inside an iron cage that will gradually get smaller and smaller until you can't even breathe."

He gave her a suspicious look. "Where is this going?"

"Calvin told me that the Council thinks you're the best candidate the Society has to take the Master's Chair."

"Damn." He looked thoroughly disgusted. "Calvin told you about that?"

"I haven't known you very long but I think he's right."

"There are others who can handle the position of Master."

"Maybe, but you're the one the Council wants." She stomped down hard on the wistful sensation unfurling deep inside. "Heck, you're perfect for the job, what with you being a Jones and a mirror talent and so good at giving orders and all."

His jaw tightened. "Jenna showed me that I wasn't nearly as good as I thought I was."

"Get real. From what you told me, it sounds like she got past all of the Society's security systems and safeguards, and I'm sure there are a number of them. You were the one who caught her, Zack. It was your talent and intelligence that prevented a Nightshade spy from marrying the next Master of the Arcane Society."

"It was so damn close," he said quietly.

"Sometimes things are close. Take what happened today, for example."

He wrapped his big hand around hers and crushed her fingers gently. "Don't worry, I won't ever forget how close that was."

"It's clear that the Society will be fighting not only for its very existence in the next few years but for the rest of us, psychic and non-psychic, as well. You said yourself it's the only organization that currently takes Nightshade seriously. Until you can line up some allies, you and your Council will have your work cut out. You can't walk away from your responsibility, and deep down, I don't think you really want to do that, anyway."

He gave her a look of sheer, wondering disbelief. "Did my grandfather send you around on a recruiting mission, by any chance?"

She smiled, trying to mask the sense of loss that was threatening to well up inside.

"No," she said. "I came to the conclusion all on my own."

He was silent for a long time—so long that she began to worry.

Eventually he stirred. "You know, an antidote to Nightshade's version of the formula would be incredibly valuable."

"For saving people like Cassidy and Niki, you mean?"

"No. Because among other things, it would send a clear message to the inner circle of Nightshade that the Society has a few tricks of its own up its sleeve. In addition, knowing that an antidote exists would help undermine Nightshade's hold over its operatives. It might encourage some defections. We could sure use some inside information."

"Hadn't thought about that." She wrapped her arms around her knees. "Face it, Jones. You were born to lead the Society in this generation."

He didn't answer. Instead she felt energy pulse, enveloping her in his exciting force field. Her own senses leaped in response.

Zack stood, doused the lights, dropped the towel and got into bed.

When he came to her he was hot to the touch and fully aroused. He trapped her legs with one muscled thigh. She heard two soft thumps and realized that

Batman and Robin had vacated the bed, no doubt annoyed by the disturbance.

And then Zack was kissing her, his mouth hard and fierce and demanding on hers. Invisible energy flared, overlapping and mingling. *His, mine and ours*, she thought. It seemed to her that when they made love their combined energy patterns extended further and deeper into the paranormal spectrum than either of them could go alone. She did not understand it; she knew only that when he made love to her she was able to savor a greater range of sensations through all her senses. In addition she was certain that she picked up some of what he was feeling, and vice versa. The effect added a dazzling dimension to their lovemaking.

He took her nipple between his teeth and tugged gently. She caught her breath as the delicious tension built swiftly.

"Tell me you feel it," he said against her breast. "Tell me I'm not alone here."

She lifted her hips against his hardened body and clung to him, glorying in the powerfully muscled contours of his back.

"Are you sure you don't read minds?" she whispered.

"Not possible." He moved down her body, dropping hot, wet kisses on her belly. "Just ask the experts."

He went lower. The next thing she knew his mouth was on the inside of her thigh. A jolt of uncertainty bordering on panic went through her. She sank her fingers into his hair, trying to tug him back up along her body.

"Zack, wait—"

"Tell me I'm not alone in this," he ordered softly.

Now his tongue was on her tight, exquisitely sensitive clitoris and she thought she would fly apart into a thousand glittering shards.

"Tell me," he repeated, sliding two fingers into her. He probed gently.

Outrageous excitement flashed through her senses. She couldn't stand this much longer, she thought. She couldn't tolerate another second of it.

"*Yes.* Yes, I feel it, too." She tightened her grip in his hair, abandoning herself to the intimate kiss. "I think the experts may have some more research to do."

An instant later her release swept through her and she came apart in his hands. Somewhere someone shrieked softly in the night. She realized vaguely that it was her own voice she heard.

Before the world had even begun to come into focus he shifted onto his back, taking her with him. His hands were damp from her body. He slid his palms down her sides and closed his fingers around her buttocks. He sheathed himself slowly, relentlessly.

She wanted to tell him it was too soon, that she was still too sensitized from the orgasm but she couldn't get the words out. She could feel him going deep, stretching her, filling her. It was too much.

"No," she gasped.

"Yes," he said.

Without warning another series of tremors spilled through her. This time he followed her over the edge, pumping heavily into her. For a timeless moment they flew together through a realm where light and darkness and every color in between swirled together in a whirlpool of sensual pleasure.

She could not have him forever, she thought. The Society had first claim on him. But she would hold on to as much of him as she could get for as long as possible.

Fifty-four

John Stilwell Nash was in the locker room of his club, dressing after an intense workout, when his phone rang. He paused, his shirt half-buttoned, and checked the coded number on the screen. He recognized it immediately. He was about to hear the results of the Oriana operation. Adrenaline and dread gripped him.

He opened the phone slowly, ambivalent about whether or not he wanted to hear good news. Good news meant that January had succeeded. Success would strengthen her position within the organization. Good news meant that she would become an even more serious threat to him. Good news meant that he would be forced to find a clever way to get rid of her without revealing himself. That would not be easy.

On the other hand, good news meant that he would be the first to get his hands on the Tallentyre information. That would give him incredible power.

"The Oriana operation has failed," the voice on the other end of the connection said. "Both operatives were apprehended by the local authorities. Criminal charges were filed."

Nash convulsively tightened his grip on the phone. The bitch had failed. . . . *Be careful what you wish for* . . .

"What about the operatives?" he asked, keeping his tone icy cold.

"Both are deteriorating rapidly. It is unlikely either will survive more than a few days at most."

He was suddenly flooded with relief, shaking with reaction. He sank down onto a bench and forced himself to breathe slowly. The bitch would soon be dead. That was worth a lot.

As badly as he wanted to obtain the information Lawrence Quinn had promised to get from Vella Tallentyre, it had become clear in the course of the operation that Cassidy Cutler was a serious threat. The great fear that had been eating at his guts for the past few weeks at last began to subside.

"What about the Tallentyre data?" he asked, concealing any hint of emotion with an effort of will. "Does it exist or was Quinn wrong?"

There was a short, ominous silence before the voice on the other end of the connection spoke again.

"We don't know yet. J&J still has a man on the ground in Oriana so we must assume that if the data does exist, it is now or soon will be in the Society's hands."

The entire room turned a bloody shade of red. He lurched to his feet, picked up the nearest object, a shoe, and hurled it at a locker.

"What's that noise?" the person on the other end asked uneasily.

. . . *Stupid, stupid, stupid. You can't lose control* . . .

"Nothing," he said, recovering his flat tone. "A shoe fell out of a locker."

"Is there someone else there, listening to this call?" Alarm flashed in the formerly cold voice.

"No, of course not. Forget it. You do realize what this means, don't you? If the Society has the Tallentyre information and if Quinn was right about its potential, we have a problem."

"Yes," the voice said.

He was suddenly sweating. This wasn't just a minor setback or even a simple failure. It could prove to be a full-blown disaster.

"I'll be in touch," he said.

He ended the call and stood, fighting to control his rage and panic. It would be okay. Cassidy Cutler had maneuvered hard to take the credit for the Oriana project. So be it. He would make damn sure all the blame fell on her. Luckily he had analyzed the risks involved ahead of time and taken care to keep his distance. He had planned to wait until success was assured before he claimed the victory.

He'd had a very close call.

One good thing had come of the mess, he reminded himself. At least he was rid of that very scary bitch.

Fifty-five

She was rinsing her hair under a hot, steamy shower, contemplating the simple pleasure of breakfast with Zack, when a cold draft warned her she was not alone in the bathroom.

"I sense another presence in this room," she said in dark, theatrical tones. "An unseen being has entered. Speak, oh, unseen being."

"You're right," Zack said, from the other side of the shower curtain. "I am going to take the Master's Chair."

She went very cold beneath the hot water. Her chest suddenly felt tight. She thrust her face under the torrent to wash away the incipient tears. She had known this was coming, she reminded herself. This was the way things had to be. It was the right way. The Society needed him. She would live in the present as long as possible and not think about the future. An affair with Zack might last a very long time. Months. Years.

Who was she kidding? Sooner or later he would marry and that would be the end of their relationship.

"That's good," she managed. "You'll make a terrific Master."

He pulled the curtain aside. She saw that he was wearing trousers but nothing else. She was very conscious of her own nudity.

"Now I want to know what you're going to do about us," he said.

Automatically she held the small washcloth in front of her breasts while she tried to come to grips with his question.

"I don't understand," she said, going blank.

"Yesterday afternoon when you were in danger, I knew it. The other night when the illusion talent attacked me, you were aware that I was in trouble."

"Weird, huh?"

"There's some kind of psychic bond between us and it's getting stronger. Don't know about you, but it sure as hell hasn't ever been like that for me before. Not with anyone else."

She blinked. "Not even with Jenna?"

"Not even close with Jenna. What about you?"

"No," she whispered. "Not with anyone."

"So, what are you going to do about it?" he asked softly.

She needed to think, to get her act together, and

she couldn't do that standing there, naked, in front of him.

"Uh, could we talk about this later?" she asked without much hope. "At breakfast, maybe?"

"This thing between us isn't going to go away," he said quietly. "I think you know that as well as I do. It runs too deep. I can feel it right down in my bones."

"Oh, Zack."

"Is that how it is for you? A bone-deep sense of connection?"

He was relentless.

She snatched the shower curtain out of his hand and yanked it closed far enough to conceal her naked body. She put her head around the edge and glowered.

"You know how I feel about you," she said crossly.

"No, I don't. I know you're attracted to me and that we're probably going to be linked for life by whatever this bond is that has developed between us but that's all I know for sure."

Exasperation flared. "For heaven's sake, I started falling in love with you that first night in Shelbyville. You must have realized that. You're a hotshot mirror talent, remember?"

He pulled the curtain back again, reached into the shower and hauled her out.

"Zack," she yelped. "You're getting all wet."

He took her spa robe off the hook and bundled her into it. Then he pulled her close.

"Being a mirror talent doesn't give me all the

answers," he said. He put his big hands under the wide collar of the robe and used it to capture and frame her face. "That's especially true when it comes to the personal stuff. The nuance problem, remember?"

"Yes," she whispered. "I remember."

"In this case it's real personal. I didn't *start* falling in love with you that first night in Shelbyville. I fell all the way. Hard. I knew you were the one the minute you opened the door of your room."

She stared at him, stunned. "You did?"

"Marry me, Raine."

She felt as if she had fallen off the edge of the world.

"That's not possible," she got out.

"Why not?"

"Because you're going to be the next Master. There is no way you can marry the daughter of one of the Society's most notorious outlaws. You know that. Your family and the Council would be horrified, to say nothing of J&J. You've got all that crap about tradition to worry about. The only feasible solution for us is an affair. And someday that will end because you'll have to marry and—"

He silenced her by pushing her up against the closed door and kissing her with calculated deliberation. When she finally gave up struggling and more or less collapsed against him, he raised his head.

"There's something you don't seem to understand

about the office of Master of the Society," he said, his voice very rough around the edges.

She swallowed hard. "What?"

"The Master is the boss."

"So?"

"So, as boss, I get to do whatever I want to do."

"After what I read about my father in that J&J file you gave me, you'd have to rewrite history to make me acceptable to the upper echelons of the Society."

He gave her a slow, sure smile. "Not a problem."

Anxiety and frustration welled up inside. Why was he torturing her like this?

"There's no way marrying me can be anything but a problem for you," she said tightly. "And for me, too. I don't want to be surrounded by people who are suspicious of me. It's been hard enough trying to avoid having folks think I'm crazy."

"Have a little faith, woman."

"Zack, you have to be realistic. No one in the Society who knows anything about my past will trust me. I'll be forever tainted by my father's illicit activities. If you marry me, the Council might not make you the next Master."

"Let me worry about that."

"But you want the job."

"Not as badly as I want you."

She was dumbfounded. "You'd walk away from the Master's Chair for me?"

"In a heartbeat."

"*Zack.*"

He laughed. "But you'd probably feel guilty if I did that, so I won't. I'll just make certain that I get the job instead. Easier that way."

"What about the matchmakers at arcanematch-dot-com?"

"They're the ones who screwed up by matching me with Jenna, remember? I sure as hell don't intend to give them a second chance to find me the perfect wife."

"You're serious about this, aren't you?"

"Given my recent personal history, marriage is one subject I take very, very seriously."

She drew a deep breath, trying to retain a hold on common sense. "This has all happened so fast. We've only known each other a few days, and under very stressful circumstances."

He gave her a considering look. "You know, if you'd been raised within the Society, you'd understand that this link between us is very, very special."

She raised her chin. "As has been noted on more than one occasion, I wasn't raised within the Society." She widened her hands. "I don't know what I'm doing here. Haven't got a clue."

"You do know that you want me, though, right?"

She squeezed her eyes tightly shut. "Yes, I want you. More than I've ever wanted anything in my whole life."

"That's enough for now."

He unzipped his pants.

She looked down, startled to realize that he was fully erect. A wave of heat rushed through her. "What are you doing?"

"I can't resist you when you're all damp from the shower like this. Gets me hot."

"Gosh, I could have sworn you said it was my hearing voices that got you hot."

"That, too. Pretty much everything about you gets me hot."

She expected him to carry her back to the bed. Instead, he reached inside her robe, gripped her rear and lifted her straight off her feet. Instinctively, she clutched his shoulders to steady herself.

"Wrap your legs around my waist," he said against her throat. The words were dark and soft and a little hoarse. "Tight."

Excitement mingled with shock, creating an erotic thrill that danced through all her senses.

She enclosed him between her thighs. He held her in place with one arm around her back. With his other hand he teased her mercilessly until she was soaking wet and desperate for him.

He braced her against the door. Then he was deep inside, impossibly full and hard. The feel of him was a delicious shock to her wildly excited senses. She sank her nails into his shoulders as he stroked rapidly in and out.

The release rocked through her almost immediately, leaving her voiceless and breathless. When he climaxed a few seconds later she knew he had been deliberately holding back, waiting for her to come first.

When it was over they remained locked in each other's arms for several long moments, breathing hard, recovering.

Then, very deliberately, Zack lowered her to her feet. He adjusted the robe around her very tenderly, gave her an understanding smile and patted her on top of her head.

"I agree," he said. "You've been under a lot of stress. You need time to get used to the idea of having me around."

Outrage replaced the warm afterglow. How dare he pat her on the head?

"You're right." She narrowed her eyes. "I do need time to think. Lots of time."

"Fine. But I'm warning you, the bond between us is only going to get stronger. You won't be able to ignore it."

She raised her brows. "How do you know that?"

"I'm psychic."

He kissed her on the tip of her nose and walked out of the bathroom.

Half an hour later, feeling only slightly more composed, she opened a can of cat food. Batman and Robin reacted to the sound of the can opener the way ancient sailors responded to the call of the sirens. They trotted enthusiastically across the kitchen to sit at her feet, gazing up at her and the open can of food with worshipful expressions.

She looked down at their little masked faces. Out of nowhere Vella's words flashed through her head.

"Everyone wears a mask," she said softly.

Zack was at the counter, making coffee. He gave her an inquiring look.

"What?" he asked.

"I think I know what Aunt Vella meant when she said to look behind Wilder Jones's mask."

Fifty-six

Zack's phone rang just as he brought the car to a halt in the drive in front of the Shelbyville house. He shut down the engine and took the call.

Raine waited, watching the gloom-drenched house through the rain-splattered windshield. Eventually Zack hit the end button.

"That was Mitchell," he said.

"Yes, I gathered that much." Raine turned toward him. "Bad news?"

"For Cassidy Cutler and Niki Plumer, yes. Both of them are showing signs of severe mental disorientation and confusion. A psychiatrist has been called in to evaluate the situation. I didn't tell Mitchell, but given J&J's recent experience with Nightshade operatives, both women are probably going to get steadily worse."

Raine shuddered. "And there's nothing anyone can do."

"No," Zack said. "Not a damn thing. But Mitchell told me something very interesting. Before she started cracking up, Niki Plumer did a lot of talking. She was enraged because she thought Cassidy Cutler was setting her up to take the fall."

"For trying to kidnap me?"

"No," Zack said. "For staging those spectacular murders that she wrote about in her books."

"Good grief. Cassidy killed those people herself?"

"And then set up the suspects for the police to find, according to Niki."

Horror shot through Raine. "Those people who were arrested for those ghastly murders—they're all innocent?"

"According to Niki they are." Zack smiled slightly. "Luckily, thanks to the molasses-like speed of the criminal justice system, none of them has made it as far as the death chamber. You'd better believe Mitchell is excited."

"I'll bet he is. If Niki told him the truth, he's just been handed the career-making case of the decade. There's a book and probably a movie deal, as well, in this thing."

"He said Plumer gave him more than enough to open an investigation. With luck and maybe a little discreet help from J&J, in a few months Mitchell will be the hero who solved several front-page crimes and got some innocent people out of jail."

"Amazing." She had been dreading the return to Shelbyville for the entire drive from Oriana but now she was suddenly feeling a lot more cheerful. "I sure hope Niki wasn't lying."

"I think there's a good chance she was telling the truth." Zack unfastened his seat belt and reached into the backseat for his jacket. He pulled it on over his shoulder holster. "She didn't have any motive to implicate herself in those murders."

"Good point." She unclipped her own seat belt, grabbed her long black raincoat and opened the door. "On that note, let's go see if I'm right about Wilder Jones's mask."

They walked quickly through the misty rain toward the entrance to the house. It was colder than it had been the last time she was there, Raine thought. The looming trees whispered in anticipation of snow.

A strip of shredded crime-scene tape fluttered from one of the posts that supported the roof over the front door. Raine paused on the step and dug out her keys.

"You're sure it's okay to go inside?" she asked.

"When I called Langdon this morning he said the forensics people had finished. He didn't have any problem with us going back into the house."

She opened the door. Cold shadows illuminated the small entry hall.

Zack looked around curiously. "Where did you pick up the bad vibes last time?"

"The kitchen and the basement. The killer used the back door."

They went past the fireplace that Vella had never used and up the stairs to the second floor. Because of her injured ankle, Raine was forced to use the banister to steady herself. She dimmed her senses as much as possible. Nevertheless, she would have preferred not to touch the wood with her bare hand. Although Vella had not left any intense hot spots, the heavily used surfaces in the house, such as railings and doorknobs, resonated faintly with the disturbing echoes generated by years of her depression, anxiety and despair.

Zack put his hand on the banister and immediately withdrew it. "I can see why you don't like this house very much."

"I wish I could sell it quickly but I'm afraid that's going to be next to impossible now. Unfortunately, the taxes don't stop just because the owner is deceased."

"Tell your real estate agent to look for a client who is interested only in the property, one who won't mind tearing down the house and building a new one."

"Good idea," she said.

"You won't get nearly as much for the place, probably a fraction of its worth, but at least you'll be out from under the taxes."

"That's all I care about now."

She hobbled to the top of the stairs and limped down the hall to the bedroom that Vella had used. The door stood ajar. She pushed it open and went inside.

The interior of the small room was even gloomier than the rest of the house. The drapes were drawn across the windows. Raine reached out to flip on the lights, automatically bracing herself for the psychic static she knew would be clinging to the switch.

Zack's hand closed abruptly around her wrist, stopping her. Startled, she turned toward him, mouth open to ask why he did not want the lights.

He shook his head once and put his fingertips to her lips.

Then she, too, heard the faint sound from downstairs. Someone had opened the kitchen door. Tension sizzled through her. Instinctively her parasenses opened wide.

"Miss Tallentyre?" Doug Spicer called. "It's me, Doug, from Spicer Properties. Where are you?"

Zack took his fingers from her mouth. Raine didn't realize how tense she had been until she suddenly went limp with relief. *Too much stress lately*, she thought.

"My real estate agent," she explained.

She took a couple of deep breaths, trying to calm her overhyped nerves, and went out onto the landing. Gripping the railing, she looked down. Zack came to stand beside her. Doug Spicer was at the foot of the stairs, one hand on the newel post. His leather briefcase was clutched tightly in his other hand.

"Hello, Doug," she said. "We just came to collect a few things of my aunt's."

He gave her a genial smile. "Saw Chief Langdon at the café this morning. He mentioned that you and a companion had phoned and told him you were on your way up here today." He switched his attention to Zack. "I don't believe we've met. Doug Spicer."

"Zack Jones," Zack said.

Doug nodded and turned his attention back to Raine. "I thought I'd drop by and let you know that I've had a nibble on the house. It's not a very impressive offer, I'm afraid, but under the circumstances, I strongly recommend that you consider it."

"Are you kidding? I'll take it, whatever it is. I can't tell you how relieved I am to hear that someone actually wants to buy this place."

"The buyer is from the Seattle area," Doug said. "Looking for a weekend house in the mountains. I was going to fax the offer to you today but since you're here, we might as well deal with it now."

"I'll be right down."

"Fine. We can work at the kitchen table. I'll get the papers ready."

He tightened his grip on his briefcase, turned and walked briskly toward the kitchen.

"Looks like this is my lucky real estate day," Raine said, starting down the stairs.

Zack caught her wrist, halting her on the top step.

"Wait here," he said softly.

She looked at him in surprise as he went quickly

past her. When he reached the bottom of the stairs he flattened his hand on the newel post where Doug's palm had been a moment earlier.

He snatched his fingers away from the wood. He swung around and started back up the stairs, taking the steps two at a time.

"Oh, shit," she whispered. "Not my lucky day, after all."

He grabbed her wrist again with one hand. He used the other to take his gun out of his shoulder holster.

"The bedroom," he said into her ear. "Hurry."

Gritting her teeth against the pain radiating from her weak ankle, she struggled to keep up with him.

They made it to within a foot of the bedroom doorway before her ankle betrayed her. She lost her balance. Zack's grip on her wrist kept her from sprawling but she nevertheless went down hard on one knee.

She glanced over her shoulder and caught a glimpse of Doug Spicer through the opening between two of the banister posts. He was just inside the kitchen, using the doorway for cover.

"*Witch!*" he screamed. He raised one hand.

Before she could process the scene and make sense of it, Zack fell on top of her, crushing the breath from her lungs. She registered a loud staccato drumbeat of noise and felt a violent shudder go through Zack.

Cold fire splashed violently through her senses. She knew intuitively that she was sharing Zack's psychic reaction to the bullet that had slammed into him.

"Zack."

He was moving, rolling with her into the bedroom. A second flurry of shots crashed through the house. She heard wood splinter.

The sensation of icy fire dissipated. She knew Zack had somehow clamped down on his senses.

Flat on his belly, he leaned through the opening and fired twice.

"Can't get a clear shot from here," he said, his voice low and harsh. "Have to wait until he comes up the stairs."

There was a long pause from down below. Then Spicer's voice, unnaturally shrill, reverberated up the staircase.

"Only one way to kill a witch," he yelled from the kitchen.

Raine glanced at Zack. Beneath the open edge of his leather jacket she could see a terrible red stain on the side of his shirt.

She started to move toward him.

He motioned her toward the window. "We'll go out that way."

"You've been hit. I need to stop the bleeding."

"Not now. Got to prioritize here."

"What are you talking about?"

Then she caught the stench of gasoline.

"Dear God," she whispered. "He's going to burn the house down with us inside. Just like he did to all the other witches."

"Move," Zack ordered. Somehow he was on his feet.

She grabbed the edge of the bedside table and staggered upright. Adrenaline made it possible to ignore the pain in her ankle. Somehow her purse had made it back into the bedroom along with her. It was lying on the floor. Age-old feminine instinct and reflex made her scoop it up.

The sight of the painting on the wall stopped her. It was an ominously smiling mask. She reached up and took it down. There was a small safe set into the wall.

Zack had the window open now. Cold air blew into the bedroom. "What the hell are you doing? Get over here."

"Just a second."

The safe was a simple, inexpensive one. She punched in the date of her own birth.

"Leave it," Zack said, throwing the emergency rope ladder over the windowsill. "Whatever is in there isn't worth your life."

But she had the door to the safe open now. She pulled out the only object, a leather-bound volume, and stuffed it into her purse.

There was a great, roaring whoosh of sound from the hallway.

"*Burn, witch!*" Spicer screamed.

Vella's many smoke alarms began to shriek.

She ran for the window. Zack practically shoved

her through the opening. She got a foot on the first rung of the emergency ladder and started down. The ladder shook and trembled but it held.

Zack followed swiftly.

She reached the ground and scurried back.

"This way." Zack stumbled a little when he stepped off the ladder. He put one hand to his side where the crimson stain was growing.

Together they half limped, half staggered toward the shelter of the small shed that had originally been built to hold firewood. Vella had used it to store garden tools. Raine gritted her teeth against the pain in her ankle, aware that Zack had to be in agony. If he could keep going, so could she.

When they reached the back of the shed they stopped. Raine could see flames and black smoke surging up into the damp sky. The fire was roaring now, a huge tyrannosaurus rex come to life and busily devouring everything in sight.

"Sit down," Raine ordered. "Before you fall down."

Zack obeyed reluctantly, unclipping his phone while he sank onto the cold ground. He leaned forward slightly, watching the burning house, gun in hand, while he talked to the 911 operator.

Raine reached inside his jacket and unfastened his blood-drenched shirt. His right side was a gory mess. It was difficult to tell exactly where the wound was. Using her fingers, she tracked a steady, welling stream of blood back to its source. When she found the raw edges of the wound that had ripped open his flesh she felt him suck in his breath.

She jerked off the long scarf she wore and wrapped it snugly around his rib cage. By the time she finished they were both covered in blood.

The house was fully engulfed now. The speed of the fire was terrifying. If it hadn't been for the phobic fear that had led Vella to install emergency fire ladders in the upstairs rooms—

No, Raine thought. *Don't go there. Thank you, Aunt Vella.*

"Spicer must have left," she whispered.

Zack shook his head once, never taking his attention off the house. "Don't think so. He can't leave. He has to be sure."

"He's crazy."

"Oh, yeah."

A few seconds later she heard Spicer's voice again. *"Die, witch. Die like she died."*

"He just noticed the rope ladder," Zack said quietly. "He's going to come unglued now."

Spicer's high, keening scream of rage rose above the thunder of the fire.

"You can't escape!" Spicer shouted. "You have to burn. It's the only way."

"He's just noticed the shed," Zack said. "He's coming this way."

She could hear sirens in the distance now. Spicer seemed oblivious, however.

"The demon always wins!" he yelled. "The demon is more powerful than you, witch."

Zack rose slowly, back pressed to the wall of the shed.

"Put the gun down, Spicer," he called. "The cops are on the way. It's over."

Spicer's response was a flurry of shots followed by an abrupt pause. She didn't know much about guns but she knew enough to realize that they occasionally needed to be reloaded.

Zack leaned around the edge of the shed and fired once.

Doug Spicer was still alive when Wayne Langdon and a deputy pulled into the drive. A fire truck followed by an aide car appeared next.

Raine didn't wait for the medics to do triage. She limped toward them, waving her arms to get their attention.

"Take care of him first," she said, pointing to Zack. She put every ounce of authority she possessed into the command. "He's the good guy."

Fifty-seven

Two hours later she sat in the reception area of the Shelbyville Community Hospital. Wayne Langdon was with her.

She was still waiting for Zack. He had been in the emergency room for what seemed an eternity. A doctor had appeared briefly to assure her that the wound looked a lot worse than it was. He explained that the bullet had passed cleanly through skin and tissue, not striking any vital organs on the way.

"A lot of stitches and some antibiotics and he'll be fine. Mr. Jones will end up with an interesting scar but no permanent damage."

Easy for him to say, she thought. She would remember the moment that Zack took a bullet for her for the rest of her life. The terrible fear that had flashed through her when she knew he'd been hit would haunt her nightmares, just as the voices did.

Someone had retaped her ankle and provided her with a pair of crutches.

"Got a full confession out of Spicer before they took him into surgery," Langdon said. "Hard to shut him up, to tell you the truth. Kept babbling about how he had to burn the witches."

"Uh-huh." Raine fiddled with her crutches, trying to get the hang of using them.

Langdon grimaced. "I appreciate that you're not saying *I told you so.*"

"Hard to resist, though."

"I'll bet." Langdon whistled softly. "Got to say, Spicer's confession couldn't have come at a better time, and that's a fact."

"Why is that?" Raine asked, glancing at her watch.

"The case against Burton Rosser was starting to unravel pretty fast. Turns out he's got an ironclad alibi for at least one of the Bonfire murders. He was doing time for burglary when the first girl was killed."

"I assume Spicer was the one who set him up?" she asked.

"Yeah. Evidently you scared the, uh, crap out of him after you discovered the girl still alive in your aunt's basement." Langdon cleared his throat. "Got the feeling that something about you made him real nervous."

"I have that effect on people sometimes. It's a gift."

Langdon looked as if he didn't know how to take that. He turned a little red and then acted as if she hadn't said anything. He cleared his throat again and hurried on with his story.

"Spicer figured the best way to protect himself from becoming a suspect was to give us a solid perp. He left the belt in Burton Rosser's house. Then he copied the photos of the victims off his own computer onto a flash storage device and loaded them onto Rosser's computer. We found the same photos on Spicer's computer a few minutes ago."

"How did he know that Rosser would make a likely-looking suspect?"

"Spicer deliberately picked someone who was even newer in town than himself. Rosser also looked good because he was a loner and there were rumors that he'd done jail time."

Her phone rang. She reached into her purse and glanced at the incoming number. Blocked.

"Hello," she said warily.

"Is this Raine Tallentyre?"

A man's voice, or maybe the voice of a really irritable bear. It was hard to tell.

"I think you have the wrong number," she said.

"Fallon Jones," the bear rumbled, sounding even more annoyed because he'd had to identify himself. "Just tried to call Zack. His phone's off. What the hell is going on?"

She gave Langdon a brief, bright smile. "Excuse me, Chief. I have to take this call."

"Sure, no problem."

She got to her feet, grabbed the crutches and limped through the sliding glass doors out onto the brick entranceway. It was cold outside, but she didn't care. She was suddenly generating more than enough heat to keep herself warm. Leaning on one of the crutches, she managed to get the phone back to her ear.

"How do you do, Mr. Jones," she said, making her voice glassy smooth. "So you're the head of the firm that ripped my family apart all those years ago."

"Huh?"

"I can't begin to tell you how pissed off I am by the sneaky, underhanded way your agent Wilder Jones conducted his so-called investigation."

"What the hell? Lady, I had nothing to do with that investigation. It went down long before my time here at J&J."

"I don't want excuses, Jones, I want abject apologies. Wilder Jones broke my aunt's heart."

"You're mad because those two had an affair?" Fallon sounded bewildered. "Are you crazy?"

"No, fortunately. No thanks to J&J or the Arcane Society."

"Now what are you talking about?"

"According to the file you had on me, it was a known fact in certain quarters within J&J that there was a high statistical probability that I had inherited a type and degree of parasensitivity that is very difficult to handle out here in the real world. Did you know that when you tell folks you hear voices they tend to treat you like you're crazy? And guess what? You often end up crazy."

"It's not my fault that your file got buried. Every file concerning your family was classified."

"Got news for you, Mr. Jones, J&J may choose to conduct its operations as if it were a clandestine government agency, but it's not. It's just one more private investigation firm, as far as I'm concerned."

"Damn it—"

"What's more, even if it was a legitimate agency of the federal government, I'd still be just as pissed."

"Calm down, Miss Tallentyre."

It was an order. She ignored it.

"I am perfectly calm, thank you. Speaking of your cavalier disregard for other people's personal privacy, I would like to add that I am not at all pleased to know that at the start of this case you had your analysts check out everything from my medical history to my personal shopping habits. Such things are supposed to be confidential, Mr. Jones."

"Put Zack on the line."

"Just so you know, I'm giving serious thought to taking J&J to court. Just imagine what a lawsuit would mean to your firm and the entire Arcane Society. Why, I'll bet if I get myself a really good lawyer and the right judge, I can force you to open up all of your so-called classified files. Think of the headlines. '*Psychic Detective Agency Maintains Secret Files on Private Citizens.*'"

"Put. Zack. On. The. Phone," Fallon ordered. "Now."

"Sorry. He's not available."

"Where is he?"

"In the emergency room."

"He's been hurt? How? What's going on there?"

"Oh, right, I guess you don't know about the latest little J&J screwup, do you? Turns out you were wrong when you confirmed that the Shelbyville cops had the serial killer in custody."

"I said the analysts estimated the probability of the cops having the right man to be ninety-six point three percent."

She made a *tut-tutting* sound. "Not good enough, Mr. Jones. Your analysts were one hundred percent wrong. The real killer took a couple of shots at us this afternoon. One of those shots hit Zack. That was before the guy tried to torch us, by the way."

"How bad?"

He sounded genuinely worried. She relented slightly.

"The doctor said he'll be okay. I'm standing outside the emergency room as we speak, waiting to find out."

"Did they get the bastard?"

"You mean, did they get the right bastard this time? The answer is yes, no thanks to J&J."

"I don't know how we missed that one. Clearly we had insufficient or false data."

"Maybe you should rely a little less on your analysts' psychic abilities and a little more on traditional methods of criminal investigation."

"It's not like we had a lot of time to check out the reports," Fallon shot back defensively. "We had other priorities, if you will recall."

She was about to fire back but she saw Zack on the other side of the sliding glass doors. He was on his feet and moving. That was a very good sign. The medics had cut off his shirt. He wore his leather jacket open over his bare chest. She could see the edge of a large white bandage on his side.

"Zack just came out of the ER," she said. "Got to go."

"Wait," Fallon said quickly. "Don't hang up. Put him on the line."

"Okay. But before I do, there's something you and I should get clear."

"What?" he asked, very wary.

"I understand that J&J answers only to the Governing Council and the Master of the Arcane Society."

"Yeah. So, what?"

"As it happens, I will soon be the wife of the next Master."

"*What?*"

"That position will give me a great deal of power, not to mention enormous influence." She waved a crutch at Zack. "Better not piss me off any more, Mr. Jones."

"Give me Zack," Fallon snarled.

Zack was through the glass doors, coming toward her.

"It's Mr. Jones of J&J," she said. "He wants to speak with you."

"Figured he'd be calling," Zack said.

"Better warn you, I just told him that you and I are going to get married."

Masculine satisfaction etched his hard face. His eyes got very, very blue.

"Well, now," he said softly. "Within the Society that pretty much amounts to a formal announcement. How'd he take it?"

"In another era I believe he would have been described as apoplectic."

"Don't worry, he'll survive."

"Zack?" Fallon's voice, emanating from the small phone, sounded faint and tinny. "Is that you?"

Zack took the phone from Raine's hand, leaned forward and kissed her very thoroughly. By the time he raised his head she was tingling from head to toe.

"Zack?" Fallon was shouting now. "You there? Talk to me, damn it."

"Later," Zack said somewhat absently into the phone. "I'm a little busy at the moment."

He ended the call, dropped the phone into a pocket and went back to kissing Raine.

Fifty-eight

They were gathered in her living room, drinking the first of the two bottles of Oregon pinot noir that Gordon had brought along. He and Andrew claimed they both needed the wine for medicinal purposes while they recovered from the shock of events. The pair occupied the sofa, the cats stretched out between them. Zack was in one of the two reading chairs. Raine took the other.

"How did you figure out where she hid the journal?" Andrew asked. "Did you know about the wall safe?"

"No." Raine looked at the leather-bound book lying on the coffee table. "But this morning I suddenly remembered the painting on the wall of her bedroom. It was the first of her mask series. "In hindsight, I realized it must have been inspired by Wilder Jones."

Gordon glanced at the volume on the coffee table. "What did you find in that journal?"

She fortified herself with a swallow of wine and set down the glass. "My father injected himself with his version of the formula."

"Damn." Gordon's silver-gray brows shot straight up. "That certainly explains a few things."

"I'll say," Andrew agreed.

"I know what you're all thinking," she said. "Judson Tallentyre sounds like the original mad scientist."

"No," Zack said. He drank some wine and lowered his glass. "Within the Arcane Society, that honor belongs to my ancestor Sylvester Jones."

Raine looked up, startled. "You're calling the founder of the Arcane Society a mad scientist?"

"Well, technically speaking, I guess you'd have to label him a mad alchemist, given that he lived in the late sixteen hundreds. Don't think the word *scientist* was used in those days. It amounts to the same thing, though. Sylvester was unquestionably brilliant, and there's no doubt but that he was a powerful sensitive. But it's also no secret, at least in the Jones family, that he was obsessed, paranoid and probably delusional, at least toward the end."

"Interesting family history," Andrew observed drily.

"Family tree is riddled with what the Society euphemistically likes to call *exotics*," Zack said. "But in Sylvester's case, I think there's a strong possibility that some of his quirks were exacerbated by the experiments he ran on himself."

Andrew frowned. "Sylvester Jones invented the original version of the formula?"

"Along with what was supposed to be the antidote," Zack said. "But in the Victorian era, the Society found out the hard way that the antidote doesn't work. In the late sixteen hundreds Sylvester died alone in his laboratory, which became his tomb. No one knows for sure what killed him, but there's a widely held theory in the family that he probably poisoned himself with his own formula and died because the antidote failed."

Gordon absently stroked Batman and looked at Raine. "I suppose your father took the risk with his version of the formula because he was convinced it would work."

"Yes." She picked up her glass and swallowed some wine. She was going to need it to get through the rest of the story. "He also injected Aunt Vella with the drug."

There was a short, horrified silence while they all absorbed that news.

Andrew closed his eyes in pain. "That probably explains a few more things."

"The drug worked," she continued evenly. "It dramatically enhanced both my aunt's and my father's psychic abilities. But Dad soon realized that there were problems. He and Aunt Vella began to have difficulty controlling their parasenses. Their normal senses were affected, as well."

"The old instability problem," Zack said.

"My father immediately stopped all research on the enhancing formula and went to work on an antidote. He believed he was making progress. During the last year of his life he worked day and night in the lab. He was desperate to save himself and Aunt Vella."

Andrew looked at her. "He found something?"

"Yes," she said. "He began giving the antidote to Aunt Vella and himself, even though it was still highly experimental. It was a course of injections designed to be taken over a period of several weeks so that the results and side effects could be closely monitored. But Dad was killed in the car accident before either of them completed the series. They were each supposed to take one more dose."

Zack went very still. "That's why the two of you went to his lab the night of the funeral."

She nodded. "Aunt Vella writes in the journal that she was desperate to take the last injection of the antidote. By then she had realized that she had been sleeping with the enemy. She knew that when Wilder found the lab, he would destroy everything in it."

"Did she get the final dose?" Gordon asked, riveted.

"Yes." Raine took another sip of wine and lowered the glass. "I remember her driving us to the lab that night. She knew the code that unlocked the door. Once we were inside, she sat me down in a chair and gave me one of my favorite books to read. It was about horses. I loved that book, but that night I couldn't concentrate."

"No mystery there," Andrew said. "You were traumatized because you had been to your father's funeral that day."

"At the lab she went into the small room where my father had installed a special refrigerator." Raine watched the flames dance in the hearth. "Wilder Jones and his men stormed through the door a short time later and started taking the place apart. Aunt Vella rushed out of the refrigerator room and scooped me up in her arms. She was crying and screaming at Wilder. The next thing I knew we were sitting in the back of the car, being driven home by one of Wilder's men."

"She took the last dose of the antidote that night," Zack said, looking very thoughtful. He switched his attention to Andrew and Gordon. "How long was it before you started seeing signs that she was in trouble?"

Andrew and Gordon exchanged looks.

"Three, maybe four months later," Gordon said. "The first episode only lasted a few days. She seemed to return to normal after that, at least for a while."

"We thought the worst had passed," Andrew explained. "But the episodes came and went with increasing frequency over the years. Each was more severe and lasted longer, leaving her a little more fragile."

"But she lived until last month." Zack leaned back in his chair, stretched out his legs and put his fingertips together. "She'd still be alive if she wasn't murdered."

"She had to be institutionalized at the end," Gordon reminded him.

"Yes, but you described her as being relatively calm and reasonably lucid during the last year of her life, thanks to Ogilvey's meds and therapy. And we know for a fact that she was able to think clearly enough on the night of her death to leave a message for Raine."

"Where are you going with this?" Raine asked.

Zack tapped his fingers together once. "I'm thinking that, although your father's version of the antidote was obviously flawed, he must have leaped a few major technical hurdles."

She frowned, baffled. "What do you mean?"

"As far as I know," Zack said, "your aunt lived longer than anyone else who was given several doses of the drug and then deprived of it. In every other instance that I am aware of, the individuals all died within days, usually by suicide. But Vella Tallentyre, for all her odd behavior, did not go insane and she did not take her own life. According to the historical records, that makes her unique."

They all absorbed that for a few minutes.

After a while, Raine stirred in her chair. "In that case, you might be interested to know that taking the last dose of the drug wasn't the only thing that Vella did that night when we went to the lab."

Zack watched her steadily. "What else did she do?"

"My father kept three sets of lab notes—one on a computer, another on a hard-copy printout and a third in his private journal. Wilder Jones knew about all three and destroyed them. But before he arrived at the lab, my aunt photocopied the pages of my father's journal that contained his antidote. She took the copies with her that night."

Zack's eyes narrowed. "According to his report, Wilder searched your aunt before he put the two of you into the car."

"I don't know if he concluded that I had been traumatized enough for one day or if he was just distracted by Vella in a hysterical rage. Whatever the case, he didn't search me. Aunt Vella hid the pages in my horse book. I'm the one who carried the formula for my father's antidote out of the lab."

They all switched their attention to the leather-bound volume lying on the coffee table.

"She took the pages from me as soon as we got home," Raine said. "I never saw them again until I opened that journal. They were tucked into the back."

Zack contemplated the flames with an enigmatic expression. "Well, one Jones family mystery has been solved."

"What's that?" Raine asked.

"It's now obvious why Uncle Wilder went over the edge during the last three months of his life. Everyone said it seemed as though he had developed a death wish. But Mom was right. There was a woman involved."

Raine looked at him. "Are you saying that you believe he fell in love with Aunt Vella?"

"I think Uncle Wilder found the love of his life but he screwed things up so badly he probably figured there was no hope. So he took that last suicide mission."

Raine thought about that for a long time.

"He shouldn't have lied to her," she said at last.

"She lied to him about the formula," Zack said.

"They lied to each other," Gordon declared grimly. "In my experience, that approach to interpersonal communication never leads to good outcomes."

Bradley Mitchell called later that night. Zack picked up the phone. Raine came out of the bathroom in her robe, just as he finished speaking. He ended the call and looked at her.

"Mitchell says that Cassidy Cutler managed to find an open window at the hospital. She jumped. Broke her neck."

Raine sank down on the edge of the bed, her hands in her lap. "Suicide."

"Yes."

"What about Niki Plumer?"

"Still alive but the doctor says she's sliding deeper and deeper into a psychotic state. She no longer speaks or communicates in any way. No one expects her to snap out of it." Zack sat down beside her and took her hand. "Same old pattern."

"Did Bradley say anything more about Cassidy Cutler being a serial killer?"

"He said the case is looking very solid."

Raine looked pleased. "This is going to make his career. And the best part is that he won't have to share the credit with a psychic sidekick."

Zack eased her back onto the bed, flattened his hands on the quilt on either side of her shoulders and loomed over her. "I sure as hell hope you're not about to tell me that you'll miss working with him. Because I'd have a real problem with that."

She put her arms around his neck. "How do you do that?"

"Do what?"

"Look ominous and dangerous and incredibly sexy all at the same time."

He appeared to give that a moment's serious contemplation. "Damned if I know. Guess it's a—"

"Gift." She laughed and pulled him closer. "It's not Bradley I'll miss. It's the work."

He kissed her lightly and raised his head. "I know. I understand how it is with our kind of talent, remember? But don't worry, as the wife of the Master of the Arcane Society and part-time consultant for J&J, you'll get your psychic fix."

She blinked. "I'm going to become a J&J agent?"

"Why not? You were born for the work."

"Uh, have you discussed this plan with Fallon Jones?"

"There's nothing to discuss. I'm the boss."

He silenced her laughter with a kiss that made the atmosphere around the bed crackle with invisible energy.

Fifty-nine

The orderly paused outside room 705 and peered through the small glass window. The patient was still asleep. In the glow of the night-light he could see her on the bed. She was in the exact same position she had been in an hour before, lying on her side, her back to the door. The sheet was pulled up over her head. She had not moved.

Now that he thought about it, it seemed to him that there was something unnatural about her stillness. He'd been on the night shift on this ward ever since she arrived a few days before. She had never slept this soundly before.

An uneasy sensation drifted through him. She was on a suicide watch but he'd worked there long enough to know that when patients were determined to take their own lives, they usually succeeded.

He entered the code that unlocked the door, moved inside the small space and went toward the bed.

"Miss Plumer? Are you awake?" He reached down to shake her shoulder.

By the time he realized that the shape on the bed had been created by pillows and folded blankets, it was too late.

He heard the faint slide of a slippered foot on the tile floor behind him. The next instant pain exploded in his head.

The world went dark.

She had chosen one of the smaller orderlies but his clothes were still much too big on her. The shirt reeked of masculine sweat and cigarette smoke. But she had learned the night routine well. All she had to do was cross the hall to the stairwell without being seen. If she made it that far, she stood an excellent chance of getting out of the building. With a little luck, no one would miss the orderly for a while.

She made it down the stairs to the employees' locker room, found the orderly's locker and removed a cap and a jacket. She shoved her hair under the cap and turned up the collar of the jacket.

A small hypnotic suggestion removed any doubts the guard at the employees' entrance had concerning the identity of the departing staff member.

A few minutes later, she was in the orderly's battered compact, driving away from the hospital. She would have to ditch the car and get another one before dawn, she decided.

She drove hard and fast, putting as much distance between herself and the hospital as possible. And while she drove she made her plans.

For all intents and purposes, the organization considered her as good as dead. That situation would change, however, as soon as someone found the unconscious orderly.

The Inner Circle would order an immediate search when word got out that she had escaped. The cops and J&J would also look for her. Niki Plumer would have to disappear in a very convincing manner, at least until she could demonstrate to the Inner Circle that John Stilwell Nash was a traitor to the organization.

When she proved that she was the only one who had recognized how truly dangerous Nash was, the director would thank her. And then he would give her Nash's position in the organization. From there it was only a few short steps to the Inner Circle and, ultimately, the director's chair.

They would wonder why she had survived being deprived of the formula, of course. Perhaps she would let them think she had some natural immunity to the side effects. Or maybe she would pretend that Nash never gave her the real drug because he feared she would become more powerful than him. Yes, that would work nicely, she thought. Nash gave her a fake version of the drug. Perfect. Another nail in his coffin.

The Inner Circle believed that she was a mid-range strategy talent who had been bumped up to a level nine by the drug. The truth was, she was a natural level-nine parahypnotist who had only pretended to be a mid-range strategist. With her abilities, it had been easy enough to swap out the little vials when she was given the first three injections of the formula, the ones designed to get her hooked. Later, when she was on her own, she had simply dumped her regular supply down the nearest drain.

She had sensed from the outset that if the organization was handing out a para-enhancement drug freely to its operatives, there had to be a serious downside. The Inner Circle would want to make sure it had a way to control the dangerously powerful talents it created.

She had been right.

She wanted to use the drug as badly as any of the others but she wasn't going to take it until she knew for certain that it was safe or that there was an antidote. She had seen for herself what the stuff was doing to John Stilwell Nash.

They said that family feuds were the nastiest quarrels.

She didn't doubt that for a moment. It would be interesting to see the expression on Nash's face when he discovered that he wasn't the only modern-day result of John Stilwell's very personal reproductive experiments back in the late 1800s.

It wasn't the strong who survived, she thought. It was the very, very smart.

Fallon Jones read the news when it came across his computer screen the following day. It was a small, insignificant item that anyone who did not have an unhealthy obsession with dots would likely have missed.

> . . . Niki Plumer, a suspect in a recent conspiracy to kidnap the mayor of Oriana, Washington, escaped from Winter Cove Psychiatric Hospital and is believed to have drowned.
>
> A woman matching Plumer's description was last seen boarding a late-night Washington State Ferry in Seattle. A car that was stolen from the hospital parking lot last night was found on board.
>
> Plumer had been on a suicide watch while undergoing psychiatric evaluation. Authorities believe she may have jumped overboard midway between Seattle and Bremerton. Her body has not been recovered.

Fallon got to his feet and went to stand at the window looking out over the fog-drenched town of Scargill Cove. He stood there for a long time, thinking about dots.

Sixty

The official headquarters of the Arcane Society, USA, was located in a generic steel-and-glass office tower in Los Angeles. It was a surprisingly small suite of offices because the Society had never been big on centralization. By definition, most of its members tended to be strong individualists who did not take well to regimentation and organization. The Council met formally in LA only a few times a year. The rest of the time they convened online or on the phone.

The decision to house the headquarters in LA was made back in the 1930s, when it had become obvious that California was the ideal place to conceal a group devoted to the weird and the bizarre. Weird and bizarre passed for normal in LA.

The good thing, Zack thought, was that after he assumed the Master's Chair, he and Raine would not have to live in this vast, sprawling city of glitz and freeways and sun. Oriana would make a fine hometown. It looked like a great place to raise kids. He and Raine were already shopping for a house.

But first he had to deal with his future Council.

At the opposite end of the table his grandfather was concluding his announcement. Tall and distinguished, Bancroft Jones radiated power, not just the paranormal stuff but the charismatic kind that seemed to infuse those who were born to lead. He was also a whip-fast and very shrewd hunter talent, even at the age of seventy-eight.

". . . And so I am pleased to announce that my grandson, Zackary Gabriel Jones, has accepted the appointment to the Master's Chair," Bancroft said.

There was an enthusiastic round of applause. The ten men and women seated at the table turned to Zack. They were all powerful sensitives of one sort or another. He also knew that each was endowed with a very broad streak of personal ambition and a remarkable non-paranormal talent for the sort of political maneuvering that had gotten them onto the Council in the first place. Dealing with them in the years ahead would be a challenge.

The middle-aged man across from Zack rose and cleared his throat.

"I know I speak for all of us when I say that we are

delighted you have decided to accept the appointment," Hector Guerrero said. "We feel it is important that you know that you were not asked to take this position merely because of your family's long and respected association with the Society."

At the far end of the table Marilyn Houston chuckled. "If all we cared about was having a Jones at the head of the Society, we had a great many of your relatives to choose from. You come from a very prolific family, sir."

There was a round of laughter. Zack acknowledged the humor with a smile.

Guerrero cleared his throat a second time and continued. "We all sense that in the next few decades the Society will face a variety of serious challenges. There are difficult, possibly even dangerous, times ahead. In addition to trying to move into the mainstream, the threat presented by Nightshade appears to be growing stronger. The organization must be defeated. If it flourishes it has the potential to not just destroy the Society but to infiltrate and manipulate our nation's leading corporations and our government."

It had been Bancroft's idea to let Guerrero, one of the most powerful and influential members of the Council, act as the closer.

"The thought of psychically enhanced Nightshade operatives becoming powerful figures in the highest circles of our land is intolerable," Guerrero warned. "The damage that could be done is inestimable. We must fight this grave threat and, for the foreseeable future at least, we must fight it largely alone."

There were a series of unhappy murmurs of agreement around the table.

"We all know that we can expect little overt assistance from the government, the establishment media or the mainstream law enforcement community," Guerrero added. "Officially, at least, most people in this country still hold the view that the paranormal is the province of science fiction, fantasy, quacks, gurus, talk-show guests and frauds. Convincing them that a secret, dangerous conspiracy composed of psychically enhanced individuals exists and must be taken seriously is probably beyond our ability, at least for now."

Without exception, those around the oval table sat tight-lipped and grim-faced.

"And so we welcome to this Council chamber a new Master who is uniquely qualified to lead us through these perilous times." Guerrero fixed Zack with piercing eyes. "We ask you to take the oath of office and assume the Master's Chair, Zackary Gabriel Jones."

Zack rose but made no move to go to the head of the table. Instead, he looked at each of the ten members in turn. Then, very deliberately, he set a folder down on the polished stone table.

"Before I take the oath," he said, "I am going to

introduce you to my fiancée, Miss Raine Tallentyre, daughter of Judson and Miranda Tallentyre."

The name hit the room with the impact of a meteor. Jaws dropped and eyes widened. Zack knew that some of those present had served on the Council when Tallentyre was kicked out of the Society. The rest were well aware of the name.

Before anyone could say a word, Bancroft opened the door to the chamber and ushered Raine into the room. .

She stopped just inside the doorway and gave everyone a cool, self-possessed nod. She was at her most austere and untouchable today in a sculpted black Armani jacket, trousers and high heels. Her dark hair was pulled straight back into an elegant knot at the nape of her neck. Her eyes were pools of mystery behind the lenses of her black-framed glasses.

How in hell did I get so lucky? Zack thought. *I will love her for the rest of my life and beyond.*

He walked around the table and took her arm, making no attempt to conceal his pride.

"Welcome, my dear. Allow me to present the members of the Governing Council of the Arcane Society, USA."

He went through the names quickly. Heads nodded stiffly. There were a few mumbled greetings. Most of the members were still speechless.

Raine gave them all her dazzling *screw you* smile.

"What a pleasure to meet all of you," she said in a perfectly neutral tone.

Zack managed, just barely, to suppress a grin. Fortunately, none of the Council members seemed to grasp the fact that they had just been dissed.

"As many of you will have guessed," he said, "my fiancée is the daughter of the Judson Tallentyre who, many years ago, was investigated by J&J for unauthorized research. That investigation led to Tallentyre being thrown out of the Society. All records of his work were destroyed."

No one moved. They all knew the story.

"What neither the Council nor J&J was aware of at the time was that the focus of Tallentyre's research was not on the founder's formula but on an antidote for it."

That garnered another round of startled murmurs.

"The only reason Tallentyre created a version of the formula was so that he could run experiments on it with his antidote," Zack said.

The faces around the table assumed various expressions ranging from confusion to dawning comprehension. At least three of the people in the room were high-level intuitives who were no doubt starting to sense where this was going.

"I'm sure all of you realize what a great strategic advantage an antidote would provide us in our battle against Nightshade," he continued. "Among other things, it would weaken the organization's hold over its operatives."

"An antidote would be a huge asset," Paul Akashida observed. "Currently, the penalty for failure or betrayal within Nightshade brings an automatic sentence of death or insanity. The existence of an antidote would make it possible to attract defectors."

Janice Forster brightened. "It might also allow us to plant a spy within the organization."

At the far end of the table Conner Price spoke up. "Hell, just the rumor of an antidote would damage the Nightshade power structure."

More excited conversation erupted around the table. Bancroft stood quietly, hands clasped behind his back, satisfaction gleaming in his eyes. He winked at Zack. The strategy was working precisely as they had planned.

Wilson Everleigh ended an animated conversation with Akashida and turned to Zack, dark features alight with anticipation. "Are you telling us Judson Tallentyre really did discover an antidote?"

"It's not perfect," Zack said. "There has been only one human trial and it was only partially successful. But preliminary analysis by our experts indicates that Tallentyre succeeded in overcoming the most critical of the technical problems that have prevented us from coming up with a true antidote."

Bancroft spoke up. "Dr. Jameson has informed me

that Tallentyre's work points in an entirely new direction. He believes that there is a very high probability that his people will be able to create a stable, effective drug to counter Nightshade's version of the founder's formula within a few months."

"This is a huge breakthrough," Guerrero announced. "It will be the first real weapon we've had to use against Nightshade. But why are we hearing about it now? Tallentyre died years ago."

Zack had been waiting for the carefully planted question. "The secret of the antidote was lost after Tallentyre died. In the course of a recent J&J investigation, however, Fallon Jones made the decision to reopen the old file on Judson Tallentyre. It turned out that there were a lot of loose ends in the case."

Bancroft took up the carefully tailored story. "Tallentyre intended to turn over the antidote to the Society but he died in an auto accident before he could tell J&J about his discovery. Most of his files were destroyed by the agents. The formula for the antidote, however, was salvaged by Tallentyre's sister. Given the manner in which her brother had been treated, she had no incentive to hand it over to us. She took her secret to the grave."

Zack looked at Raine. It was her turn.

She studied the group around the table. "That folder on the table contains copies of the final report of J&J's new investigation into my father's activities. It is true that he was consumed by his research and followed his passion into unauthorized areas. But J&J has determined that he never intended to use the formula for criminal purposes."

"All Tallentyre cared about was the science behind the drug," Zack said. "It was his in-depth understanding of the biochemistry of the founder's formula that allowed him to do the groundbreaking work on an antidote."

"Hold on here," Janice Forster interrupted. "You said the antidote was lost."

"It was until after Vella Tallentyre's death," Zack said. "But a few weeks ago it turned up among her personal effects, all of which were left to my fiancée."

Everyone's attention was suddenly riveted on Raine.

Raine gave the group another smile. This one was a lot warmer, Zack noticed.

"I have decided to hand over the formula for the antidote to the Arcane Society," she said. "I trust you will all see that it is used wisely. It is what my father would have wanted."

The table was engulfed with another burst of excited conversation.

Zack leaned a little closer to Raine.

"That, babe, is how you rewrite history," he said into her ear.

She laughed. "I do love you, Zackary Gabriel Jones."

"I love you, Raine Tallentyre."

He kissed her in front of his grandfather and the

entire assembled Council. A round of applause went up. He felt the vibrant energy of love shimmering in the air, knew that Raine felt it, too. They would share it for the rest of their lives.

KEEP READING FOR A SPECIAL PREVIEW OF

The Perfect Poison

A NOVEL OF THE ARCANE SOCIETY
BY AMANDA QUICK

Lucinda stopped a few feet away from the dead man, trying to ignore the fierce undercurrents of tension that raged through the elegant library.

The constable and the members of the grieving family were well aware of who she was. They watched her with a mixture of macabre fascination and barely concealed horror. She could hardly blame them. As the woman the press had once featured in a lurid scandal and a tale of shocking murder, she was not welcome in polite society.

"I do not believe this," the attractive, newly minted widow exclaimed. "Inspector Spellar, how dare you bring that woman into this household!"

"This will only take a moment," Spellar said. He inclined his head toward Lucinda. "If you would be so kind as to give me your opinion, Miss Bromley."

Lucinda was careful to keep her expression cool and composed. Later the family members would no doubt whisper to their friends and associates that she had appeared as cold as ice, just as the newspapers and the penny dreadfuls had portrayed her.

As it happened, the thought of what she was about to do actually did chill her to the bone. She would much rather be home in her conservatory, enveloped by the scents, colors and energy of her beloved plants. But for some reason she could not explain, she found herself drawn to the work that she occasionally did for Spellar.

"Certainly, Inspector," she said. "That is why I'm here, is it not? I think we can safely say that I was not invited for tea."

There was a gasp from the widow's spinster sister, a severe-looking woman who had been introduced as Hannah Rathbone.

"Outrageous," Hannah snapped. "Have you no sense of the proprieties, Miss Bromley? A gentleman is dead. The least you can do is behave in a dignified manner and leave this household as quickly as possible."

Spellar gave Lucinda a veiled look, pleading silently with her to watch her tongue. She sighed and closed her mouth. The last thing she wanted to do was jeopardize his investigation or cause him to think twice about requesting her advice in the future.

At first glance one would be highly unlikely to guess Spellar's profession. He was a comfortably stout man with a benign, cheerful countenance, a voluminous mustache and a thin ring of graying hair, all of which served to distract others from the sharp, insightful intelligence in his blue-green eyes.

Few who were not well acquainted with him would guess that he possessed a true talent for noticing even the smallest clues at a murder scene. It was a psychical gift. But there were limits to his abilities. He could not detect any but the most obvious cases of poisoning.

Fairburn's body lay in the middle of the vast floral carpet. Spellar stepped forward and reached down to pull aside the sheet that someone had drawn over the dead man.

Lady Fairburn burst into a fresh cascade of sobs.

"Is this really necessary?" she cried brokenly.

Hannah Rathbone gathered her into her arms.

"There, there, Annie," she comforted. "You must calm yourself. You know your nerves are very delicate."

The third family member in the room, Hamilton Fairburn, set his well-modeled jaw in grim lines. A handsome man in his midtwenties, he was Fairburn's son by a previous marriage. According to Spellar, it had been Hamilton who had insisted on summoning an inspector from Scotland Yard. When Fairburn had recognized Lucinda's name, however, he had been aghast. Nevertheless, although he could have refused to allow her into the mansion, he had not done so. He wanted the investigation to go forward, she thought, even at the cost of having such a notorious female in his house.

Lucinda walked toward the body, bracing herself for the disturbing sensations that always accompanied an encounter with the dead. No amount of preparation could entirely dampen the disorienting sense of utter emptiness that swept over her when she looked down at the figure on the floor. Whoever and whatever Fairburn had been while he was alive, that essence was gone.

She knew, however, that traces of evidence that might provide clues to the manner of his death still clung to the scene. Spellar would certainly spot most of them. But if there was any indication of poison, it was her mission to detect it. The psychical residue of toxic substances remained not only on the body but on anything the individual had touched in those last moments.

There was often other, very unpleasant and much more obvious evidence as well. In her experience most people who died after ingesting poison became violently ill before expiring. There were always exceptions, of course. A long, slow, steady diet of arsenic did not usually produce such dramatic results at the end.

But there was no indication that Lord Fairburn

had suffered from bouts of nausea before he died. His death could have been attributed to a stroke or heart attack. Most families who moved in elevated circles, as the Fairburns did, would have preferred to accept such a diagnosis and thereby avoid the publicity that inevitably attended a murder investigation. She wondered what had made Hamilton Fairburn send a message to Scotland Yard. Clearly he had his suspicions.

She concentrated for a moment on visual cues but they told her little. The dead man's skin had turned a stark, ashen shade. His eyes were open, staring at nothing. His lips were parted in a last gasp. She noticed that he had been older than his wife by at least a couple of decades. That was not an unusual circumstance when a wealthy widower remarried.

Very deliberately she stripped off her thin leather gloves. It was not always necessary to touch the body but direct physical contact made it easier to pick up nuances and faint traces of energy that she might not notice otherwise.

There was another round of shocked gasps from Lady Fairburn and Hannah Rathbone. Hamilton's mouth tightened. She knew that they had all seen the ring on her finger, the one the sensation press claimed she had used to conceal the poison that had killed her fiancé.

She leaned down and lightly brushed her fingertips across the dead man's forehead. Simultaneously, she opened her senses.

At once the atmosphere of the library shifted in subtle ways. The scents that emanated from the large jar of potpourri swept over her in a heavy wave, a combination of dried geraniums, rose petals, cloves, orange peel, allspice and violets.

The colors of the roses in two tall, stately vases intensified dramatically, exhibiting strange hues for which there were no names. While the petals were still bright and velvety, the unmistakable reek of decay was clearly detectable. She had never understood why anyone would want to decorate a room with cut flowers. They might be beautiful for a short time but they were, by definition, in the process of dying. As far as she was concerned, the only suitable place for them was in a graveyard. If one wished to preserve the potency of a plant or bloom or herb, one dried it, she thought, annoyed.

The sad-looking filmy fern trapped behind the glass front of the Wardian case was dying. She doubted the exquisitely delicate little *Trichomanes speciosum* would last the month. She had to resist the urge to rescue it. There was scarcely a household in the country that did not boast a fern in the drawing room, she reminded herself. One could not save all of them. The fern craze had been going strong for several years now. There was even a name for it—pteridomania.

With the ease of long practice, she suppressed the distracting energy and colors of the plant life in the room and concentrated on the body. A faint residue of unwholesome energy slithered across her senses. With her talent she could detect almost any type of poison because of the way the energy of toxic substances infused the atmosphere. But her true expertise was in the realm of those poisons that had their origins in the botanical kingdom.

She knew at once that Fairburn had, indeed, ingested poison, just as Spellar had suspected. What stunned her were the faint traces of a certain, very rare species of fern. A cold chill of panic trickled through her.

She took a moment or two longer than necessary with the body, pretending to concentrate on her analysis. In reality she used the time to catch her breath and steady her nerves. *Stay calm. Do not show any emotion.*

When she was certain that she had herself under control, she straightened and looked at Spellar.

"You are right to be suspicious, sir," she said in what she hoped were professional tones. "He ate or drank something quite poisonous shortly before he died."

Lady Fairburn gave out a shrill cry of ladylike anguish. "It is just as I feared. My beloved husband took his own life. How could he do this to me?"

She collapsed into a graceful faint.

"Annie!" Hannah exclaimed.

She dropped to her knees beside her sister and removed a dainty vial from the decorative chatelaine at her waist. She pulled out the stopper and waved the vinaigrette under Lady Fairburn's nose. The smelling salts proved effective immediately. The widow's eyes fluttered.

Hamilton Fairburn's expression hardened into grim outrage. "Are you saying that my father committed suicide, Miss Bromley?"

She closed down her senses and looked at him across the vast expanse of the carpet. "I never said that he deliberately took the poison, sir. Whether he took it by accident or by design is for the police to determine."

Hannah fixed on her with a seething glare. "Who are you to declare his lordship's death a case of poison? You are certainly not a doctor, Miss Bromley. Indeed, we all know exactly what you are. How dare you come into this household and hurl accusations about?"

Lucinda felt her temper stir. This was the unpleasant aspect of her consulting work. The public was consumed with a great fear of poison, thanks to the sensation press, which had developed a morbid infatuation with the subject in recent years.

"I did not come here to make accusations," Lucinda said, fighting to keep her voice even. "Inspector Spellar requested my opinion. I have given it. Now, if you will excuse me, I will take my leave."

Spellar stepped forward. "I will escort you outside to your carriage, Miss Bromley."

"Thank you, Inspector."

They left the library and went into the front hall, where they found the housekeeper and butler waiting. Both individuals were steeped in anxiety. The rest of what was no doubt a very large household staff remained discreetly out of sight. Lucinda did not blame them. When there was a question of poison, the servants were often the first to come under suspicion.

The butler hurried to open the door. Lucinda went out onto the steps. Spellar followed. They were met with a wall of gray. It was midafternoon but the fog was so thick that it masked the small park in the center of the square and veiled the fine town houses on the opposite side. Lucinda's private carriage waited in the street. Shute, her coachman, lounged nearby. He came away from the railing when he saw her and opened the door of the vehicle.

"I do not envy you this case, Inspector Spellar," she said quietly.

"So it was poison," Spellar said. "Thought as much."

"Unfortunately nothing so simple as arsenic, I'm afraid. You will not be able to apply Mr. Marsh's test to prove your case."

"I regret to say that arsenic has fallen somewhat out of favor of late now that the general public is aware that there is a test to detect it."

"Do not despair, sir. It is an old standby and will always be popular if for no other reason than that it is widely available and, if administered with patience over a long period of time, produces symptoms that can readily be attributed to any number of fatal diseases. There is a reason, after all, why the French call it inheritance powder."

"True enough." Spellar grimaced. "One can only wonder how many elderly parents and inconvenient spouses have been sped on their way to the Other World by that means. Well, if not arsenic, what then? I did not detect the smell of bitter almonds or notice any of the other symptoms of cyanide."

"I'm certain that the poison was botanical in origin. It was based on the castor bean, which, as I'm sure you know, is highly toxic."

Spellar's forehead creased. "I was under the impression that castor-bean poisoning produced violent illness before it killed. Lord Fairburn showed no indication of that sort of sickness."

She chose her words with great caution, anxious to give Spellar as much of the truth as possible. "Whoever brewed the poison managed to refine the most lethal aspects of the plant in such a way as to produce a highly toxic substance that was extremely potent and very fast acting. Lord Fairburn's heart stopped before his body even had a chance to try to expel the potion."

"You sound impressed, Miss Bromley." Spellar's bushy brows bunched together. "I take it that the skill required to prepare such a poison would be uncommon?"

For an instant his talent for keen observation sparked in his eyes. It disappeared almost immediately beneath the bland, slightly bumbling facade he affected. But she knew now that she had to be very careful.

"Extremely uncommon," she said briskly. "Only a scientist or chemist of some genius could have concocted that poison."

"Psychical genius?" Spellar asked quietly.

"Possibly." She sighed. "I will be honest, Inspector. I have never before encountered this particular blend of ingredients in any poison." And that, she thought, was no more or less than the absolute truth.

"I see." Spellar assumed a resigned air. "I suppose I shall have to start with the apothecary shops, for all the good it will do. There has always been a lively underground trade in poisons carried on in such establishments. A would-be widow can purchase a toxic substance quite easily. When the husband drops dead she can claim that it was an accident. She bought the stuff to kill the rats. It was just unfortunate that her spouse accidentally drank some of it."

"There are thousands of apothecary shops in London."

He snorted. "Not to mention the establishments that sell herbs and patent medicines. But I may be able to narrow the list of possibilities by concentrating on shops near this address."

She pulled on her gloves. "You are convinced this is murder, then? Not a suicide?"

The sharp gleam came and went again in Spellar's eyes. "This is murder, all right," he said softly. "I can feel it."

She shivered, not doubting his intuition for a second.

"One cannot help but observe that Lady Fairburn will look quite attractive in mourning," she said.

Spellar smiled slightly. "The same thought occurred to me as well."

"Do you think she killed him?"

"It would not be the first time that an unhappy young wife who longed to be both free and wealthy fed poison to her much older husband." He rocked on his heels once or twice. "But there are other possibilities in that household. First, I must find the source of the poison."

Her insides tightened. She fought to keep the fear out of her expression. "Yes, of course. Good luck, Inspector."

"Thank you for coming here today." He lowered his voice. "I apologize for the rudeness that you were obliged to endure in the Fairburn household."

"That was in no way your fault." She smiled slightly. "We both know that I am accustomed to such behavior."

"That does not make it any more tolerable." Spellar's expression turned uncharacteristically somber. "The fact that you are willing to expose yourself to such behavior in order to assist me from time to time puts me all the more deeply into your debt."

"Nonsense. We share a common goal. Neither of us wishes to see killers walk free. But I fear you have your work cut out for you this time."

"So it would seem. Good day, Miss Bromley."

He assisted her up into the dainty little cab, closed the door and stepped back. She settled against the cushions, pulled the folds of her cloak snugly around her and gazed out at the sea of fog.

The traces of the fern that she had detected in the poison had unnerved her as nothing else had since the death of her father. There was only one specimen of *Ameliopteris amazoniensis* in all of England. Until last month it had been growing in her private conservatory.

NEW YORK TIMES BESTSELLING AUTHOR

JAYNE ANN KRENTZ

"Jayne Ann Krentz is a woman who knows
her way around a thrilling plot."
—The Huffington Post

For a complete list of titles,
please visit prh.com/jayneannkrentz